Twice *as* Nice
Amish
Romance Collection

Featuring Two Delightful Stories

Twice *as* Nice
Amish
Romance Collection

WANDA &
BRUNSTETTER
& JEAN BRUNSTETTER

BARBOUR BOOKS
An Imprint of Barbour Publishing, Inc.

The Lopsided Christmas Cake © 2015 by Wanda E. Brunstetter and Jean Brunstetter
The Farmers' Market Mishap © 2017 by Wanda E. Brunstetter and Jean Brunstetter

Print ISBN 978-1-64352-677-5

eBook Editions:
Adobe Digital Edition (.epub) 978-1-64352-679-9
Kindle and MobiPocket Edition (.prc) 978-1-64352-678-2

All scripture quotations are taken from the King James Version of the Bible.

This book is a work of fiction. Names, characters, places, and incidents are either products of the author's imagination or used fictitiously. Any similarity to actual people, organizations, and/or events is purely coincidental.

Published by Barbour Books, an imprint of Barbour Publishing, Inc., 1810 Barbour Drive, Uhrichsville, OH 44683, www.barbourbooks.com

Our mission is to inspire the world with the life-changing message of the Bible.

Member of the
Evangelical Christian
Publishers Association

Printed in the United States of America.

The Lopsided Christmas Cake

Dedication

To our husbands, Richard Sr. and Richard Jr.
We appreciate your love and support.
A special thanks to Mary Alice Yoder for
your friendship and helpfulness.

*He that handleth a matter wisely shall find good:
and whoso trusteth in the LORD, happy is he.*
PROVERBS 16:20

Prologue

Sullivan, Illinois

Elma Hochstetler sat quietly beside her twin sister, Thelma, as their somber father read his parents' will. He'd found it last week after the funeral but had waited until now to read it to them.

Dad leaned forward, looking right at the twins. "Girls, it appears that you two have inherited my folks' house, as well as their store."

The twins gasped in unison.

"Once your *daed* has talked to a lawyer and the paperwork has been finalized, you can sell both places," Mom interjected.

Dad touched Mom's arm. "Kathryn, I think this is something we ought to let the girls decide."

Tears threatened to spill from Elma's eyes as she allowed Dad's words to sink in. It had been difficult to accept that her grandparents had been killed when their horse and buggy were hit by a truck. Hearing this news was an even greater shock. Elma had assumed that Dad, being their only son, would inherit their estate. Why would Grandma and Grandpa want her and Thelma to have it?

Full of questions, Elma squeezed her sister's hand. "What do you think we should do about this?"

Tears glistened in Thelma's blue eyes. She drew in a quick breath. "If Grandma and Grandpa wanted us to have their house and store, I think we should honor their wishes."

"But you can't move all the way to Indiana. We rely on you both to help at our store here." Mom's forehead wrinkled. "Besides, your grandparents didn't run things the way we do."

"You worry too much, Kathryn." Dad removed his glasses. "We'll hire a couple of girls to work in our store. The twins can run my folks' business however they want." He looked at Elma and Thelma. "In fact, I think you ought to go there as soon as possible."

Mom's brown eyes widened. "Why, Jacob? What's the rush? This is a big decision."

"It's not good to leave my parents' house sitting empty too long. And my folks' store needs to be up and running again. Their community relies on it." Dad rose to his feet. "I'm going out to the phone shack and call one of our drivers. Thelma and Elma, you need to get packed."

Drying her tears, Thelma smiled. "This could be an adventure. I don't know about you, Elma, but it feels right to me."

Elma nodded slowly, although she felt overwhelmed. Looking around their parents' living room, a lump formed in her throat. This was the only home she and her sister had ever known. Taking over their grandparents' place in Topeka meant she and Thelma would have to move three hundred miles away. Fortunately, they had experience running a store, since they'd been helping at their parents' general store from the time they were girls. But they weren't girls anymore. Although they looked much younger, Elma and Thelma had turned thirty-two last month. They still lived at home, and neither of them was married or even had a serious boyfriend. There really was nothing keeping them here. The question was, would they be able to take on such a monumental task by themselves?

Chapter 1

Topeka, Indiana
Three days later

Standing in the front yard, while gazing at their grandparents' rambling old two-story house, all Elma Hochstetler could do was shake her head in disbelief. Glancing toward the road as their driver disappeared, Elma bit her lip. *This is it. There's no going back.*

Overcome with emotion, she turned to face Thelma. "I can't believe this place is really ours."

Holding the orange-and-white cat that had sauntered up to them, Thelma nodded.

Everything from the weeds choking out the garden to the sagging front porch and peeling paint spoke of one thing—work. The barn and other outbuildings were run-down too. Since this was the first week of September, Elma knew they would have to get some of the outside chores done before the harsh winter set in.

How quiet it was. She hadn't noticed that before when they'd visited Grandpa and Grandma. Their grandparents' home was on a side road, with farms on both sides of it. The home across the street had a FOR SALE sign out front.

As they stepped onto the porch, Thelma paused and tipped her head. "Listen to the tinkle of Grandma's wind chimes."

Barely noticing the chimes, Elma pointed to the eaves above the porch. "Oh my. There's an ugly brown spider up there."

"It's nothing to worry about. I'll take care of it later." Thelma stroked the cat's head. "I think it'll be fun to fix this place up."

Elma shook her head. "Fun? You think all the effort it will take to get this place livable is going to be fun? I'd call it work. And some of it will take money we don't have."

"You're right, but we can have fun in the process." Thelma's exuberance was almost contagious. But then, even when the twins were children Thelma hadn't worried about things. "Free-spirited." That's what Dad called Thelma, while he'd labeled Elma as "the serious one." While the physically identical twins shared the same petite frame, blue eyes, and chestnut brown hair, their personalities didn't always mesh.

I suppose I am too serious, Elma thought ruefully. *But someone has to stay focused. It takes organization to keep things running smoothly. If I followed my twin sister's path, we'd spend every day looking through rose-colored glasses.*

Thelma released the cat and slipped her arm around Elma's waist. "We've always done everything together, right?"

Elma could only nod, watching a clump of cat hair float through the air.

"Together, we'll turn this place back into what it used to be before Grandma and Grandpa got too old to keep everything up."

Thelma smiled. "We'll make this a *glicklich* adventure."

Elma knew her sister had good intentions and was thinking positively. Even though the situation looked overwhelming, perhaps Thelma was right. "*Jah*, we'll make it successful," Elma said. "The first thing we should do is go grocery shopping, because I'm sure there's not much fresh food in Grandma's kitchen."

⌁

"I think we should've accepted Mom's offer to help us organize this place," Thelma said as she mopped the kitchen floor the following day.

"This is *our* project." After disposing of some out-of-date canned fruit and vegetables they'd found in a cupboard, Elma placed the empty jars in the sink. "Besides, Mom has plenty to do at home, taking care of the house and helping Dad at the store. They'll be coming here in a few weeks to visit. I want to surprise them with all we've gotten done."

Thelma grimaced. "They'll be surprised all right. Mom will wonder why we don't sell this place and move back home."

"Hey, where's that positive attitude you had yesterday? This is our home now," Elma reminded. "Grandma and Grandpa's store is our only source of income." She opened another jar and dumped the contents into the garbage can. "Can you believe all the green beans Grandma canned two summers ago? It's a shame to waste all this food."

"It is a waste, but it's not safe to eat something that old." Thelma plugged her nose. "Smell that musty odor?" She drew the curtain aside that hid the items under the sink. "Uh-oh. It looks like the pipe's been leaking for some time. Grandma must have tied this old thin rag around it to stifle the dripping. Eww...it's soaking wet." Thelma rubbed her hands over her apron and pointed to something else. "There's a coffee can under the pipe to catch the water. It's nearly full."

"You'd better dump it. We should get that fixed as soon as possible, but for now we should find a thicker piece of material to secure around the leak." Elma pushed her dress sleeves up. "I've started a list of things that need to be done. It would be good if you started a list too in case I miss anything."

Thelma scrunched her nose. "Oh no. Not more lists!"

"They do help when there's so much to be done."

"I suppose. One thing I know we need to do is paint." Thelma gestured to the wall behind the woodstove. It was coated with soot.

"You're right," Elma agreed. "I think most of the rooms in this house could use some paint. That alone will help to spruce things up."

Thelma pushed a piece of her hair back under the black scarf covering her bun. Then she gestured to the missing handles on a few of the cupboard doors. "The whole place seems to be falling apart. Didn't Grandpa fix anything?"

"He and Grandma were old. Their health was slipping before the accident." Elma spoke in a quieter tone, tears welling in her eyes. "I think it was too much for him to keep up."

"You're probably right," Thelma agreed, "but wouldn't you think they would have sold the place and moved to Sullivan to be closer to family?"

"Remember, Dad tried to talk them into moving." Elma rinsed another jar. "But our grandparents were too independent to budge. They would probably still be running their store if the accident hadn't happened. Besides, it can't be easy selling the home you've always known." Tears clung to her lashes. She would miss seeing them. Grandpa told funny jokes. Grandma knew how to cook better than anyone and always had a delicious treat waiting whenever the twins came to visit.

Unfortunately, due to how busy they'd been at their folks' store, the twins hadn't made a trip to see their grandparents for two years. That saddened Elma, because she and Thelma hadn't been able to see Grandma and Grandpa before they'd died. But knowing they'd been entrusted with this old house and the store fueled her determination to make a go of it.

"Guess I can't blame Grandma and Grandpa for staying put," Thelma admitted. "This place was special to them. It was their home for as long as I can remember." She pushed the mop under the table. "It's hard for older people to lose their independence and rely on others." She sighed. "I don't look forward to getting old."

"Try not to worry about aging," Elma said. "Let's take one day at a time and try to—"

"Enjoy the moments we have on earth." Thelma finished her sister's sentence and set the mop aside. "I don't know about you, but I'm tired of working. With all the organizing and decluttering, we'll never find time to do anything fun."

Elma flapped her hand. "Oh, sure we will. The holidays will be coming soon. There'll be all sorts of fun things to do."

"Like what?"

"We can go Christmas caroling. If we get enough snow, we can get that old sleigh out of Grandpa's barn."

Thelma perked up. "A sleigh ride sounds fun. We can put bells on the horse's harness, and sing Christmas songs, like Grandpa used to do when we were little."

"Don't forget the holiday baking we'll get to do," Elma put in. "We can make Grandma's special Christmas cake—you know, the one she used to fix whenever we came to visit during the holidays."

"I've always liked that special cake with Jell-O in it." Thelma gestured to the woodstove across the room. "If we have to use that old relic, everything we make will probably flop. Besides, I'm not the world's best baker."

"We can't afford to buy a propane-operated stove right now. We'll make the best of what we have." Elma had removed another jar from the cupboard when she spotted a little gray mouse skittering across the floor.

Startled, she loosened her grip on the jar, sending it crashing to the floor. "*Ach!* Did you see that?"

"See what?"

Elma dashed into the utility room, grabbing the broom. Instead of cleaning the mess, she shoved it under the stove, swishing it back and forth.

"What are you doing, and what did you see?"

"There's a *maus* in here! Didn't you see it?"

"No, I didn't, and you won't get it with that. We need to bring in one of the *katze*. Grandpa always said his cats were good mousers."

Elma grimaced. "You know I don't like katze in the house."

"Would you rather have a maus?"

Elma shook her head vigorously. "They're *ekelhaft* little creatures."

"If you think they're disgusting, then let me bring in a cat."

"Okay." Elma grabbed a dustpan. She swept up the broken glass and beans. "After he gets the maus, make sure he goes outside."

When Thelma stepped outside, she spotted one of the cats curled in a ball on the saggy porch. "Come with me, Tiger." She bent down and picked up the cat. "You have a job to do in the kitchen. I'll bet you'll appreciate the meal." Even though one of the neighbors had been feeding the animals since her grandparents had died, this cat looked scrawny.

Meow! Tiger opened his eyes, looking at Thelma as if to say, "Why'd you wake me?"

Thelma took the cat inside and set him on the floor near the stove. "Get the mouse, boy!"

Elma's gaze went to the ceiling. "You think he's gonna listen to you?"

"Tiger may not understand what I said, but if that mouse moves, the cat will spring into action." Thelma stood back with her arms folded, waiting to see what would happen.

"Tiger?"

"Jah. That's what I named him because of his color. I think it fits. Don't you?"

"I guess so."

Tiger sat a few seconds then turned toward a moth that had flown into the room. Thelma ducked. She'd never cared much for moths, especially when they flew toward her face. Tiger took off in good form, heading for his prey that now hovered over the bucket of ashes near the stove. The cat leaped into the air and upset the container.

"*Die katz laaft im esch!*" Elma shouted.

Thelma groaned. Her sister was right—Tiger walked in the cinders and had caught his airborne snack. She knew if she didn't get him quick, he'd be tracking the mess all over her clean floor.

Thelma dashed across the room, but when she was about to grab the cat, the mouse shot out from under the stove. Elma shrieked and jumped on a chair. Dropping the moth, Tiger chased the mouse. Thelma raced for the door. Jerking it open, she was relieved when the mouse made its escape. Tiger followed. Slamming the door, she turned to face her sister. "You can come down now. It's safe."

"For now, anyway," Elma muttered, stepping down from the chair. "If there's one maus in the house, there's bound to be more. What if there's a whole family of them?"

"Maybe I should bring Tiger back in," Thelma suggested.

Elma shook her head. "Not now. I think we've done enough here this morning. Let's finish cleaning this mess. Then we can fix lunch. When we're done eating, we can head over to the store to see what needs to be done there."

When they'd finished cleaning the floor, Elma stepped out of the room and came back with a notebook. "Here's the list I started. I'll make another one when we go out to the store."

"Pretty soon we'll have so many lists you won't know which one to look at," Thelma teased; then she got serious. "Do you think we should hire someone to help us in the store? That would give us more time to do some other things around here."

Elma shook her head. "Maybe later. Right now we can't afford to hire anyone." She opened the refrigerator, glad they'd had time yesterday to pick up a few things at the grocery store. "What kind of sandwich would you like—ham or bologna?"

Thelma shrugged. "I don't care. You choose."

Elma took out the packages of lunch meat. "I'm hungry enough to eat two sandwiches, so let's have both."

"Sounds good to me." Thelma got out the bread.

Elma placed the lunch meat on the counter and opened the packages.

"You know, Thelma, I've been thinking that it's good for us to be on our own. After all, we're not *kinner* anymore. We need to prove to ourselves, and also to Mom and Dad, that we can make a go of things."

"You're right." Thelma gave Elma's arm a tender squeeze. "With the Lord's help, we can handle most anything."

Chapter 2

"I wonder if we'll ever get this yard in shape." Elma kicked some scattered leaves as they walked past a dead bush. "There's so much to do here; I feel overwhelmed by it all."

Thelma clasped her sister's arm. "Don't worry so much. It'll get done in good time."

"I hope so, but that's our first priority." Elma motioned to the general store, several feet behind the house. According to Grandpa, with the help of his friends, he built the store a few years after he and Grandma were married.

When Thelma heard chickens clucking, she glanced to the left. "I just remembered, we didn't check for eggs last night. Think I'd better do that right now."

"Go ahead. I'll head over to the store and start organizing some of the shelves." Elma took a few steps in that direction but turned around. "Don't be long. There's lots of work, and it's going to take both of us."

"Don't worry. It won't take much time to gather a few eggs. I'll join you shortly."

After Elma walked away, Thelma headed for the chicken coop. *My sister worries too much. People shopped at Grandpa and Grandma's store when it wasn't perfectly organized. If we don't have everything just so, I'm sure it won't affect our business.*

Thelma thought about her folks' store back home and how, between Mom and Elma, everything was kept neat and tidy. One or both of them seemed to be constantly cleaning and organizing. Thelma had never enjoyed cleaning that much. Organizing was definitely not her thing. She'd rather wait on customers so she could visit.

When Thelma opened the door to the coop, she was greeted by several cackling hens. She remembered collecting eggs with Grandpa when she was a little girl. He would talk about a few of his favorite chickens and had even given them names.

Thelma fed the chickens first and gave them fresh water. When that was done, she grabbed a basket and filled it with eggs. It was fun to see the different colors. Not all the chickens were the same, and not all of the eggs were white. Some hens laid eggs in various colors. She was surprised to see any eggs at all, since one of Grandma's neighbors had been taking care of the animals. Perhaps, since they knew Thelma and Elma would arrive yesterday, they hadn't collected any more eggs.

Thelma hummed, reaching under a stubborn hen that wouldn't move off its nest. *Bawk! Bawk!* The chicken ruffled her feathers and hopped to the floor, looking back at Thelma as if to say, "How dare you steal my egg."

Thelma looked out the small window facing the corral. She saw Rusty, the horse Grandpa bought a few months before he died. His old horse, Cutter, had been pulling their rig the day of the accident and was killed. That left only Rusty available to the twins. Unfortunately, he was still a bit green and would be a challenge. *One more problem,* she thought.

Satisfied that she'd gotten all the eggs, Thelma moved toward the door. "Oh great," she chided herself when she realized that she'd left it open. "Sure hope none of the chickens got out."

Thelma's brows furrowed as she stepped outside and saw chickens roaming all over the yard. "Good grief! Now I have chickens to round up."

She set the basket on the ground and moved toward the nearest chicken. Apparently, the hen didn't want to be caught, because it took off like a flash. The other chickens scattered too.

The chickens really didn't need to be in the coop all day. She'd wait until nightfall, when they would be subject to predators, to put the birds back in their coop. They'd be easier to catch when it started getting dark, and she'd have Elma's help.

Thelma grabbed the basket and hurried into the house. She took care of the eggs first then paused for a drink of water. After working in the kitchen most of the morning, Thelma was tired. Too bad Elma wanted to work at the store right now. Thelma wanted to sit outside and work on the gloves she'd begun knitting for Mom's Christmas gift.

Maybe I'll get my knitting out now and do a couple of rows, she decided. *If I sit a few minutes, I'll have more energy to help Elma clean the store.*

❧

Elma swiped a trickle of sweat on her forehead and pushed a wayward hair under her scarf. If the store had been open for business today she would have worn her stiff white head covering. But with all the sweeping and dusting she'd been doing, her normal covering would have gotten dirty.

Elma glanced at the battery-operated clocks near the door. She'd been in the store over an hour already. Where was Thelma?

"She probably got distracted, like she often does," Elma mumbled. "Guess I'd better find her." She set her broom aside and hurried from the store, leaving the door open to air the place out. Glancing toward the chicken coop, she noticed the door was open. Surely, Thelma couldn't still be gathering eggs.

Elma stepped into the coop. No sign of her sister there—only a couple of hens on their nests. *Thelma must be in the house. Doing what, I can't imagine.*

When Elma entered the house, she was surprised to see Thelma sitting in Grandma's rocking chair, clicking away with her knitting needles.

"What are you doing?" Elma stepped in front of Thelma.

Thelma blinked rapidly, her cheeks turning pink. "I—I was tired and sat down with my knitting to relax a few minutes."

Elma's hands went straight to her hips. "I thought you were coming out to the store to help me. If we don't get the place cleaned and organized, we'll never be ready to open for business."

"I know, and I'm sorry. I lost track of time."

"I don't see how this is going to work if you get distracted so easily and leave me to manage things by myself."

"I'll try to do better." Thelma set her knitting aside. "Let's head to the store."

Elma opened the door and squealed when Tiger brushed her ankles as he darted into the house. "Oh great, now we have a *katz* to catch."

"Let's leave him here while we're at the store," Thelma suggested. "If there's another maus, he might catch it and we won't have to worry about setting any traps."

Elma shook her head. "We can't leave the cat in the house unattended. After what he did earlier, who knows what kind of mess he could make. Besides, he's shedding. I don't want cat hair in the house."

"I could stay and catch the cat."

"Oh sure, and leave me to do all the work? No way! We'll both try to capture the cat."

Elma and Thelma went through the house, calling for Tiger, but he seemed to have disappeared.

"Now what?" Elma frowned.

Thelma shrugged. "Tiger's bound to come out sometime. He can't stay hidden forever. I suppose we could stay here and work in the store later."

"The longer we put that off, the longer it'll be till we can hang the OPEN sign in the front window." Elma released a frustrated sigh. "As much as I dislike the idea, I think we'd better leave the cat in the house. Hopefully, he's found a place to sleep and won't wake up for a while."

"If that's what you want to do." Thelma turned toward the door. "I promise, the first chance I get I'll look for a brush and go over his coat real good. And don't worry, I'll do that outside."

Elma followed her, making sure to close the door. The last thing they needed was another cat getting in—or a bunch of chickens.

As they neared the store, Elma halted. "Look, Thelma, there are two horse and buggies at the hitching rail."

"Oh good, we have company!" Thelma grinned. "Maybe some of our neighbors have come to get acquainted."

Elma groaned. "More than likely we have customers who think the store is open. This is not what we needed today, Sister."

Chapter 3

When Thelma entered the store, she was excited to see four women and five young children. She recognized Sadie Yoder from Grandma and Grandpa's funeral. Perhaps she'd met the other women too, but the day of the funeral had been such a blur. She'd been introduced to so many people she couldn't remember them all.

"Hello, everyone." Thelma smiled, and her voice grew louder. "It's nice to see you." She glanced at Elma and noticed that her smile appeared to be forced. Wasn't she happy to see all these people?

"As soon as we saw the store's open door, we figured you were open." Sadie held a cardboard box. "When we heard you were coming, we decided to bring you some food. It's our way of welcoming you to the area."

"That's right," another woman, who introduced herself as Doris Miller, spoke up. "Mine is still in my buggy, and so are the boxes Clara Lehman and Mary Lambright brought." She gestured to the other two friends. One of them had two small boys with her, and the other had two girls and a boy. The children all appeared to be under the age of six, which meant they hadn't started school yet.

Looking at their cute little faces, Thelma couldn't help feeling a bit envious. She loved children and longed to be a wife and mother, but as the years slipped by, she'd begun to lose hope. She'd had a few suitors, and so had Elma, but none of the men had seemed quite right for them. And they'd never been courted at the same time. Thelma still remembered as a little girl promising her sister that she would never get married unless Elma was getting married too.

Glancing back at her sister, Thelma was relieved to see Elma's relaxed expression. "*Danki.* That's so kind of you," Elma said. "If you'd like to bring your food items to the house, I'll get them put away."

"That's fine," Sadie replied. "We'll see that everything is taken in." She and Doris followed Elma outside, but the other two women and their children remained in the store. Thelma wondered if they wanted to visit or planned to do some shopping. She hoped that wasn't the case, because Elma had made it clear this morning that they wouldn't open until the cleaning and organizing was done.

Thelma turned to Clara and asked, "Do you live nearby?"

Clara shook her head. "Our home is several miles away. Having three little ones, I don't make trips to the store as often as I'd like." She glanced toward the stacked material. "I need some fabric. Is it all right if my kinner look at your children's books while I choose the cloth?"

Thelma nodded. What else could she do? It wouldn't be right to turn the woman down.

"Do you still carry vitamins here?" Mary asked.

"Umm. . .I'm not sure. We haven't had a chance to take inventory yet, but you're welcome to look around."

"I'll do that." Mary motioned to her boys. "Is it okay if Philip and Richard look at the children's books too?"

"That's fine with me," Thelma replied. "In fact, I'll take a book off the shelf and read them a story."

As Mary and Clara started shopping, Thelma placed a braided throw rug on the floor. After the children took a seat, she found an appropriate book and sat beside them. "Solomon Lapp was a very smart boy," she began reading in Pennsylvania Dutch, so the children would understand. "He always got the best grades in school. He fed the cows faster than his five brothers. He gathered eggs quicker than his three sisters."

The children giggled when Thelma showed them a picture of Solomon riding his scooter. She loved to see them enjoying the story and wished she could sit with these sweet children the rest of the day.

ം

"You can set the boxes on the table," Elma said when she entered the kitchen with Sadie and Doris. "Again, it was so thoughtful of you to think of me and my sister this way."

Sadie, the older woman, touched Elma's arm. "We were all saddened when your grandparents passed away, but we're glad you and your sister have taken over their place." Her hazel eyes clouded, and she wiped a tear that had dribbled down her cheek.

"Jah," Doris agreed. "We are so glad you're here." She pushed her metal-framed glasses back in place. "I didn't know your grandparents as well as some of the others, because my husband and I are new to the area. But from what we've heard, they were both a blessing to this community."

Elma's throat tightened. She had to fight to control her emotions. The kind things these women said about Grandma and Grandpa made her miss them even more.

Refocusing her thoughts, she unloaded the boxes. They held everything from home-canned fruits and vegetables to casserole dishes, packages of meat, and several kinds of desserts.

Sadie passed Elma another item. "If there's anything we can help you with, please don't hesitate to ask."

"Danki," Elma said. "We'll let you know if we need any help."

She had put the last item in the refrigerator, when Tiger darted into the room—chasing a mouse of all things. *Oh no, not now!* Not wanting to embarrass herself, Elma fought the urge to scream and hop onto a chair.

As though this was an everyday occurrence, Doris chuckled. "Would you look at that?"

Sadie laughed too, and Elma sighed with relief. Either these ladies were very kind or had dealt with mouse issues before.

By this time, Tiger had run the mouse into the utility room. Elma cringed when she heard a thud. A few seconds later, the cat appeared, carrying the rodent in his mouth. The women giggled as the cat sat before them, apparently waiting for their approval. Even Elma thought it was rather cute.

"Good work, kitty." Sadie jerked the back door open. "Now take your prize outside."

As if he understood, Tiger bounded out the door.

"Don't worry," Sadie assured Elma. "We get mice at our place from time to time too. That's why we keep a few katze around."

Desperate for a change of subject, Elma said, "Maybe we should head back to the store and see what the others are doing."

When they entered the store, Elma saw Thelma on the floor reading to the children. They seemed to be totally engrossed as she read about a young boy named Solomon. Even the children's mothers, who stood nearby, listened. This was nothing new. Elma remembered how many times in their store back home, her sister had entertained some of the little ones while their mothers shopped. It was a nice gesture, but Elma hoped Thelma wouldn't get into the habit of doing that here. They had only the two of them running the store, so they both needed to wait on people.

❧

That evening, after the supper dishes were done, the twins built a fire in the fireplace and settled into the living room to relax. Thelma picked up her knitting to work on Mom's gloves, when Elma suggested they try one of the desserts they'd been given today. She went to the kitchen and returned with a bunch of peanut butter cookies on a crystal platter Grandma had often used when the twins had come to visit. Thelma remembered it well because of a small chip on one corner.

"I have some water heating on the stove for tea." Elma placed the platter on the coffee table. "Is the gas lamp giving you enough light?"

"Jah, it's plenty."

"It looks like you're squinting. Would you like to borrow my reading glasses?"

Thelma shook her head. "No, I'm fine."

The teakettle whistled, and Elma returned to the kitchen.

"Do you need any help?" Thelma called.

"I can manage."

While her sister was getting the tea, Thelma put her knitting down and glanced around. With the exception of the linoleum in the kitchen and bathroom, the rooms in this house had hardwood floors.

Her gaze came to rest on the small table beside her chair, draped with one of Grandma's handmade doilies. This old house had a story to tell—their grandparents' story. Each piece of furniture and every room held a special memory. To Thelma it felt like a second home. She was anxious to see what new memories she and Elma would make here.

When Elma returned with two cups, she handed one to Thelma and took a seat on the sofa. "I'd like to discuss something with you."

Thelma tilted her head. "What's that?"

"Remember how at our folks' store, you often entertained the kinner who came in with their parents?"

"Like I did today. Those children were so cute. I think they really enjoyed the story."

"I'm sure they did, but there are only two of us running the store." Elma leaned slightly forward. "I think it would be best if we both stick to waiting on customers and let the parents deal with their children."

Thelma's shoulders slumped. "I'm sorry. I'll try to remember that." Her sister was right, but oh, how she would miss spending time with the children. Taking over Grandma and Grandpa's store meant more responsibilities for her and Elma. Things would be different from now on. Back home in their parents' store, Thelma had always mixed a bit of fun with work. She hoped, even though it was only the two of them now, that the fun wouldn't be completely lost.

"I appreciate that," Elma said. "So how would you like to go shopping tomorrow in Shipshe?"

Thelma smiled, remembering how often Grandpa had used that shortened version of the name Shipshewana. The town had several good places to shop and eat. "That's a good idea." She reached for a cookie. "Maybe I'll look for the paint we need."

Elma smiled. "I could use a new pair of shoes. Of course, they'll have to be on sale."

Thelma took a sip of tea. "There's one thing we need to consider."

"What's that?"

"Shipshe's ten miles away. It's a bit far to ride our bikes. That means we'll have to get out Grandma and Grandpa's old buggy and take—"

"Rusty," they said in unison.

Elma frowned. "We haven't used him yet. I hope that horse behaves himself."

Chapter 4

The next morning, Elma was surprised to see Tiger lying under the kitchen table. He looked a bit better since Thelma had brushed him the evening before. She'd thought her sister had put the cat out before they went to bed last night. But at least he'd slept in the kitchen, where they'd already seen two mice.

When Elma reached under the table, the cat opened his eyes and stretched. "Come on, Tiger, out you go. You're not going to stay in the house while Thelma and I are shopping today."

Elma picked up Tiger, opened the back door, and set him on the porch. She stopped for a moment to take a deep breath of cold air. Was that frost she saw on the grass? Could the warmer days of summer be gone already?

She grabbed an armful of wood and hauled it inside to feed the wood-stove. Elma rubbed her arms. The overnight temperatures had dropped, leaving it a bit chilly inside. Soon, the pleasant sound of wood snapping and popping filled the air. A sudden wave of sadness flowed over her. She thought about all the times she and Thelma had warmed themselves in front of this stove when they were children. Grabbing the edge of her apron, she wiped her eyes. Elma didn't think she'd ever get used to cooking or baking in the old relic. Due to their lack of money right now, it could be some time before they'd be able to buy a stove like they had at home. But at least this one heated the kitchen. *Maybe that's why Grandpa and Grandma held on to this old thing. Grandma had gotten used to cooking on it, and it does possess a certain unique charm.*

After Elma was sure the fire was going, she got out the loaf of banana bread one of the women had given them yesterday. It would go well with the eggs she'd boiled last night, along with a cup of hot tea.

As Elma set the table, she rubbed her fingers over one of the plates. Another memory flashed across her mind. Grandma always made fluffy pancakes when the family came to visit. Pancakes were one of Elma's favorite breakfast foods. When she was younger, she often ate as many as six for breakfast. "I'll have to see if I can find Grandma's recipe," she murmured.

Her thoughts turned to how things had turned out after she and Thelma had found customers waiting at the store yesterday afternoon. It was nice to get acquainted with some of the women from their area, and even nicer to know that they lived in such a caring community. Elma was pleased to have met such kind ladies. How glad she was that they hadn't made an issue of Tiger chasing that mouse. *Maybe I shouldn't have worried about it either. I know I can be a bit fussy sometimes.*

When Elma first realized that some of the women wanted to shop, she wasn't too happy about it. She and Thelma still hadn't cleaned or organized much, not to mention taking inventory. But after reminding herself that they needed some money coming in, she'd gratefully accepted their cash and checks. Since the news was out that the twins had inherited their grandparents' store, she figured the best thing to do was keep the store open during the weekdays. They could reorder supplies and do their cleaning and organizing in the evenings. Of course Thelma, who was taking a shower right now, had other thoughts about that. She'd made it clear that she wanted her evenings free to knit or do other things. Thelma even said she didn't think the store was as bad as Elma thought. She couldn't see any need to organize, since their customers probably knew where things were already. Elma didn't agree.

Knowing she needed to get busy, Elma checked the firebox on the stove. It had heated up nicely, and the kitchen was getting warmer. Now if Thelma would get here, they could eat breakfast and get on with their day. They'd decided to put the CLOSED sign in the store window today, and she was anxious to leave for Shipshe. Then later, if there was time, she hoped to sort through some things in their store to see what may have expired and need to be thrown away.

A bloodcurdling scream reached the kitchen. Dropping the silverware on the table, Elma raced from the room and dashed down the hall. "Thelma, what's wrong?" she hollered, pounding on the bathroom door.

"Except for the cold water that was running down on me, I'm okay." Thelma's voice boomed through the closed door. "It went from lukewarm to ice cold. Let me tell you: it's the coldest and quickest shower I've ever had to take."

"Sorry. When you screamed, I was worried that you'd been hurt."

"No, I'm fine—just feel like I'm gonna freeze to death."

Elma sighed with relief. She was glad Thelma wasn't in serious danger, but they did need to address their inadequate hot water supply. "I have breakfast ready," Elma said through the door. "So unless you need something, I'll see you in the kitchen."

"Go ahead. I'll be there shortly."

❧

When Thelma entered the kitchen a short time later, she was still shivering. "Did the water turn cold like that when you took your shower?" she asked.

Elma shook her head. "No, but it wasn't hot either. I wonder if the water tank may be going out."

"One more thing we'll have to fix." Thelma rubbed her hands over her arms. "Look at me. My arms are full of goose bumps."

"Put this on." Elma grabbed a sweater and handed it to Thelma. "You may want to stand by the stove. It's warming up nicely in here."

"Is that frost I see out the window?" Thelma asked before slipping into the sweater and moving closer to the stove.

"Seems to be. I think we'll be seeing fewer warm, summery days now that fall is approaching."

"At least this old stove is good for something." Thelma scooted closer to the source of heat.

"Jah, but if we get more money coming in soon, I'd really like to replace it." Elma took a seat at the table. "I have everything set out, so whenever you're warm enough we can eat breakfast."

Thelma stood near the stove a few more minutes then joined Elma. Bowing her head, she silently prayed, *Heavenly Father, thank You for this food and the hands that prepared it. Please keep us safe as we travel to Shipshe today, and let this be a good day. Amen.*

⌒

LaGrange, Indiana

Joseph Beechy opened the door to his harness shop and drew in a deep breath. The odor of leather and pungent dye filled the room. These were aromas he was accustomed to, as he'd been making and repairing harnesses and other leather items since he'd graduated from the eighth grade. Of course, that had been a good many years ago, since Joseph would be turning thirty-eight the first week of December.

"Thirty-eight years old and still a bachelor," Joseph muttered as he turned on the gas lamps overhead. "Guess I'm destined to remain single."

It was hard to admit, but Joseph had never developed a serious relationship with any of the young women he'd known. He had been interested in a few of them; although his shyness had always gotten in the way. His face would heat up and he'd start to stutter whenever he approached any single women who'd caught his eye. Maybe it was best that he'd never married. Life was less complicated that way—although he did long for a wife and children and had even prayed for that.

Maybe it's my ears women don't like, he thought, tugging on one of his earlobes. Though Joseph's ears were an average size, they stuck out slightly. He'd always been self-conscious about them. Of course, it hadn't helped that some of the scholars who'd attended school with him made fun of his ears. They never dared to do it when the teacher was around, but that hadn't stopped them from teasing Joseph when they had Joseph alone. Had it not been for his older brother, Eli, standing up for him, Joseph would have probably been taunted even more.

Eli and their sister, Katie, were both married and each had four children. As much as Joseph enjoyed spending time with his nieces and nephews, he felt left out. It was a reminder that he'd probably never have a family of his own. Of course, if Joseph should ever find the woman of his dreams, he might step out of his comfort zone and at least try to approach her without making a fool of himself. *Finding the woman of my dreams? That'll probably never happen.*

Joseph's gaze came to rest on the loosely rolled leather pouring out of the shelves along one side of his shop. In an area near his workbench, bits of leather scraps lay piled on the cement floor. If his mother walked in right now, she would probably scold Joseph for not cleaning up after himself. Since this was his place of business, he figured he had the right to decide how it should look. Maybe that was another good thing about not being married. If he had a wife, she might come into the shop and tell him to clean the place up.

Moving over to some open boxes full of snaps, rings, buckles, and rivets, Joseph rolled up his shirtsleeves, deciding that he needed to quit thinking and get to work. He'd connected the breast strap of a harness to a large three-way snap, when his good friend Delbert Gingerich entered the shop.

Delbert's long legs took him quickly across the room. "*Wie geht's?*" he asked, stepping over a pile of dirty leather straps and buckles.

"I'm doin' fairly well, Dell. How about yourself?"

"Can't complain." Delbert gestured to the harness Joseph held. "Looks like you're hard at work here, Joe."

"As a matter of fact, I'm just gettin' started." Joseph grinned. He and Delbert had been friends since they were teenagers. When Delbert started calling him "Joe," he'd given his friend the nickname "Dell." Since neither of them was married, they often did things together, like fishing, playing horseshoes, or having a good game of Ping-Pong. Of course Delbert, having longer, stronger arms, usually won at horseshoes. But Joseph almost always caught the biggest fish. While the men shared common interests, they had very different personalities and appearances. Delbert had blond hair, sky-blue eyes, and dimples that would turn any woman's head. Joseph's red hair and freckles made him feel homely in comparison, but that didn't matter much since Delbert seemed more interested in making his woodworking business successful than in looking for a wife. And while Delbert was outgoing and competitive, Joseph was timid and didn't care whether he won or lost at most games they played.

"What brings you by this morning?" Joseph asked.

Delbert snapped his suspenders. "I'm heading to Shipshe to pick up a few things and thought you might like to go along for the ride."

Joseph shook his head. "I've got too much to do here to be going on any joyrides."

"I'll treat you to lunch." He thumped Joseph's back. "How's that sound?"

"Where are you planning to eat?"

Delbert shrugged. "Oh, I don't know. I'm thinking maybe the Blue Gate."

Joseph looked down at the stain on his trousers. "Naw, that place is too nice for a working fellow like me."

"How about Wana Cup Restaurant? It's fairly casual."

"Jah, and they do have some pretty good pies and homemade ice cream."

Delbert bobbed his head. "That's right, they sure do. So are you willing to leave your work for a while and go to Shipshe with me?"

"Jah, sure, why not?" He set the harness on the workbench. "My work will be waiting for me when I get back."

⁂

As she and Thelma headed for Shipshewana in their grandparents' closed-in buggy, Elma gripped Rusty's reins. Grandpa's open buggy, which he and Grandma had been riding in when their accident occurred, had been demolished. Thinking about it now sent shivers up Elma's spine. She'd give anything if she could bring her grandparents back and make everything as it once was. *I still wonder why they left their home, the store, and all their possessions to me and Thelma. I wish* that *would have been stated in their will.*

"What are you thinking about?" Thelma asked, breaking into Elma's thoughts.

"How do you know I was thinking about anything?"

Thelma gave Elma a gentle nudge. "You had that 'I'm mulling things over' look."

Elma snickered. "Since you know me that well, maybe you can figure out what I was thinking."

"Grandma and Grandpa?"

"Jah. Riding in their buggy makes me miss them even more."

"I know what you mean." Thelma gestured to the horse. "At least Rusty's cooperating."

As if he had heard her, the horse picked up speed. Elma tried to hold him back, but a car coming from the opposite direction honked, causing Rusty to go wild. When the horse darted into the other lane, she screamed. A vision of her grandparents flashed before her eyes. Was this what it was like before their buggy got hit? Elma knew if she didn't get control of the horse, they were going to collide with the oncoming car.

Chapter 5

Rusty's hooves slammed down on the pavement. He whinnied then shook his head with force as steam surged from his flaring nostrils. Elma's heart pounded as she gripped the reins with all her might, trying to guide him back to the right side of the road. The stubborn horse planted his feet firmly and wouldn't budge. She could almost hear her father's voice telling her to hold on tight and let Rusty know who was boss. Fortunately, the oncoming car had pulled over to the side of the road and stopped.

Elma had been around horses since she was a girl. She and Thelma had been given a pony and a cart for their tenth birthday. They'd begun driving a full-size horse and buggy by their early teens. But she'd never been this frightened or felt that she had so little control. Struggling with a sense of panic, Elma looked at her sister. "I can't make him go."

"Let me see what I can do." Thelma hopped out of the buggy and grabbed the horse's bridle. Rusty kept trying to shake his head, but Thelma held firm, while talking to him in a calm tone and stroking his side. Eventually, she was able to lead him and the buggy to the right-hand shoulder of the road.

The car moved on, and Elma breathed a sigh of relief. Her hands shook so hard she could barely hold on to the reins. She didn't want to go to Shipshewana now, but turning the horse around and heading back home was frightening too. What if Rusty acted up again? The next time it might not end so well.

Thelma opened the door on Elma's side of the buggy. "Slide over,

Sister. I'll take over now. I can see that you need a break."

"Maybe we should go home and forget about shopping. I'm not sure we can trust Rusty to get us to Shipshe."

"We'll be fine. He needs to know who's in control. Besides, this is Rusty's first trip out since we moved here, and he's not used to us yet. We'll have to use him more and our bikes less."

Elma slid to the passenger's side and handed Thelma the reins. Closing her eyes, she prayed, asking God to give them a safe trip.

With an air of confidence, Thelma directed Rusty onto the road. So far, the horse was behaving himself, but Elma kept praying. Thelma had always been the braver one, but in the past, they'd both done well with horses. Now, Elma wasn't sure she could ever drive Rusty again. It was a good thing the woman who'd driven them from Sullivan to Topeka had a van, so they'd been able to bring their bikes. Despite what Thelma said, Elma planned on using her bicycle for her main mode of transportation. Of course, she wouldn't be able to ride it when the weather turned bad or if she had to travel a long ways.

She glanced over at Thelma and was amazed to see her relaxed expression. "I wonder if this cooler weather has anything to do with Rusty acting up. If it does, then with winter coming he'll probably get worse."

Thelma shook her head. "I don't think that's the horse's problem. He just needs a lot of work."

"None of our horses ever acted like that when we hooked them to our buggy. Maybe we ought to sell Rusty and have one of our horses from home brought to us."

"That would be expensive. I'm sure once we've worked with Rusty awhile, he'll be fine."

"I don't want to work with this horse." Elma shook her head forcibly. "He's too spirited and unpredictable."

"Which will make him more of a challenge." Thelma's brows pulled in.

"Right. That's why we need to sell him."

Thelma let go of the reins with one hand and reached over to pat Elma's arm. "Let me take care of Rusty. I'm up to the challenge."

Shipshewana

When Thelma guided Rusty into the parking lot behind Yoder's Complex, she felt relief. She'd been able to get them the rest of the way without a problem, but she'd been nervous—although she hadn't let on to Elma. "Are you okay?" she asked her sister, noticing that her face was quite pale.

Elma slowly nodded. "I'm relieved to be here. You did an amazing job with Rusty. He didn't act up for you at all."

Thelma patted her sister's cold hand. "I did what needed to be done. Do you want to secure Rusty to the hitching rail, or shall I?"

"I'll take care of it." Elma stepped out of the buggy and walked up to Rusty.

As Thelma watched, she heard her sister scold the horse. "You scared me something awful. Don't ever do that again."

Rusty jerked his head back, pawed the pavement, and snorted.

Thelma knew Elma was afraid of the horse, but she had to get past it, or the animal would sense her fear and get worse.

Once Elma secured the horse, Thelma got out. "Where shall we go first?" she asked.

"I'd like to look in Yoder's Department Store for a pair of black dress shoes. When we were here two years ago, they had a good supply, so I'm hoping they'll have the plain style and size that I need. When I'm done there, I may run across the street to Spector's and see what kind of material they have."

"Why would you want to do that when we have material at our store?"

"We're getting low on some colors. If I find the color I want, I may buy enough to make a new dress. I still have some birthday money left."

"That's fine. While you're trying on shoes, I'll go across the hall to the hardware store and look for paint."

"Why don't we get something to drink first?" Elma suggested. "I could use a cup of herbal tea to help me relax."

The twins headed for Yoder's. After they'd ordered their tea, they sat in the restaurant and talked about all the things they'd need to do before their folks came to visit.

"It'll be great to see Mom and Dad again," Elma said. "But in some ways I wish they weren't coming so soon."

Thelma quirked an eyebrow. "Really? How come?"

"We haven't accomplished much of anything so far. Now that we're feeling the necessity of keeping the store open during the week, it's doubtful that we'll get much done at the house."

"We'll do what we can. I'm sure Mom and Dad won't expect everything to be perfect."

"I guess you're right, but I do want to show them that we've made some headway." Elma set her empty cup down at the same time as Thelma. "Are you ready to go shopping?"

Thelma chuckled. "Jah, sure. We can meet back at the buggy. After that, unless we want to do more shopping, we can go somewhere for lunch."

"Maybe we could stop over at Jo-Jo's and get a soft pretzel," Elma suggested. "That would be cheaper than buying a whole meal, and almost as filling."

"Okay. See you later."

When Thelma entered the hardware store, she spotted some puzzles. Thinking it could be fun for her and Elma to work on one during cold winter evenings, she took one off the shelf. Placing it in her basket, she moved on to look at some bird feeders and seed. Grandma had always enjoyed watching the birds, and several feeders were hanging in the yard. Thelma had seen some birdseed in the barn yesterday, but she hadn't taken the time to fill any of the feeders. Maybe she'd do it when they got home later today.

Moving on, she noticed an Amish man with sandyblond hair also looking at feeders. He was obviously not married because he had no beard. When he glanced her way, she quickly looked in another direction. She certainly didn't want him to catch her staring.

Remembering that they also needed some batteries, Thelma hurried off. When she located the right size for their flashlights, she added a package to her basket. She stopped to glance briefly at some sleds, but they wouldn't have need of anything like that until it snowed. When it did, if they found the time to go sledding, they could use the old ones hanging in Grandpa's barn.

Thelma had begun her search for paint, when she spotted two Amish women. One she didn't recognize, but the other woman was Sadie Yoder. "It's nice to see you again," Thelma said, walking over to Sadie.

Sadie smiled. "It's nice to see you too. Now, which twin are you?"

"I'm Thelma."

Sadie studied Thelma a few seconds, making her feel like a bug under a microscope. "I'm sure I'll remember who's who after I get to know you better. You and your sister look so much alike, it's hard to tell you apart."

"People have been getting us mixed up since we were kinner," Thelma responded.

"Is Elma here with you?" Sadie questioned.

"She's across the hall, looking for shoes."

"Oh, I see. Well Thelma, I'd like you to meet our bishop's wife, Lena Chupp. You didn't get to meet her the day of your grandparents' funeral because she was home with the flu."

The elderly woman smiled and greeted Thelma. "I'm sorry about your grandparents. They will be missed in our community." Thelma's throat constricted as Lena held on to her hand. "We're glad to have you and your sister in our church district and look forward to seeing you at the service this Sunday."

"Where will it be held?" Until now, Thelma hadn't thought about this Sunday and whether it would be a day of worship or an off-Sunday. Her only excuse was that she had so much on her mind.

"The service will be at Herschel Miller's," Sadie spoke up. "You met his wife, Doris, yesterday." She reached into her black leather purse and pulled out a tablet and pen. "I'll write their address down for you."

Thelma visited with the women a few more minutes, and after saying that she and Elma would see them on Sunday, she headed to the checkout counter to pay for her purchases.

As Thelma approached the counter, she was surprised to see the blond-haired Amish man waiting there as well. His arms were full, and she wondered why he hadn't picked up a basket to put his things in. An elderly man stood in front of him with several items. Since there was only one clerk, Thelma figured it could be several minutes before she or the blond man were waited on.

He kept fidgeting and glancing over his shoulder. Suddenly the man turned, bumping Thelma's arm.

"Oops. Sorry," he mumbled, trying to juggle the other items as the tape measure fell from his grasp. The next thing Thelma knew all of his purchases were on the floor.

Setting her basket down, Thelma leaned over to help him pick them up, but in doing so, they bumped heads.

"Sorry about that. Are you all right?" His shimmering blue eyes revealed the depth of his concern.

Rubbing her forehead, to be sure a lump wasn't forming, Thelma could only manage a nod.

The man smiled, revealing deep dimples in both cheeks. "Guess this is my day for being clumsy. This morning, I dropped a carton of milk when I was fixing breakfast."

"It's okay. No harm done," Thelma murmured. It had been awhile since she'd met a man with such pretty blue eyes. They weren't an average shade of blue, like hers and Elma's. This man's eyes reminded her of a clear blue lake, glistening on a summer day.

He motioned to her basket. "Guess I should've gotten one of those instead of trying to carry everything myself."

Averting her gaze, Thelma reached for the tape measure still lying on the floor, but she ended up grasping his hand as he picked up the object.

"Oh, I'm sorry. It seems like I'm the clumsy one now." Thelma's face flooded with heat. "At least nothing appears to be broken."

"No, everything seems to be fine." He picked up the rest of his things and stood.

As Thelma clambered to her feet, she rubbed her hand down the side of her dress, still feeling the warmth from his hand when she'd accidently grasped it.

The older gentleman had finished checking out, so the blond-haired man put his purchases on the counter. After he paid for them, he gave Thelma a nod and left the store.

She paid for her things and was about to walk away, when she noticed a piece of paper on the floor. Thinking the man must have dropped it, she picked it up, but by then he was out of sight. *This looks interesting,* Thelma thought, realizing it was a flyer advertising a cooking show. The event would take place in Shipshewana the following month. Everything the contestants made would be auctioned off and go to the winning bidders. The proceeds would go to several families in the community with medical expenses. Since the Amish didn't carry health insurance, they relied on events such as this to help in emergencies. Thelma thought this might be something she and Elma should take part in. It was for a good cause, and since they were now part of the Amish community in this area, they should do something to help.

❧

Delbert had crossed the street to meet Joseph for lunch, when he saw an Amish woman going into Spector's. He was surprised to see that it was the same young woman he'd bumped into at the hardware store. "That's strange. I thought she was wearing a green dress."

"Who were you talking to?" Joseph bumped Delbert's arm.

Startled, Delbert whirled around. "What are you doing sneaking up on me like that?"

"I wasn't sneaking. I finished what little shopping I decided to do and thought we were supposed to meet here before we went to lunch."

Delbert's face heated. "We were. . . . I mean. . ." He didn't know why he felt so flustered all of a sudden.

"So who were you talking to?" Joseph asked.

"No one. I mean, I was talking to myself." Delbert pointed to Spector's. "Did you see a woman go in there a few minutes ago?"

Joseph shook his head. "Nope. Can't say as I did."

"I bumped into her at Yoder's Hardware, and I thought she was wearing a green dress. But when I saw her again, I realized her dress was blue."

Joseph thumped Delbert's shoulder. "What's going on here, friend? Are you interested in that woman?"

"Course not. I don't even know her. Never saw her till today, in fact." Delbert scratched his head. "I wonder if she's married."

Joseph punched Delbert's arm. "Don't get any ideas. Remember, we're both confirmed bachelors."

Chapter 6

Topeka

Wwhat are you thinking about, Thelma?" Elma asked as they ate breakfast Sunday morning. "You look like you're five hundred miles away."

Staring out the window, Thelma sighed and glanced back at her sister. "No, not five hundred—maybe ten miles or so."

Elma's eyebrows lifted. "What do you mean?"

"Oh, nothing." She picked up her glass of apple juice and took a drink. She wasn't about to tell Elma she'd seen an attractive Amish man at the hardware store the other day and couldn't quit thinking about him. Elma would tease her. Besides, it wasn't likely she'd see the man again, much less get to know him.

"You must have been thinking about something or you wouldn't have been staring off into space." Elma reached for the salt shaker and sprinkled some on her scrambled eggs. "But if you'd rather not talk about it, that's okay with me."

"It's nothing, really." Thelma didn't like where this conversation was headed, so she quickly changed the subject. "When we were in Shipshe the other day, I picked up some candy. Think I'll put it in my purse and hand it out to the kinner who are in church today."

Elma smiled. "The children in our church district in Sullivan always enjoyed it when you gave out candy, so I'm sure the ones here will like it too. By the way, did you get the paint you went after?"

"Uh-oh. Guess I got sidetracked and forgot. I'll have to make another trip to Shipshe sometime this week." Thelma went to get her purse from a wall peg near the back door. Then she grabbed the bag of candy from the cupboard. When she opened her purse to put the candy in, she noticed the cooking show flyer she'd put in there and forgotten about. "Look at this, Sister," she said, bringing it back to the table with her. "I found it on the floor in Yoder's Hardware the other day."

Elma took the flyer and put her reading glasses on. "'Shipshewana Cooking Show. All contestants who enter will have their baked or cooked item auctioned off.'" She removed her glasses and squinted as she looked at Thelma. "This looks interesting, but why are you showing it to me?"

"Didn't you read the rest of the flyer? The proceeds from the auction will help people in the community who have medical expenses. It's for a good cause."

Elma moved her head slowly up and down as she placed the piece of paper on the table. "I saw that, and if we have time we might go to the event and give a donation of whatever we can afford."

"Oh no," Thelma said, her excitement mounting as she thought more about this. "I think we should make something that will be auctioned off. We could make a dessert from Grandma's favorite recipe book."

"That's a nice thought, but with all we have to do here and at the store, we don't have the time for something like that."

Thelma motioned to the flyer. "The cooking show doesn't take place until the first Saturday of October, so we'd have almost a month to figure out what we want to make and get it done. We could take an evening, and instead of working on the puzzle, or me knitting, we could bake something. It wouldn't hurt for us to close the store that day either, so we could attend the event." Thelma paused to catch her breath then kept going with enthusiasm, her voice growing louder. "It would be a nice way for us to contribute to a good cause. I'm sure others in our community here in Topeka will be attending the show that day."

"You sound pretty excited about this. I'll give it some thought. Right now though, we need to finish our breakfast so we can be on our way to church." Elma drank the rest of her juice. "It wouldn't be good for us to be late on our first Sunday attending services here."

Thelma glanced at the battery-operated clock on the wall behind them, noting that it was only seven o'clock. "I'm sure we'll get there in plenty of time. By the way, did you find the shoes you were hunting for at the store in Shipshe?"

Elma stuck out her foot. "Jah. I'm wearing them. I also found some material for a new dress in the color I wanted."

"That's good to hear. At least one of us got what we went after."

Elma looked at the table and frowned. "I wish the Millers' place was close enough for us to walk." She picked up her readers and put them in her eyeglass case. "I can't say that I'm looking forward to going anywhere again with that unpredictable horse."

Thelma reached over and patted her sister's hand. "Not to worry. I'll be in the driver's seat the whole way." She leaned back in her chair, enjoying the warmth of the stove. The sun's light poured into the kitchen, adding a warm, golden glow. "I'll take charge of driving Rusty until you feel ready to sit in the driver's seat again."

Elma sighed. "That's a relief. After what happened with Rusty the other day, I'm in no hurry to drive again."

Thelma tipped her head. "Did you hear that noise?"

"What? I didn't hear anything."

"It sounded like a cat shrieking, and I think it was coming from the basement." Thelma stood. "Maybe we should go check."

"Why don't you go while I do the dishes? It's almost time to leave for church, and if we both go to the basement, we'll have to leave the dishes till we get home this afternoon." Elma glanced at her new shoes. "Sure hope I chose the right size shoes. These are pinching my toes a bit."

"Sorry about that. Maybe you ought to take them back."

"No, I think they'll be okay once I break them in."

"Okay, whatever you think best. I'm gonna run down to the basement and check on that noise."

Thelma grabbed a flashlight, clicked it on, and started down the basement steps. When she reached the bottom, she turned on one of the gas lamps. Nothing seemed out of the ordinary. It was quiet. *That's sure strange. I was almost sure I heard a cat.*

"Tiger, are you down here?" She clapped her hands. "Here, kitty, kitty." No response.

Holding the flashlight in front of her and swatting a few cobwebs out of the way, Thelma began searching, while calling for the cat. *I guess one of these days we'll have to clean this basement, or the spiders are going to take over.*

Behind the stairs, she still saw nothing then ducked, but it was too late. "Eww..." She'd walked headlong into a dirty web. Quickly, she pulled away the silken strands gummed to her cap and forehead. "Come on, kitty. Where are you?" she called again. "You don't have to hide from me." If it was Tiger, the friendliest of all the cats, she was sure he would have responded—unless he was trapped.

"Here, kitty. Where are you, kitty?" Thelma stood still and listened, but except for her sister humming upstairs and the sound of water flowing through the pipes, she still heard nothing. Her nose twitched. *This place smells like a combination of dust and mildew. It really needs a thorough cleaning.*

"Thelma, are you coming?" Elma shouted from above. "If we don't leave now, we are definitely going to be late!"

"Okay, I'm on my way." Thelma headed up the stairs, wondering if she had imagined the noise.

Back in the kitchen, she'd put the flashlight away and had turned to head out of the room, when Elma pointed at her. "You must have brushed against something downstairs. There's a smudge on your dress."

Thelma brushed it away. "Looks like dust. There are plenty of cobwebs in the basement. Someday we'll need to go down there and clean."

"We'll add that to our ever-growing list of to-dos." Elma sighed. "Before we go, did you remember to turn off the gas lamp in the basement?"

Thelma bobbed her head. "At least, I think I did." She tapped her chin. "You know, I can't remember doing that. I'd better run back down and make sure it's off."

Elma sighed. "Really, Sister, I wish you would try to stay a little more focused."

"Sorry about that. I was listening for the noise I heard. Plus trying not to eat any spiders," she added under her breath.

"Did you find out what it was?"

"No, I didn't hear it again, and when I looked around with the flashlight, I didn't see anything out of the ordinary either." Before Elma could comment, Thelma grabbed the flashlight and headed back downstairs.

As soon as Thelma reached the bottom, she saw that she had left the gas lamp on. She reached up to turn it off, when she heard that same catlike screech. The sound came from way back in one corner of the basement. Shining her flashlight, she discovered one of the cats in a small wooden box full of rags. Beside it was a tiny kitten, and it appeared as if the little one had recently been born. No doubt, the mama cat would deliver more babies soon.

Thelma clasped her hand over her mouth. *Oh my! If Elma finds out about this, she'll want to move the cats out to the barn. Well, she can't know. I'll have to keep it a secret and find a way to keep Elma from coming down here until the cats are old enough to go outside. Maybe I shouldn't have said anything about cleaning the basement.*

❧

As the twins headed for church with their unpredictable horse, Elma tried to relax. Rusty was doing much better for Thelma than he had done for her the other day. *He must have sensed my fear,* Elma thought. *I'm glad my sister isn't afraid and was willing to drive.* The thought of sitting in the driver's seat, trying to keep control of the horse they'd inherited sent shivers up the back of Elma's neck. She knew she had to get past her fear or she'd never be able to drive their buggy, but right now she couldn't deal with that. Maybe once Thelma got Rusty tamed a bit, Elma would try taking him out again. Of course, she'd make sure her sister was along, in case there was a problem.

As they approached the Millers' home, Rusty picked up speed. He'd apparently gone there before with Grandpa in the driver's seat and was anxious to get there again. It made Elma wonder if Rusty was anxious to see some special horse at the Millers'.

Even with her nervousness over the horse, she noticed how pretty the Millers' farm was, nestled back in, off the road.

"Can't you make him go any slower?" Elma asked as Thelma directed the horse up the driveway. "Look at the dust he's kicking up behind us. People will think we're crazy, approaching like this."

"I'm trying to, but Rusty seems quite excited."

Elma noticed that her sister was holding the reins pretty tight, and it looked like she was gritting her teeth. Maybe she wasn't as confident driving this aggravating horse as she'd let on.

"Whoa, Rusty!" The twins called in unison.

Thelma pulled back on the reins, and the horse came to a stop a foot or so from the barn. She looked over at Elma and smiled. "We're here!"

Elma released a quick breath. "Jah, and thank the Lord we didn't run into the barn."

After one of the young men came up to greet them and took Rusty away to be watered and stabled, Elma walked across the yard with Thelma. Several women were clustered outside on the lawn near a large white building that Elma assumed was Mr. Miller's workshop. A group of men stood chatting in a line on the other side of the shop door.

As the twins were greeted by each of the women, Elma recognized several from the day of their grandparents' funeral. Sadie Yoder introduced Elma to Lena Chupp and Lena introduced the twins to the other women they didn't know.

Shortly before nine o'clock, they entered the shop and took their seats. At a quick glance, Elma could see the shop was as neat and orderly inside as it was outside. It had obviously been thoroughly cleaned before the benches were set up for service.

Soon after, the men came in. The ministers and older men entered first, followed by young married men, and then the youth and young boys. The men sat on the opposite side of the room from the women, facing one another.

The service began with a song from their ancient Amish hymnal, the *Ausbund*. One of the men led off, carrying the first few notes, and then everyone else joined him. Soon after the singing began, the ministers left the building to discuss who would preach and to offer instructional classes to any candidates for baptism. An hour or so later, the ministers returned. When the singing ended a short time later, the first minister rose to begin his sermon, which lasted about twenty minutes. It still amazed Elma how the bishop and other ministers could preach without any notes on readings mostly found in the New Testament.

By the time the second minister, their bishop, rose to speak, Elma was struggling to keep from yawning out loud. She clasped her hand over her mouth and hoped no one was looking at her. They shouldn't be, after all; everyone was supposed to be focused on the one delivering the message. With eyes feeling heavy, Elma's head lowered then bobbed up again. *Oh no, I can't fall asleep. Guess I shouldn't have stayed up so late last night working on that new puzzle Thelma bought. On top of that, I'm exhausted from everything we did this past week. It's all catching up with me, I guess.*

Elma glanced at Thelma. She seemed to be wide awake and listening intently to what Homer Chupp, the elderly bishop, was saying. He was preaching from the book of Luke, chapter 18, and had quoted verse 27, which Elma had read the other day: "And he said, The things which are impossible with men are possible with God."

Given everything she and her sister were facing, Elma needed the reminder that nothing was impossible with God. They would try to do their best, seek His wisdom in all their business dealings, and trust Him to take care of their needs.

As the bishop's message continued, Elma struggled to keep her eyes open. At one point she was about to nod off, when Thelma's elbow connected with her arm. Elma's eyes snapped open and she sat up straight. She hoped she hadn't missed anything important. *What am I thinking?* she asked herself. *Everything that happens during our three-hour Sunday services is important—especially the Bible verses that are quoted during the message.*

Elma did better after that, but by the time Homer Chupp's message was over and the last song had been sung, she felt drowsy again. Hopefully after the meal, she and Thelma could be on their way home, because Elma needed a nap.

When it came time for the twins to sit down to the light meal that had been prepared, Elma felt a headache coming on. She didn't say anything, however, because Thelma seemed so eager to visit and make new friends. As soon as Thelma finished eating a few pieces of bread, spread with sweetened peanut butter, she offered to hold a young woman's baby so the mother could eat with both hands free. After putting some peanut butter on her own piece of bread, Elma realized that she wasn't the least bit hungry. Out of politeness, she nibbled on the bread, but set it down and took a sip of water instead. As the pain increased, she brought her hand up to the back of her neck and massaged it for a bit. It didn't help much, and she felt more uncomfortable by the minute.

When the woman who'd introduced herself as Nancy finished eating and took the baby back, Elma leaned over and whispered to Thelma, "Are you ready to leave now? I'd like to go home and take a nap."

"In a minute," Thelma said. "I haven't given out the candy I brought to any of the kinner." She hopped up and headed across the yard to where a group of children played a game of tag. They stopped immediately when she showed them the bag of candy, and it wasn't long before several more children showed up. Once all the candy had been passed out, Thelma went over to the swing set and started pushing one of the little girls who'd been at the store this past week.

Elma groaned inwardly, while rubbing her forehead. At this rate, they'd never get home. She feared that if they didn't leave soon, she could lose what little was in her stomach, because what had started out to be a normal headache was now turning into a pounding migraine.

Nancy leaned over and asked, "Are you all right? You look pale, and I noticed you rubbing your head."

"I've been fighting a *koppweh*, and it's turned into a migraine," Elma admitted.

Doris Miller came over. "Why don't you go inside and lie down for a while? You can rest in the downstairs guest room."

"I appreciate the offer, but I think it would be best if my sister and I head for home."

Elma told the women goodbye and headed across the yard to where Thelma was visiting with the children. "Sorry for interrupting, but I'm not feeling well. We need to go home."

"Oh, I'm sorry, Elma; I didn't know. I'll see about getting the horse right away."

Thelma hurried off and Elma headed straight for the buggy. When she got inside, she took her sunglasses out of her purse. The glare of the sun was intense and magnified the throbbing in her head. She blinked her eyes rapidly. Even her vision was blurring. Holding her stomach as a wave of nausea coursed through it, she hoped Thelma would return soon.

Elma moaned. *Why now?* She had hoped to enjoy today, since it was their first church service here and a chance to meet more of those in their community. Now, as she waited in the buggy, trying to think of things besides the pain in her head, waves of haziness clouded her vision. She closed her eyes to ward off the dizziness. *What is taking my sister so long? I hope she hasn't stopped to talk to anyone.*

Several minutes later, Thelma led Rusty to the front of the buggy.

The same Amish boy who had greeted them this morning was with her. He took care of getting the horse hitched while Thelma climbed into the driver's seat.

As they headed down the driveway, Elma's stomach gave a lurch. "Sister, you'd better pull over. I'm gonna be sick."

Chapter 7

"K*otz es raus, no fiehlscht besser!*" Thelma hollered as her sister bent over a clump of weeds. She'd told Elma to vomit it out, knowing it would make her feel better. Of course, it might not do much for her headache.

When Elma returned to the buggy a few minutes later, her face was pale as goat's milk. "I'm glad I didn't do that in front of the others. It would have been so humiliating."

"I'm sorry you're not feeling well. When we get home, you should go straight to bed."

"I surely won't argue with that. Resting in a darkened room is the only way I'll be able to get rid of this headache."

Thelma gave Elma's arm a gentle pat. "Don't worry about anything. As soon as we get home, you can head to the house. I'll take care of Rusty's needs and feed the chickens, as well as the cats. We were in such a hurry this morning, I forgot to do that."

"Danki." Elma leaned her head back and closed her eyes. Thelma hoped they'd make it home without her sister getting sick to her stomach again.

Please, Lord, let Rusty behave himself on the way home, Thelma silently prayed as she directed the horse onto the main road. With Elma feeling so poorly, this would not be a good time for him to act up.

❧

When Thelma guided Rusty into their yard, Elma felt relieved. Not only had the horse obeyed Thelma's commands, but Elma was simply glad to be home. Her stomach still churned a bit, and her head felt like it could explode, but at least she could finally lie down in her room. As soon as Thelma pulled Rusty to the hitching rail, Elma climbed out of the buggy. As hard as this simple task was, she managed to quickly secure the horse then gave her sister a wave and headed for the house. She walked slowly, not only because each step she took seemed to intensify the pain but also because she felt wobbly from the dizziness.

Stepping onto the porch, she was greeted by Tiger meowing and rubbing against her leg. "Go away," she muttered. "I'm not going to pet you, and you're not coming in."

Elma opened the door and slipped inside before the cat could make its move. She wished they'd never started letting him in at all, because now he expected it. *If we see any more mice, then he can come in,* Elma thought as she hung her black outer bonnet on a wall peg.

She went to the kitchen and got a glass of water then made her way carefully up the stairs. When she entered her room, she took off her dress and slipped into her nightgown. After she'd released her hair from its bun, she crawled into bed. Sleep was what she needed—quiet, uninterrupted sleep.

Elma was on the verge of dozing off, when Thelma tapped on her door. "Are you okay? Do you need anything? Should I fix you a cup of tea?"

Elma groaned. "No thanks. I just need some sleep."

"Oh, all right. I'm going downstairs now, but I'll check on you later."

Elma knew her sister meant well, but she wished she hadn't bothered her. Thelma wasn't prone to migraines, so she didn't fully understand what they were like. For Elma, they usually came on when she hadn't had enough sleep or was really stressed about something. She certainly had plenty of reasons to feel anxious right now—not only about the store and the home they'd inherited but also about their unpredictable horse.

As Thelma moved through the hall, past both her and Elma's bedrooms, her gaze came to rest on the large jar of marbles sitting on the floor at the end of the hall. Grandpa had collected marbles and had several jars scattered around the house. Some were in the way, as this one was.

Think I'll move that jar into the spare bedroom for now, Thelma decided.

Elma and I can decide what to do with it later on, but at least it won't be a danger to us anymore.

At first, Thelma tried to lift the cumbersome jar, but it was too heavy. *Maybe I'll try to slide it over there.* Leaning over, she grabbed the top of the jar and tipped it slightly in order to get a good grip. Moving backward, she slid it across the floor. She was almost to the guest room when she realized the door was closed. Trying to steady the jar with one hand, she reached up with the other hand to open the door. She turned the knob, but it wouldn't open. Then she remembered that this particular door had a tendency to stick. She pushed again, a little harder. As the door suddenly gave way, Thelma lost her balance, and the jar slipped from her grasp, crashing to the floor. Fortunately, the jar was intact, but marbles of all sizes and colors rolled everywhere along the hardwood floor, some even bouncing down the stairs.

Thelma's finger went to her lips, as if that would somehow muffle the racket and not disturb her sister. Thelma watched helplessly as the marbles finally rolled to a stop. Hunching her shoulders and holding her breath as everything grew quiet again, she squeezed her eyes shut and waited.

"What's going on out there?" Elma called from her room.

"Don't come out!" Thelma hollered, wishing her sister hadn't been disturbed. "I dropped a jar, and marbles are everywhere. It's not safe. Let me sweep the marbles into the guest room and pick up the strays. I'll let you know when it's safe to come out."

"Okay. Be careful, Thelma. You don't want to slip and fall."

"I'll watch what I'm doing."

"Do you need any help?"

"No, I can manage. Please, stay in your room and rest." Thankful that they had a broom in the upstairs utility closet, Thelma took it out. After she'd opened the door to the spare room, she laid a small cardboard box on its side and swept the marbles inside. She would figure out what to do with them some other time.

Looking around the room at the boxes and other items scattered about, Thelma realized they would never have it cleaned up in time for Mom and Dad to sleep here. They'd have to use Grandma and Grandpa's old room downstairs. That would be more convenient anyway, since it was close to the bathroom. She hoped it wouldn't make Dad feel sad to sleep in his parents' bed.

e⌢⌣

After Thelma had picked up the stray marbles that had rolled down the steps, she headed outside to the coop to feed the chickens and check for eggs. When that was done, she set the basket filled with six eggs on the back porch and headed across the yard.

Breathing the earthy scent lingering in the air, Thelma headed toward the barn. Even though it was in need of a new coat of red paint, the building itself would probably be around for a good many years.

When she entered the barn and headed for Rusty's stall, he kicked the wall in front of him. "Now calm down, boy. Your meal is on the way." Thelma grabbed a hefty chunk of alfalfa hay and placed it in the horse's feeding trough. "How's it going, Rusty?"

The horse nickered.

Thelma smiled and patted him gently up by his ear. "It's your dinnertime, and now the barn cats need some food too." She left his stall, making sure the latch was secure on his door.

After she'd fed and watered the cats, she took a seat on a bale of straw. Leaning against another bale, she sat quietly listening and watching the animals crunching on their food. They all appeared to be content, like she was, breathing in the pleasant grassy aroma in the barn. Thelma missed the way things had been when her grandparents were living. Looking over at Cutter's empty stall made this moment quite difficult to bear. She fought back tears as she continued to sit and reminisce. Finally, she rose, brushed her sweater and dress off, and headed back to the house.

Once inside, she took care of the eggs then fixed herself a glass of chocolate milk and went to the living room to relax. The past week had been busy, and it was nice sitting here in the quiet and solitude.

Thelma reached for Grandma's Bible lying on the table beside her. Opening it to a page marked with a ribbon, she read Proverbs 16:20 out loud: " 'He that handleth a matter wisely shall find good: and whoso trusteth in the LORD, happy is he.' "

What a good verse this is for us right now, Thelma thought. *I need to commit it to memory.*

Hearing a noise from below, Thelma suddenly remembered the mother cat and baby she'd found in the basement. She needed to check on them and feed the mama cat.

Setting the Bible aside and slipping into her sweater again, Thelma went back out to the barn. When she returned to the house, she was relieved to see that Elma hadn't gotten up yet. It wouldn't be good if she had to explain what she was doing with a sack of cat food. She'd never understood why her sister didn't care much for cats.

Thelma went to the kitchen and grabbed her flashlight then made her way down to the basement. As soon as she descended the last step, she heard mewing. Taking a quick peek, she saw that the mama cat now had four babies. "I brought you some nourishment, Misty." Thelma chose that name because the cat had light gray fur. She poured food into the dish she'd brought along and set it near Misty. The cat sniffed it and then started chomping. While Misty ate, Thelma filled another bowl with water from the utility sink. Some dirty clothes were in the laundry basket, and Thelma was glad the cat hadn't climbed in that to give birth to her babies.

Passing the hot water tank on her way to give Misty her drink, Thelma noticed a small puddle. She hoped the tank wasn't leaking. Perhaps some water had sloshed out of the washing machine when she'd washed a few towels yesterday. But if that were the case, wouldn't there be moisture in other places too?

Thelma gave Misty a drink then grabbed an old rag and sopped up the water. If it had come from the old tank, it would probably happen again. She'd check it the next time she came down. Thelma sighed. *One more thing to remember.*

LaGrange

Joseph leaned back in his chair, locking his fingers behind his head as he visited with Delbert after the noon meal following the church service in their district. They'd stayed longer than usual today, enjoying the fellowship with members of their community.

"Those were good messages our ministers preached today," Joseph said. "The one our bishop preached about being trustworthy and keeping our promises really spoke to me."

Delbert nodded, stroking his chin. "The promises we render to unbelievers can make a difference in how they view us as Christians."

"That's true. If we say we're gonna do something and don't follow through, it makes us appear dishonest." Joseph reached for his coffee cup and took a drink. "The other sermon, about helping others when we see a need, was important too."

"Jah."

"Speaking of helping others," Joseph said, "when we were in Shipshe the other day, I picked up a flyer about a cooking show that will take place next month. It's for a good cause. Would you like to go there with me?"

Delbert grinned. "You know, now that you mentioned it, I picked up the same flyer. I must have dropped it somewhere though, 'cause when I got home, it wasn't with my purchases."

"Did you plan to go?"

"Sure, if something else doesn't come up."

Joseph snapped his fingers. "Say, I have an idea. Since you're a pretty fair cook, maybe you could make something and have it auctioned off."

"No way! I'd have to not only make something ahead of time and bring it to the event, but I'd be required to stand in front of everyone and make the recipe from scratch." Delbert shook his head vigorously. "I wouldn't mind bringin' something to auction off, but I could never prepare it in front of a large crowd."

Joseph tapped his friend's arm. "Okay, Dell, forget I mentioned that part, but if you're not busy that day, you can join me, because I plan to go."

"Jah, okay." Delbert smiled. "As you said, it is for a good cause. Maybe we'll find something we'd both like to bid on that day."

Chapter 8

Topeka

The next morning, Thelma had breakfast ready when Elma entered the kitchen. "Did you sleep well?" Thelma asked. "Is your koppweh gone?"

Elma walked over to the window and looked out. "Jah, my headache is gone. It upsets me when I get a migraine like that, because it puts me down, sometimes for hours."

"I'm sorry you have to deal with those. I can't imagine what it must be like. Even when I get a sinus headache, it's rough."

Elma sat down at the table. "I'm glad headaches like that are one thing we don't have in common. I sure wouldn't want you to go through such pain—not to mention getting sick to your stomach."

"Thank the good Lord your headache is over. Shall we pray?"

Elma nodded, and they both bowed their heads. *Heavenly Father,* Thelma prayed, *please guide and direct our lives this week and keep our friends and family safe. Bless this food to the nourishment of our bodies. Amen.*

When they had both finished praying, Thelma smiled and handed her sister a bowl of oatmeal. "I hope this isn't too sticky. I think I'm getting the hang of cooking on top of the stove, but sometimes the kettle heats up too quickly and everything sticks to the bottom."

Elma added a pat of butter and some brown sugar to her bowl and stirred it around. Then she poured a little milk over the top and took a bite. "It tastes fine to me."

"Oh good." Thelma put butter in her bowl of cereal as well, only she added a hefty dash of cinnamon along with several scoops of brown sugar before finishing it off with milk.

Elma's brows wrinkled. "That's a lot of sugar you've added to your hot cereal."

"You're right; I probably shouldn't have gotten so carried away." Thelma grinned as she stirred the toppings into the oatmeal. "I wish we had some raisins to add. That would be healthy and tasty."

"We'll get some the next time we go for groceries," Elma said. "As soon as we're finished eating though, I think I'll go down to the basement and wash some clothes before it's time to open the store. Since it's raining lightly this morning, I'll hang everything on the line in the basement."

Feeling a sense of panic, Thelma's grin faded, and her eyes widened. "There's no reason for you to do that. You had a rough day yesterday and need to take it easy. Let me do the laundry."

"After lying around most of yesterday, I'm anxious to do something." Elma cleared her throat. "Besides, I'm fine now, and since we'll be working in the store most of the day, I definitely won't be taking it easy."

"That may be true, but it's all the more reason to let me wash our clothes," Thelma insisted. If Elma went to the basement, she'd probably hear Misty or her kittens, and that was the last thing Thelma needed.

"Okay, if you insist." Elma drank some of her coffee. "While you're doing that, I'll go over some of my lists to make sure I haven't forgotten to write down anything important that needs to be done. Have you been adding things to your list?"

"I've been trying," Thelma replied. *Should I say anything about the puddle I found near the hot water tank? No, my sister will want to go down there and check on it herself. That would be another opportunity for her to discover the mama cat and her kittens. I'll wait.*

Thelma smiled. "When we're both done with our chores in here, we can head over to the store."

"What about the outside chores?" Elma questioned. "Do you want me to feed the chickens and gather eggs while you take care of the barn cats and Rusty?"

Thelma touched her sister's arm. "Already taken care of. I did those things while you were taking your shower."

"Jah, and a cold shower it was." Elma grimaced. "I had only been showering a few minutes before the water went from lukewarm to cold.

I'm afraid it won't be long and we'll have to replace that old water tank in the basement."

"Maybe it only needs some adjustments or a new element," Thelma was quick to say. "We'll ask Dad to take a look at it after the folks get here next week."

Elma's eyes brightened. "I can't believe they'll be here so soon. Won't it be great to see them again?"

Thelma nodded. "I hope Mom doesn't try to talk us out of staying here. She wasn't too happy when she found out Grandpa and Grandma had left us their place."

"That's true, but she's had some time to get used to the idea, so maybe she won't even bring up the notion of us selling this place and moving back home." Elma blotted her lips with her napkin. "I hope not, because even though we've had a few bumps in the road, I already feel like this is our home."

"Me too. It's good that we're both in agreement because we could never do all this work without each other's help." Thelma spooned a small bite of cereal into her mouth. "Yum. This tastes *appeditlich*. Too bad it takes so much effort to cook on that old stove."

"You're right. It is delicious." Elma poured a little more milk over her oatmeal. "As the old saying goes, 'Anything good takes effort.'"

⁊

When Thelma got to the basement, she turned on the gas lamps then checked on the cats and gave the mama some food. She also made sure to give Misty a litter box filled with shredded newspapers she'd found stacked along one wall in the basement. It seemed that her grandparents liked to save everything.

Thelma stood watching the cute little kittens for a few minutes. Their eyes wouldn't open for at least ten days, but somehow they managed to wiggle their little bodies around. Moving over to the wringer washing machine, she started filling the tub with water and poured in the detergent. While the water went in, she put some sheets in the machine. The tub still had a lot of room, so she retrieved some dirty towels from the laundry basket and added them as well. Thelma leaned over and looked under the washer, making sure the hose was inside the floor drain. *Sure wouldn't want water running out the hose and having a big mess to mop up,* she thought.

"Do you need any help with the clothes?" Elma hollered down the basement stairs.

Thelma cupped her hands around her mouth. "Danki anyway, but I'm fine on my own. Keep doing what you're doing. I'll be up as soon as I get the clothes hung on the line."

Thelma watched the clothes agitating for a moment. Then she grabbed the broom and brushed away the cobwebs overhead as she moved around the washroom. Smiling, she was pleased that at least this area was a bit tidier.

❧

Elma had put her notepad away when Thelma came upstairs. "It's still raining lightly, so we may need our umbrellas."

"Okay. I'll get one for each of us." Thelma went to the utility room and returned with two black umbrellas. She handed one to Elma and opened the back door.

"Looks like it might let up soon," Elma commented as they headed to the store. "See that blue patch of sky?" She pointed to the east.

"I see that, but even if it quits raining, it feels like it's going to be a chilly day. Oh, and look who's following us—Tiger the cat." Thelma's umbrella bumped into Elma's, knocking it out of her hand and onto the ground. "Oops! Sorry about that. Here, take mine." Thelma handed her umbrella to Elma, and then stepping around her, she grabbed the one that had fallen.

Elma smiled. "Danki. No harm done."

They stepped onto the porch, and when Elma unlocked the door, she paused. "We'll be inside most of the day, so we won't even notice the weather." She entered the store, and Thelma followed.

"It's a bit dampish in here." Thelma rubbed her arms. "I've got goose bumps already."

"Guess one of us should have come out earlier and gotten that little woodstove going."

"You know what?" Thelma whirled around. "One of us really needs to go out to the phone shack and check for messages."

"I suppose that would be a good idea," Elma agreed.

"I'll go, unless you want to."

"No, you go ahead. I want to get this stove going so we have some heat in here. Then I need to do more inventory before any customers show up."

"Okay, I'll be back soon."

"Oh great!" Elma pointed. "You left the door open, and the cat got in. We'd better get him quick before he hides, or we'll be stuck with that critter in our store all day."

"I'll take care of it." Thelma scooped up the cat and carried him outside, along with her umbrella. "All's good," she said before closing the door behind her.

Elma put her umbrella behind the counter and saw a box of starter sticks to get a fire going. She'd also noticed a small pile of wood stacked outside by the side of the store. That must have been where Grandpa kept the wood they used for the stove.

Elma finished lighting a few of the fire sticks she'd put inside the stove and sniffed. Glancing back at the stove, she noticed smoke coming out through the door, and also from the area where the pipe connected. Quickly, she ran to the bathroom and filled a jar with water. Dashing back to the stove, she doused the fire. Luckily, it hadn't been burning long enough to make the stove or the pipe hot.

Elma wasn't sure she was doing the right thing, but she detached the pipe where it connected to the stove then twisted it off at the top where it connected to another section that went through the store's roof. "Let's see if there's anything blocking this straight part," she muttered, holding the pipe up and looking through it. Elma shrieked as an empty bird's nest fell onto the floor. Instinctively, she looked up the pipe, which was a big mistake. At that instant, a puff of soot swooshed onto her face.

"Ach no!" Elma sputtered, blowing a cloud of soot off her lips. "Just look at me. And look at my dress!" Running her hands over the front, smearing more dark powdery ash all over the material, all she could do was stand there with her mouth open.

"What happened to you?" Thelma looked stunned as she came into the store.

"I—I started to light the stove, and all this smoke poured out." Elma swiped the back of her hand over her mouth. "Then, after I put out the fire, I took the pipe off and this fell out." Holding up the bird's nest and motioning to her dress, she grimaced. "You can see what happened next."

Thelma snickered; then her face sobered. "You'd better go back to the house, change out of that dress, and get washed up. While you're gone, I'll clean up in here. Hopefully I'll have it done by the time you get back."

"Danki, Thelma. I'll be back as soon as possible."

❧

When Elma returned to the store half an hour later, she was surprised to see Thelma standing behind the counter, smiling. "Surprise! It's all done." Thelma pointed to the stove. Not only had Thelma cleaned up the mess, but she had the stovepipe back on and a cozy fire going. "It should warm up quickly now."

Elma smiled. "Danki. You're such a big help."

"By the way, what did you do with your dress?" Thelma asked.

Elma sighed. "It's soaking in a bucket of water in the utility room. I'm not sure if that poor dress will ever be the same; it's such a mess. I may replace it with the new dress I still haven't made. Of course," she quickly added, "I have other work dresses I can wear."

"That's true, and at least this all happened when there were no customers in the store. That could have been quite embarrassing."

"You're right." Elma couldn't help giggling. She could only imagine how silly she must have looked, standing there with soot all over her while holding a bird's nest.

"Guess we'd better get busy," Thelma said.

Elma picked up a tablet, preparing to write down whatever needed to be ordered. She'd only made it to the first aisle, when Thelma came by. "I forgot to tell you. When I went to the phone shack I saw someone across the street looking at the house that's for sale."

"Are they Amish or English?"

"Amish. I saw them walking around the yard, and I noticed that the woman's skirt is pleated." Thelma's forehead wrinkled. "I don't think I've ever seen an Amish woman's dress with pleats."

"She's probably from the Graybill area," Elma said. "Didn't someone tell us that many of the Amish women who live there wear skirts like that?"

Thelma tipped her head. "I can't remember. . .maybe." She frowned, brushing at some stray cat hairs on her sweater. "Tiger can sure shed. Guess when I find the time I'll have to brush him again."

"That may help some, but it'll be a constant chore. One more reason I don't like having cats indoors."

Thelma shrugged. "Anyway, it will be nice if we get new neighbors soon. I'll be anxious to get acquainted."

"You'll have plenty of time for that if they buy the house."

"That's true."

"By the way, were there any important messages?" Elma asked.

"Not a one." Thelma snapped her fingers. "Guess I should have checked for mail when I went to the phone shack. I'll do that now."

♲

Thelma was almost to the mailbox when she noticed Mary Lambright riding past on her bike. Her little boy Richard was in a child's seat on the back. Thelma hollered a greeting to them and waved. Mary and Richard waved back. It had quit raining, but the roads were slightly wet.

Smiling, Thelma stepped up to the box. She was about to reach inside, when she heard a horn honk, followed by the spine-tingling sound of brakes squealing—then a bloodcurdling scream. Thelma rushed out and looked up the road. Mary and Richard lay sprawled on the ground, next to the bike. With her heart in her throat, Thelma dashed to the accident. *Please, God, let them be all right.*

Chapter 9

Thelma dropped to her knees beside Mary and Richard. The driver of the car, a young woman, got out and rushed over. "Oh my! Are either of you hurt?" The woman's voice trembled as she knelt next to Thelma.

"I'm all right—just a few scrapes on my knees and hands," Mary said. "But I'm worried about my little boy." She gestured to Richard, still strapped in his seat at the back of her bike, sobbing and holding his gravel-embedded arm.

"This was my fault," the woman said. "I shouldn't have honked the horn when I saw your bike."

Thelma winced when she saw the way Richard's arm was twisted. "I think his arm is broken," she whispered to Mary. "We have to get him out of that seat. You'll need to take him to the medical clinic and have it X-rayed."

Mary's fingers trembled as she struggled with the safety strap.

"Here, let me try," Thelma offered.

"We can cut the strap with the scissors I have in my purse," the English woman said. "I can call 911 or drive you there. I'll call my boss and let him know I'm gonna be late for work."

Mary nodded. "I'd appreciate the scissors—and a ride to the clinic."

Thelma cut the strap away, and Mary took her son out of the seat. Gathering her son carefully into her arms, Mary said, "It'll be okay, son. The doctor will take good care of you."

While the young woman made the phone call, Thelma held Richard, and Mary climbed into the backseat of the car. Then Thelma gingerly handed the boy to his mother. It was hard seeing the little tyke grimace in pain.

"I'll take your bike to my place, and someone from your family can pick it up later on." Thelma spoke in a reassuring tone.

Tears gathered in Mary's eyes. "Danki, Elma. My husband, Dan, is at work right now, and my *mamm's* home with our other son, Philip. It probably won't be till sometime this evening that Dan can come by with our market wagon to pick up my bike."

Thelma was on the verge of correcting Mary, but right now it didn't matter that the woman had mixed her up with Elma. She was used to that. Even some people back home who had known them for years couldn't tell the twins apart. The only thing that mattered was getting Richard's arm looked at. "This evening will be fine. Mary, if you'll give me your address, I'll go to your house and let your mamm know what's happened so she doesn't worry because you haven't returned home."

"That would be most appreciated." Mary's voice was full of emotion.

Thelma gave Mary's arm a tender squeeze. "I'll be praying for Richard."

"Danki." Mary dabbed at the tears on her pale cheeks; then she reached into her purse and took out a notepad and pen. After she wrote down the address, she tore off a piece of paper and handed it to Thelma. "Please tell my mamm not to worry but to pray that Richard's arm does not have a serious break."

"I will," Thelma promised. "And I'll be praying myself."

e⅃◡

Elma peered out the front window of the store, wondering where Thelma was. She'd been gone a lot longer than necessary to get the mail. *I wonder if my sister got sidetracked again.* She opened the door and stuck her head out but saw no sign of Thelma in the yard or down the driveway. If Elma hadn't been concerned that a customer could show up, she would have walked out to the mailbox to see if her sister was still there.

I'll give her a few more minutes, she decided, *but if she doesn't show up soon I'll put the* CLOSED *sign in the window and see if I can find her.*

Elma went back to inventorying the shelves and was about to start on the next row of kitchen items when the front door opened and Thelma rushed in.

"You'll never believe what happened out there," she panted.

"What is it?" Elma asked. "You look *umgerrent*."

"I am upset. Mary Lambright was on her bicycle with her son Richard on the seat behind her, and. . ." Thelma paused to take a breath. "A car almost hit her, and she and Richard fell off the bike." She moved over to stand beside the woodstove.

"Oh dear," Elma gasped. "Were either of them hurt?"

"Mary was scraped up, and it looked like the little boy's arm was broken. The driver of the car is taking them to the medical clinic. I brought Mary's bike back here. Her husband will pick it up later. Oh, and Mary gave me her address, so I promised to go over to her house and let her mamm know what happened. She's there with Mary's other son, Philip." Thelma was talking so fast Elma could hardly keep up with her.

"I'm sorry to hear about the accident but grateful that it wasn't any worse." Elma thought about her grandparents' fatality. Whether riding in a buggy, on a bicycle, or walking, there was always the danger of being hit by a car.

"I know, but even though the little guy's injuries weren't life threatening, he was frightened and obviously in pain." Thelma fiddled with the paper she held.

"I imagine he would be. Remember when we were eight and I fell from the loft in Dad's barn and broke my *gnechel*? That hurt."

Thelma nodded. "We were all glad it was only your ankle that was broken. You could have been killed, falling a distance like that."

"God watched out for me that day. There's no doubt about it."

Thelma glanced around. "How are things here? Have you gotten much inventory done?"

"Some, but I still have several more shelves to get to, not to mention all the things that are in the store's basement."

"Have you had any customers yet?"

Elma shook her head. "Maybe it's going to be a slow day and we can spend it taking stock of all the things we need to order."

"I know one thing. . . The buggy could use a little cleaning, outside and in. With the rain we've gotten, plus the dust in the air, our rig is looking a bit neglected."

"You're right," Elma agreed. "That's one more thing I'll need to add to my list."

Moving away from the stove, Thelma said, "Since there are no customers at the moment, I'd better head over to Mary's house and let her mamm know what happened."

"Does Mary live far from here?" Elma asked.

"From the address she gave me, I'd say it's about a mile or so."

"That shouldn't take you too long, if you go on your bike."

Thelma paused and shifted her weight from one foot to the other. "Actually, I thought I'd take the horse and buggy and make a stop at the hardware store in town."

Elma's forehead wrinkled. "How come?"

"Remember that paint I forgot to get in Shipshe last week?"

"Jah."

"If I don't get it now, we'll never have the kitchen painted before Mom and Dad get here."

Elma pursed her lips. "You're right about that. Guess I can get by awhile longer without your help."

"There's one more errand I'll need to run," Thelma said.

"What's that?"

"Before I came back to the store, I checked phone messages again. There was a new one from the people who own the meat locker in town." Thelma grimaced. "They said Grandpa and Grandma's bill hadn't been paid for this month. They asked whether we want to pay it or come by and get what's left in the locker they'd rented."

Elma groaned. "Oh great. I wonder what that will cost. Will it never end?"

Thelma shrugged, turning her hands palms up. "Guess I could go by there and clear out their locker, but I'm not sure how much there is. We may not have room for all of it in the small freezer section of our refrigerator, but we'll slip in whatever we can. Maybe we can precook part of the meat to have for some of the meals we'll be fixing this week."

"You're right," Elma agreed. "Did they say how much the rent would be for the next month?"

"Jah. It's twenty-two dollars. Can we afford that right now?"

"I guess we'll have to." Elma went to the battery-operated cash register behind the counter and took out a twenty dollar bill, plus two ones. "Here you go."

"I'll need some money for the paint too," Thelma reminded.

"Oh, that's right." She handed Thelma another fifty dollars. "I hope this will be enough. If it's not, then get one gallon for now."

"Okay. I'd better get going then." Thelma turned toward the door, glancing at the sky. "Maybe I'll take an umbrella. It was clearing up a little while ago, but I see a few more dark clouds." She slipped on her outer bonnet and grabbed the umbrella.

Elma touched her arm. "Are you sure you want to take Rusty?"

"It's the only way I can take the buggy, and there's no way I'm going to ride my bike that far, not to mention needing a place to put the paint." Thelma paused. "I'll probably bring home some meat from the locker too. Anyway, Rusty needs to earn his keep around here. He should be worked as much as possible. Otherwise, he may get worse, and I won't let him do that. Dad would want us to hang in there and keep showing Rusty who's boss. Right, Sister?"

Elma hesitated then nodded. "Okay, see you later then."

"I'll be back as soon as I can."

When Thelma went out the door, Elma leaned against the counter and sighed. "I hope I gave Thelma enough money. Even more than that, I hope and pray the horse behaves."

Chapter 10

When Thelma left Mary's house, after notifying Richard's grand-mother that he had broken his arm, she headed toward town. She felt a little nervous when she halted Rusty at the first stop sign and he started tossing his head from side to side.

"Calm down," Thelma said soothingly. "We can't go till it's safe." Once she was sure no cars were coming, she guided the horse to make a right-hand turn onto the highway that would take them to the stores in Topeka. Rusty moved at a pretty good clip, but as long as he wasn't running out of control, she didn't mind. The quicker she got to town, the quicker she'd get back to the store to help Elma. At least the trip to the local hardware store wouldn't be as long as it would have been if she'd gone all the way to Shipshewana.

The clouds that had looked threatening when she'd first left home were now breaking apart, letting peeks of sunshine through. Thelma was glad it had quit raining. That made it easier to see, and with less water on the pavement, Rusty was not as likely to spook.

As she drew closer to town, Thelma thought about Richard and won-dered how things were going at the clinic. Had he seen the doctor yet? If his arm was broken, would they be able to take care of it there, or would Mary have to take her son to the closest hospital?

If it doesn't take too long at the hardware store and frozen food locker, maybe I'll stop by the clinic before I go home, Thelma thought. *That way, I'll know for sure what happened to Mary's little boy.*

Joseph had spent the last few hours in Topeka, visiting with the Amish man who owned the harness shop. The man had more business than he could handle and wondered if he could send some customers to Joseph. Never one to turn down a job opportunity, Joseph had eagerly agreed.

Guess I won't need to stop by the office for The Connection *magazine to run an ad like I'd planned,* Joseph thought as he left the harness shop. *Maybe another time, if business gets slow.*

Thinking he ought to make a quick stop at the hardware store to pick up some paint for his bedroom, Joseph directed his horse and buggy in that direction. The horse, which had been moving along steadily, suddenly broke into a canter. "Whoa, boy! Slow down!" Joseph pulled on the reins.

The horse slowed, and in no time, Joseph had the animal under control.

When he entered the hardware store a short time later, he noticed a young Amish woman standing near the aisle where the paint was kept, tapping her chin as she studied the cans.

When he approached, she looked up at him and smiled, revealing a small dimple in her right cheek. "Do you know much about paint?" she asked.

He shrugged. "A l–little." *Oh great. Don't start stuttering now.* Tripping over his words was something Joseph did only when he felt nervous, and for some reason that's how he felt at the moment. The dumb thing was he didn't even know why. He'd never met this woman with the pretty blue eyes before and might never see her again. Besides, a woman as attractive as her was probably married.

"The wording is so small; I'm having a hard time reading the instructions and recommendations on the paint cans. Would you be able to tell me what kind of paint would be best to use in a kitchen?"

"Umm. . ." Joseph cleared his throat and swallowed. He hoped he wasn't going to stutter again. "I'd say a latex/enamel would be a good choice." *Whew. So far, so good.* Joseph pointed to one of the cans. "What color do you want?"

She pursed her lips while studying the various colors available. "I've been looking at these color samples. I'm thinking an off-white would be best."

He gave a nod. "Makes sense to me."

"I appreciate the advice." She smiled, picked up two cans of paint, and headed to the checkout counter.

"Good luck with your project." Joseph gave her one last glance and moved on to pick out his paint.

⸿

When Thelma started for the door, carrying the paint she'd purchased, she caught sight of a flyer taped to the inside of the store window. It was the same as the one she'd picked up in Shipshewana, telling about the upcoming cooking show. She felt certain it was something Elma would want to do with her. After all, who wouldn't want to help a good cause such as this? *Think I'll call the phone number on the flyer and let the person in charge know that my sister and I would like to make something to be auctioned off. I also have one other important call to make.*

She'd barely stepped outside when the red-haired Amish man she'd spoken to about the paint came out the door holding a paintbrush. He approached her in a shy manner, and with a little stutter in his voice, he said, "I—I think this is yours. It was left on the c—counter inside."

Thelma's cheeks warmed as she took the paintbrush from him. "Guess I was in such a hurry, I forgot." For some strange reason it was all she could do to keep from tripping over her own words. Forcing herself to look away from his steady gaze, Thelma glanced to her left. She was stunned to see Rusty prancing up the street, pulling her buggy. "Oh my!" She pointed in that direction. "That's my horse and buggy, with no driver. I must not have tied him securely enough."

The redheaded man sprang into action. As he dashed up the street, his straw hat blew off, landing on the pavement, but he kept running and never looked back. Another Amish man who sported a full beard and had been standing nearby joined the chase as well. With her heart beating wildly, all Thelma could do was stand there, powerless, and watch. What a day full of mishaps this had turned out to be.

By some miracle, the two men managed to get hold of Rusty. Several minutes later, they brought him back to Thelma. She breathed a sigh of relief. Never in a million years had she expected that her and Elma's move to Topeka would bring so much drama.

"Danki," she told the men. "I fear that unpredictable horse would have run into the next county if you two hadn't caught him when you did."

"I'm glad I could help," the older of the two men said, still trying to catch his breath.

The man with red hair gave a nod. "He gave us quite a chase."

Thelma couldn't help but notice how the man's freckles stood out against his rosy cheeks. Despite the fact that his ears stuck out a bit, she thought he was rather good looking. Not in a dashing sort of way, like the blond-haired man she'd bumped heads with at Yoder's Hardware last week, but in a boyish sort of way she found appealing. She knew he wasn't married because he was clean shaven. *Stop thinking such crazy thoughts,* Thelma reprimanded herself. *My focus should be on all that Elma and I need to get done before Mom and Dad arrive, not thinking about men I don't even know.*

"Would one of you mind holding my horse awhile longer, so I can get the paint and brush put in the buggy?" Thelma asked the men.

"I'd be happy to do that," the bearded man spoke up.

After giving the horse's nose a gentle pat, the younger man with red hair stepped away from Rusty. "I'm glad everything's under control, so I'll be on my way." He gave Thelma a quick nod and hurried off down the street.

Thelma put her purchases on the floor of the passenger's side then stepped into the driver's seat. Gathering up the reins, she waved at the bearded Amish man and headed down the street in the direction of the building where her grandparents had rented a freezer. "Okay, Rusty, you've had your fun for the day. Now you'd better be good."

Fortunately, Rusty behaved himself, and in no time Thelma was guiding the horse up to the hitching rail. She made sure he was securely tied and hurried inside the building. After paying for this month's rent, she removed a few packages of meat from the freezer and placed them in a cooler in the back of her buggy. The meat would come in handy when their parents were here next week. Thelma and Elma would be able to make a variety of dishes with the ground beef. She'd also brought a roast, some stew meat, a couple of steaks, and some breakfast sausage. *If we need any more meat while Mom and Dad are here, at least it's not far to go to get more.*

From there, Thelma headed to the clinic, where she found Mary sitting in the waiting room. "How's Richard?" Thelma asked, taking a seat beside Mary.

"His arm is broken," Mary replied. "The doctor is putting the cast on now. I came out here to call my driver for a ride home."

"Have you already done that? If not, I could take you."

Mary smiled. "I appreciate the offer, but Carolyn is already on the way."

"Oh, okay." Thelma glanced at the clock on the far wall. As much as she would like to stay until Richard came out, she'd been gone over two hours and knew she really should get home. "I'll try to stop by your place sometime tomorrow to see how Richard is doing," she told Mary.

Mary nodded. "That'd be nice. I'm sure he'd like that."

"See you tomorrow then." Thelma gave Mary's arm a gentle squeeze and headed out the door.

☙

By the time Thelma guided Rusty off the road and onto their driveway, she was more than ready to get out. She'd struggled to keep him under control the whole way home. She wondered how long it would be before he settled down and became easier to deal with. Pearl, their horse back home, had never been this testy. From the day she and Elma had first gotten the gentle mare, she'd always been easy to handle.

Remembering the phone calls she wanted to make, Thelma stopped the horse outside the phone shack and secured him to a post. She stepped into the small building and dialed the first number. After she'd made both calls, she untied the horse and hopped back into the buggy. As she directed Rusty up the driveway toward the barn, Thelma noticed three buggies parked outside the store. *Oh great. I wonder how many customers there are and how long they've been here. I'll bet Elma is upset with me for being gone so long and leaving her here to run things by herself.*

Thelma jumped out of the buggy and quickly took care of Rusty. Once she'd put him in the corral, she grabbed the cooler of meat and took it to the house to put in the refrigerator. She would get the paint out of the buggy later.

Standing in the kitchen, staring at the basement door, Thelma was tempted to make a quick trip down to check on Misty and her babies but figured it was best to get right over to the store. Still, she paused to listen and was satisfied that all was quiet.

In addition to helping Elma wait on customers, Thelma was anxious to tell her sister what she'd found out about Mary's son. It would be best not to say anything about Rusty taking off when she was in town. And she wouldn't bother to mention how skittish he'd acted on the way home. No point making Elma more afraid of the horse than she already was. And Thelma would certainly not tell her sister about one of the phone calls she'd made.

Chapter 11

"I can't believe Mom and Dad will be here this evening," Elma told Thelma as they cleaned the kitchen floor and counters.

"I know," Thelma agreed, "and I'm glad we managed to get the kitchen painted before they arrive. How exciting it will be to have them here. They'll be the first guests to stay with us as new owners of this house." Her bubbly words bounced off the walls. "Hey Sister, we can have them sign the guest book when they arrive. There'll be all new memories to make while they're here." She pushed the soapy mop around the kitchen floor.

"We've worked so hard getting ready for their arrival, yet there's still so much to be done." Elma sighed, pinning a wayward strand of hair back under her headscarf. "I think every bone in my body aches."

"Mine too." Thelma set the mop aside, rubbing her neck. "I'm glad we decided to close the store today so we could take care of any last-minute things that needed to be done here at the house." She smiled. "And I'm glad I went over to see how little Richard was doing last week, because there hasn't been time this week, with all we've needed to do."

"I keep forgetting to ask. Did he like the book and candy you took him?"

Thelma nodded. "He especially liked *The Wisdom of Solomon* because it's a picture book, so he can look at the drawings and know what's happening in the story, even though he can't read yet."

"That's nice." Elma gestured to the stove. "Have you thought about what we could fix for supper this evening? I'm sure Mom and Dad will be here before it's time to eat."

"I thought maybe we could fix some savory stew. There's a recipe for it in one of Grandma's cookbooks, and we have some stew meat I brought home last week from the freezer they rented. I put it, along with the rest of the meat, in the smaller freezer compartment of our refrigerator. If I get it out now, I don't think it'll take long to thaw."

"That's a good idea." Elma put her cleaning supplies away. "While you get the meat, I'll cut some vegetables for the stew."

"Don't you want to wait till the meat has thawed?"

Elma shook her head. "It'll save time if I do it now. Once I get the veggies cut, I'll refrigerate them until it's time to start the stew."

"Guess that makes sense." Thelma took the package of meat from the freezer and placed it in a bowl of cool water. "Think I'll go to the basement and do a little more cleaning down there before it's time to start lunch."

Elma tipped her head. "I don't think Mom and Dad will be doing much in the basement while they're here, so that's not really a priority right now."

"Mom may go down to wash clothes, and I want Dad to look at the water tank," Thelma replied. "Sure don't want them walking through cobwebs or getting their clothes dusty."

Elma shrugged. "You're right."

When Thelma left the kitchen, Elma took out some carrots, celery, potatoes, and onions and placed them on the counter beside the cutting board. As she washed the vegetables in the sink, she thought about her sister and the strange way she'd been acting for the past week. For some reason, Thelma kept making unnecessary trips to the basement. At least Elma saw them as unnecessary. It was one thing to go down there to wash clothes, but Thelma had already done so much cleaning downstairs that the place had to be spick-and-span by now. *And why, every time I say I'm going to the basement, does she offer to go in my place?*

⁓

After Thelma fed Misty and filled her bowl with fresh water, she knelt beside the box and petted the kittens. They were so cute and soft. One kitten was gray like its mother, one was all white, and two resembled a black barn cat Thelma had named Shadow. No doubt, he was the father. Thelma felt guilty for keeping the cats a secret, and she didn't know how much longer she could prevent Elma from coming down to the basement.

The one thing she had on her side was that her sister had so many other things to keep her busy.

In addition to trying to get things organized at the store, both she and Elma had spent some time each evening going through some of their grandparents' things. They'd decided to put some of Grandpa's marbles in one of Grandma's old canning jars Thelma had found in the basement. She'd placed it in the middle of the kitchen table as a centerpiece. To some, it may look ordinary, but to Thelma it was a sentimental reminder of her grandparents. She was sure that Elma felt the same. It was fun to look at the variety of marbles in different sizes. Some were clear, some were solid colors, and other marbles had a pattern inside. Since Grandpa had collected so many marbles, she and her sister decided to put the rest of them in glass jars and try to sell them at the store. In the hall closet upstairs, among the other linens, they'd found a box of beautiful pillowcases Grandma had embroidered. They looked as if they'd never been used. Each set had been beautifully wrapped in white tissue paper and neatly folded in the box. Because there were too many for the twins to use, they would ask Mom if she'd like to have a couple of sets. The rest of the pillowcases they would sell.

I can't worry about that now, she told herself. *I have to get back upstairs and see what else needs to be done.* Thelma grabbed the little garbage can and emptied the contents into a small cardboard box. Still holding on to the box, she knelt down and took one last look at the kittens. After scratching Misty behind the ears, Thelma rose to her feet, turned off the gas lamps, and headed upstairs.

"How are things going with the stew?" Thelma asked later that afternoon. "Do you think it'll be done before our folks get here?"

Elma lifted the kettle lid and pierced a piece of carrot with a fork. "The vegetables are tender. Think I'll move the kettle to the back of the stove so the stew will stay warm but won't keep cooking. Otherwise, everything will turn to mush." She glanced at the clock. "It's four thirty. I wish we knew exactly what time to expect them, because there's no point baking the biscuits until we see—"

"The whites of their eyes," Thelma finished Elma's sentence and giggled. "I've always thought that saying was kind of *schpassich*."

Elma snickered. "It is rather funny."

At the sound of a vehicle coming up the driveway, the twins both looked out the window. "It's Mom and Dad. I recognize their driver's van." Elma clutched her sister's hand. "Is that a horse trailer the van is pulling?"

"It looks like it to me." Taking Elma's hand, Thelma opened the door.

By the time the twins stepped outside, their parents had gotten out of the van. "It's so good to see you!" Thelma and Elma said simultaneously as they hugged Mom and Dad.

"It's good to see you too," their folks agreed.

"I have a surprise for you," Dad said as he and his driver, Dave Henderson, went to the back of the van. A few minutes later, Dad came back, leading a dark gray mare. "Look who missed you," he said with a big grin.

"It's Pearl!" Elma was so excited to see their own horse that her tears started to flow. "What made you bring Pearl with you? Not that I mind—I'm thrilled."

Dad motioned to Thelma. "Your sister had something to do with it, but I'll let her explain."

While gently stroking Pearl's neck, as the mare nuzzled her hand, Elma looked over at Thelma.

Her sister smiled. "I called Dad a week ago and told him about Rusty's antics. Since I've been worried about you having to drive that unpredictable horse, I asked if Dad would bring Pearl."

"Oh Sister, I'm so glad you did this for me." Elma's eyes revealed the depth of her emotions.

"It wasn't all me. Mom and Dad did the biggest part in making this happen," Thelma said.

Full of gratitude, Elma gave Thelma a hug, and then she embraced her parents again. "Danki to all of you for being so thoughtful and thinking of me." In addition to having missed the docile mare she and Thelma had shared for the last seven years, she would feel a lot safer driving this horse. Her sister and parents had lifted a huge weight from Elma's shoulders. There would be plenty of room for Pearl in Cutter's old stall. Maybe now Thelma would be willing to sell Rusty. But she would wait to bring that subject up some other time. Right now, all

Elma wanted to do was spend time with her folks.

That evening, as they sat around the kitchen table eating supper, Thelma felt a sense of satisfaction. Not only had she surprised her sister by seeing that their horse had been brought here, but they had a whole week to visit with Mom and Dad.

"This stew sure is tasty," Dad smacked his lips. "Whoever made it did a fine job."

"I can't take the credit," Thelma spoke up. "Elma did most of the work on the stew. All I really did was take out the meat to thaw." She cringed, motioning to the overly brown biscuits. "I was responsible for those, but I think that old woodstove's oven is more to blame for them getting too brown."

"Maybe the thermometer isn't working," Mom said. "You may need to buy a new one."

"Do you think it's as simple as that?" Elma asked with a hopeful expression.

Mom nodded. "When I was young, my mamm had a woodstove in her kitchen, and I had to learn to cook on it."

"Really? You never told us that before," Thelma said.

Mom smiled and patted Thelma's hand. "Maybe tomorrow we'll make a batch of chocolate chip cookies."

"While you ladies are doing that, I'll see about fixing the leak I discovered under the kitchen sink," Dad said.

Elma's cheeks turned pink. "You know about that?"

He gave a nod. "In addition to the odor of mildew, when I pulled the curtain back to look under the sink for some hand cleaner awhile ago, I saw the tape you have wrapped around the pipe." He jiggled his eyebrows playfully. "Masking tape doesn't hold up too well when there's a leak."

Elma looked at Thelma and rolled her eyes. "Is that what you wrapped the pipe with?"

Feeling rather foolish, Thelma could only nod.

"It's okay," Dad reassured her. "I will not only see that the pipe is fixed, but I'll repair the hole in the floor beneath it."

Mom's eyebrows shot up. "There's a hole in the floor? Oh Jacob, this old house must be falling apart." She pointed to the missing handles on a few of the cupboards. "And those aren't the only things that need fixing. When we stepped onto the porch to come inside this afternoon, I felt like I might fall through one of those squeaky boards."

"Actually, we've started making lists of things we've found that need to be fixed or replaced," Elma explained. "Unfortunately, our lists keep growing, and we've only been here two weeks."

"The place does need some fixing up, but I'm sure that it has a few good years left." Dad looked over at the twins and winked. "I won't be able to fix everything for you, but I'll get as much done as I can while your mamm and I are here—the most important things, at least."

"Danki, Dad. We appreciate that," the twins both said.

I wonder if I should tell Dad about the hot water tank right now, Thelma thought. *Guess I'll wait until later this evening to say anything. If I bring it up now, Mom will probably get upset. I can see by her expression and the tone of her voice that she thinks we made a mistake trying to take over this place. Well, we're determined to make a go of it, and nothing she can say will change our minds.* Thelma glanced at her sister. *At least I hope Elma's not having any second thoughts.*

Chapter 12

Kathryn shivered as she stepped out of the bathroom and into the bedroom next door. "Did you have any hot water when you took a shower?" she asked her husband.

Jacob shook his head. "I wouldn't say it was hot. More like lukewarm."

She rubbed her hands over her arms. "Mine was slightly warm for a few minutes, but then it turned cold. There must be something wrong with the water tank."

"I'll go down to the basement and take a look at it in the morning," he said. "We had a long day traveling and stayed up late visiting with the twins. It's time for you and me to go to bed."

Kathryn yawned, turning back the covers. "You're right. Tomorrow will be a busy day, and we need to be well rested. Those girls of ours need all the help they can get. While we're here, I want to help out as much as possible."

"Same here. I noticed that there's a lot of outside work to be done."

"I wish we could be with the twins longer than a week." Her brows furrowed. "I'm worried about them, Jacob. They took on a huge task when they moved here, and to do it all by themselves, well, I think it's way too much. If they had husbands it wouldn't be so bad, but at the rate things are going, it doesn't look like either of them will ever get married."

"Never say never." Jacob placed his hands gently on her shoulders. "You worry too much, Kathryn. If the good Lord wants our daughters to have mates, then it will happen in His time. And as far as them taking on the job of running my folks' store and keeping up with this place...I think they're up to the challenge. They made it through two weeks. Even with all they've found wrong so far, it sounds like they're determined to make it work. We should be pleased to have daughters who don't give up so easily." He bent his head and kissed Kathryn's cheek. "Now let's go to bed and try to get a good night's sleep." Jacob waited for her to climb into bed before he turned off the gas lamp.

Kathryn drew in a deep breath and released it slowly. *Jacob may think the twins are up to the challenge, but I'm their mother, and I could tell the minute we got here that they're both exhausted. If I have anything to say about it, Thelma and Elma will be home before Christmas.*

❧

"Are you girls having trouble with your water tank?" Dad asked the following morning during breakfast. "Your mamm had a cold shower last night."

Thelma gulped. Last night she'd planned to ask Dad to take a look at it but had gotten so caught up in visiting and completely forgot. "I know, and I'm sorry about that, Mom." She handed Dad a fresh cup of coffee. "It's not heating like it should. The other day I noticed a puddle of water in the basement near the tank."

"Really?" Elma turned from the stove, where she was frying sausage. "How come you never mentioned it to me?"

"You knew about the cold showers," Thelma reminded.

"Jah, but this is the first I've heard about water on the basement floor." Elma frowned.

"I only saw it one time and figured it could have been from something else."

"I'll go down and take a look as soon as breakfast is over." Dad reached over and tapped Elma's arm as she set the pan of breakfast sausage on a pot holder in the middle of the table.

"I'll go with you," Thelma was quick to say. She still hadn't told Elma about Misty and the kittens. She sure didn't want her finding out about them today. With Mom here, she'd probably side with Elma, and the kittens would have to be taken out to the barn. Ever since the twins were little, it seemed like Mom sided more with Elma on things than she did

Thelma. It wasn't that she loved Elma more; they just had similar likes and dislikes.

Wanting to change the subject, Thelma brought up the box of pillowcases they'd found in the upstairs closet.

"That's right." Elma glanced at Mom and Dad before starting to fry some eggs to go with the sausage. "We found this box of beautiful pillowcases Grandma must have embroidered. They look like they've never been used."

"There are several sets of them, and we'll keep a few," Thelma added. "But before we sell any of them in the store, we thought maybe you and Mom would like to have some, since your mamm embroidered them." She brought over a plate of toast and handed it to Dad.

Before Dad could respond, Mom said, "I would think about that before you decide to sell any of them. Your daed and I could use some new pillowcases, so I may take a few sets. Why don't you and Elma keep the rest? You could regret it later on if you sell them."

"Mom may be right," Elma said while using a spatula to put an egg on each of their plates. "Maybe we should keep all of the pillowcases—in case we ever get married."

Thelma nodded. "She did do a beautiful job on them, and who knows, we may have a use for them sometime in the future."

Thelma and Elma pulled out chairs and sat down at the same time. "I'm glad we talked about this," Elma said. "Sometimes I'm too quick to get rid of things; then later, I regret my decision."

"I think we've all done that at one time or another," Dad commented; then he bowed his head. "Let's pray."

When the prayers ended, they visited some more. Thelma was in a good mood, happy that she hadn't burned the toast. But all too soon, the joy of the moment was gone when Mom, who had poured herself a glass of orange juice, let out an ear-piercing scream. "Ach, there's a *gross* maus eating the bread we left on the counter!"

All heads turned in the direction she was pointing. "That's not a big mouse," Dad said, his eyes widening. "It's a *ratt*!"

"A rat?" Mom and Elma shouted in unison. Faces pale, they both jumped on their chairs, jarring the kitchen table. Mom's orange juice spilled, and Elma's fork flew off her plate and clanked on the floor.

Thelma groaned. It was bad enough that they'd had some mice in their house. Now this?

"I'll take care of that unwanted creature!" Dad leaped out of his chair, grabbed a broom from the utility room, and rushed back to the kitchen. By the time he came in, however, the rat had dived to the floor.

Fearful that it would run under the table, Thelma lifted her feet. Dad swung the broom, but the rat was too fast. It quickly disappeared under the curtain beneath the kitchen sink. Dad jerked the material open, but the rat, thumping its tail, made its escape through the hole in the floor.

"Oh great." Mom pressed her hand to her forehead and moaned. "As if things aren't bad enough around here already, now the girls have a ratt in their home."

"Calm down, Kathryn." Dad held up his hand. "I'll hitch Pearl to the twins' buggy and go to the hardware store today. I'm sure I can buy a rat trap there. Better yet, I'll take Rusty. From what Thelma said when she called us the other day, it sounds like that spunky horse could use some more time on the road." He chuckled, looking over at Mom. "So far there hasn't been a dull moment around this place."

"Then we. . .we'd better all go." Mom's voice trembled as she continued to stand on her chair. "Because I'm certainly not going to stay here with a rat!"

"Before anything else, I'll throw out that bread. Also, I'd better use some disinfectant wipes on the whole counter. Who knows where that dirty rat has been?" Elma picked up the bread bag and tossed it into the garbage can. "We'd best not leave any more food out unless it's in a sealed container."

"That would be a smart idea," Mom agreed. "Besides, who knows what kind of diseases that thing may be carrying around? I hope we can catch it before we leave for home."

Dad gave a nod. "Not to worry. I'm sure we'll get that rat caught in no time at all."

"Mom, why don't you come out to the store with me and Thelma?" Elma suggested. "We still have a lot of work to do out there, and we need to be there for at least part of the day because we may get some customers." Glancing at the curtain beneath the sink, she lowered herself into her chair.

Mom nodded and sat down as well. "That's a good idea. I'd be happy to help with whatever needs to be done in the store."

"Would you two mind if I go with Dad after I get the counter cleaned?" Thelma asked, looking at Elma and then their mother.

"That's fine with me," Elma said with a nod.

Dad put the broom away and took a seat at the table. "Before we go anywhere, I'm going to finish my breakfast. Then I'll see about closing up that hole in the floor under the sink. After that, I'll head down to the basement and take a look at the water tank."

"Did Grandma and Grandpa have rats to deal with?" Thelma asked.

Dad shrugged. "I don't know. If they did, they never said anything about it to me. Maybe with their house sitting empty for a few weeks after their death, the mice and rat moved in."

Elma frowned. "They can't move out soon enough to suit me."

⁂

While Elma helped Mom do the breakfast dishes, she kept glancing down, fearful that the rat might make another appearance, even though Dad had put a temporary patch of wood over the hole before he and Thelma went downstairs. She couldn't believe all the problems she and her sister had encountered since they'd moved to Topeka. Was there no end in sight? How glad she was that the rat had appeared when Dad was here. She had every confidence that he would get rid of it too. Elma knew the unwanted creature had made its escape and disappeared down the hole in the kitchen floor. But the route it took would put it somewhere in the basement. She hoped her sister would keep a watchful eye on her surroundings and be wary of that rat and its creepy long tail.

Mom reached for a dish to dry as she looked over at Elma. "You girls really ought to sell this place and move back home. It's not safe here, and there's too much work."

"I don't think we're in any grave danger," Elma said, "but you're right, there's a lot of work to be done."

"So you'll consider selling?" Mom's expression was hopeful.

Elma shook her head. "Thelma and I both want to make a go of this venture. It's become a challenge for us that we can't back away from. Can you understand that?"

Mom pursed her lips. "Not really, but it's your life and your decision, so I'll try to keep my opinions to myself."

Elma smiled. "We don't mind your opinion on things, but we also need your support."

"You've got it." Mom glanced at the clock. "I wonder what's taking your daed and *schweschder* so long. Seems like they've been down in that basement quite a while."

"Should we check on them?" Elma asked.

Mom nodded. "The dishes are done now anyway, so jah, I think we should go downstairs."

✑

"What are you two still doing down here?"

Thelma jumped at the sound of her sister's voice. "Oh, umm. . . Dad was checking the water tank."

"That's true," Dad said, "and I discovered that in addition to the gas burner being shot, the bottom of the tank is rusting out. I'm afraid you're gonna have to get a new one."

Elma's mouth formed an O. "That'll probably be expensive. I don't think we can afford it right now."

"What other choice do we have?" Thelma asked. "We can't keep taking cold showers."

"Not to worry," Dad said. "I'll pay for a new tank. Think I'd better call my driver at the place he's staying in Middlebury and see if he can take me to Goshen to get a new one today." He looked at Thelma. "Instead of going to the hardware store here in Topeka, I can pick up a rat trap while I'm in Goshen. Do you still want to go with me?"

She nodded. "I sure do. And danki, Dad, for offering to get that for us."

"No problem; I'm glad to help out."

Suddenly, Misty appeared, meowing and swishing her tail against Elma's legs.

Elma jumped back. "Ach, what's this katz doing down here?" She eyed Thelma suspiciously. "Did you bring her into the house?"

Thelma shook her head. "Remember that noise I heard last week before we left for church?"

"Jah, but when you came down here you said you couldn't find anything."

"I didn't at first. Not until I came back down again." Thelma moistened her lips with the tip of her tongue. "What I discovered that second time was Misty, and she had given birth to a *bussli*."

Elma blinked. "There's a kitten down here too?"

"Not just one. Misty had more." Thelma held up four fingers then watched as her mother crouched down to look at the kittens. Gingerly picking one up, she held it close to her chest, petting it carefully.

"Well, they can't stay." Elma shook her head. "The mother cat and her babies need to be out in the barn."

"I disagree," Mom said as she stood. "If you've had mice and now a rat in the house, the logical thing to do is keep some katze around. Look at this cute little thing." She nuzzled the ball of fur against her cheek. "You don't really want to take them to the barn, do you, Elma?"

Dad, who hadn't said a word so far, spoke up. "Your mamm's right, Elma. Having a cat in the house is a good way to keep rodents away."

Thelma was surprised to see her mother cooing over the kitten. And she certainly never expected Mom to side with her on this issue. She was glad Dad was in agreement too.

Elma sighed. "I suppose you're right, but we don't need five katze in here." She gestured to Misty, who had moved over to rub against Thelma's leg.

Thelma bent down to pet the cat; then she too picked up one of the kittens. "As soon as the kittens are old enough to be weaned, I'll see if I can find them all homes. Then we can let either Misty or Tiger come into the house for at least part of each day."

Elma frowned. "I'm not thrilled about the idea, but it looks like I don't have much choice in the matter."

Mom slipped her arm around Elma's waist. "You'll get used to the idea, dear, especially if the katz catches that old ratt."

"I can't wait for that."

Chapter 13

Thelma kept her eyes closed and breathed slowly in and out, trying to make herself relax, but sleep wouldn't come. The last time she'd looked at the clock beside her bed, she'd realized she had been lying in bed for more than an hour. She couldn't stop thinking about the events of the day. Her brain felt like it was going in fast motion. *I hope I can fall asleep soon, or I'll be exhausted in the morning.*

Slowly, she pushed back the covers and went to stand by the window. The moon wasn't full yet, but bright enough to illuminate her room and create shadows in the yard below. Lifting the window a ways, Thelma breathed in the cool night air. The only sound was a lone katydid singing as if it were still August. It was the middle of September, and the weather had been giving little hints of what was soon to follow.

Thelma yawned and rubbed her arms, shivering from the chill. She lowered the window and climbed back into bed. Breathing in deeply, smelling the fresh air that now lingered in her room, she rolled onto her side, hugging her pillow. Closing her eyes, she smiled, thinking how nice it was having Mom and Dad here. It almost made her feel like a child again, with no worries. But she didn't want their visit to be all work like it had been today. While Dad and Thelma were in Goshen, Elma and Mom had worked in the store, cleaning, organizing, and waiting on customers. After Dad and Thelma came back, Thelma had fixed sandwiches and brought lunch out to the store. When they'd finished eating, Dad set up the water tank. How nice it was to finally have hot water.

The big old rat still hadn't been caught, but Dad had set a trap for it, and they'd let Tiger into the house before going to bed. Hopefully, the long-tailed creepy critter would be gone by morning.

Thelma reflected once again on how Mom had sided with her about having a cat in the house. Poor Elma still wasn't happy about it, but at least she'd accepted the idea. With the fear her sister had over mice and rats, it was a wonder she didn't insist on having several cats around, even if she was afraid of them scratching her. "Give them a wide berth, and they'll leave you alone." That's what Dad had always said about the cats they had at home. Of course, those felines he was referring to stayed outside for the most part.

Before heading to bed, Elma told Thelma that Mom had tried to talk her into moving back home. Thelma had been pleased to hear that her sister told Mom she was committed to making things work here.

As a sense of drowsiness came over her, Thelma pulled the blanket up to her chin and snuggled against her pillow. She'd started to drift off, when a loud clatter, followed by a catlike shriek, brought her straight up. As the noise continued, she leaned forward, realizing that it was coming from somewhere downstairs—the kitchen, perhaps.

Thelma climbed out of bed, put her robe and slippers on, and grabbed a flashlight. She clicked it on, but the beam grew dim. "Oh great! This thing is useless, and I have no batteries up here." Thelma hit the flashlight a few times, hoping it would brighten the beam, but all that did was make the light go completely out, so she dropped it onto her bed. Using the glow of the moon shining through her window, she carefully made her way to the door. Her curiosity about the ruckus downstairs was enough to give her the determination to try and navigate her way down the steps.

When Thelma stepped out of her room, she nearly bumped into Elma outside her bedroom door. "Where's your flashlight, Sister?" Elma whispered.

"Ach my! You startled me. It's on my bed. The batteries must be low because it isn't bright enough to help anyone." Thelma also spoke in a quiet tone.

"Did you hear that noise?" Elma rasped. "What's going on downstairs? It woke me out of a sound sleep."

"I–I'm not sure, but I think we'd better check it out."

"Let me get my flashlight first," Elma said. "We'd probably fall down the steps without some light to guide us."

"Okay. I'll wait right here till you get back."

When Elma returned with her flashlight, she led the way and Thelma followed. "I wonder if all that commotion woke our folks."

"I wouldn't be surprised," Elma responded. "I don't see how anyone could sleep with all that racket."

As Elma led the way with her flashlight, the twins went carefully down the stairs, where they met Mom and Dad, both heading for the kitchen. When they all stepped into the room, and Elma turned on the gas lamp, Thelma gasped. Tiger was on the counter near the sink. The cat's rigid frame moved in closer to his prey, while he growled and hissed. Tiger seemed larger than he was, hunching his back as he swatted and nipped at the rat. The next thing she knew, the fat rodent was in the sink. Like a flash, Tiger jumped in there too. A few seconds later, the cat leaped out of the sink with the rat in his mouth. When Tiger's paws hit the floor, his head jerked forward, and he dropped the rat.

Mom and Elma both screamed as the rat zipped under the table, with the cat in hot pursuit.

"I'll get the broom!" Dad shouted, while Mom and Elma each grabbed hold of a chair and climbed up on the seat.

Unsure of what to do, Thelma stood off to one side so she wouldn't get hit when Dad returned, swinging that broom.

By the time Dad came back, Tiger had caught the rat again, and the rodent was dead.

Thelma breathed a sigh of relief. At least that problem had been solved.

⁂

"What are you baking?" Elma asked when she entered the kitchen that Wednesday morning and found Thelma putting something into the oven.

Thelma closed the oven door and smiled when she turned to face Elma. "I mixed a batch of dough for surprise muffins. I put a teaspoon of strawberry jam in the center of each muffin."

"Sounds good. Should I fix some oatmeal to go with them, or would scrambled eggs be better?"

"We have a lot of eggs in the refrigerator, so I think you should scramble some eggs."

"Okay." Elma went to get the eggs. "I'm surprised Mom and Dad aren't up yet. They're usually such early risers."

"I know, but with all the ruckus last night, between the cat and the rat, we were all up later than normal."

Elma took the egg carton over to the counter—a place she'd made sure to clean thoroughly before going to bed last night. Who knew what kind of horrible germs that old rat had left behind, not to mention the cat's dirty paws? "It's hard for me to say this, but I'm glad we let Tiger come into the house last evening. As far as I'm concerned, he can come in every night."

Thelma smiled. "I'm glad we're in agreement on this. Between him being up here, and Misty in the basement, we shouldn't have any more mice or rats to deal with from now on."

Elma wrinkled her nose. "I certainly hope not. Those creatures are *ekelhaft*."

"I agree. They're downright disgusting." Thelma went to the cupboard and took out four plates. "Guess I'll set the table while the muffins are baking."

"Should I wait to cook the *oier* till Mom and Dad are up?" Elma asked. "I sure wouldn't want to serve them cold eggs."

"That's probably a good idea." Thelma motioned to the teakettle whistling on the stovetop. "Let's have a cup of tea while we're waiting for them."

"That'd be nice." Elma beat the eggs and added some milk, then she set the mixture aside and took a seat at the table, while Thelma fixed their tea.

"Poor Grandma and Grandpa. So much needed to be done around this place. I guess it was too much for them to keep up." Elma blew on her cup of tea. "I wish Mom and Dad didn't have to go home next week. They've been such a big help already, and since there's so much yet to be done, a lot more could be accomplished if they could stay longer."

"You're right," Thelma agreed, "but they have a store to run and need to get back to Sullivan. Plus, I don't want them working the whole time they're here, but it seems that's what they want to do for most of their visit."

"I know, and we can't reject their offer of help. That would hurt their feelings." Elma sighed. "I'm sure going to miss them when they leave."

"Are you feeling homesick?"

"Maybe a little. I was doing fine till Mom and Dad came. Then I started missing the familiarity of home and being with our folks."

Thelma patted Elma's arm. "I'm sure things will be better once we develop some close friendships here. It's not like we can never visit Mom and Dad again. They said they'd try to come here for Christmas, and if they can't, then maybe we can hire a driver and go there."

"What's that smell?" Mom sniffed the air as she entered the room. "Is something burning?"

Thelma jumped up. "Ach, my muffins! I hope they're not ruined." She dashed across the room, grabbed a pot holder, and flung open the oven door. A puff of smoke billowed out. Thelma groaned while waving the smoke away with the pot holder. "Oh no, they're not fit for any of us to eat!" She set a folded towel on the counter and placed the muffins on that.

Elma grimaced. Even the tops of the muffins were burned.

"Look at it this way," Mom said cheerfully. "The *hinkel* will have something to nibble on."

Elma snickered, but Thelma frowned. "I'm not sure even the chickens would eat these," she muttered, dumping the muffins into a plastic container. "I should have kept an eye on that oven. Now, thanks to me, we won't be eating my surprise muffins."

"It's all right, Sister. It could have happened to me. We'll still have scrambled eggs." Elma pointed to the bowl of eggs she'd mixed up.

"You know what I think you girls need?" Mom moved over to the stove.

"What's that?" they asked.

"A lesson in cooking on an antique woodstove."

"Or maybe," Dad said, entering the kitchen, "what our daughters need is for each of them to find a husband who can cook."

LaGrange

Joseph's hands shook as he fumbled with the harness he was working on. He'd made oatmeal for breakfast and had managed to scorch it, so he'd ended up eating nothing and drinking three cups of coffee instead. Not the best way to begin his day, but with all the work he had facing him, he didn't want to take the time to cook another batch of oatmeal.

"Probably would have ruined that too," he muttered under his breath. He heard a commotion outside and stopped to look out the window. Usually when someone came to visit, his dog, Ginger, alerted him. Grinning, he watched the golden retriever sitting at the base of the oak tree in the yard between his house and shop. With tail wagging, the dog kept her head tipped toward the branches high in the tree.

Glancing up, Joseph saw a big black crow, squawking loudly as it looked down at Ginger. "Crazy critters," Joseph muttered. He tapped on the window. "Knock off the noise, Ginger!"

As the crow flew off and the dog wandered toward the barn, Joseph returned to the table. Normally, Ginger's barking didn't get on his nerves, but today he felt kind of gloomy and a bit lonely too. He had been on his own since he'd bought the small log cabin house and harness shop eight years ago. Even though his folks and sister, Katie, lived in the area, their homes weren't close enough that he could take his meals with them every day. In addition to Joseph's inability to cook, he tended to be a procrastinator, which meant he often put off grocery shopping. That led to the problem of not having enough food in the house, which was the situation he'd been faced with this morning. At first, Joseph had planned to fry some eggs, but when he'd opened the refrigerator, there weren't any eggs. His next choice was cold cereal, but there wasn't any milk.

As Joseph sat holding his cup of coffee, a thought popped into his head. *I think there's a package of cheese and crackers in my other jacket that I wore last week.* Setting his mug on the workbench, he walked over to the coatrack. He put his hand into the pocket, but it came up empty. Joseph checked the other pocket, and this time he pulled out the sealed snack. "Wish this were a hot meal instead of cold crackers," he mumbled, heading back to the bench.

Mom would say I was being too picky. Joseph bent down to pick up a leather strap from the floor. *And if Katie had been in my kitchen this morning, she would have said that I needed to find a good* fraa *who could cook.* He sucked in his bottom lip. *Maybe I do need a wife, but who's gonna want someone with ears that stick out and who can't talk to a woman without stuttering?*

Chapter 14

Topeka

I can't believe it's time for us to go home." Mom dabbed at the tears on her cheeks. "It seems like we just got here, yet it's been a whole week."

"Jah, and about all we did was work. I wish we had an extra week to sit and visit," Thelma said in a tone of regret.

"Don't worry about that," Mom assured her. "There will be plenty of other times to visit."

"I hope so." Elma shivered as she stood between Mom and Thelma, while Dad put their suitcases in their driver's van. Not only was it four in the morning, but a steady breeze made the air quite chilly. "I feel bad that you wouldn't let us fix you some breakfast before you leave."

"That's okay," Dad called. "We'll be stopping somewhere to eat along the way, and we appreciate the fruit you gave us to snack on."

Elma tried not to cry as she held Mom's hand. "We'll miss you and Dad, and we appreciate all the things you did to help out."

"It was our pleasure." Mom sniffed. "If you need anything, please let us know."

Dad came around from the back of the van and gave each of the twins a hug. Then he reached into his pocket and handed Thelma some cash. "This should give you enough to hire someone to do a few repairs around here. I'd start with that saggy porch, if I were you."

"Danki, Dad," Elma and Thelma said.

"If you need more, let me know." Dad turned to Mom then. "Are you ready to hit the road, Kathryn?"

"Not really," she said tearfully, "but I know we need to go."

The twins hugged their parents one last time and waved as the van pulled out of the yard.

Elma slipped her arm around Thelma's waist. "We need to get to work, or we'll be blubbering and wiping tears away the rest of the day."

"I agree. It will be easier not to miss them if we keep busy." Thelma sighed. "I sure hope they can come here for Christmas."

"Same here."

Thelma held the money Dad had given her. "Now that Dad gave us this, should we see about hiring someone to do the porch?"

"Jah, but we have so many other things going on right now, I think we should wait on that awhile."

"You mean like canning the rest of the beets you and Mom picked yesterday?"

Elma nodded. "Mom was certainly a big help in the kitchen and out here." She gestured to their weed-free garden.

"I hope we can remember everything she told us about cooking and baking with that old woodstove," Thelma said. "I'm wondering if we should have written it all down."

"You may be right," Elma said as they walked toward the house. "The biscuits I baked last night turned out pretty tasty, thanks to Dad putting in a new stove thermometer."

When they entered the house, Thelma touched Elma's arm and said, "Speaking of baking, I keep forgetting to tell you that I signed us up for the cooking show that takes place the first Saturday of October."

Elma's mouth dropped open. "You did what?"

"I signed us up for the—"

"Without asking me?" Elma could hardly believe her sister would do something like that.

"When I told you about the cooking show, you seemed interested, so I assumed—"

"You should never assume anything." Elma strode into the kitchen and flopped into a chair at the table. "And I think you misunderstood what I said before, which was that I would give it some thought."

"Have you?" Thelma's wide-eyed expression and air of enthusiasm made it hard to say no.

"I don't see how we can bake anything when we haven't truly mastered that old stove." Elma placed her hand above her eyes. "Besides, we are up to here with other projects to do."

"I know, but this is for such a good cause. I'm sure we can find something special to make. If we do everything Mom said with the stove, I think it will turn out fine."

Elma drew in a quick breath and released it slowly. She'd always had a hard time saying no to her sister. "Oh, all right. I'll do the cooking show with you."

Thelma clapped her hands. "Great! Why don't we try making Grandma's Christmas cake? In fact, since it's so early and we don't have to open the store for a few hours, we can make the cake right now."

Elma pushed away from the table. "If you insist, but let's get some breakfast first, because I'm *hungerich*."

"I'm hungry too." Thelma opened the refrigerator door. "We still have plenty of eggs. Do you want them fried, boiled, scrambled, or poached?"

"Why don't you boil them this time?" Elma suggested. "If you do several, we can have them for a midday snack or sliced on a salad."

"That's what I'll do then." Thelma took out a carton of eggs. "Do you want to get out the ingredients for the cake, while I put the eggs on to boil?"

"Sure." Elma left her seat and took out Grandma's cookbook to look for the recipe. Then she went to the cupboard and gathered all the ingredients. "I'm glad we bought some Jell-O last week when we went shopping, or we wouldn't be able to make this cake."

"That's true. The red and green Jell-O ingredients are what make the cake taste moist and look so colorful and appealing." Thelma grinned. "I'll bet this cake will bring a fairly good price when the bidding starts. I mean, who wouldn't want a delicious festive cake such as this to get them in the mood for Christmas?"

"It's hard to think about Christmas when we have so many other things to do," Elma said, placing a measuring cup on the counter. "I know some of the stores start decorating for the holiday as early as October, but it's not until after Thanksgiving that we even start making out Christmas cards. And we never do any holiday baking until a week before Christmas."

"That's true, but this is different, and our cake will be different, because

I'm sure it'll be something that no one else will have at the cooking show to auction off."

Elma shrugged. "I hope you're right about that."

&

Thelma had put the cake in the oven when she heard the rumble of a vehicle coming up the driveway. "Someone's here," she called to Elma, who had gone to the living room to gather up some throw rugs. Since they'd been letting Tiger in every night, Elma shook the rugs every morning as soon as they put the cat outside, saying that he'd left cat hair behind.

When her sister made no response, Thelma closed the oven door and went to the kitchen window to look out. A delivery truck was coming up the driveway, and when it passed the house, she realized it must be heading for the store.

Cupping her hands around her mouth, she hollered a little louder. "It's a delivery truck, Elma—probably bringing some of the things we ordered for the store. I'm going out there to open the store and tell the driver where to set the boxes. Could you check on the cake while I'm gone?"

Elma mumbled something, so Thelma figured she must have understood what she'd said. Grabbing a sweater from the back of her kitchen chair, Thelma dashed out the back door. She'd only made it as far as the barn when she realized that her half-slip was sliding down her legs. "Oh my!" Quickly, she opened the barn door and stepped inside. "Now wouldn't that have been embarrassing if my slip had done that when I got to the store? Or I could have tripped on it coming across the yard." She pulled the slip back in place. Thelma couldn't figure out why that had happened. She'd never had one of her slips fall off before. *Maybe I've lost some weight since moving here. I'd better try to eat a little more, and for sure, I'll need to take in the waistband on my slip so that doesn't happen again.*

Continuing on to the store, walking a little slower this time, Thelma made sure to keep her hands pressed firmly against her waist. When she got back to the house, she'd either look for a slip that fit better or pin this one so it was a bit tighter.

When Thelma got to the store, the delivery truck was parked near the basement door. She waved to the driver and shouted, "I'll unlock the door and let you in."

"No problem," the young English man hollered back.

After Thelma unlocked the door, she told him to bring the boxes inside. "You can stack them over there." She motioned to a corner of the basement where some empty cardboard boxes sat.

While the delivery man brought in the boxes, Thelma stood off to one side so she wouldn't be in his way. Since she wasn't walking, she felt certain that her slip would stay in place.

"Do you have a restroom I can use?" the man asked. "I drank too much coffee this morning."

Thelma motioned to the steps leading to the main part of the store. "There's a bathroom upstairs."

"Okay, thanks." He started for the stairs but paused. "Oh, there's one more box on my truck. I'll get it as soon as I'm done in the restroom."

"That's okay," Thelma was quick to say. "I'll go out and get it."

"Are you sure? I mean—"

"It's no problem at all."

When the man went upstairs, Thelma headed outside and climbed into the back of his truck. It didn't take her long to spot the box that was theirs because it was clearly marked. The only problem was she would have to move two boxes that were on top of it. That should be easy enough.

Boy was I ever wrong. Thelma grunted as she struggled to pick up the box on top. *What in the world could be in here that's making it so heavy?*

෴

When Elma stepped onto the back porch to shake the last rug, she spotted a delivery truck parked near the basement entrance of the store. *I'd better go let him in.* "Thelma," she hollered, sticking her head through the open door, "I'm going out to the store to let the driver in."

Hoping her sister had heard, Elma sprinted across the yard and up the path that led to the store. When she got there, she was surprised to see the door open. *Now that's strange. I wonder if we left it open last night.*

Stepping inside, she almost collided with a tall English man. "Oops, sorry," he said. "I didn't realize you'd come back already."

Elma tipped her head. *Come back from where? Does he mean come back from the house?* Before she could voice her thoughts, however, he handed her the shipping invoice and headed out the door. "I think that's everything. See you next time."

As he was getting in the truck, Elma glanced out the open door and gasped. There sat Thelma in the back of his truck, holding a box in her lap.

"Wait up!" Elma shouted, running out the door as the truck started pulling away. "My sister's in the back of your truck!"

The truck kept moving, and Elma chased after it, waving and hollering for the driver to stop. He was about to pull out on the main road, when the truck came to a halt. The young man rolled down his window. "What's going on? Did I forget one of your packages?"

"Not a package." Elma pointed to the back of his truck. "My sister—she's inside your truck." The young man hopped out and ran to the back. He looked at Thelma, whose face was red as a ripe cherry, then he looked back at Elma. "There are two of you?"

Elma nodded. "We're twins."

His brows furrowed as he turned back to Thelma. "What are you doing in my truck?"

"I told you I'd get the last package while you used the restroom, remember?"

He scratched the side of his head. "Oh, yeah, that's right. When I came out of the restroom and saw the person I thought was you in the store, I figured you'd brought the package in."

"It's right here." Thelma handed Elma the box. "It was under two other packages, but they were heavy, so I had a hard time getting it at first."

"Don't ever do that again," he muttered. "From now on, I'll take care of getting all the packages out of the truck. It's actually company policy not to let anyone but the driver in the truck. If your sister hadn't hollered for me to stop, you may have ended up in Michigan before the day was out, and then I would have been in a heap of trouble."

"Sorry about that." Wearing a sheepish expression, Thelma stepped down from the truck, holding the sides of her dress. She headed back to the house, while Elma took the box into the store.

When Thelma opened the door to the house, she was greeted by a haze of smoke. "What's going on?" It didn't take her long to realize the smoke was coming from the kitchen.

Coughing, while covering her nose with her hands, she raced into the room. Seeing smoke billowing from the stove, she jerked the oven door open. "Oh no!" The cake in the pans looked like two blobs of charcoal.

Thelma grabbed two pot holders and removed the pans then carried them out to the porch. After resting them on the pot holders on the porch floor, she raced back inside and opened all the downstairs windows. When she went back outside, Elma was walking toward the house.

"What happened?" Elma asked, pointing to the cake pans.

"The cake is ruined. The layers were left in the oven too long. Didn't you check on them like I asked you?"

Elma's brows furrowed. "When was that?"

"Before I went out to the store to let the delivery man in." Thelma folded her arms. "I told you I was going and asked you to check on the cake."

Elma groaned. "I was singing while gathering the rugs. Guess I didn't hear you. Then when I took the rugs outside to shake them and realized a delivery truck was waiting at the store, I hollered at you so you'd know I was going. I assumed you'd be checking on the cake and taking it out of the oven when it was done."

"Well, I guess you didn't hear me, and I certainly didn't hear you, because I was already at the store."

Elma sank into one of the wicker chairs on the porch. "If we try to make that cake again, I fear something else may happen. Participating in the cooking show is not a good idea, Sister. Is there any way we can get out of it?"

Thelma shook her head determinedly. "And let the community down? No way! We're gonna make that cake, and it will turn out fine."

Chapter 15

I really wish we weren't obligated to do that cooking show tomorrow," Elma said as her sister took out the ingredients for Grandma's Christmas cake. "We had a busy day at the store, and I'm so tired I can barely keep my eyes open, let alone stay awake long enough to bake a cake."

"Why don't you go up to bed, while I bake the cake?" Thelma suggested.

Elma yawned. "Are you sure about that? I wouldn't feel right about leaving you down here by yourself with that old thing." She gestured to the woodstove. "Remember what happened the last time we used the oven to do a trial run on this cake. Plus, the kitchen took awhile to air out from that burnt smell. If that happens again, we sure couldn't take a coal-black cake to the cooking show to be auctioned."

"I'll be fine," Thelma said. "I know better than to leave the room while the cake is baking. I'll sit out here in the kitchen and get some knitting done till the cake is ready to come out of the oven."

Still feeling a bit hesitant, Elma smiled and said, "Okay. Danki, Sister."

Thelma gave Elma a hug. "Sleep well, and I'll see you in the morning. We have a big day ahead of us, but I'm sure it'll be fun and rewarding."

Elma wasn't sure about the fun part, but she knew that a charity event such as this was important. She hoped she wasn't doing the wrong thing by going to bed early and leaving Thelma to bake the cake by herself.

⁓

Thelma was excited about making Grandma's Christmas cake. In addition to the cake itself, two flavors of Jell-O would be used for the filling, with whipped topping and cream cheese for the frosting.

Humming to herself, she followed the directions in Grandma's recipe book then greased the bottom of two nine-inch round pans. "This will be a piece of cake," she murmured, grinning at her pun.

The directions said to bake the cake at 350 degrees for thirty to thirty-five minutes or until done. For the woodstove, that meant she didn't want the oven to get too hot. Placing the cake pans carefully into the oven, Thelma closed the door, set the wind-up timer, and took a seat at the table with a cup of tea and her knitting project. When her folks were visiting, she'd kept her knitting needles and yarn in her room so Mom wouldn't see the gloves she was making for Christmas.

Sure hope our folks can come here for Christmas, Thelma thought as her needles began clicking. She paused for a sip of tea. *I wonder what it'll be like if Elma and I have to spend the holiday alone?* In all the twins' thirty-two years, they'd never been away from their parents for Christmas. It had been so wonderful having them here. As Thelma sat in the quietness of the kitchen, it felt abnormally empty.

The sweet scent of vanilla tickled Thelma's nose as the cakes continued baking. The aroma made her think of Christmas. She reflected on all the Christmases they'd come here to spend with Grandma and Grandpa. The same cake recipe and this old oven were working together once again.

Thelma's gaze settled on the kitchen cupboards. She was glad Dad had been able to put handles on the ones that had been missing. It not only looked better, but it was easier to open the doors too.

Wondering if Grandma had ever sat here sewing while waiting for something in the oven to finish, Thelma resumed knitting. Pretty soon, the timer went off. Grasping one of the oven mitts she'd set out, Thelma opened the oven door and poked a toothpick into each of the cake pans. It came out clean both times, so she was sure they were done. Best of all, neither looked overly brown. *Whew! That's a relief! I'll bet Grandma would be proud of me, and so would Mom.*

She grabbed the other mitt and removed the hot pans from the oven, placing each on its own cooling rack. Then, before she went back to her knitting, Thelma stood over the cakes and inhaled deeply as the steamy aroma rose from both pans. The whole kitchen smelled like Grandma's Christmas cake. Thelma figured any minute now, Elma would appear, since the cake's inviting smell seemed to be wafting through the house.

Thelma tilted her head, waiting to hear footsteps coming down the stairs. No sign of Elma though. *She must be in a sound sleep.*

Half an hour later, Thelma checked the cake pans. They were still slightly warm, but she figured it would be okay to add the Jell-O now. After poking several holes in the first one, she mixed the red Jell-O and carefully spooned the crimson liquid over the top. Then she did the same with the other cake, spooning the warm green Jell-O over that half. When that was done, she covered both cakes with plastic wrap and set them in the refrigerator to cool more thoroughly. The recipe said the cakes should be refrigerated overnight or for a few hours.

I'll probably stay up and finish the cake tonight she told herself. *Otherwise there will be too much to do in the morning.*

Thelma left the kitchen and let Tiger in for the night. She wasn't surprised to find him sitting by the back door. When she opened it, he meowed loudly then pranced inside as though he owned the place. With his tail in the air, Tiger strutted around the living room, purring, until he finally settled down on one of the throw rugs and fell asleep.

Thelma went back to the kitchen and glanced at the clock. It was nine o'clock, so at eleven she would take the pans from the refrigerator, remove the cake rounds, and put them together with filling between each layer. Once the top and sides of the cake had been frosted, she planned to add some red and green sprinkles to make it look more festive. That's what Grandma had always done when she made her special Christmas cake.

Think I'll go downstairs and see how the kittens are doing, Thelma decided. She grabbed her flashlight and headed down the stairs, careful to close the door behind her. If Tiger should awaken, she didn't want him going to the basement and disturbing Misty and her babies.

When Thelma reached the bottom of the stairs, she turned on the overhead gas lamp and headed toward the back of the basement. The kittens' eyes were open now, and they'd become quite active. Thelma knew it wouldn't be long and they'd be getting out of the box. She would either have to find a taller box for them or put up some kind of a barricade. It wouldn't be good to have them wandering all over the basement and possibly getting stuck behind something. They could get hurt.

Leaning down, she scooped up one of the kittens. It purred as she rubbed its head gently against her chin. "All *bopplin* are cute," she murmured. "Human babies more so than others." Unexpected tears sprang to Thelma's eyes. If she remained single the rest of her life, she would never experience the joy of being a mother. *Lord, help me not to long for something I may never have,* she prayed silently.

The words of Philippians 4:11 came to mind: *"For I have learned, in whatsoever state I am, therewith to be content."*

Feeling somewhat better, Thelma remained with the kittens and their mother awhile longer before going back upstairs. Knowing she needed to wash up after handling the cats, she went to the bathroom, where she removed some loose cat hair from her dress and washed her hands.

When she returned to the kitchen, she opened the refrigerator to check on the cakes. It was ten thirty, and she was beginning to feel tired, so she decided to take the cakes out of their pans, since they seemed to have cooled sufficiently. Using a spatula to loosen the cakes, she slid the first one onto a plate. After mixing the whipped topping with the creamed cheese, as per the directions in Grandma's cookbook, she spread some of the creamy white mixture on the first cake round. Then she took out the second cake round and placed it on top of the first.

"Ach!" Thelma gasped. "The top of the cake looks a bit lopsided. I'll need to do something about that."

She pursed her lips. Maybe it wouldn't be too difficult. All she needed to do was add more frosting to the side that looked uneven. "Easy as pie. . . I mean cake." Thelma chuckled as she piled more frosting on the cake and spread it over the area that needed it the most. "Not too bad. I think it looks fine. I'll add a bit more and then do the sides."

Thelma had only added a little frosting to the sides, when Tiger darted into the room and leaped onto the counter, knocking over the bowl. Before Thelma could grab him, the cat swished his paw through the frosting. The next thing she knew, the bowl had rolled off the counter and landed upside down on the floor.

"Oh no! Get down, you bad cat!" Thelma groaned as Tiger leaped onto the floor and licked the frosting smeared on his paws. "I can't use that topping now." She didn't have another tub of whipped cream, and no creamed cheese either, so there was no way she could make another batch of icing. About all Thelma could do at this point was to add some sprinkles on the top, which she did right away. Once that was done, the cake looked a little better, though not the way she remembered Grandma's Christmas cake, which had always looked perfect.

"It'll have to do." Thelma put the cake inside a plastic container and attached the lid. When she went to place it in the refrigerator she realized that the receptacle was too big. Placing it back on the counter, Thelma rearranged some of the items in the refrigerator. Then she picked up the container and tried once more. This time it fit, but with only an inch to spare.

She and Elma would only have to demonstrate how to bake the cake tomorrow then show this cake to the audience so they could see the finished product. She would simply explain that it was lacking some of the frosting.

Of course, she thought as she turned off the gas lamp, *I still haven't told Elma that we'll be expected to stand up in front of everyone and do all the prep work for the cake. If she knew that, she'd probably refuse to go.*

Chapter 16

When Elma entered the kitchen the next morning, she found her sister fixing a pot of tea. *"Guder mariye."*

"Good morning." Thelma smiled. "You look rested. Did you sleep well last night?"

"Jah, I did. How about you?"

"Not as soundly as I would have liked, but it's my fault for getting to bed late."

"How come you stayed up?" Elma questioned.

"I was frosting the cake." Thelma grabbed a couple of floral-patterned cups from the cupboard and set them by the plates on the table. "The icing I sampled was quite tasty. Even the cat had a taste of it."

"I'm glad the frosting was good, but how'd the cake turn out?" Elma sniffed the delicious aroma of peppermint tea. "It didn't get too done, I hope."

Thelma shook her head. "When the cake was finished it was a warm golden brown." She motioned to the boiled eggs on the table. "I think we'd better eat so we can get ready to go to Shipshe. We don't want to be late this morning."

Elma sighed. "About the only good part of going there today is knowing that we'll be taking Pearl and not Rusty."

"Actually, we won't be taking Pearl after all."

"How come?" Elma's shoulders slumped a bit.

"When I went out to the barn earlier to get her, I discovered that she'd thrown a shoe."

"That's not good." Elma frowned. "I don't want to take Rusty."

"I know, and I'll call the local farrier as soon as we get home." Thelma gave Elma's arm a light tap. "Don't worry. I'll be in the driver's seat. I'm gonna follow the advice Dad gave me when he was here."

"What advice was that?"

"I'll take control and let Rusty know that he has to obey my commands."

"I hope it works, because I'm not in the mood for his antics this morning." Though Elma wasn't happy about taking Rusty, at least the responsibility of getting him there was not hers. She hoped he would behave himself this time.

⟡

The twins were halfway to Shipshewana when Rusty started lunging and lurching.

"What is that horse's problem?" Elma touched her sister's arm.

"I have no idea, but he'd better settle down." Thelma's jaw clenched so hard, Elma could hear her teeth snap together.

Elma's back hurt as she sat firmly on the seat. "Maybe we should turn around and go home."

With a determined expression, Thelma shook her head. "I'm sure he'll settle down. Hold on to your seat so you don't get jostled." Her stern, take-control voice kicked in, and Thelma handled Rusty in a manner a lot like Dad would have used.

Elma did as her sister suggested, the whole time praying they would get to their destination safely. Finally—and much to Elma's relief—the horse settled down. When they pulled up to the hitching rail near the Shipshewana Event Center, Elma climbed out of the buggy and secured Rusty.

"I'll get the cake from the back," Thelma said after she'd stepped down from her seat. "Oh, and Sister, before we go in, there's something I need to tell you."

"What's that?" Elma asked.

"When our names are called and we have to take our cake onstage before the bidding starts, we'll need to demonstrate how to make the cake first."

Elma stiffened and her mouth went dry. "Are you saying we have to make the cake in front of all those people?"

Thelma gave a quick nod.

"But we don't have the necessary ingredients for that. All we brought was the finished cake, which, by the way, I haven't seen yet."

Thelma patted Elma's arm. "You'll see it when I take it out of the container, but that won't happen till we've finished our demonstration."

"Which we can't do without the ingredients," Elma reminded.

"I brought them along." Thelma motioned to the back of the buggy. "They're in that cardboard box with the cake. When I went to the grocery store in Topeka the other day, I got enough flour, milk, and other ingredients we need for the cake." She smiled. "I even brought a large bowl, wooden spoon, and a wire whisk along."

"What about the whipped topping and cream cheese to frost the cake?"

"We won't have to worry about that part. All we have to show the audience is how to mix the cake, put it into the pans, and place it in the oven. Then we'll take our finished cake out of the container and show them that," Thelma explained. "Now would you like to carry the box, or should I?"

"I'll do it," Elma mumbled. It all sounded simple enough, but a sense of panic set in. The thought of cooking in front of a group of people, many of whom they would not know, made Elma nervous. She wondered if they'd made a big mistake coming here today.

⁓

"Let's take a seat in the front row so we can see everything and be close to the stage," Thelma suggested when they entered the building. Already, hundreds of people were milling around.

"I wish we could sit in the back and watch the proceedings." Elma's voice trembled a bit. "Look at all these people. I had no idea this event would draw such a big crowd."

"If we sit in the back, we'll have farther to walk when our names are called." Thelma tugged on her sister's arm. "Let's look for a good seat before they're all gone."

When the twins found chairs in the first row, Elma set the box on the floor by her feet.

Looking at the stage in front of them, Thelma saw a stove with an oven, a long table, and several plastic bins full of cooking supplies, as well as a large pitcher of water.

The room was astir with people chatting and others still straggling in, looking for a place to sit or stand. Finally, things settled down as a tall English woman took the stage and turned on a microphone. Elma leaned close to Thelma and whispered, "We won't have to say anything while we're mixing the ingredients for the cake, I hope."

All Thelma could do was shrug, for the woman in charge had begun speaking. "Welcome to our cooking show charity event," she said. "We appreciate all of you who came out today. This event is something special for our community, since the money is going to a good cause. Because of that, we hope you will be generous with your bids and enjoy the show."

Everyone clapped. Once the applause died down, the woman continued. "Thank you for such a warm welcome. To begin our program, we have two single ladies from Topeka. Elma and Thelma Hochstetler, would you please come up?"

"Here we go." Elma picked up the box, and Thelma followed onto the stage. "I didn't know we'd be the first ones," Elma whispered.

Thelma put on her best smile. "Don't worry. Afterward we can relax and watch everyone else."

Elma's face turned ashen when the host handed her the microphone. "Please tell us a little about your dessert and why you chose to make it today."

Thelma thought she could hear her sister's knees knocking as she said in a quavering voice, "This is our Grandma's Christmas cake. We chose it in memory of her."

The audience clapped, and Thelma noticed pink splotches had erupted on Elma's cheeks. Her own face felt warm too.

After Thelma placed the ingredients on the table, Elma picked up the recipe card. As she read the instructions, Thelma measured the ingredients. *So far, so good.*

Glancing at the audience, Thelma's throat constricted. So many people, and they were all watching her and Elma. She didn't realize being the center of attention would make her this nervous. Averting her gaze, she hurriedly mixed the flour and other dry ingredients. In the process,

Thelma ended up with a puff of white on her dress, and some settled on her arm. Brushing it away, she looked at the snickering audience again. All eyes seemed to be focused on them.

"Be careful, Sister," Elma warned. "You're getting flour all over the place. By the way, you need to add the eggs and milk."

"I—I know. I feel like I'm all thumbs right now," Thelma muttered under her breath.

"It's okay. It's okay. Try to stay calm," Elma whispered. But her words were not reassuring.

Thelma frantically grabbed more flour and dumped it into the bowl.

"Sister, you're not making bread."

Thelma snickered. She didn't know what else to do.

Then, in her nervous state, she managed to spill what was left in the bag of flour onto the floor. "Oh no!"

At the same time, the twins leaned down to reach for an egg and bumped heads. When they stood, they rubbed the spots of impact simultaneously. Another round of chuckles came from the crowd, making Thelma even more nervous.

With shaky fingers, she managed to crack the eggs into the bowl, but the shells fell in as well. "Oh my word!" Thelma's cheeks felt like they were on fire as she hastily picked out the pieces. This was not going well. She could only imagine what people must be thinking. *They probably think we're a couple of bumbling* dummkepp *who don't know a thing about baking a cake.*

"Is there anything I can do to help?" the host of the show asked.

As Thelma shook her head, Elma rolled her eyes.

"Pour the milk," Elma said impatiently, nudging Thelma's arm.

"I will. Don't rush me." Thelma picked up the carton of milk, but her hands shook so badly, she ended up pouring all of it into the bowl.

"Oh no, that's too much." Elma handed Thelma the microphone and grabbed the wire whisk. "Let me take over now."

"I don't see how you're gonna fix that mess, Sister," Thelma said, her mouth too close to the mic. Her eyes widened, and the audience roared.

When Elma stirred the batter, a glob splattered up and stuck to the end of her nose.

Thelma's chuckle resonated through the microphone, as she pointed at Elma. Despite their best efforts, this was turning into an unrehearsed skit.

⟪⟫

"I know that young woman—or at least one of them," Delbert said, bumping Joseph with his elbow.

Joseph's forehead wrinkled. "I know one of 'em too. Well, maybe not *know*, but I did meet her at the hardware store in Topeka a few weeks ago."

"I met one of the twins at the hardware store here in Shipshe." Delbert rubbed his chin. "Didn't realize there were two of them though. Thought I was seein' one woman in two places."

"They must be identical, because they sure look alike." Joseph leaned forward in his chair. "I'm tryin' to figure out which one of 'em I saw in Topeka."

"They're sure funny." Delbert chuckled when the twin wearing the green dress stuck her hand in the bowl to fish out the spoon her sister had dropped. "I wonder if they're really that clumsy or just puttin' on an act to get the spectators enthused so they'll make a high bid on their cake."

"I don't know." Joseph leaned close to Delbert's ear. "I really want that cake."

Delbert looked at Joseph as though he had two heads. "You haven't even seen it yet."

"I know, but I want to meet that young woman."

"Which one?"

"The one who's holding the microphone now. Don't know why, but the more I watch her, the more I'm thinkin' she's the woman I met in Topeka."

"Oh boy." Delbert grunted. "What are we dealin' with here—love at first sight?"

Joseph shook his head. "I'd like the chance to get to know her, and that won't happen unless I get the cake." The determined set of his friend's jaw told Delbert that Joseph was serious about this.

"After the cooking show's over, go on up and talk to her, Joe."

Joseph slunk down in his chair. "I can't do that, Dell. She'd think I was too bold. But if I bid on her cake and win, I'll have a reason to speak with her when I get the cake."

Delbert shrugged. "Suit yourself. If you want the cake, go ahead and bid. But if I were you, I'd at least wait till they show the audience what the finished cake looks like. You might not even want it."

"But if I do, would you bid on it for me?"

Delbert's eyebrows rose. "Why would I bid on it? You're the one who wants it."

"I—I know, but if I try to call out a bid, I'll get tongue-tied and start stuttering."

"Here's what I've got to say about that. If you really want to meet the girl, then you'll call out the bid, even if you have to trip over your own tongue."

Joseph kept his gaze straight ahead. He'd wait until he saw the finished cake and then try to persuade his friend to do the bidding. After all, Dell had told him several times that he'd do almost anything for him.

Chapter 17

The cake pans were finally in the oven, and it was time for Thelma to remove the cake they had brought from its container. Placing it on the table, she faced the audience, removed the lid, and lifted the cake plate out. "Oh no," she murmured, staring in disbelief. Their cake was even more lopsided than it had been last night. The trip to Shipshewana, with Rusty acting up, had obviously not helped.

Thelma looked at Elma, who was clearly upset. "What happened to our cake?" Elma whispered, giving her a sidelong glance. "It looks *baremlich.*"

Thelma couldn't argue with that; the cake did look terrible. Not only was the top lopsided, but the frosting barely covered the sides. What icing was left on the cake seemed to have accumulated on the plate, around the base. The cake must not have been cool enough, which had caused the frosting to run. *No one will ever bid on this now. We ought to leave the stage,* Thelma thought. *I'll explain things later,* she mouthed to Elma.

A middle-aged English man approached the stage with some paperwork. He talked to the woman in charge, and when they parted, he grabbed the microphone.

"All right now, who'll start the bidding with five dollars?" he shouted.

Thelma gulped, feeling trapped by the audience. There was no way they could leave the stage—at least not until they'd become thoroughly embarrassed, because she was certain no one would place even one bid on this pitiful cake. *I should have listened to my sister and gotten out of this event.*

111

Joseph leaned over and whispered something.

"What was that, Joe?" Delbert asked.

Joseph's ears turned pink, like they always did when he was embarrassed. "I need you to bid on the cake for me."

Delbert frowned. "Why would you want a lopsided cake?"

"It's for a good cause, and I want to meet that girl. Come on, Dell. I'll give you the money for it."

"Okay, but you're gonna owe me for this." Delbert lifted his hand. "Five dollars!"

"I'll make it ten!"

Delbert looked at Joseph, and they both looked around the room. Where had that deep voice come from, upping the bid?

"Fifteen," Joseph whispered. "Hurry, Dell, do it now."

"Fifteen dollars!" Delbert shouted. Looking at Joseph, he chuckled. "Think I'm getting into this bidding game, especially since I'm spending your money."

"Twenty!" the other bidder hollered.

Delbert looked at his buddy again, and when Joseph nodded, Delbert raised his hand and upped the bid—this time for thirty dollars.

Excitement wafted over the crowd. Some people even clapped.

"Fifty dollars!" the other man shouted, louder this time. Was there no stopping this fellow? Why was he so desperate to have a pathetic-looking cake?

"Go higher," Joseph prompted, bumping Delbert's arm. "Take it up to sixty."

Delbert raised his hand again. "Sixty dollars!"

"Seventy!"

Joseph, rocking back and forth in his chair, looked almost desperate. "Go to eighty. I—I want that c–cake." He wiped his sweaty forehead. The poor guy had started stuttering. Delbert knew he'd better get that cake, no matter what it cost. He cupped his hands around his mouth and shouted, "Eighty dollars!"

By this time, the audience was in an uproar. Some people stood, and even more applauded. Delbert and Joseph kept their eyes on the auctioneer.

"Eighty dollars once. . . Eighty dollars twice. . . Do we have another bid on this unusual cake?"

Delbert watched the two women onstage, holding the cake with quizzical expressions. They were probably as surprised as the audience that two men were bidding on their crazy-looking dessert.

"I'll make it ninety!" the other bidder bellowed.

The crowd whooped and hollered even louder. Several started shouting, "Higher! Higher! Higher!"

Delbert looked at Joseph. "Now what?" He glanced around, trying to see who was bidding against him, but it was so crowded, he couldn't tell.

"Go again, Dell. Make it one hundred." Joseph pointed his finger toward the ceiling. "Raise the bid. Hurry, please."

Delbert's hand shot up. "One hundred dollars!"

"One hundred going once. . . One hundred going twice. . ."

Delbert held his breath, waiting to see if the deep voice would speak again and outbid him, but all was quiet.

"Sold—to the man wearing a blue shirt in the fourth row!"

"Th–that's you," Joseph said a bit too loud, jumping up. "You won the cake!"

The audience clapped again. Those folks closest to Delbert congratulated him. Someone patted his shoulder. Joseph slunk down in his seat. The auctioneer slowly shook his head. Delbert was glad it was over.

❧

Now a part of the audience again, Elma sat next to her sister, watching the rest of the contestants. After each demonstration and bidding was completed, she was surprised to see that, so far, their cake had brought in the most money.

Glancing around the crowd then settling her gaze a few rows back on the Amish man who'd won their cake, Elma quickly turned her attention back to the stage, embarrassed when he caught her staring. "Do you think this show will be over soon?" she whispered to Thelma.

"Aren't you having a good time?"

Elma fidgeted in her chair. "Guess I am, but my stomach is starting to growl, and I can't stop thinking of all the things that need to be done at home."

Thelma patted Elma's hand. "This is the last item up for bid. As soon as it's over, we can give our cake to the man who won it then get a little something to eat before we run a few errands and head for home."

Elma's nerves escalated. If standing onstage in front of all those people hadn't been bad enough, now they'd have to give the lopsided cake to the man who'd bid that outrageous price of one hundred dollars.

ᘓᗡ

When the cooking show let out, Joseph asked Delbert if he would go with him to speak to the twins, because he was too nervous to speak to them alone.

"I suppose I should," Delbert said. "I must admit, once I got into that bidding war, it became an exciting game—especially when the crowd starting urging me on. And after all I went through to get you that cake, I'd like the chance to meet those twins. When the woman in charge first introduced them, she said they were single."

"Which of the women are you interested in?" Joseph hoped it wasn't the same twin he had his eye on. But they looked so much alike, he couldn't be sure which one he'd met in Topeka. *What if I can't talk to her without stuttering?*

Delbert shrugged. "I'm not sure which one I met before. Right now I'm thinking the more serious one."

"Not the twin who was holding the lopsided cake?"

"Nope. Did you see the look of disapproval on her sister's face when she took that dessert out of its container?"

Joseph nodded. "I wonder how it got that way."

"We'll never know if we don't talk to them." Delbert thumped Joseph's back. "I see 'em by the table where all the other baked goods are. Let's head over there now."

When the men approached Thelma and Elma, Joseph couldn't think of a single thing to say. He stared at the twins, feeling rather foolish.

"I'm Delbert Gingerich, and this is my friend, Joseph Beechy," Delbert spoke up. "I'm the one who gave the winning bid, but it was really for him."

Joseph's face felt like it was on fire.

"That was an interesting presentation you ladies gave." Delbert chuckled. "The humor you added really got the audience enthused. Did you plan it that way?"

The twins looked at each other with strange expressions. Then the one wearing the green dress spoke up. "It was definitely not planned. I think I speak for my sister when I say that we were both nervous wrecks."

"That's right," the other twin agreed. "We've never cooked anything in a public setting before. I was surprised that anyone even bid on our crazy-looking cake, much less paid so much for it."

Joseph, finally finding his voice, said, "It didn't l–look like you were n–nervous." *Not like I feel right now,* he mentally added.

"Which one of you is Elma and which one is Thelma?" Delbert asked.

"I'm Elma," the twin wearing the blue dress said. "And this is my sister, Thelma."

Delbert moved closer to the twins. "If I'm not mistaken, I bumped into one of you at Yoder's Hardware about a month ago."

"That was me," Thelma spoke up. "It was when you were waiting at the checkout counter and you dropped your things."

Delbert snickered. "That was pretty clumsy of me."

"I met one of y–you too," Joseph stuttered. "It was—"

"At the hardware store in Topeka." Thelma finished his sentence. "That was me as well."

Elma smiled. "Apparently, you've both met my sister before."

"Where do you live?" Delbert asked.

"Our home is in Topeka," Elma said. "We moved there from Sullivan, Illinois, after our grandparents died. They left us their house and variety store. Where do you men live?"

"We're both from LaGrange," Delbert said before Joseph could find his voice. It seemed like Delbert was taking over the conversation. Joseph sure hoped his friend wasn't interested in Thelma.

They talked awhile longer, and then Delbert suggested that Joseph pick up the cake so they could get going.

"We should probably go too," Thelma said. "We want to grab a bite to eat and then head for home soon after. Our grandparents' house is pretty run-down and in need of repairs. We may paint the living room this afternoon."

Delbert reached into his pocket and pulled out a business card. "I'm a carpenter with my own woodworking business. If you need any repairs done that involve carpentry, please consider giving me a call."

Elma smiled. "You may be hearing from us."

As the men turned away, Joseph nudged Delbert's arm. "If they call you to go look at their place, I'd like to go along." He walked with a spring in his step.

Delbert grinned and thumped Joseph's shoulder. "Sure, no problem."

As Thelma and Elma headed for home after a quick bite to eat, they talked and even laughed about their lopsided cake. "At first I was mortified," Elma said. "But everything turned out pretty well in the end. I feel good knowing that our contribution went to a good cause."

"Jah." Thelma held firmly to Rusty's reins. "In addition to our cake going for such a high bid, we got to meet two very nice fellows." She glanced over at Elma. "Do you think we should call Delbert and see how much he would charge to fix our sagging front porch?"

Elma nodded. "Since Dad gave us that money, maybe we can afford to hire Delbert to do the work. In addition to making our place look nicer, it'll be a lot safer."

"You're right," Thelma agreed. "Honestly, I fear that someone will step right through the old wood and get hurt."

Elma sat up straight and loosened her sweater. "Whew! It's sure getting warm in this buggy."

I wish it were Joseph we'd be calling to work on our house, Thelma thought. *But I'd better accept the fact that I might never see him again.*

Chapter 18

The following Saturday, when Elma came into the house after checking messages in the phone shack, she smiled at Thelma and said, "Remember when I left a message for Delbert Gingerich the other day?"

Thelma placed a clean dish in the drying rack. "Jah. Did you hear something back from him?"

"I did. His message said that he would be out later today."

Thelma smiled, putting a freshly washed glass on the rack. "That's good to hear. I hope he's willing to fix our porch and that it won't cost too much. It would be nice if we didn't have to use all the money Dad gave us on just one project." She rinsed some pieces of silverware and set them in the dish drainer to dry.

"I agree. If Delbert's able to do it and we have some money left over, maybe we can ask him to do a few other projects."

Thelma grabbed a clean dish towel and began drying the dishes. "That would be good."

"It will be nice to see him again. He seemed like a pleasant man." Elma grabbed her to-do list and took a seat at the table. "What do you think would be the second thing we could ask him to do?"

Thelma finished drying a glass and put in the cupboard. "How about putting on some nice cabinet doors beneath this old sink? That would look better than the outdated curtain."

"You're right, Sister. That would be a good thing to have done." Elma jotted it down.

"So it's Delbert you're interested in, and not his friend Joseph?"

Elma tapped her pencil against her chin. "What makes you think I'm interested in Delbert?"

"You said it would be nice to see him again, and—"

"Now don't get any silly ideas," Elma interrupted. "He will be coming here to work, not for courting."

Thelma set her dish towel aside and sat across from Elma. "If he showed an interest in you, what would you do?"

Elma blinked her eyes rapidly. "I really can't say, since that hasn't happened."

"But if it did?" Thelma persisted.

"I give up!" Elma lifted her hands in the air. "I can tell that you're not going to drop this subject till I come up with an answer."

"That's right."

"If Delbert were to show some interest in me, I may be interested too. But I'd have to get to know him first to see how well we're suited." Elma leaned closer to Thelma. "Is that the answer you were looking for?"

Thelma grinned, bobbing her head. "Of course, it would be more fun if we both had suitors. Think of all the things we could do as courting couples."

"Maybe Delbert could fix you up with his friend Joseph. You did mention the other day that you thought he was *gutguckich*." Elma tugged the tie on her headscarf.

"I didn't say he was handsome. I said he was cute. Delbert's the handsome one, with that shiny blond hair."

"You're right about that." Elma placed her pencil on the table. "We can't sit here all day and talk about something that may never happen. We need to get out to the store before any customers show up."

"Okay, but I'm going to check on the horses first. I want to make sure that Pearl is happy in her new home."

"Speaking of Pearl," Elma said, as Thelma started for the door, "since she got new shoes put on last Monday, we can use her instead of Rusty when we need to go somewhere."

Thelma shook her head. "If he's not worked with, he'll never become fully road trained. You can take Pearl whenever you need to go somewhere with the buggy, but I'll keep using Rusty." Her face brightened. "I haven't given up hope on him yet, and I'm going to hang in there till I produce a wonderful buggy horse. Besides, I'm getting more confident each time I take him out."

"That's your choice," Elma said, "but you need to be careful, because you never know what that animal might do."

"I know, and I will be careful." Thelma smiled and scooted out the door.

⸎

The twins had closed the store for the day, when Delbert showed up. Thelma was surprised and pleased to see that Joseph was with him.

Looking shyly at Thelma, Joseph mumbled, "I—I came along 'cause Delbert owes me a meal."

"That's right," Delbert agreed. "We're planning to eat at Tiffany's here in Topeka."

"We've never eaten there," Thelma said, "but we hear they have good food."

"If you have no other plans, maybe you'd like to join us for supper," Delbert suggested.

Elma was about to say that she planned to fix a meat loaf, but Thelma spoke first. "We'd be happy to go to Tiffany's, wouldn't we, Sister?"

Feeling like a bug trapped in a spider's web, all Elma could do was nod. It wasn't that she didn't want to go to supper with these men. She simply felt like things were moving too fast. After all, they'd only met Joseph and Delbert last week, and here the men were asking them to share a meal at a restaurant. Maybe Delbert was only being polite. It could be that after Joseph said they were going out to eat, Delbert felt obligated to invite the twins to join them. But there was no point in mulling this over; she and Thelma had already agreed to go.

"Maybe I should take a look at your porch," Delbert suggested.

"That's a good idea," Thelma spoke up. "Let's head over there now."

When they stepped onto the porch, Delbert released a low whistle. "This is sagging pretty badly." He kicked at a couple of boards with the toe of his boot. "I'd say several pieces of this wood are rotted."

Elma cringed. "Does that mean it's going to be expensive to fix?"

"Not necessarily," he replied. "It's gonna depend on what I find when I start tearing into it. I can give you an estimate, but it might go over that amount. I'll try to work within your budget though."

Thelma smiled. "We appreciate that. Don't we, Sister?"

"Of course." Elma wondered if they should have gotten another carpenter to look at the porch too, but if Delbert did the job, it would give her a chance to get to know him better. She could tell from the rosy color on her sister's cheeks that she was glad Joseph had come along with Delbert today too.

***

When they entered Tiffany's, Joseph made sure he was sitting across the table from Thelma, which put Delbert across from Elma. Earlier at the twins' house, he wasn't sure which twin was who, because they looked so much alike. But after listening to them, he quickly realized that Thelma was more talkative and had a sense of humor.

Despite Joseph's shyness, on the buggy ride over, he'd managed to carry on a conversation with Thelma but mostly because she had so much to say. He wondered, now that they were at the restaurant, if she would continue to carry the conversation, or was she all talked out?

"How did the painting go last week, when you went home after the show?" Joseph managed to ask.

"It went pretty well," Thelma replied. "We got all the furniture moved to the middle of the room, and with two of us painting, we had the walls done in a few hours. The color looks nice too—like the shade of wheat."

When their waitress, a middle-aged Amish woman, came to take their order, everyone agreed that they would have the all-you-can-eat buffet. "Oh, and could you please bring some extra napkins?" Thelma asked.

"No problem. I'll grab you some and bring out your waters." She stuffed her pencil in her apron pocket and headed off toward the kitchen.

"Should we pray now, before we go to the buffet?" Delbert asked.

Joseph bobbed his head. "That's a good idea."

All heads bowed, and when Joseph opened his eyes, their waitress returned with glasses of water. She also handed Thelma a whole stack of napkins.

Thelma snickered. "I wonder why she gave me so many. Maybe I look like a messy person."

"I'm sure she was only being helpful." Elma patted her sister's hand.

"And I doubt she thought they were just for you."

Thelma handed each of them three napkins and laid the rest beside her plate. Then they made their way to the buffet.

When they returned to the table with their plates full of fried chicken, mashed potatoes, roast beef, corn, and noodles, Joseph was more than ready to eat. Just smelling the delicious food made his mouth water.

"Too bad they're out of the butterfly shrimp," Delbert commented. "I was kinda hoping for that. Truth is, I like all kinds of seafood."

"Same here," Thelma agreed. "And I like freshwater fish too."

"Do you ever go fishing?" Joseph asked, and he didn't even stutter.

She nodded enthusiastically. "Ever since I was a little girl and my daed took me out to the lake near our home, I've been hooked on fishing." She covered her mouth and giggled.

Joseph laughed too. He enjoyed Thelma's humor. She was bubbly, and the more he was with her, the more relaxed he became. Not only that, but she was a fine-looking woman. *I wonder how old she and her sister are? Do I dare ask?* Deciding that it would be too bold, he said instead, "If you and Elma aren't busy, maybe you'd like to go fishing with me and Delbert. We're planning to go next Saturday. Would that be a good day for you?"

"Oh, we'd love to go!" Thelma's face broke into a wide smile. "Wouldn't we, Sister?"

Elma, looking none too enthused, slowly nodded. "I—I suppose we could do that, but we'd have to close the store that day."

"That shouldn't be a problem," Thelma said, before taking a drink of water. "We closed it to go to the cooking show, and since it'll be open for business Monday through Friday, I think we deserve a little break, don't you?"

Again Elma nodded, but Joseph sensed she'd rather not go. *Maybe I shouldn't have said anything, but I'd like the chance to get to know Thelma better. Since we all like to fish, it should be a fun day.* He glanced at Delbert and realized that his friend hadn't made a single comment about taking the twins fishing. *I wonder if he'd prefer that they not go. Or maybe he's too busy eating his fried chicken to join the conversation right now.*

Joseph was having such a good time that he really didn't care what Delbert thought. Besides, the fishing trip would give Delbert a chance to get to know Elma better too.

At home after the men dropped the twins off, Thelma brought up the topic of Joseph and Delbert. "You were kind of quiet during supper," she said, sipping her cup of chamomile tea while holding a peanut butter cookie. "Weren't you having a good time?"

"It was fine. I enjoyed the meal." Elma blew on her tea. "I only wish you hadn't told Joseph that we'd go fishing with them." She sighed, finally taking her first cookie. "You know I don't like to fish. I don't have the patience for it."

"Don't worry about fishing. You can bring a book along. Anyway, it'll be a chance for us to get to know Delbert and Joseph better." Thelma smiled. "I think Joe likes me, Sister. And I have a hunch that Delbert may be a good match for you."

Finished with her snack, Elma said, "I'll admit, I am attracted to his good looks, but I don't know yet whether he and I are compatible."

"Which is why we need to go fishing with them. It'll be a relaxing, fun day—the perfect opportunity to visit and get to know what they're like."

"I suppose."

Thelma placed her hand over Elma's and gave it a gentle squeeze. "You know, this could be our one hope of finding husbands."

Elma finished drinking her tea. "We'll have to wait and see about that."

Chapter 19

How come you're bringing all of that?"Thelma asked when she noticed Elma stuffing several items into two large tote bags she'd placed on the kitchen table.

Elma blinked, as though surprised at Thelma's question. "We might need all these things. Remember, Mom would say that you never know what can occur on any outing, and being prepared is always good." Elma stood by her totes with her arms folded. "Did you remember to check on all the animals this morning?"

"Jah, I did. They are fed and content, and so are the mama cat and her babies in the basement."

"What about the eggs? Did you collect them like usual?"

Thelma nodded with a sigh. "I did all of that. And why do you always have to remind me of everything?"

"Because you're often preoccupied—this morning, more than usual."

Thelma lifted her gaze to the ceiling. In addition to a first-aid kit, her sister had packed bug spray, disinfectant wipes, blankets, sunglasses, and two umbrellas. "I'm glad we were able to get our fishing licenses earlier this week, and I'm looking forward to meeting Joseph and Delbert at the pond they told us about. If they were picking us up and we went in one buggy, there might not be room for all those things." Thelma glanced at the totes again.

Elma simply went to the refrigerator and took out the sandwiches she'd made to share with the men for lunch. Along with those, the twins were bringing potato chips, pretzels, cut-up veggies, and grapes. For dessert, they'd baked chocolate chip cookies. Delbert had volunteered to bring beverages, and Joseph would provide the fishing bait.

Thelma had been looking forward to this day ever since they'd made plans with the guys a week ago. Even though she'd only met Joseph, she found him to be quite pleasant. He seemed a bit shy and, except for small talk, hadn't said a lot during their meal at Tiffany's. Maybe that was because she had monopolized too much of the conversation. Joseph was a good listener though. He seemed interested in everything she'd said. It was a good thing she and Elma had chosen to wear different-colored dresses today. That would help the guys to keep them straight. Thelma had double-checked the way she looked this morning, as she wanted to make a nice impression on Joseph. She was even debating about going back to the bathroom and checking one more time to make sure her head covering was on straight.

"I am not really that interested in fishing." Elma broke into Thelma's thoughts.

"Then why'd you agree to go?"

"I did it for you—because I know you like to fish." Elma paused and put a package of paper plates in the wicker basket, along with the chips and cookies. The sandwiches would go in their small cooler. "And I can tell you're smitten with Joseph."

Thelma tipped her head. "Aren't you interested in Delbert? Have you forgotten so soon how handsome he is?"

"You're right, but good looks are not that important." Elma smiled. "I would like the chance to get to know him better though."

"Then it's settled. I have a feeling that by the end of the day, we'll both know more about those men."

◌◠◞

LaGrange

"This will be a great day for fishing, and the weather is looking favorable. The sun is shining, and I'm feelin' the warmth," Joseph said as he climbed into Delbert's buggy, which looked sharp and clean, as usual. Recently, Delbert had installed a new heater in the dash of his buggy, but they wouldn't need that today. If Joseph didn't know better, he'd think it was late summer, instead of the middle of October.

124

Truth was, all week Joseph had been looking forward to this day and getting an opportunity to spend it with Thelma. While he didn't know much about her yet, she'd said she liked to fish. He hoped they'd get some time alone to visit and that he'd discover other things they both liked.

Delbert took up the reins. "Let's hope the fish are biting and the women bring something good for lunch."

"I'm sure they will." Joseph smiled. "Thelma said she was going to bake chocolate chip cookies."

"Sure hope they look better than that crazy cake she and her sister made."

"The cake may not have looked so good, but it sure was tasty. You're lucky I shared it with you."

Delbert guided his horse onto the main road. "You almost had to share it, since I'm the one who got that lopsided dessert for you."

"That's true." Joseph rubbed his chin. "You know, we never did ask the twins how that cake ended up looking so uneven or why the whole thing wasn't frosted."

Delbert thumped Joseph's arm. "Not a problem. You can ask them today."

"You don't think they'll forget about meeting us, do you?"

"Naw. I'm sure they'll remember."

"Can't you make your horse go any faster?" Joseph couldn't help feeling impatient.

"Hold your horses. Snickers is going fast enough." Delbert chuckled. "I want to stop at the store and get some sweet tea."

"What if the twins aren't able to find the pond we told 'em about?" Joseph continued to stroke his chin, trying to keep from becoming too antsy. At least he'd remembered to shave this morning. He'd been so excited about seeing Thelma again he'd almost left the house without doing that. "Maybe we should have gone over to their place to pick them up."

"I gave them good instructions," Delbert said. "Since the small fishing hole is halfway between LaGrange and Topeka, it only made sense that we should meet them there. Now, quit fretting and relax."

❧

As soon as Elma pulled Pearl into the designated spot where Delbert and Joseph had said they would meet, Thelma climbed down and secured the horse to a tree. It was nice that Elma had driven today. She seemed happy to have Pearl pulling their buggy too. *I'm glad I told Dad about Elma's fear of Rusty and he decided to bring our docile, dependable horse.*

"Are you sure this is the right pond?" Elma asked when she joined Thelma by the tree. "I don't see any sign of the men, and no one else seems to be here fishing either." She made a sweeping gesture of the area.

"We followed Delbert's directions, so this has to be the place." Thelma didn't admit it, but she was a little worried too that they might be at the wrong pond.

"Let's leave everything in the buggy till the men arrive. I wouldn't want to have to put it all away if they don't show up." Elma opened the bag of grapes and popped one into her mouth.

"You're right." Thelma walked around for a bit, surveying the pond and enjoying the warmth of the day. It was interesting how the weather could change so quickly. Yesterday it had been chilly with a bit of rain, and now this morning, the sun shone brightly. The sun's warmth felt so good. *How silly of Elma to bring those umbrellas along*, she mused. *I doubt we'll see any rain today.*

❧

Elma swatted at a bothersome fly as she stood stroking Pearl's mane. Even the fly was fooled by the temperatures, but Elma was glad the gnats and most of the other aggravating bugs were gone. *I wonder how long we should wait. If they don't get here soon, maybe we should return home, because I sure don't want to drive my poor horse all over the place in search of the right pond.*

She glanced at Thelma, who stood near the water's edge, looking up at the sky. Elma looked up too. The sky was as blue as ever, without the hint of a cloud. Even so, it might not be like that later in the day, which was the reason she'd come prepared. Her sister may think she was silly bringing all those other things as well, but Elma thought it was good to be prepared for any given situation. Besides, they had plenty of room in their buggy, so what did it hurt?

Tired of waiting, she was about to suggest they go home, when a horse and buggy rolled into the clearing. It was Delbert and Joseph. "Sister, they're here!"

Thelma came running with an eager expression. "Oh good. Now we can begin fishing!"

Elma gritted her teeth. *Oh good. I can't wait.*

"So glad you two were able to find this place," Joseph said, smiling at Thelma. At least he thought it was her. When she spoke, he was sure he would know for certain, but he wished the twins didn't look so much alike. It was confusing.

"It wasn't hard at all, was it, Elma?"

Elma shook her head "We had no problem finding the pond, but when we got here and saw no sign of you and Delbert, we wondered if we were at the wrong place."

"Sorry we're a bit late," Delbert spoke up. "We stopped by the store on the way here so we could pick up some bottles of sweet tea." He gestured to the cooler Joseph was lifting out of the buggy. "I packed water, and Joe brought some bait, but we thought the tea would go good with our lunch."

Joseph grinned. *The one in the dark blue dress is Thelma all right.* Elma had worn a gray dress this morning. Since they hadn't dressed alike, it would be easier to tell them apart. "I hope you and your sister don't mind, but I brought Ginger along. She loves to go fishing with me and shouldn't be any problem at all."

"It's fine with me," Thelma spoke up.

Elma leaned down to pet the dog's head. "What a beautiful golden retriever."

"She's also very gentle and has been a great companion for me," Joseph said.

"I hope you'll enjoy what we brought to eat," Thelma said. "If not, then maybe the dog will eat it."

Elma rolled her eyes.

"I'm sure it'll be good." Joseph thumped his stomach. "Thinkin' about food makes me hungerich."

Delbert bumped Joseph's arm. "Let's get to fishin'. That oughta take your mind off your hungry stomach."

Joseph chuckled when his stomach growled in protest. "Sure hope so." He glanced over at the twins who were busy taking things out of their buggy. "Do you need any help?"

"I think maybe we do," Thelma said. "I have our picnic basket and a small cooler, and Elma brought two hefty tote bags along."

"That's right," Elma agreed. "In addition to blankets for us to sit on, I packed bug spray, sunglasses, umbrellas, a first-aid kit, plus a few other items."

Delbert frowned while swatting at the back of his neck, where a fly had landed. "How come you brought so much stuff? All we really need is the food, beverages, and fishing gear. Oh, and of course, my favorite fishing chair."

Elma's eyebrows shot up. "You brought your own chair?"

"Sure did." Delbert reached into the buggy and pulled out a canvas folding chair. "I always fish better when I'm sittin' on this."

Elma looked at the chair then quickly pulled a blanket out of one of the tote bags. "I'd rather sit on this."

"You don't say," Delbert was quick to reply.

Joseph pulled at his collar, which suddenly seemed too tight. Was he imagining it, or was there a bit of friction going on between his friend and Elma? He hoped that wasn't the case, because in order to keep seeing Thelma, he needed Delbert to go out with her twin.

Chapter 20

As Thelma sat on a log beside Joseph, holding her fishing pole, she looked over her shoulder and frowned. Elma sat on the blanket by herself, with a pen and crossword-puzzle magazine in her hand. *My sister will never get to know Delbert that way,* she fretted. He'd been kind enough to bring four poles and had even baited Elma's hook, but she showed no interest in fishing. *I need to think of something to get them together. Maybe when we eat lunch it'll go better.*

"By the way," Delbert said, looking at Thelma from where he sat on his chair. "If you and Elma still want me to fix your front porch, I'd be free to start on Monday."

"I believe we do. Isn't that right, Elma?" Thelma called to her sister.

"What was that?" Elma leaned slightly forward, putting the magazine down. "I was so engrossed in this puzzle that I didn't hear what was said."

"Delbert said he'd be free to start on our porch this coming Monday. We still want him to do the job, right?"

Elma nodded. "Definitely. It needs to be done, and soon."

"Great then. I'll be over early that morning."

"How early?" Elma asked. "We open the store at nine."

"I'll be there before then, in case you want to ask me any questions." Delbert looked at Thelma and smiled. "And if I have any questions, I'll come up to the store to speak with whichever of you isn't busy."

"That should work out fine," Thelma said.

"By the way. . ." Joseph moved a little closer to Thelma. Then Ginger got up and moved a little closer to Joseph, nudging his hand for some attention. "I keep forgetting to tell you that I enjoyed eating the cake you made for the charity event. It was sure tasty."

Thelma's face heated. "Danki, Joseph. I'm glad the way it looked didn't affect the taste."

"We never got to ask," Delbert said, "but how did the cake end up looking that way?"

"I had baked it the night before, and when I put the top layer on, one side looked lopsided," Thelma explained. "So to fix that problem, I added more frosting to one side of the top." She grimaced. "That may have been okay, but just then, our cat jumped up and got in the bowl of icing, so I couldn't use what was left. Then on the way to Shipshewana, our horse started acting up, lurching and lunging. I believe that's what made the cake look even worse."

"It was an embarrassment." Elma joined them at the pond's edge. "What I'd like to know, Delbert, is why you bid on our cake. I mean, lots of the other desserts looked much better than ours."

Delbert pointed at Joseph. "I did it for my good friend here. He wanted that cake and asked me to bid on it for him."

More than a little surprised, Thelma turned to face Joseph. "If you really wanted it, then why didn't you bid on it yourself?"

Joseph's ears turned pink, and so did his cheeks, making his freckles stand out. "I. . .uh. . .the thing is. . . I—I knew if I tried to call out a bid, I'd trip over my own t–tongue, like I'm doin' right now."

"But why did you want a lopsided cake?" Elma asked, lowering herself to the log beside Thelma.

Joseph dropped his gaze to the ground, rocking slightly back and forth. "I—I wanted to m–meet Thelma."

Thelma's eyes opened wide. She hardly knew what to say. It made her feel good to know that Joseph had wanted to meet her, but to pay that much for their cake?

"And don't forget," Delbert said, "the cooking show was for a good cause."

"That's true," Elma agreed. "And we hope the proceeds from the auction brought in a lot of money."

"I don't know how much exactly, but I heard it was a success." Delbert's fishing pole jerked. He leaped to his feet. "I've got a bite, but I'm thinkin' it might be a sucker. If so, I'll throw it back in."

Thelma sat quietly, watching Delbert reel in his fish, unable to look at Joseph. He hadn't said a word since he'd announced that he'd asked his friend to bid on the cake so he could meet Thelma. She figured he was embarrassed, and she wished she could say something to make him feel better, but what? She couldn't blurt out that she was glad he'd wanted to meet her. Or was there something else she could say?

"Ginger is sure a nice dog. How long have you had her?" Thelma decided to ask.

"Six years already—since she was a puppy." Joseph looked tenderly at the dog. Thelma could tell they were true companions as Ginger laid her head in Joseph's lap. "After I bought my place two years before that, I missed having a dog around."

"She certainly is well behaved," Elma said.

He gave a nod. "Has been from the very beginning."

"Danki for inviting us to go fishing with you today." Leaning over, so she was closer to Joseph's ear, Thelma whispered, "I'm glad you asked Delbert to bid on the cake. If you hadn't, we wouldn't be sitting here right now, enjoying this lovely day."

He lifted his head and smiled at her. "Maybe we can do this again sometime. If not before winter sets in, then maybe come spring."

Thelma nodded. "I'd like that, Joseph." She knew now that he truly must be interested in her, or why would he have mentioned that?

Elma rose from her seat. "I think I'll go for a walk."

By now, Delbert had thrown the fish back in the pond and was about to put more bait on his hook when Joseph stood. "Why don't you go with her, Dell? It'll give you two a chance to get better acquainted. And take Ginger along. I think she could use some exercise."

"I suppose I may as well take a walk, since the good fish aren't biting anyway." Delbert turned to face Elma. "Should we go right or left?"

"Since you know the area and I don't, why don't you choose?" She smiled up at him.

"Let's head in this direction." Delbert pointed to the left.

Elma patted her leg. "Come on, Ginger!" The dog jumped up and came right over, her tail swishing about.

As Elma followed Delbert down a dirt path, she noticed several kinds of wildflowers. "Those are so *schee*."

Delbert stopped walking and turned to face her. "What's pretty?"

"Those." Elma pointed to the flowers.

"Ah, I see." He motioned to a pile of colored leaves. "I think those are equally schee."

Elma nodded. Apparently Delbert enjoyed the colors found in nature. It was nice to know they had that in common.

"How come you're not fishing today?" he asked as they continued walking.

"To be perfectly honest, I've never had that much interest in the sport. I enjoy eating some fish, but I don't have the patience to sit and wait for a fish to bite."

"It does take patience," he agreed. "But you know what they say: 'Good things come to those who wait.'"

Elma smiled in response.

"Don't know about you, but I'm about ready to eat. Should we head back so we can have lunch?"

"That's fine with me."

When they returned to the place where they'd left Joseph and Thelma, Elma was surprised to see how close they were sitting on that log. They both had their lines in the water and were chattering away like a pair of blue jays that had known each other for a long time.

"You're back so soon?" Thelma asked, looking up at Elma.

Delbert bobbed his head. "We decided it was time for lunch." He stood close to Joseph, and Ginger came and sat between them. "Have you caught anything yet?"

"No," Joseph replied, "but Thelma and I have been havin' a good conversation."

"I'm glad, but you can visit while we eat." Delbert opened his cooler. "I'll get out the beverages. Who wants a bottle of sweet tea?"

"I'll stick with water," Elma said as she spread the other blanket on the ground. She assumed she and Thelma would sit there and the men could share the blanket she'd sat on earlier.

But before she could make a move, Thelma knelt on the blanket closest to the picnic basket and began taking out the paper plates and napkins. Then Joseph, who had just finished putting Ginger's food out, plopped down right beside her.

"Is it okay if I sit here?" he asked.

"Of course." Thelma handed him a paper plate and passed a couple of others to Elma and Delbert, along with napkins.

Elma took the sandwiches from the cooler she and Thelma had brought and gave one to everyone. "I hope you like ham and cheese," she said. "We have some potato chips too."

"Ham and cheese sounds good to me." Delbert plopped his sandwich on the paper plate and plunked down in his folding chair, leaving Elma to sit on her blanket alone.

"Shall we pray?" Thelma suggested.

All heads bowed, and when their prayers ended, Delbert gave Elma a bottle of water. "What would you like, Thelma—water or sweet tea?"

"I think I'd like the tea."

"Oh Sister, there's a lot of *zucker* in one of those bottles. I've read the labels before and it—"

"Unless she has diabetes or something, a little sugar won't hurt her." Delbert handed Thelma some sweet tea. "How about you, Joe? What would you like to drink?"

"If there's enough sweet tea, I'll have one of those."

"No problem. I bought four bottles, thinkin' we'd each have one."

"If there were no zucker added, I might have taken one," Elma was quick to say. She didn't want Delbert to think she was ungrateful. She passed around the chips, veggies, and grapes to everyone.

As they ate, the twins talked about their grandparents' house and how much work it needed. "Sometimes it seems a bit overwhelming," Elma said, "but we've decided to take one project at a time."

"Come Monday, Delbert will be taking care of one of your problems," Joseph looked at Thelma. "If there are other things you need that don't involve carpentry, let me know. I'd be glad to help."

"Danki, we'll keep that in mind," Thelma responded.

When they finished with the sandwiches and other food, Thelma opened the wicker basket again and took out the cookies. "I hope you and

Delbert like chocolate chip," she said, offering the cookies to Joseph. He took a couple and passed the container to Delbert.

Delbert grabbed one and held it up, his brows scrunching together. "They look like they're a bit burned on the bottom."

Thelma's face turned red. "Sorry about that. It's hard to judge how long things should bake in our old oven. It's a relic. Someday, if we start making enough money from the store, we hope to get a new stove."

"Our oven is heated with wood, not propane," Elma clarified.

"That explains everything." Delbert grunted. "I'll scrape off the dark part." He took out his fishing knife, poured some of his tea over it, wiped it on his trousers, and scraped away the dark part on the cookie.

Eww, Elma thought. *That really grosses me out.* She looked over at Thelma and discreetly pointed at Delbert's knife.

Thelma shrugged. Didn't this man's lack of manners bother her at all?

"That was a good meal, and I thank you for it." Delbert dropped the paper plate in a paper sack Elma had set out and rose to his feet. "Think I'll try my hand at fishin' again."

"I don't think that's such a good idea." Elma pointed to the darkening sky. "I felt a few raindrops, and it's likely to get worse."

Delbert waved his hand. "A few drops of rain won't hurt us. I can't leave here without getting at least one fish." He looked at Joseph. "How 'bout you? Aren't you gonna fish for a while too?"

Joseph looked at Thelma. "Do you want to fish some more?"

She smiled and nodded. "I'm in no hurry to go home."

"Okay, you three can fish, and I'll put our lunch basket away." Elma gathered everything up and got out her umbrella. She had a feeling these few drops of rain would soon become a full-blown rainstorm.

When more raindrops fell, Elma said she thought they should go.

"Let's wait and see how bad it gets." Delbert reached for some bait and was on the verge of putting it on his hook when a clap of thunder sounded. Everyone jumped, and Delbert hollered, "Ouch! I've got a fishhook stuck in my thumb!"

Chapter 21

Topeka

"Delbert's here," Thelma said, peering out the kitchen window. "He came early, like he said. The rig he came in today, Sister, is far more untidy than the one he had at the pond. Guess that's probably because this is Delbert's work buggy."

Elma, who had been folding a dish towel, joined Thelma at the window. "You're right. Guess I'd better go out and explain to him what needs to be done."

Thelma pressed her hands against her hips. "Delbert's a *schreiner*, Sister. I'm sure he knows what to do."

"Just because he's a carpenter doesn't mean he will know what we want to have done," Elma argued.

"I thought we already told him when he came to look at the saggy porch."

"We did, but I've thought of a couple other things since then." Elma grabbed her sweater and scooted out the door. She stepped onto the porch, being careful not to trip on any of the loose boards. She paused to breathe in the fresh autumn air. "Look at God's handiwork," she murmured. Everything from the golden leaves to the mixture of colorful mums filled her senses.

Elma watched Delbert unhook his horse from the rig and waited while he walked Snickers over to their corral. A few minutes later, Delbert joined her on the porch, carrying his tool belt. "Guder mariye," he said. "Beautiful morning, isn't it?"

"Good morning, and jah, I was taking it all in and thinking the same thing. By the way, before I forget, how is your thumb?"

He held up his hand. "Still hurts a bit, but it'll be fine with the bandage I'm wearing."

"I hope you put some disinfectant on it after you got home Saturday."

He nodded. "I've got more stuff in my work buggy, so as soon as I take it out, I'll get busy on your porch."

"Before you get started, I wanted to point something out." Elma motioned to the handrail. "In addition to the boards in the porch floor, I'd like that replaced too."

He looked at her quizzically. "Are you sure? It looks like it's still in fairly good shape."

She shook her head. "No, it's not. See, right there, some of the wood is beginning to split."

Delbert leaned down and studied the area she was referring to. "Hmm. . . I can probably fix that with some putty and wood glue."

"I'd rather it be replaced."

He shrugged. "Okay, if that's what you want. Anything else?"

"I do have a few other tasks in mind, but maybe you should get this project done first." Elma was about to step back inside, when she thought of something else. "Thelma and I will be at the store most of the day, but we'll leave the front door unlocked so you can go in to use the bathroom or get a drink of water. One of us will come up to the house around noon to fix you some lunch."

"There's no need for that," he said. "I brought my own lunch along."

"Okay. I'll see you later then." With a quick smile, she went back into the house.

It was getting close to noon and Delbert was thinking about stopping for lunch, when Elma showed up. He knew it was her because she'd been wearing a dark maroon dress when she'd spoken to him earlier.

"How's it going?" she asked, moving toward the porch steps.

"It's going okay, but you'd better not come up here." He motioned to the boards he'd pried loose. "Oh, and I'm afraid I've got bad news."

Her forehead creased. "What's that?"

"You have a problem with carpenter ants."

"Oh dear." Elma clasped her hand over her mouth. "How bad is it?"

"Pretty bad." Delbert gestured from one end of the porch to the other. "They're about everywhere, I'm afraid." He lifted his hammer and smacked a big black ant crawling near his boot.

"I wonder how they got into the porch."

"Carpenter ants build their nests in wood, so they're often found in and around homes. They don't actually eat the wood, but they bore through the wood, making a place for their nest."

"Oh. So maybe that's not so bad."

"It can be. Carpenter ants can find their way into your home and even get into your food and water sources, so they need to be taken care of." He smacked another crawling bug. "Have you seen any sign of them in the house?"

Elma shook her head and mumbled something about a rat and some mice.

"You've got a rodent problem too?"

Her face flamed. "We did, but our katze have taken care of that." Wrinkles formed above her brows. "What are we supposed to do about the ants?"

"The first thing will be to kill them off. You could call a professional company to come out and do that, but it'll be expensive, and they might not get out here right away."

"Would you be able to get rid of the ants?" she asked.

He nodded. "I can get some bait from the hardware store to lure them out, then trail 'em back to the nest so I can figure out exactly where they're hiding."

"Can you do it without using anything toxic? My folks have always tried to use organic methods, even when dealing with bugs and other critters that have invaded our garden. All natural is better than taking the chance of poisoning a pet or any kinner that may be playing in the yard."

Reaching under his straw hat, Delbert scratched his head. "How often do you have children in your yard?"

"Well, maybe not here, but they do come to the store with their parents, and if one were to wander down to the house, then. . ."

Delbert lifted his hands in defeat. "Okay, I get it. I'll make sure to use tamper-resistant bait stations."

"Will it be toxic?"

"Jah, but it'll be safer because—"

"Is there anything natural you can try?" she questioned.

"I've used a boric acid bait before. I'll mix one-third powdered sugar with two-thirds boric acid, fill some bottle caps with the mixture, and set it down around the areas where I've seen the ants. When they return the next time, it will kill the ants that are already in the nest. See, the boric acid penetrates the insect's body and dissolves in there."

Elma wrinkled her nose. "That sounds ekelhaft."

"It may be disgusting, but if it gets rid of your ant problem without using poison, then you oughta be glad." He stepped off the porch. "Unless you have some boric acid here, I'd better run into town to get some."

"I'm sure we don't have any of that, but we do have some powdered sugar."

"Great. If you'll have that sitting out for me, I'll mix up the stuff when I get back."

"I'll make sure it's ready. I'll leave the powdered sugar on the kitchen counter. Until you get the porch finished, my sister and I will only use the back door."

"That's a good idea. See you later then," Delbert called over his shoulder as he headed for his horse and buggy.

When Delbert came back an hour and a half later, he found a box of powdered sugar and a large measuring cup on the kitchen counter with a note attached, telling him what it was for. "Like I needed that," Delbert mumbled. "Does she think I'm *dumm*?"

Grasping the note, he read it out loud. "Before you leave for the day could you please come up to the store? There is something else I'd like you to do."

"What does she want now? I'm not even done with the porch."

Delbert wondered whether Elma was always so demanding or if she had singled him out. Maybe demanding wasn't the right word. Elma was a little too opinionated to suit Delbert. She reminded him of his ex-girlfriend, Mattie, who'd wanted to make Delbert become the kind of man she thought he should be. Her constant suggestions and opinions about what he should or shouldn't do had caused him to finally break things off and give up on marriage. Of course, having put up with five somewhat bossy older sisters when he was growing up hadn't helped either. But Delbert thought he ought to at least give Elma a chance, since Joseph was set on establishing a relationship with Thelma and wanted him to be a part of the foursome. He'd give her the benefit of the doubt and see what happened. After all, she was pretty cute.

Delbert's nose twitched and he sneezed. He went to the sink to get a drink and sneezed a few more times. *Achoo! Achoo! Achoo!* He reached for a paper towel and wiped his nose as his eyes began to water.

Meow! Meow!

Delbert looked down and scowled at the cat rubbing against his leg. No wonder he'd sneezed. "Go on, get!" he said, moving to one side.

The cat followed, meowing up at him as though it wanted something. Whatever it was, the feline wouldn't get it from Delbert. He was allergic to cats and couldn't get anywhere near one without his nose acting up. Sometimes when his allergies got real bad, he would become so stuffed up he could barely breathe. He wasn't going to stay in here any longer. He needed to get back outside.

❦

"I've done as much on your porch as I can for today," Delbert said when he entered the twins' store. "I need to be in Shipshe soon to bid on another job."

"Oh, before you go," Elma said, "there's something else my sister and I would like to have done."

"You said something about that in your note." Delbert pulled out his hanky and wiped his nose.

"Do you have a cold?" Elma asked, stepping out from behind the counter where she stood with her twin sister.

"Nope. I'm allergic to *katze*."

"There's no cat in here," Thelma spoke up. "Although we probably will bring the *busslin* out when it's time to find them all homes."

Delbert grimaced. "Kittens? Do you have kittens in your house? I thought it was just the one cat."

"What one cat?" Elma asked. "Were you in the basement? That's where the kittens and mama cat are."

Delbert shook his head. "I was in the kitchen getting a drink when this orange-and-white cat rubbed against my trousers. It made me sneeze." If there were more cats in the basement, he wouldn't go down there.

Thelma pressed her fingers to her lips. "Uh-oh. I must have forgotten to put Tiger out this morning. I'd better do that right now, before he makes a mess in the house." She slipped past Elma and rushed out the door.

Delbert moved across the room and leaned on the counter. "What else are you wantin' me to do?"

"There's a piece of fabric hanging below the kitchen sink. Thelma and I would like to have it replaced with real wooden doors." Elma smiled— that oh so sweet smile that made him feel like he couldn't say anything but yes.

"It's in the kitchen, huh?"

"That's what I just said."

He paused to blow his nose then returned his hanky to his pocket. "Will the cat be in there when I'm workin'?"

"Oh no, I'll make sure he's not."

"That's good, 'cause if he were, I'd probably have to wear a dust mask so I wouldn't have to breathe all that cat dander." Delbert paused to rub his eyes.

"I'm sorry you were exposed to Tiger. We'll make sure it doesn't happen again."

Delbert coughed then smiled. "Okay. When did you want me to start on the cabinet doors?"

"There's no real rush. Whenever you finish with the porch. And if you have work for other people that needs to be done first, that's all right too."

"I'll get it done as soon as I can." Delbert glanced to his left and noticed a rack full of candy. "Got any jelly beans over there?" he asked, gesturing to the candy.

"I believe so," Elma replied, "but I'm not sure how fresh they are. Thelma and I are still in the process of taking inventory of all the stock in our store. We haven't done the candy rack yet."

"Think I'll go have a look-see anyhow." Delbert strode over to the candy and plucked off a package of mixed jelly beans. The black licorice–flavored ones looked especially enticing. "I'll take these. How much do I owe you?" he asked, plopping the bag on the counter.

"Let me see if there's an expiration date on them." She picked up the bag and slipped on her reading glasses. It seemed odd to Delbert that a young woman her age would have a need for reading glasses. Come to think of it, he wasn't sure how old she and her sister were. In the few times they'd been together, the subject hadn't come up. Delbert guessed they were probably in their mid to late twenties. He thought about asking Elma her age, but a customer had entered the store, and she looked like she wanted to ask Elma a question.

"So how much for the jelly beans?" he quickly asked.

She pressed her lips together, staring at the package. "You know, Delbert, eating too much zucker is bad for your health."

Delbert's fingers curled into a ball, biting into his palms. Did Elma think she was his mother? One minute she could be so nice, then the next, she was downright irritating. Making no reference to her comment, he said, "How much do they cost?"

"Since you seem determined to have them, and since the expiration date was three months ago, I'll give you the jelly beans for free."

"Really?"

She nodded.

"Danki. I'll be back sometime tomorrow to finish the porch." He picked up the bag of candy and headed for the door, feeling a little better toward Elma than he had before. Now that he knew they sold jelly beans in this store, he'd make sure to visit more often.

Chapter 22

LaGrange

A re you ready for a rousing game of Ping-Pong?" Joseph asked when he arrived at Delbert's on Friday night.

Delbert grinned. "More to the point, are you ready to lose?"

"We'll have to wait and see about that." Joseph removed his jacket and hung it over the back of a chair.

"Should we get started now, or did you want a cup of coffee first?" Delbert asked. "I've got a pot heatin' on the stove."

"Maybe I will have a cup." Joseph followed Delbert into the kitchen and took a seat at the table, while Delbert got out the mugs and poured the coffee. "Sure was a colorful week, with autumn leaves at their peak."

"You're right, and this is my favorite time of the year." Delbert glanced out the window and yawned. "You want a cinnamon roll?"

"Did you bake 'em?"

Delbert shook his head. "I've been too busy this week to do any baking." He handed Joseph a cup and placed several cinnamon rolls on the table.

"Busy workin' in your shop? Or workin' on somebody's home?"

"I worked at my shop a few days, but the rest of the week I was in Topeka, at the Hochstetler twins' place."

Joseph set his cup down and plopped his elbows on the table, eager to hear about the twins—especially Thelma. "How'd it go over there?" He helped himself to a roll.

"I got their porch done, and then I made a couple of doors for under the kitchen sink."

"Sounds like you've been busy."

"Jah."

"Did you see Thelma?"

Delbert grabbed a cinnamon roll, broke it in half, and dunked the piece in his hot coffee. "Not so much. Saw a lot of Elma though."

Joseph smiled, biting into the soft, sweet pastry. "That's good to hear."

Delbert shook his head. "No, not really." He finished up his last piece of the cinnamon roll.

"Seeing Elma isn't good?" Joseph couldn't hide his confusion. "But you said before that you thought she was pretty." He took a sip of his steaming hot coffee.

"She is, but she doesn't like to fish, and on top of that, she sometimes gets on my nerves."

"Oh really? Why's that?" Joseph blew on the coffee.

Delbert reached for another roll. "She says things to irritate me and offers her opinion on how I should do things. No wonder she's not married."

"I wouldn't talk about who's not married, if I were you. In case you haven't looked in the mirror lately, you're over thirty and still not sportin' a beard."

Delbert jerked his head around to meet Joseph's gaze. "That's right. I'm still single, and I kinda like it that way." He took another bite of the pastry he held.

Joseph leaned forward. "Are you sure? Don't you think havin' a wife and family would be nice?"

Delbert just drank down his coffee and grabbed another cinnamon roll.

"Maybe you're too set in your ways."

"That could be." Delbert pushed away from the table, licking some of the icing that had stuck to his fingers. "I'd best go wash my hands." He got up and went to the sink. After he'd washed and dried his hands, he returned to the table. "Are you ready to play that game of table tennis now?"

"Not quite. I haven't finished my coffee yet." Truth was, Joseph felt like he and Delbert were already playing a type of ping-pong.

Delbert went to the stove and got a refill then sat back down.

"I've been thinking that maybe we could see if Thelma and Elma would like to come over to my house for pizza next Friday night. We could play a few board games after we eat."

"I don't think so, Joe. Elma gets on my nerves. She even made an issue of me eating jelly beans the other day." Delbert grimaced. "Made me feel like a little boy being scolded for having too much candy."

"You should take that as a good sign."

Delbert's eyebrows pulled together. "Good sign of what?"

"That she likes you and cares about your welfare. Too much zucker can be bad, you know."

"I don't eat too much sugar. Besides, she's not with me all the time, so there's no way she can know how much sugar I eat." Delbert folded his arms. "If you want to keep seeing Thelma, that's fine by me, but I think I'm done pursuing Elma."

Joseph sat rigidly in his chair as a sense of panic set in. "Aw, come on, Dell. You don't know Elma all that well yet. I think you need to give her a chance."

Delbert slowly shook his head. "I don't know about that."

Joseph leaned closer to Delbert. "Won't you go out with her a couple more times, even if it's only as a friend? I want to keep seeing Thelma, and I really need you with me."

"You don't need me in order to see Thelma."

"Jah, I do, because I still feel a little awkward and tongue-tied when I'm around her. Besides, after you get to know Elma a little better, maybe you'll decide that she's the right girl for you." Joseph's stomach tightened. If Delbert gave up on seeing Elma, he didn't know what he would do. Could he really find the courage to court Thelma on his own?

Delbert sighed. "I'll give it some thought. Now are we gonna play Ping-Pong or what?"

"Sure, and if you wanna serve first, that's fine by me."

⁂

Topeka

"Did you happen to notice that the FOR SALE sign is back on the house across the street?" Elma took a seat in her favorite chair. "The sign did read SALE PENDING before. I wonder what happened with the potential buyers. It's such a nice place too."

"That's right. I thought the family from Graybill was interested in getting that house." Thelma shifted a bit on Grandpa's old chair. "I guess it wasn't meant to be. When the time is right, maybe someone else will buy the house."

"What are you knitting?" Elma asked, noticing Thelma's yarn. "It doesn't look like gloves for Mom. The yarn is a different color."

"No, it's not. I finished those several days ago." Thelma held up the ball of blue yarn. "I'm making a stocking cap for Joseph."

"Really?" Elma placed the dress she was hemming in her lap. "Are you serious about him? I mean, you've only gone out with him a few times."

"I know, but I really like Joe. I may give him the cap for Christmas."

"What do we have here, Sister—a case of love at first sight, the way it was for Mom and Dad?"

Thelma's heart raced a bit, and she felt the heat of a blush. "Maybe, but I'm not sure how he feels about me."

"If the dreamy-eyed look he gets when he's with you is any indication, then I'd say you have nothing to worry about." Elma grinned and picked up her mending.

Thelma smiled in response, feeling relaxed. "How about you and Delbert? He's been over here quite a bit in the last week, and it seemed like you were talking to him a lot."

Elma sighed. "I don't think he likes me, Thelma."

Thelma's eyes widened. "What makes you say that?"

"He seems irritated whenever I ask him a question."

"He was probably preoccupied. After all, he did come here to work."

Elma threaded her needle. "I know, but it was more than that. I just feel that we don't communicate well or really have much in common."

"Dad and Mom don't have a lot of things in common, but they've been happily married for thirty-four years."

"Can we change the subject?" She stood. "It's getting chilly in here. Think I'll throw another log on the fire."

"Want me to do that so you can keep working on your new dress? You'll probably want to wear it to church this Sunday."

"You're right. I do. And if you're sure you don't mind, it would be nice if you put the next log on the fire."

"I don't mind at all." Thelma set her knitting aside and crossed the room. She'd picked up a piece of wood when she heard a loud *meow*. "Uh-oh. I'll bet that's Tiger. I forgot to let him in this evening. And by the way, I found a good-sized box in the back of the store earlier today. It's perfect for Misty and her growing kittens. Before long, we'll be able to take them out to the store to try and find them new homes. I hope you won't mind, but I'd like to keep one of Misty's kittens."

Elma wrinkled her nose. "Another cat? Oh Sister, don't you think we have enough of those already?"

"Maybe, but they do keep the mice down."

"True."

"I've grown attached to the little cuties but mostly the white-colored female in the group." Thelma yearned to keep the kitten.

"Okay. I guess one more katz won't matter. As you said, having the katze keeps down the mice. But one thing to consider is that Delbert is allergic to cats. We can't allow Tiger in the house when Delbert is here, but it'll just be till he's done working for us."

"I thought he was done. He fixed the front porch and put the doors under the kitchen sink. Isn't that all you asked him to do?"

"At first it was, but then I asked if he would fix the loose railing going upstairs to the bedrooms, and I'm thinking we may want him to replace the broken lock on the kitchen window. There's also that door upstairs that catches."

Thelma smiled. "I'm thinking from your expression that you're worried about Delbert. Does that mean you like him a lot?"

"I can't say that. I don't want him having an allergic attack when he's trying to work on our house."

"He won't be coming here tonight, so I'm gonna let Tiger in." Thelma tossed the wood on the fire and opened the front door. She hoped things would work out between her sister and Delbert, because if Elma didn't have a man friend, then Thelma wouldn't either. It wouldn't be fair, and besides, she'd made that childhood promise not to get married unless Elma was too.

Chapter 23

"I am sure looking forward to this evening," Thelma said as she and Elma climbed into their buggy the next Friday. "It'll be fun to see where Joseph lives and spend the evening with him and Delbert."

Elma sighed. "I suppose, although I was honestly looking forward to a restful evening at home. It's been a busy week at the store, and I'm tired." She picked up the reins and got Pearl moving. "Brr... You can tell it's November, even though it's only the first week."

"If the night air doesn't do it, I'll bet you'll perk up as soon as we eat and play a few board games. I know how much you enjoy the competition."

"That's true. A good game of Rook or Settlers is always fun." She yawned. "I hope you're not planning to stay too late."

Thelma touched Elma's arm. "We can go whenever you like. Just say the word and I'll be ready to head for home."

Elma had a feeling that wouldn't turn out to be the case. Knowing her sister, they'd probably be there until quite late, since Thelma liked to socialize. *I hope she doesn't get any ideas about the two of us doing some silly skit tonight.* Thelma had always enjoyed putting on skits when they got together with a group of friends or attended some family function. Elma always went along with it because she didn't want people to think she was a poor sport or too serious about things. Tonight though, with two men they were getting to know, Elma wouldn't feel comfortable trying to make Delbert and Joseph laugh by acting out one of the skits they'd done in the past.

Clucking at Pearl, Elma watched as the steam blew from the horse's nostrils when she picked up a little more speed. *Maybe if we keep busy playing board games, the subject of skits won't come up.*

⁓

LaGrange

"Yum. Those pizzas baking in my oven sure smell good," Joseph said to Delbert as they worked together at setting the table. "Danki for helping me make them."

"Not a problem," Delbert replied. "I'm happy to do it."

"You know your way around the kitchen a lot better than I do." Joseph placed four glasses on the table and glanced at the clock on the far wall.

"Living on your own as long as you've been, I would have thought you'd be a pro by now." Delbert enjoyed teasing his friend.

"You'd sure think so, wouldn't you?" Shrugging his shoulders, Joseph looked toward the window. "I was expecting Thelma and Elma to be here by now. Hope they don't have any trouble finding my place. Since it's the only house on this road that looks like a log cabin, it shouldn't be too hard to find."

"It's a crisp, clear night, so if you gave them good directions, they shouldn't have a problem." Delbert thumped Joseph's back. "Try not to worry."

"I've been looking forward to this all week, and I want everything to go right."

"You're one big bundle of nerves. It'll be fine. You'll see." Delbert gestured around the room. "You got the place all clean and tidy, so relax."

Joseph smiled. "By the way, danki for agreeing to get together with Elma again. I think it should be a relaxing evening for all of us."

"If things don't go well tonight, you're gonna owe me big—maybe another meal out at my favorite restaurant." Delbert chuckled as he went to get the hot pepper flakes from the refrigerator. He wasn't so sure this evening would be relaxing but looked forward to eating that pepperoni pizza and drinking a tall glass of the cold cider he'd brought along. Thelma had left a message for Joseph, accepting the supper invitation and saying that she and Elma would bring a dessert. He hoped it would be something he liked and not more overly baked cookies.

Why can't Elma be more laid back like her sister? he wondered. *She always seems so uptight. It gets on my nerves when she's so free with her opinion. Joseph's lucky to have found a girl like Thelma.*

"I think they may be here. I heard a horse whinny outside." Joseph went to the window to look out.

Delbert laughed. "I sure hope it was outside."

"Very funny." Joseph opened the back door. "I'll go take care of their horse."

After Joseph went outside, Delbert opened the oven door and checked on the pizza. It was a good thing Elma and Thelma were here, because the pizza was almost done. *Probably should've waited till they showed up to bake the pizza,* he told himself, *but I figured they'd be here before now.*

Delbert closed the oven door and turned the oven down. Then he went to the refrigerator and took out the tossed green salad he'd also made, placing it on the table.

One of the twins entered the kitchen. "Good evening, Delbert. The pizza smells good." She stepped up to the stove. "I don't mean to sound envious, but I wish we had an oven like yours."

"I'm sure it's a challenge to use your old woodstove for cooking." He stood by the table, holding the pot holders.

"Jah," she said, holding out a container. "Here are some pumpkin whoopie pies I picked up at the bakery today, since neither Thelma nor I had time to do any baking this week."

"That's great." Delbert now knew that he was talking to Elma. "You can set them over there on the counter." His mouth watered, thinking about how good those cookies were going to taste. "Pumpkin's one of my favorite kinds of whoopie pies. Course I like chocolate, banana, and lemon too. Anything sweet and it's all right by me."

Elma set the container down and turned to face him. "You certainly have a sweet tooth, don't you?"

"Guess I do." He put the pot holders away.

"Have you ever considered how much damage all that sugar can do to your body?"

He shrugged. "Nope, sure haven't."

"Well, maybe you should."

Delbert grunted. If this was what he could expect all evening, he might go home early instead of spending the night at Joseph's like he'd planned. They were going fishing on Saturday and he had brought his fishing gear along, but they could always meet in the morning. Joseph had suggested they invite the twins again, but Delbert talked him out of it, saying he thought they'd get more fishing done if it was just the two of them.

"What kind of pizza did you make?" Elma asked.

Delbert opened the oven door. "It's ready, so I hope Thelma and Joseph come in soon."

She bent down to observe the pizza. "Is that pepperoni?"

"Yep. It's Joe's and my favorite kind."

She wrinkled her nose. "Is that the only topping you have?"

"What's wrong? Don't you like pepperoni?" He turned off the oven and closed the door.

"To be honest, it's not one of my favorites."

"Sorry about that. When Thelma told Joe she liked pepperoni, I figured with you being twins that you would too."

"We may look alike and enjoy some of the same things, but we're not identical in every sense of the word."

"What kind of pizza do you like?" he asked, studying the curve of her pretty face.

"I really enjoy a vegetarian pizza, but plain cheese is okay too."

Delbert motioned to the bowl he'd set on the table. "There's plenty of salad, so maybe you can fill up on that."

She offered him a quick smile. "Maybe I will try one piece of pizza, since Joseph worked so hard making it for us."

Delbert leaned against the cupboard and folded his arms. "Actually, I did most of the work. Joe's not much of a cook, so he asked me to help him make the pizza."

Her eyes widened. "I—I didn't realize that. I'll definitely try a piece then."

Just then the back door creaked as it opened, and Joseph and Thelma stepped in, both smiling from ear to ear. *Those two are obviously crazy about each other,* Delbert mused. *I have a feeling by next year at this time my good friend may be growing a* baart. He stroked his own chin. *Wonder how I'd look wearin' a beard.*

As they sat around the table a short time later, Elma found herself enjoying the meal. The salad was delicious, with lots of cut-up veggies in it, as well as green lettuce leaves. She had to admit that even the pizza was pretty good. Of course, she picked off the pieces of pepperoni and fed them to Joseph's dog, who lay under the table. While she didn't care much for cats, Elma did have a soft spot for dogs—especially one as pretty as Ginger.

"Would you like to try some of this crushed pepper to sprinkle on your next slice of pizza?" Delbert asked, looking at the twins. "It adds a little kick to—"

Before he could finish his sentence, Elma took the bottle and shook a fair amount on.

"You may want to—"

Eagerly taking a bite, Elma felt the heat rise from her throat as she swallowed the piece of pizza. An uncontrollable cough started as she tried to catch her breath, while tears flowed down her cheeks.

"Here, Sister, drink some of this." Thelma handed Elma a cup of cider.

After Elma drank some of the cold cider, she looked at Delbert and frowned. "You should have warned me that it was so hot."

"Tried, but you put those hot pepper sprinkles on so fast. By the time you took a bite, it was too late." Delbert picked up his napkin and fanned Elma's face with it, which only made her more irritated. "You only have to use a little of that stuff to enhance the flavor of the pizza. Are you all right now?" he asked.

"I'll be fine." Elma brushed the flakes off the rest of her pizza. Glancing to her left where Delbert sat, Elma noticed that he had a glob of cheese stuck to his chin. Wondering if she should say anything, she kept staring at him.

"What's wrong?" Delbert asked, sprinkling a little more pepper on his pizza. "Why are you lookin' at me so strangely? Are you waiting for me to choke?"

Before she could say anything, Joseph snickered and pointed at Delbert's chin.

Delbert swiped his hand across it, leaving the sticky cheese on his fingers. Everyone laughed. It was then that Elma saw a splotch of pizza sauce on Delbert's shirt, but she decided not to mention it. If someone else did, that was one thing, but she didn't want to seem overly critical. She wouldn't have minded getting back at Delbert after choking on the hot pepper, but in truth, it was her own fault. For Thelma's sake, she needed to be on her best behavior this evening.

"Say, I was wondering, Delbert, would you have the time to stain our barn before winter sets in?" Elma asked.

He added more salad to his plate. "Sure, that shouldn't be a problem."

"Maybe I'll come along and lend a hand," Joseph was quick to say. "With two of us working, the barn will get done faster."

Thelma smiled. "That would be great. We'll pay you both of course."

Joseph shook his head. "There's no need for that. You can pay Delbert if you want to, but I'm more than happy to do it for free."

Delbert cast Joseph a quick glance. He shrugged and said, "Guess I can do the same."

After they finished the meal and the dishes were done, Joseph brought out a couple of games. "What should we play first?" he asked. "Uno or Rook?"

"I vote for Uno," Thelma said.

Joseph looked over at her and smiled. "That's what it'll be then. Unless Dell and Elma don't want to play that."

"I think we should let our supper settle a bit and then eat dessert," Elma said.

Thelma and Joseph bobbed their heads, but Delbert's forehead wrinkled. He looked disappointed. Joseph didn't seem to notice though, as he shuffled the cards and dealt, placing the cards facedown. The rest of them he put facedown in the center of the table. Then he turned one card over so the game could begin.

"You go first, Thelma," he said, "since you're sitting to my left."

Thelma picked up her cards and studied them. "I don't have a card to match the color or number of the one you laid down, so I guess it's my sister's turn."

"Don't forget to draw a card," Elma reminded.

"Oh, that's right." Thelma drew a card off the pile in the center of the table.

Then Elma took her turn and discarded one of her cards. Delbert played a reverse card, so it was Elma's turn again.

The game continued, until Elma had one card left. "Uno!" she shouted.

Delbert looked at her suspiciously. "Already? We haven't been playing that long."

She stiffened. "I hope you're not accusing me of cheating."

"Course not," he said, shaking his head. "I was merely making a statement."

On Elma's next turn, she laid down a wild card, her last one.

Thelma moaned. "I still have seven cards left."

"I have five." Joseph looked at Delbert. "How many do you have?"

Delbert tossed his cards on the table. "Too many, and it's all because somebody kept playing 'draw two' cards that were meant for me." He looked at Elma.

"Sorry," she mumbled. "I had to play the cards I had."

"Let's play again." Joseph gathered up the cards and handed them to Thelma. She shuffled and dealt, and the game started. This time Delbert won.

Elma won the next game and Delbert the game after that.

Thelma looked at Joseph. "I think we're both losing this game."

"It doesn't matter," he said, smiling at her. "It's fun for us all to be together." Pushing his chair back, he stood. "Maybe we oughta have some dessert now. Who wants coffee to go with the whoopie pies?"

All hands shot up.

"Do you need some help?" Thelma asked.

"Sure, you can set out the whoopies," he replied.

"I'll bring in another log for the fireplace." Delbert pushed back his chair then jumped when Ginger let out a *yip*. "Sorry, girl. I didn't see you behind my chair." He bent down to pet the dog's head.

"You have to watch when there's a pet in the house," Elma said. "They can get underfoot without you even knowing it."

"I'm sure Ginger knows I didn't do it on purpose." Delbert headed for the door without putting on a jacket.

While Joseph and Thelma got things ready, Elma tried to think of something to say when Delbert came back with the wood. She probably shouldn't have said anything when Joseph's dog yipped. Without a doubt, she felt uncomfortable around him tonight. More so than the other times they'd been together. Was there the remotest possibility that they could become a couple?

Chapter 24

"That was such a nice evening, wasn't it?" Joseph said after the twins left. "Thelma is fun to be with. Some of the jokes she told had me laughing so hard my sides ached."

"She was pretty funny," Delbert agreed. "I wish Elma were more like her."

Joseph's eyebrows shot up. "You're interested in Thelma?"

"I didn't say I was interested in her. Said I wished Elma were more like her."

"So you're not interested in Thelma?"

Delbert shook his head and thumped Joseph's shoulder. "Don't look so *naerfich*. I'm not gonna steal your *aldi*."

"Whew, that's a relief! I wasn't nervous, but I'll admit, you had me worried there for a minute." Joseph released a deep breath. "I do think of Thelma as my girlfriend now."

Delbert snickered. "I kind of got that impression. Now don't do anything to mess it up."

Joseph winced. "Did I say or do something wrong tonight?"

"Not that I know of. You and Thelma seemed to get along fine." Delbert grimaced. "I, on the other hand, had a few issues with Elma."

"Really? I thought everything was going okay. What kind of issues did you have with her?"

"For one thing, when we were playing the last game of the night, Elma made a big deal out of me not drinking my coffee before it got cold." Delbert talked in a high-pitched tone, trying to imitate Elma's voice. " 'Oh Delbert, aren't you going to drink your coffee? It's probably cold by now.'"

"Guess I didn't hear her say that," Joseph said. "What'd you say?"

"I said, 'Maybe I like it cold.' " Delbert shifted in his chair. "Oh, and when we were playing the games, Elma was very competitive."

"And you weren't?"

Delbert shrugged. "Maybe a little. I've never met a woman who acted that way when it came to playing a game."

"Everyone's different, and some people take their game playing more seriously. Look how Elma choked on the hot pepper flakes you suggested she use on her pizza. Maybe you should have explained it before handing her the bottle."

"Guess that's true. But she took it so fast and then took a bite even faster. I had no time to warn her." Delbert rose from his chair, abruptly changing the subject. "I don't know about you, but I'm bushed. Think I'll head to bed. See you in the morning."

Joseph gave a nod. "I'll be up bright and early."

⁍

"Are you feeling all right? You're awfully quiet," Thelma said as she and Elma traveled home from Joseph's. Thelma was driving Pearl, since Elma said she didn't feel like it.

"I'm tired, and I've got the beginning of a koppweh."

"Oh no. I hope it's not another migraine coming on."

"It's not bad yet," Elma responded. "I'm sure with some aspirin and a good night's rest I'll feel better in the morning."

Thelma reached across the seat and patted her sister's arm. "Did you enjoy yourself tonight?"

"It was fun playing games, but I think Delbert was upset that I won so often."

"Most men are competitive. He probably couldn't deal with losing to a woman." Thelma smiled. "Delbert's sure a lot different than Joseph. Joe always seems so easygoing."

"That's true," Elma agreed. "You're lucky to have found him."

"I think it's more that he found me. But then, Delbert found you as well."

156

"Humph! Well, the least he could have done was warn me about those pepper flakes in time. I thought I would choke to death, it was so hot."

"In Delbert's defense, you did take the bottle from him rather fast, and you put an awful lot of the stuff on your pizza," Thelma said. "I think he was getting ready to warn you, but you didn't give him much of a chance. You bit into that pizza so quickly, even I was surprised."

"I was only trying to show Delbert that I was receptive to his suggestion."

"In any event, I don't think the evening was a total flop, do you?"

Elma shrugged as she sat quietly beside Thelma.

"You seemed to enjoy petting Joe's dog tonight," Thelma commented.

"Jah. Ginger's a nice *hund*."

"She seems to have taken to you as well."

Elma laughed. "That's probably because I was feeding her pieces of pepperoni under the table."

Thelma gasped. "You did that?"

"Didn't you notice?"

"No, can't say that I did."

"Probably because your focus was on Joseph all night."

Do I detect a bit of jealousy in my sister's tone? Thelma wondered. *If she and Delbert would set their differences aside and focus on each other's positive qualities, they could have a nice relationship too. Sure wish I could say or do something to make that happen.*

Topeka

When Elma woke up the following morning, she knew there was no way she could work in the store, because her head pulsated with pain. It was even worse than the night before. It wouldn't be good to put the Closed sign in the window, like they had on the Saturday they'd gone fishing with Delbert and Joseph. They had quickly discovered that for some folks in their community, Saturday was the only day they could shop. *I wonder if Thelma could handle things by herself.*

Elma forced herself to climb out of bed and went into the hall to knock on Thelma's bedroom door. She hoped her sister hadn't already gone downstairs, because given the way her head pounded and her stomach felt nauseous, she would need help making her way down those stairs to the bathroom. She'd just made it to Thelma's door when it opened and Thelma stepped out. "Oh Sister, I didn't know you were standing there. Are you all right? You don't look so well."

"My headache is worse than it was last night," Elma explained, "and I don't think I can work at the store today."

"It's okay," Thelma assured her. "I'll manage on my own. You should go rest on the sofa so you don't have to go up and down the stairs today."

"Are you sure? Maybe we should close the store."

Thelma shook her head. "As you have said many times, we need the money. Besides, if we close, any people coming in today will be disappointed."

"You're right. I feel bad about leaving you all alone to run the store, but I don't have it in me this morning to work."

Thelma patted Elma's arm gently. "I'll be fine, and if things get too crazy, I'll close up early."

"If I feel better before the day is out, I'll come out to the store." Elma gave her sister a hug.

Thelma had only been at the store fifteen minutes when Mary came by with little Richard and Philip. Thelma smiled when the boys plopped down on the braided rug near the children's books. Each of them picked out a book while their mother did her shopping. She was glad to see that Richard's arm had healed and he was no longer wearing a cast. "Would you like a piece of candy?" she asked, holding out a small chocolate bar for each of them. The brothers nodded and eagerly took the candy. "Danki," they said.

Once more, Thelma found herself longing to be a mother. *If Joseph and I got married, I wonder what our children would look like. Would they have his red hair and freckles, or would they resemble me?* She shook her head. *I need to get back to work and quit daydreaming about Joe. He may not even be entertaining the idea of marriage.* The words of Proverbs 16:20 that she'd read in Grandma's Bible and committed to memory came to mind. "I need to trust You, Lord," she whispered.

All morning Thelma was busy at the store, but by noon things had slowed down. Without customers for the moment, she decided to put the CLOSED sign in the window and go check on Elma. She was just getting ready to do that, when Elma showed up.

"How's it going?" they asked in unison.

Thelma laughed. "A few minutes ago it was real busy in here. How are you feeling right now?"

"Much better." Elma lifted the basket she held. "I brought lunch out for us, and I'm ready to help you here for the rest of the day."

"Danki for that. I've been having hunger pangs for the last hour or so."

"Why don't we go to the back room to eat, since there's a table and chairs in there. If someone comes into the store, I'm sure we'll hear them."

"Sounds good to me."

Elma moved toward the counter and pointed to a stack of material. "Is this here for a reason?"

"It was left from the fabric I cut for Mary Lambright. I got too busy to put it away."

"What about these?" Elma picked up a stack of books that were hidden under the material.

"Another woman, whom I've never met, was going to buy some books but changed her mind."

Elma handed the basket to Thelma. "Why don't you take this to the back room? After I put the fabric and books away, I'll meet you there."

Thelma was on the verge of telling her sister that putting those items away could wait until after they'd eaten, but Elma, being such a tidy person, would never rest until the counter was clean. "Okay," she responded. "I'll take everything out of the basket and set it on the table. We'll eat as soon as you get there."

LaGrange

"The weather isn't as warm as the last time we were here." Joseph grimaced as a chill ran down his back.

"It's a lot colder," Delbert agreed. "Glad it wasn't like this when we brought Elma and Thelma here. I'm sure Elma would have complained." He looked out over the pond. "I'm not even sure if the fish will bite today. They probably won't be hungry."

"Speaking of food, have you made any plans for Thanksgiving?" Joseph asked as he sat on a rock near the edge of the pond.

"Not yet, but that's still a few weeks away."

"True, but there's nothing like planning ahead."

Delbert chuckled. "So now you're into planning ahead, huh? Used to be that you just did things as they came along."

"People change." Joseph reached over and patted his dog's head. Ginger grunted and looked up at him with soulful brown eyes.

"What are your plans for Thanksgiving?" Delbert baited his hook.

"Mom's planning a dinner, and she said I could invite Thelma." Joseph grinned. When he'd told his parents about meeting Thelma and going out with her a few times, Mom had eagerly suggested he invite his new girlfriend to dinner, saying she and Dad would be anxious to meet her.

"What about Elma?" Delbert asked. "I doubt that Thelma would come without her twin sister."

"Of course Elma will be included. My invitation will be to her, and you too."

Delbert popped a piece of gum into his mouth and starting chomping. "Am I supposed to be Elma's date?"

Joseph shrugged. "Only if you wanna be. It will be another opportunity for you to get to know her better."

"I guess you're right, but the way things have gone so far between us, I don't think there's much hope of us having a permanent relationship."

Joseph felt bad hearing that. Even though he hadn't known Thelma very long, he was convinced that he'd found the woman God intended him to have. He wished that was the case for his friend Delbert too.

Chapter 25

Topeka

"Sister, I don't feel so well." Clutching her stomach, Thelma sank to the couch.

Elma did the same. "I don't feel well either. I think we may be coming down with the flu that's been going around."

Thelma nodded slowly. "Given all the people we come in contact with at the store, we could have easily picked up the bug."

"What are your symptoms?" Elma asked.

"Besides my stomach doing flip-flops, my body aches, and I feel hot and sweaty."

"Same here. Unless we feel better than this in the morning, I don't see any way we can go to Mr. and Mrs. Beechy's house for the Thanksgiving meal."

Thelma leaned her head against the sofa and moaned. "As much as I was looking forward to going, we can't take the chance of exposing the others to whatever is plaguing us right now."

"Maybe you should let Joseph know we won't be there. Then we need to go to bed."

"You're right. If we don't show up, he's bound to be worried." Thelma forced herself to stand up then shuffled across the room. "I'll grab a flashlight and go out to the phone shack to make the call. I hope Joseph checks his messages in the morning."

❧

Elma hated being sick, but she was actually glad they wouldn't be going to the Beechys' tomorrow for Thanksgiving. Truthfully, she would rather

161

make dinner here, for just her and Thelma. As it was, it looked like the only thing they'd be eating was some hot chicken noodle soup—and that was only if they could keep it down.

As Elma pulled back the covers and crawled into bed, a shiver went through her. If she and Thelma were at home right now, Mom would be fussing over them, making sure they had plenty of liquids to keep them hydrated.

I wonder what Mom and Dad will be doing tomorrow. I'll bet they'll have a big Thanksgiving meal at one of Mom's sisters'. Or maybe Mom is cooking and some of the family will come to their house to eat.

Huddling under the blankets, tears moistened Elma's cheeks as she thought about all the delicious food she and Thelma had helped Mom prepare for past Thanksgiving meals. In addition to the turkey, there had been plenty of buttery mashed potatoes, tart cranberry sauce, and moist stuffing. She could almost see the steam rising from the brown glazed turkey as Dad carved thick slices for each of their plates.

As she drifted off to sleep, Elma said a silent prayer: *Heavenly Father, please bless Mom and Dad and those who will share a meal at their table tomorrow. Help Thelma and me to feel better. Guide and direct our lives, and give us wisdom in all matters.*

⁂

LaGrange

As Joseph left for his folks' the following morning, he thought about checking phone messages but decided it could wait until he got home. Since this was Thanksgiving, it was doubtful that anyone would call him anyway. He sure looked forward to eating dinner at his folks', but the best part was being able to introduce them to Thelma and her twin sister. He knew they would like her, and Elma too. *Sure wish Delbert had strong feelings for Elma, the way I do for Thelma,* he thought.

Over the last couple of weeks, he and Delbert had gone several more places with the girls, including a day of shopping that included lunch at the Blue Gate Restaurant. Each time they were together, Joseph felt a stronger connection to Thelma. He was almost sure that if things kept going this way, he would eventually ask her to marry him—if he could get up the nerve. He'd been doing better about not stuttering when he spoke to Thelma, but when it came to offering a marriage proposal, he would trip over his words so badly that she wouldn't even know what he said.

Delbert and I have been doing things together for a long time. It won't be the same if I get married and he doesn't. Joseph thumped his head. *Why am I even thinking such thoughts? I haven't been courting Thelma that long and don't really know how she feels about me.*

As Joseph's horse and buggy rounded the next bend, he made a decision. If he got the chance to speak with Thelma alone today, he would gather his courage and express how he felt about her. "Sure hope I don't lose my nerve."

⸎

"I'm glad you joined us today," Joseph's mother, Dora, said when Delbert entered their home.

He smiled, sniffing the air appreciatively. "I'm glad you invited me. Since I have no family living close by, I'd have probably been at home, eating alone. And I sure wouldn't have fixed a big Thanksgiving dinner."

She gave his arm a gentle squeeze. "You've been a good friend to Joseph, and we think of you as family."

"Speaking of Joseph, is he here yet? I didn't see his rig parked outside."

Dora motioned to the door leading to the living room. "He's in there with his daed. The reason you didn't see his buggy is because it's in the shed. Since my son will be spending the night, he figured he'd get the buggy out of the weather."

"That's a good idea," Delbert said. "I hear it's supposed to snow either tonight or tomorrow."

"You're welcome to spend the night too."

"That's nice of you, but I'll probably head for home sometime later this evening." Delbert moved across the room. "Guess I'll head into the other room and see what Joe's up to."

"Would you tell him and his daed that the turkey is almost done? We'll eat as soon as Elma and Thelma get here. I'm so glad you and Joseph have both found girlfriends. I'm looking forward to meeting them." A wide smile spread over Dora's freckled face. There was no doubt about it—Joseph had inherited his mother's red hair and fair complexion.

Delbert was tempted to tell Joseph's mother that Elma wasn't his girl-friend but saw no point in going into that right now. Instead, he excused himself and left the kitchen.

When Delbert entered the living room, he found Joseph and his father, Vern, visiting on the sofa. "Oh good, you're here." Joseph stood. "Did you see any sign of Elma and Thelma on the road?"

Delbert shook his head, taking a seat in the recliner across from them. "I'm surprised they aren't here already."

"Me too," Joseph agreed. "Sure hope they were able to follow my directions to Mom and Dad's house. It's not that hard to find, but if they took a wrong turn, they may be lost."

"You worry too much, son." Vern looked at Delbert and grinned. "It's good to see you."

Delbert smiled. "Same here."

Joseph pulled out his pocket watch to check the time. "I'm wondering what we should do about dinner if the twins don't get here soon."

"Your mamm hasn't said it's time to eat yet, so I wouldn't worry about that." Delbert smiled. "Speaking of the twins, I'm glad we got their barn stained last week. With the snow that's predicted, if we hadn't done it then, it may have had to wait till spring."

"That's true," Joseph agreed. "But come spring, I think we ought to see about painting the house for them, don't you?" He stretched his legs.

Delbert nodded. "Their place is looking better and better."

"I was talking to Joe before you got here about those young women you two have been courting," Vern spoke up. "Told him I think it's nice that you both have girlfriends now." He scratched his balding head. "Makes me wonder which of you will get married first."

Joseph's ears turned pink. Delbert jumped up and moved closer to the fireplace. The last thing he wanted was to talk about marriage.

"All I've got to say," Vern continued, "is that it's about time."

Dora stepped into the room then and announced that the turkey was done. "Since your lady friends aren't here yet, I'll try to keep everything warm. But at some point we may have to eat without them." She brushed her hands on her apron. "If they arrive after we've already started eating, or even have finished the meal, there will be plenty of food left over to feed them."

Joseph stood and began to pace. "Thelma and Elma should have been here long before this. There's no way I can eat till they get here."

"Maybe they're not coming," Delbert said. "Could be that something came up to keep them at home."

"I can't imagine what it would be." Joseph moved over to stand beside Delbert. "If they weren't coming, I'm sure Thelma would have called."

"Does she have our phone number?" Dora asked.

"No, but she has mine, and—" Joseph stopped talking and grabbed his jacket and hat.

"Where are you going?" Dora called when Joseph was almost to the door.

"I didn't check my phone messages last night or this morning. I'm heading back to my house right now to see if there's any word from Thelma or her sister."

"Hold up," Delbert said, "I'll go with you. We can take my rig."

❧

When Delbert pulled his horse and buggy next to Joseph's phone shack, Joseph hopped out and hurried inside. He flipped on the battery-operated light and took a seat. He was relieved when he found a message from Thelma but concerned when she said in a weak voice that she and her sister had come down with the flu and wouldn't be able to join them for Thanksgiving. He'd so wanted her to meet Mom and Dad.

Joseph picked up the receiver and dialed her number. When her answering machine came on, he left a message, saying if she needed anything to let him know and that he'd come by sometime tomorrow to check on them. Then he got back into Delbert's buggy. "The twins are *grank*. They have the flu and won't be coming to dinner. I'm really disappointed."

"Sorry to hear they're sick," Delbert said, "but there will be other times when you and Thelma can get together."

"I hope so." Joseph folded his arms and stared straight ahead, barely aware that a few snowflakes had begun falling. He had no appetite for food, but Mom had worked hard fixing the meal. So he'd force himself to eat a decent-sized portion and try not to worry about the twins.

As he and Delbert headed back to his parents' home, the road was quickly covered with a white film of crystals. What a beautiful night this would have been to go on a buggy ride with Thelma.

Chapter 26

Topeka

By Monday morning, the twins felt well enough to work in the store, although they were both still a little weak. Joseph had come by on Friday. He'd been nice enough to drop off a basket with leftovers from their Thanksgiving meal. After eating soup for three days, the leftovers she and Elma had heated for Sunday's meal tasted so good. Thelma had called and left a message for Joseph this morning, letting him know that she and Elma were fully recovered, and saying how much they'd enjoyed the food. She had been so disappointed that they'd missed Thanksgiving and the opportunity to meet Joseph's parents.

Pulling her thoughts back to the task at hand, Thelma glanced in the box she held and smiled as she waited for her sister to unlock the store. She and Elma had decided to bring the kittens to the store, hoping to give them away. It was getting to be a challenge going down to the basement with a basket of laundry and trying not to step on a kitten.

Thelma placed the box near the front door and went to straighten some bolts of material. As she worked, she reflected on her relationship with Joseph. The more time they spent together, the more she found herself falling in love with him. She continued to fantasize about what it would be like to be his wife and knew that should he ever ask her to marry him, her answer would be yes. Of course, that would depend on how things progressed with Elma and Delbert. So far, their relationship didn't seem to be going anywhere, but Thelma continued to hope things would get better.

They must feel something for each other, Thelma thought, *or they wouldn't keep double-dating with us.*

"Two of the busslin are gone."

Thelma jumped at the sound of her sister's voice. The last time she'd seen Elma, she'd been at the front counter, waiting on a customer. "Really? Who took them?"

"Mary Lambright. She wanted the kittens for Richard and Philip."

"I'm sure the boys will be happy about that." Thelma smiled. "Danki for letting me keep the little white bussli I named Snowball."

"I didn't *let* you, Sister. You made that decision yourself. I just went along with it." Elma reached for the same bolt of material Thelma had straightened.

"What are you going to do with that?" Thelma questioned, waiting for her sister to redo the roll of cloth.

"I'm taking it up front. Doris Miller is here, and she asked if we had any fabric this color."

"Okay. I'm almost done here, so if you need any help, let me know."

"I will."

When Elma walked away, Thelma went back to straightening the bolts. She'd finished the last one when Delbert showed up.

"I'm surprised to see you," she said. "Are you doing more work for us today?"

He shook his head. "I dropped by to—"

"Did Joseph come too?" Thelma hoped she didn't sound overly anxious.

"No, I'm alone." Delbert removed his hat. "Came by to invite you to the surprise birthday party I'm throwin' for Joe this Friday evening. I know he'd be disappointed if you weren't there."

Thelma smiled, resting her hand against her hip. "That sounds like fun. My sister and I would like to come. Is there anything we can bring?"

Delbert rubbed his chin. "How about a salad?"

Thelma bobbed her head. "That shouldn't be a problem. I'll either make a fruit or potato salad. Or maybe we'll bring both. Would that be okay?"

Delbert shrugged. "Sure, that'd be fine." He shuffled his feet a few times. "Guess I'd better be on my way. I have a few stops I need to make here in Topeka before I head back to LaGrange."

"What time should we be there?" Thelma asked, following him to the front of the store.

"Six o'clock. Joe's supposed to show up at my house at six thirty. He thinks the two of us are going out to a restaurant to eat." Delbert put his hat back on his head. "His birthday's Saturday, so I don't think he'll catch on."

"But won't he see all the buggies parked in your yard when he gets to your house?"

"I don't think so. I'm asking everyone to park around back. Make sure you get to my place no later than six." He opened the door and paused.

"Okay. Elma and I will see you Friday evening then."

"If you see Joe between now and then, don't let the cat outta the bag. I want him to be surprised."

"I won't say a word."

When Delbert left, Thelma returned to the fabric aisle and stood there with a big grin. She could hardly wait to see Joseph again and planned to use the stocking cap she'd knitted him for Christmas as a birthday gift instead.

Elma came over. "You're wearing a huge smile. What's going on? I saw Delbert leave. What did I miss?"

"He came by to invite us to Joseph's surprise birthday party on Friday night." Thelma clasped her hands together.

"What did you tell him?"

"I said we'd be happy to attend, and I offered to bring two salads." Thelma tipped her head. "You do want to go, I hope, because I wouldn't feel right about going without you."

Elma smiled. "Of course I'll go. Joseph is my friend too."

∽

LaGrange

"I wonder why they didn't have this party tomorrow afternoon," Elma said as she guided Pearl down the road leading to Delbert's house. "This time of the year, it gets dark early. It's not the safest time to be on the road with a buggy."

"I guess having it tonight was the only way they could surprise him," Thelma said. "Are you anxious to see Delbert?"

Elma clenched her teeth, ignoring her sister's question. She knew Delbert well enough to know they had no future together. She was fairly certain he felt that way too. One thing Elma knew was that her sister was smitten with Joseph. *Maybe she will end up marrying him. That would sure make our mamm happy. It would give her and Dad the hope of becoming grandparents.*

"I don't see any buggies," Elma commented as she directed Pearl up Delbert's driveway. "Could we be the first ones here?"

"I doubt it. Delbert said he was asking everyone to park their rigs around back." Thelma spoke with an air of excitement.

"Guess we'd better head there too."

⸎

When Thelma and Elma entered the house, Thelma saw several other people. Delbert made the introductions, and Thelma was pleased to finally meet Joseph's parents.

"I'm Joe's sister, Katie," a pretty young woman with auburn hair said, extending her hand to Elma. "You must be Thelma."

Elma shook her head and motioned to Thelma. "I'm Elma. She's Thelma."

Katie's cheeks darkened. "Ach, you two look so much alike. How does my brother tell you apart?"

Thelma snickered. "He's gotten us mixed up a couple of times, but since he knows me better now, he can usually tell by talking to me."

"It's nice to meet you both." Katie gestured to the tall man by her side. "This is my husband, Abe, and the little girl he's holding is our two-year-old daughter, Amanda."

"She's so sweet." Thelma reached out and took the child's hand, noting how soft it was.

"Should we take our salads to the kitchen?" Elma asked, looking at Delbert.

He nodded. "Jah, that'd be good. You can put them in the refrigerator."

Thelma followed Elma to the kitchen, where Joseph's mother and his aunt Linda had gone. After they put their salads away, Thelma turned to Dora and asked, "Is there anything we can do to help?"

"I found a package of sweet tea in Delbert's cupboard," Dora replied.

"There's a metal spoon and a pitcher on the counter."

Thelma opened the powdered mix and dumped it into the glass container. Then she went to the sink and filled it with water. "I want to thank you for sharing your Thanksgiving food with me and my sister. It sure tasted good when we were finally able to eat it."

"I'm glad you and Elma are over the flu. That can get pretty nasty." Dora smiled as she put some cheese and crackers on a platter.

As Thelma stirred the mixture, someone shouted from the living room that Joseph's horse and buggy had pulled in. Hurrying to finish the job, Thelma stirred so hard that a chunk of glass broke. Sticky sweet tea spilled out all over the table and dripped onto the floor. Some also splashed on her arm. "What have I done?"

"Let me help you." Elma stepped forward and helped Thelma clean up the mess, while Katie threw away the glass pitcher. Then they all rushed into the living room in time to see Joseph enter. "Surprise! Happy birthday!" everyone hollered.

Chapter 27

Joseph was surprised to see all these people in Delbert's house. He hardly knew what to say. He wasn't used to being the center of attention and knew his face and ears must be as red as his hair.

Delbert thumped Joseph's back and grinned. "Are you surprised, my friend?"

All Joseph could do was nod as his gaze traveled around the room. All his friends and family were there except his brother Eli, who lived in Ohio. Most importantly though, Thelma and her sister had come. He knew who Thelma was too for Elma had a small scar on her right elbow, which he caught sight of right away, since her arms were folded. The twins were wearing different colored dresses as well—Thelma in dark blue and Elma in green.

"I—I never expected this," Joseph stammered, looking at Delbert. "I thought the two of us were going out to eat."

"We're gonna eat here." Delbert gestured to everyone. "They all want to help celebrate your *gebottsdaag*."

"But my birthday's not till tomorrow."

Delbert slung his arm over Joseph's shoulder. "I know that, Joe, but I figured you might have made plans to spend your birthday with your *aldi*."

Truth was, Joseph hadn't made any plans for his birthday. For that matter, he'd made no mention of it to Thelma. "Well, I. . .uh. . ."

"Sorry, friend. I didn't mean to embarrass you," Delbert said quietly. Then he turned to the crowd and said, "Now that our guest of honor is here, why don't we eat?"

"That sounds good to me." Joseph's father led the way to the table.

Joseph moved quickly across the room to where Thelma stood beside Katie. "I'm glad you're here. Would you sit beside me, Thelma?"

"I'm not Thelma," she said with a small laugh, pointing. "She's over there."

Joseph looked across the table and saw the woman he'd thought was Elma sitting beside his mother.

"I—I saw that small scar on her arm, and I thought. . ."

"What you saw was a tea stain on my sister's arm," Elma explained.

Joseph touched his hot cheeks. He felt like a dunce. On top of that, his eyes must be going bad. How could he have mistaken the sweet tea on Thelma's arm for a scar? Making his way to the opposite side of the table, he quickly took a seat on the other side of her.

She smiled and said, "Happy birthday, Joseph."

"Danki. Have you met my mamm?"

Thelma nodded. "I met both of your parents, as well as your sister and her family, after Elma and I got here." She smiled. "Your niece is so sweet."

And so are you. Joseph could only nod. He knew better than to blurt out his thoughts in front of everyone. He wasn't even sure he could say that privately to Thelma.

After their silent prayer, Joseph enjoyed visiting as he ate his meal. He was impressed with how well Thelma got along with his young niece. *She would make such a good mother,* he thought.

When the meal was over, Joseph's mother brought out a chocolate cake—his favorite. Then Joseph blushed even more when everyone sang "Happy Birthday." Afterward, his sister cut the cake while Delbert got out vanilla ice cream and several kinds of toppings. Following that, Joseph received presents from some who had come to the party, as well as many birthday cards. His best gift was the stocking cap Thelma had knitted. With the weather turning colder now, he'd be able to wear it right away. Not only that, but it made him feel special, knowing she'd probably put a lot of time into making it.

While the guests mingled in the kitchen and living room, Joseph and Thelma remained at the table. Joseph didn't know where he got the courage, but so that no one else would see, he reached under the table and took hold of Thelma's warm hand. Holding his breath, he slowly turned and looked into her ocean-blue eyes. He was glad when she held his gaze, gently squeezing his fingers in return.

"Let's play a game of Ping-Pong," Delbert suggested. "We can play doubles. How's that sound, Joe?"

Joseph and Thelma jumped up, releasing each other's hands. "That sounds like fun." Joseph looked briefly at Thelma, noticing that her cheeks were a rosy pink. "Thelma and I can be on one side, and you and Elma on the other."

❧

Delbert couldn't believe that every time the ball came his way, Elma reached over and smacked it. The only good part of having her as his partner was that he and Elma were winning. But it would be nice if he got the opportunity to hit the ball once in a while. To make matters worse, Thelma and Joseph didn't seem to be trying that hard to win. They spent more time talking to each other and less time paying attention to what was going on. There was no doubt about it—his friend Joe was in love.

When the twins said it was time to leave, Joseph put on his new cap and said that he would walk Thelma to the buggy. "I think it would be nice if you walked with Elma too," he whispered to Delbert.

Delbert went reluctantly. They walked across the yard, crunching their way through the fresh-fallen snow. A few days ago, the temperatures had dropped when another clipper system pushed through. Delbert slowed his pace, hoping Elma would do the same. "Can I speak with you for a few minutes?"

"Certainly. Can we talk while I hitch my horse to the buggy?"

"That would be fine. I'll help you with the chore." Delbert glanced over his shoulder and saw Joseph and Thelma disappear behind the back of the buggy. No doubt he too wanted to spend some time with his date alone—only for a different reason.

As they began their task, Delbert leaned closer to Elma and said quietly, "I've been thinking and praying about us."

"Oh?" With the moon's brightness, he could see her curious expression.

"Whenever we're together, there seems to be a lot of tension between us. Have you felt it too?" He looked straight into her eyes.

"Jah."

"I think we should stop seeing each other socially."

Elma let out a quick breath of air. "I'm actually quite relieved we are having this conversation. I agree. . .we can't take this relationship any further."

Delbert's shoulders relaxed. "We tried to make it work, and to be honest, toward the end, I was putting Joe's needs ahead of my own."

She tipped her head and looked at him quizzically. "What do you mean?"

"Joe needed to gain self-confidence with Thelma. As he often did in the past, Joe leaned on me for support."

"Were you only going out with me to please Joseph?"

"Not in the beginning, but as time went on and I realized that you and I aren't suited, I continued to double-date because it was what Joe wanted."

"I see." She lowered her gaze to the ground.

He touched her arm. "I hope you're not upset."

She lifted her head to look at him again. "No, I understand, because truthfully, I agreed to keep seeing you to make my sister happy."

"Guess that makes us even then, huh?"

She gave a nod. "Putting others ahead of ourselves is a wonderful act of love and friendship. But at times we need to think about our own needs too."

"I agree, and I'm glad we had this talk." Delbert felt like the weight of the world had been lifted from his shoulders.

⟋⟍

Feeling suddenly unsure of himself, Joseph reached out and took Thelma's hand as they stood behind the sisters' buggy. "I had a lot of fun tonight, and I'm glad you could be here to help celebrate my birthday."

"I'm glad too. Except for splattering myself with tea, I had an enjoyable time."

Joseph's heart pounded as he took a step closer. "Y–you're a very special girl, and I–I'm in love with you." He wished he could quiet his racing heart and speak without stumbling over his words.

"I love you too, Joseph." Thelma's voice was soft, and he stood staring at her beautiful face illuminated by the light of the moon. Then gathering his courage, Joseph drew Thelma into his arms and kissed her sweet lips. He was glad when she responded by kissing him back. Oh, what he wouldn't give to hold her like this every night for the rest of his life. But it was too soon to speak of marriage. Or was it?

"The horse is hitched, and we're ready to go, Sister," Elma called, interrupting the joy of the moment.

"All right, I'm coming." Thelma stared up at Joseph. "I guess it's time for us to go."

"I'll call or come by soon," Joseph said, walking her to the passenger's side of the buggy.

She smiled. "I'd like that."

As the twins drove away, Joseph waved until they were out of sight. "Say, I have an idea," he said as he and Delbert walked back to the house. "Why don't we invite the twins to join us for supper tomorrow evening? Since that's my actual birthday, it would be nice if the four of us could spend it together, don't you think?"

Delbert stopped walking and turned to face Joseph. "Umm. . .there's something you should know."

"What's that?"

"I won't be seeing Elma socially anymore. Before you say anything else, you need to know that it was a mutual decision. Elma and I discussed it while we were hitching her horse to the buggy."

Joseph was disappointed to hear this. He'd really hoped Delbert and Elma would work things out. He wondered if his friend was being too picky, looking for little things he didn't like about Elma so he wouldn't have to give up his freedom. What was so great about living by himself anyway? Wouldn't Delbert be happier if he had a wife and children? Maybe not. Perhaps it wasn't meant for Delbert to be married.

☙

"I feel so excited," Thelma said as she and Elma baked a batch of ginger cookies the following evening.

"What are you excited about?" Elma removed a cookie sheet from the oven.

Thelma pointed to the kitchen window. "Look at all that snow out there. It's so beautiful—just perfect for a sleigh ride."

Elma smiled. "Do you think we should get that old sleigh of Grandpa's out of the barn and let Pearl take us for a ride?"

Thelma drew in her lower lip. "It may be better to take Rusty, since he has more stamina than Pearl. And you know, since I've been working with him, he's better behaved."

Elma placed the cookies on a cooling rack. "I suppose it'll be okay to take Rusty, as long as you're driving."

"I was thinking of inviting Joseph and Delbert to join us. I'm sure one of them would be willing to sit in the driver's seat."

Elma frowned. "I thought it would just be the two of us."

"I think it would be more fun if the four of us went. Wouldn't you enjoy a romantic sleigh ride with Delbert?"

Elma sighed and sank into a chair at the table. "There's something I need to tell you, Sister."

"What's that?" Thelma sat too.

"After praying about it, I made a decision concerning Delbert." Elma brushed a splotch of flour from her apron. "We're not suited. I won't be going out with him anymore."

Thelma's heart gave a lurch. "Are you sure? I mean, won't you give it a little more time?"

Elma shook her head. "I've been with Delbert enough times to know that he's not the man God has for me."

Thelma realized now it had been wishful thinking on her part. If Elma had prayed about this, then it must not be God's will for her to be with Delbert. *Guess I won't be seeing Joseph anymore either.* Thelma's throat constricted. *It wouldn't be fair to break my promise and leave Elma all alone. But, oh, I will surely miss him.*

If she lived to be one hundred, Thelma would never forget the gentle touch of his lips against hers as they'd stood at the back of the buggy. She touched Elma's arm. "I guess the four of us won't be going for a romantic sleigh ride, after all."

"You and Joseph can still go. It can be a romantic evening for the two of you."

Thelma pushed away from the table and stood. "I think we ought to get the rest of these *kichlin* baked." Anything to keep from thinking about Joseph.

Chapter 28

"You have a message from Joseph," Elma told Thelma when she came into the house the following Friday morning, after going to the phone shack.

Thelma turned from the sink where she'd been washing dishes. "What did he say?"

"Said he wanted to take you out to supper this evening, and he wondered why you haven't returned any of his calls this week." Elma removed her shawl and draped it over the back of a chair. "I'd like to know that too."

Thelma shrugged. "We've been busy at the store. With Christmas a couple of weeks away, people have been coming in to buy gifts and other things."

"I know we've been busy, but not so much that it would keep you from returning Joseph's calls."

Thelma reached for a wet glass to dry.

"There's a lot of snow on the ground, and it looks so beautiful. Wouldn't you enjoy going on a sleigh ride with Joseph?"

Putting the dried glass away, Thelma merely shrugged.

Elma moved over to the sink. "Are you avoiding Joseph? Has he said or done something to upset you, Sister?"

"Not really. I don't think things are going to work for him and me though."

"Why not?"

"We're two very different people. He's kind of quiet, and I'm always talking." Thelma grabbed a cup from the dish rack and continued her work.

"That shouldn't prevent you from having a relationship. Look at Mom and Dad. Their personalities are different, but they have a good marriage. Haven't you ever heard the expression 'Opposites attract'?"

Thelma set the cup on the counter. "Sure, but it doesn't work for everybody. Look at you and Delbert."

"It was different for us. It wasn't just our different personalities. We grated on each other's nerves." Elma put her hand on Thelma's arm. "Are you going to return Joseph's call?"

Feeling as if she were backed into a corner, Thelma nodded. "I'll go out to the phone shack and do it now."

⁂

As Thelma crunched her way through the snow, she tried to figure out what message to leave for Joseph. Should she come right out and say she didn't want to see him anymore, or would it be best to make up some excuse?

Thelma stepped into the phone shack. The fluttering in her stomach didn't help as she dialed Joseph's number. When his voice mail picked up she said: "Hello, Joseph, this is Thelma. I'm sorry for not returning your calls. We've been busy at the store this week." She paused and moistened her chapped lips with the tip of her tongue, struggling for words that wouldn't be a lie. "I—I appreciate the invitation to have supper with you, but I won't be able to go anywhere this evening. I hope you have a blessed Christmas with your family."

When Thelma hung up the phone, tears sprang to her eyes. Giving up her relationship with Joseph was one of the hardest things she'd ever done. Sometimes though, sacrifices needed to be made for the benefit of someone else, and this was one of those times.

⁂

"Are you sure you can manage on your own for a while?" Thelma asked around noon when she and Elma were working in the store.

Elma nodded. "I'll be fine. One of us needs to get to the post office and mail Mom and Dad's Christmas package."

Thelma's shoulders drooped. "I feel bad that they probably aren't coming here to celebrate with us, after all. It'll be a lonely day without them."

"I agree, and I'll miss them too. But this time of the year, the weather can change people's plans. The area around Sullivan is getting hit with cold weather right now. Mom said in her last message that a lot of snow has fallen there already and more is expected between now and Christmas." Elma tried to sound cheerful for her sister's sake, but the thought of spending Christmas without their folks made her feel sad too. Thanksgiving was bad enough, since it was the first holiday away from their parents, but now she'd have to find a way to get through Christmas too.

Thelma sighed. "Snow is pretty, but sometimes I wish our winters were warm like they are in Florida."

"Say, I have an idea." Elma placed her hand on Thelma's shoulder. "Why don't you invite Joseph to join us for Christmas dinner?"

Thelma looked toward the pile of mail that also needed to be taken to the post office. "I'm sure he's made plans to be with his family that day."

"Has he asked you to join them?"

"No, and even if he had, I wouldn't go." She dropped her gaze to the floor.

"Why not, for goodness' sake?"

"I wouldn't think of leaving you home by yourself on Christmas Day." Thelma slipped into her coat, gathered up the mail, and started for the door.

"Wait a minute," Elma called. "You forgot something." She held up her sister's black outer bonnet.

Thelma came back and got it. "Danki. I'll try not to be gone too long."

"Hold on. Don't forget this." Elma held up the package they were mailing to Mom and Dad.

"Oops. Not sure where my mind is today. Guess I left it in the bed this morning." Thelma shrugged her shoulders as she tucked the package under her arm.

"Be careful out there. The roads may be icy," Elma called, watching Thelma go out the door.

Something is not right with my sister, Elma thought as she grabbed the bottle of spray cleaner and a towel to wipe down the front counter.

No one else was in the store. The only noise Elma heard was the crackling of wood from the small woodstove. Elma relished this time of solitude when she could be by herself to reflect on all the good things the Lord had done for her and Thelma. *I'm beginning to see why Grandma and Grandpa left us their home and store. They wanted to teach us to be responsible and make it on our own. Of course someday, if Thelma marries Joseph, I will be living by myself, and I'll have more solitude than I know what to do with.*

The thought of living alone frightened her a bit, since she'd always had Thelma with her, but Elma had always known that someday one of them would fall in love, get married, and move away. She wasn't totally prepared for that yet. In her heart she'd always hoped that she and her twin would find their one true love at the same time. She knew it was a silly dream. Simply because she and Thelma were twins didn't mean they had to do everything exactly alike or at the same time. God had created them to be two individuals, and if they didn't begin a life of their own with a man they loved, they'd stay like they were now—two old-maid sisters always hoping for the love of a man. Or worse yet, blaming one or the other, years down the road, because it had never happened.

Elma's musings were interrupted when she heard the front door open, followed by the sound of heavy footsteps. She looked up and was surprised to see Joseph wearing the stocking cap Thelma had made him.

"I got your message, and I'd like to know what's going on," he said, stepping up to the counter.

Elma's forehead wrinkled. "What message?"

"Are you really too busy to go out with me, or have I done something wrong?" Joseph put both hands on the counter.

Elma's eyes widened. "Oh Joseph, you've got the wrong twin. I'm Elma."

Red blotches erupted on Joseph's cheeks. "Oh great. I've done it again." He glanced around. "Is Thelma here? I need to talk to her."

Elma shook her head. "She went to the post office awhile ago."

"When will she be back?" He sounded desperate.

"I'm not sure. But would you mind telling me what my sister's message said?"

"She said she's been too busy to call me all week and that she's not able to go out to supper with me tonight." He paused and pulled his cap down over his ears. "Have I done something to offend her? Has she said anything to you?"

"No, not really, but I have my suspicions."

"What does that mean?"

Elma leaned forward. "Listen, Joe, my sister and I will be hosting a Christmas caroling party with some of the young people in our district next Friday evening. I'd like you to be there."

"Are—are you sure?" Joseph stammered. "What if my being there upsets Thelma?"

"It won't. Trust me." Elma gave him what she hoped was a reassuring smile. "Everything is going to work out for the best."

Chapter 29

LaGrange

More snow had fallen in the area, and Joseph wondered if the caroling party was still on. He assumed it was, because he'd checked his messages before hitching his horse to the buggy, and the only one was from a customer, asking if his harness was done.

Joseph looked forward to this evening and being with Thelma. It would be the first time he'd been with her when Delbert wasn't around. He still felt bad that things hadn't worked out between Delbert and Elma. He'd really hoped his friend would find a wife and settle down, but maybe Delbert was too set in his ways.

As Joseph's rig drew closer to Topeka, his hands began to sweat. *What if Thelma isn't happy to see me? I hope Elma told her I was coming.*

❧

Topeka

"Herschel Miller is here with his large open wagon and two draft horses," Thelma announced when she looked out the kitchen window and saw him coming up the driveway.

Elma joined her at the window. "It was nice of him to do that, because there wouldn't have been room for all of us to go caroling in Grandpa's sleigh."

"You're right about that. Guess we ought to take the sleigh out by ourselves sometime this winter though." Thelma sighed. She'd been looking forward to doing that with Joseph. *Stop thinking about him,* she chided herself. *Focus on the fun we're going to have this evening.* She drew a sad face on the moisture collected on the pane of glass then quickly wiped it off, drying the rest of the window with a piece of cloth.

Thelma looked at Elma, hoping she hadn't noticed, and at the same time they said, "We'd best get ready."

Elma laughed. "We still need to get our coats, outer bonnets, gloves, and boots."

"Let's do that right now." Thelma followed Elma into the utility room, and once they'd gotten their things, they returned to the kitchen to make sure everything was ready.

"I think we have everything ready for our refreshment time after we get back from caroling." Cookies, pretzels, and popcorn were set out on the table. They would also build a bonfire and roast hot dogs.

"Do you know how many are coming?" Thelma asked.

"I think there will be twenty of us."

Thelma smiled. "A nice big group to sing the Christmas songs we all know and love. I hope the places we stop by will enjoy hearing the music."

"I'm sure they will, Sister. Whenever we went caroling back home, everyone we sang to seemed to appreciate it."

A knock sounded on the door, and Thelma went to open it. Herschel greeted her with a friendly smile. "I'm glad you two are doing this for our *younga*," he said. "It's a perfect night for a caroling party."

"We're happy to do it." Thelma opened the door wider. "Why don't you come inside until everyone gets here? There's hot coffee on the stove."

"That sounds nice." Herschel sat down after she handed him a cup of coffee. "Danki."

The three of them visited around the kitchen table until the young people showed up. Then Thelma and Elma put on their outer garments and followed Herschel outside.

Soon everyone climbed onto the back of the wagon and took seats on bales of straw. Thelma was about to get on when she spotted another horse and buggy pulling in. "I thought everyone was here," she said, looking at Elma.

A few seconds later, Joseph got out and tied his horse to the hitching rail. "What's he doing here, Sister? Did you know he was coming?"

Elma nodded and lowered her voice. "He stopped by the store last week, and I invited him to join us this evening."

"Don't you think you should have said something to me about that?" Thelma couldn't imagine why Elma would invite Joseph to the caroling party and not tell her.

Elma slipped her arm around Thelma's waist and gave her a squeeze. "Relax, and enjoy the evening."

Thelma shivered and pulled her coat tighter around her neck. *How can I relax with Joseph heading toward me?*

❧

"Thelma?" Joseph asked, stepping up to the woman he believed was his girlfriend.

"Jah, it's me. Did you think I was Elma?"

"No. Yes." He pulled his knitted cap over his ears, knowing they must be pink. "Well, I wasn't sure. When I came by the store last week I—I thought she was you." *Don't start stuttering now, Joseph.* He reached out and touched her arm. "It's good to see you, Thelma. I've been looking forward to tonight ever since Elma invited me to go caroling with you."

"Speaking of caroling, we'd better get on the wagon before they take off without us."

Joseph grinned. "Let's go!" He hopped up and reached his hand out to Thelma, helping her onto the wagon as well. He patted the seat beside him. When she joined him on the bale of straw, he noticed that she didn't seem like her usual cheerful self. He couldn't put his finger on it, but thinking it would be best not to say anything in front of everyone, he let it go. "Here, you may need this as we begin moving down the road." Joseph placed a blanket across Thelma's lap.

She offered him a smile and seemed to relax a bit. "You're welcome to share it with me."

Joseph pulled part of the blanket over his knees, and a few minutes later they were on their way.

The joyful group laughed, visited, and sang as they traveled the roads, taking them through downtown Topeka and onto several of the back roads. They stopped by some church members' homes, serenading them with Christmas songs. Joseph was having a good time, and Thelma seemed to be as well. At one point, she'd even leaned close to him and said, "You have a nice singing voice, Joe."

He smiled. "I enjoy singing Christmas songs." *Especially when I'm with you,* he added silently. Joseph thought the chilly winter's night was perfect weather for Christmas caroling.

"Look over there." Joseph pointed at a curious raccoon watching them pass before disappearing behind some bushes.

Thelma sighed. "It's a beautiful night."

Nothing is as beautiful as you, Joseph thought, wishing he could say it out loud. Right now, he would give anything to be alone with Thelma.

When their driver announced that the next place would be their last stop, Joseph felt disappointed. He didn't want the evening to end. He hoped before he left that he could talk privately with Thelma.

Elma asked if everyone was hungry and said when they returned to her and Thelma's house, they'd build a bonfire and roast hot dogs. Joseph was happy about that. Not because he was hungry, but because it would give him more time with Thelma. It was strange how she was acting tonight—one minute quiet and aloof—the next minute laughing.

"It doesn't look like anyone is home here," one of the young men shouted. "See, there's no light in any of the windows."

"Look, there's a katz!" Thelma pointed to the cat sitting on the front porch. The feline's gray coat was illuminated by the light of the silvery moon.

"Should we sing to the katz?" someone shouted.

"Why not?" another person responded.

Everyone began singing, "We wish you a blessed Christmas. . . We wish you a blessed Christmas. . . We wish you a blessed Christmas and a joyous New Year!"

The front door opened, and an elderly Amish man with a cane stepped out, holding a flashlight. Joseph didn't recognize him, but then he didn't know that many people living in Topeka.

To Joseph's surprise, the man stepped off his porch and started singing to the carolers. His cat came over to him and rubbed against his leg. Thelma laughed and joined him in song. Soon, the others accompanied them as well. Joseph could hardly wait to see what the rest of the night would bring.

Chapter 30

Although Thelma enjoyed being with Joseph, she knew she couldn't count on more evenings like this. Before the night was over, she would have to tell Joseph that she couldn't see him again. He may not understand if she tried to explain that unless her sister was being courted by a man, there was no way she could keep seeing him. Most people did not understand the bond identical twins had.

Thelma tried not to think about it as the lively group sang their way back to her and Elma's house. But the closer they got, the more apprehensive she felt. By the time Herschel guided his team up their driveway, Thelma had broken out in a cold sweat. Clutching the scarf around her neck didn't seem to help the chill that went straight to her bones. *I should have told Joseph that I couldn't see him anymore when I left him a message last week. That would have been easier than saying it to his face.*

She thought once again about the kiss they'd shared after Joseph's birthday party, and wished now she hadn't let it happen. If she'd only known then that Elma wouldn't be seeing Delbert anymore, she would have ended it with Joseph that night. There was no point in thinking about that now. She needed to get through this evening without breaking down.

When the wagon came to a stop, Joseph hopped down and extended his hand to Thelma. Once she was on the ground, he put his hand gently behind her back as they walked through the yard.

"Would you like me to get a fire started?" Joseph asked Thelma.

She nodded. "That would be nice."

"Would you like to help me with that?" he questioned.

She swallowed hard, barely able to look at him. "I need to go inside and help Elma get the hot dogs and other things out. I'm sure some of the young men will help you gather wood for the fire."

Joseph gave her a heart-melting smile and headed across the yard to a group of young men who had starting making snowballs. "No snowball games tonight," he called. "We need to get a fire going so we can eat."

As the evening wore on, Thelma grew quieter. She could barely eat her hot dog, much less enjoy any of the cookies. All she could think about was how attentive Joseph was being and how much she dreaded telling him goodbye. At least he wasn't part of their church district and she wouldn't have to see him every other Sunday. That would have made things even more difficult.

"You've been awfully quiet since we got back from caroling," Joseph said, interrupting Thelma's thoughts. "Are you feeling all right?"

"I'm fine. Just tired is all."

"It looks like things are winding down now and most of the young people are going home." Joseph touched her arm. "If it's okay, I'd like to stay until everyone is gone so we can talk."

"That's fine. I'd like to speak with you as well."

Half an hour later, everyone had gone and Thelma began to gather the paper plates and other things left over from the meal they'd shared around the bonfire.

"Don't worry about that, Sister," Elma said. "I'll take care of cleaning up. Sit and enjoy the last of the glowing embers with Joseph." Elma scooped everything into a wicker basket and hurried inside before Thelma could formulate a response. She wondered if her sister knew what she was about to tell Joseph and wanted to give her time to do it. Quite often when either Thelma or Elma planned to do something, the other twin had a feeling about it—almost as though they could read each other's minds.

Joseph moved his folding chair closer to Thelma's. "There's something I want to say," he said, taking her hand.

"I—I need to tell you something too," she murmured. "But you can go first."

Joseph cleared his throat a couple of times. "We've only known each other a few months, and it's probably too soon to be talking about marriage, but—"

"Joseph, things are not going to work out for us. After tonight, I won't be able to see you again."

"Why, Thelma? You said you loved me the other night. And you let me kiss you."

Tears sprang to her eyes. "You may not understand, but I can't have a relationship with you when my sister has no one."

"You're right, I don't understand. I love you, Thelma, and I think God brought us together."

"I love you too, but Elma and I have a special bond. When we were little girls we talked about what it would be like when we fell in love and got married." Thelma paused and swiped at the tears rolling down her cheeks. "We promised each other that until we both found the right man, neither of us would get married."

"Are you saying that you won't marry me unless Elma falls in love with a man and they make plans to be married?" The wrinkles across Joseph's forehead revealed his confusion.

Thelma nodded slowly. "But that may never happen, and you need to be free to find the right woman, so—"

"He already has, and you, Thelma, are being ridiculous!"

Thelma whirled around, surprised to see her sister standing behind her, hands on both hips. "You. . .you startled me, Elma. I thought you were in the house."

"I was, but I remembered that I'd left my gloves lying on the log. So I came back out to get them." Elma moved around to stand in front of Thelma. Then she leaned down and looked directly at her. "That was a silly promise we made to each other when we were kinner, and I won't allow you to sacrifice the love you have found with Joseph when it's completely unnecessary." She paused, placing her hands on Thelma's shoulders. "I was perfectly happy before I met Delbert, and I will be fine on my own. In fact, you and Joseph have my blessing. I would be miserable if I were the cause of you two breaking up."

Thelma didn't know what to say. Could she really marry Joseph and leave her sister alone? Would that even be fair?

Elma gestured to Joseph, asking them both to stand. Then she took Thelma's hand and placed it in Joseph's. "You two make a good couple. I truly believe you belong together. Now, I'm going to get my gloves and leave you alone to work things out." She smiled, grabbed her gloves, and went back to the house.

Joseph turned to face Thelma. "What do you have to say about that?"

She smiled through her tears. "I've always tried to please my sister, and if she really wants us to keep courting, then I guess I can't argue with that."

Joseph bent his head and captured her lips in a sweet, gentle kiss. "And to think, we never would have met if you hadn't made that crazy-looking lopsided cake. I believe this is going to be my best Christmas yet. By next year at this time, I hope we can be married."

"I know this will be a good Christmas too." Thelma's smile widened. "I love you, Joseph."

Filled with such happiness as she'd never felt before, Thelma barely noticed how the moon encased them in its brilliant light. All she felt was the warmth of Joseph's arms holding her close as she leaned her head against his chest. *And maybe,* she thought, *by next year, my sister will have found the man of her dreams too.*

Epilogue

As Thelma sat quietly beside Joseph at their bride-and-groom's corner table, she thought about the changes that had occurred over the past year. Most important was that her and Joseph's hearts and lives were now joined through the love of God. Not only had she and Joseph been married this morning, with both of their families present, but tomorrow they would be moving into the house across the street from Elma. Joseph had recently sold his business in LaGrange and purchased the harness shop in Topeka, since the previous owner was ready to retire.

"What a glorious day this has been," Thelma whispered to Joseph.

"Jah. Even our wedding cake is perfect for us," he joked, pointing to the lopsided cake sitting before them.

She laughed. "This time it's Elma's fault. She said the cake batter didn't rise evenly, but I have to wonder if she made it this way on purpose to remind us of how we first met."

"You could be right. And speaking of Elma..." Joseph gestured to the table where Thelma's twin sister sat. "Who's that man she's talking to?"

"Oh, you mean the one sitting between her and Delbert?"

"Jah, I don't recognize him."

"That's Delbert's cousin, Myron Bontrager. He's visiting Delbert, so that's why he's here."

Joseph's eyebrows scrunched together. "I've heard Dell mention his cousin once or twice, saying that he too is a bachelor, but this is the only time I've ever seen him. From what I understand, he lives in southern Indiana. I wonder if this is his first visit to the area."

Thelma shook her head. "No, it's not. When Delbert introduced Myron to me awhile ago, he said he'd been here last October."

"Really? Dell never mentioned that."

"And here's the surprising part."

Joseph leaned closer.

"Myron is the other person who was bidding on our lopsided Christmas cake at the cooking show."

"What?" Joseph's eyes widened.

"It's true. When Myron saw our lopsided wedding cake today, he admitted he was the bidder and said he'd only wanted the cake so he could meet me and Elma." Thelma smiled, watching her sister and Myron in deep conversation. "When Myron realized it was his own cousin he'd been bidding against, he finally gave up and let Delbert win. Delbert didn't know Myron was there that day until he confessed it to him later on."

"I'm glad he let Delbert win." Looking lovingly at Thelma, Joseph added, "I wonder if there's a chance that your sister and Dell's cousin could get together. They're both smiling pretty good right now."

Thelma reached under the table and took hold of her groom's hand. "Now wouldn't it be something if our lopsided cake brought another couple together?"

Grandma's Christmas Cake

Ingredients:

3 cups sifted cake flour
2½ teaspoons baking
   powder
½ teaspoon salt
1¾ cups sugar
⅔ cup butter
2 eggs
1½ teaspoons vanilla

1¼ cups milk
1 small (3 ounce) box
   red Jell-O
1 small (3 ounce) box
   green Jell-O
1 (8 ounce) tub Cool
   Whip

Preheat oven to 350 degrees. Sift flour, baking powder, and salt together in bowl and set aside. In mixing bowl, cream sugar and butter. Add eggs and vanilla. Beat until fluffy, scraping down sides of bowl frequently. Slowly beat in flour mixture alternately with milk. Mix batter thoroughly and pour into two greased and floured 9-inch round pans.

Bake for 30 to 35 minutes or until done. Cool. Prick cakes several times with fork and leave in pans. Dissolve red Jell-O in 1 cup boiling water and carefully pour over one cake. Dissolve green Jell-O in 1 cup boiling water and pour over other cake. Refrigerate overnight or for a few hours.

Take cakes out of pans using spatula and put on plate, one on top of the other, spreading filling between layers (see recipe below). Frost cake with 1 tub Cool Whip. Decorate with red and green sprinkles if desired.

Filling:

1 (8 ounce) package
   cream cheese, softened

1 (8 ounce) tub Cool
   Whip

In bowl, mix cream cheese and Cool Whip until thoroughly combined.

The Farmers' Market Mishap

Dedication

To Miriam Brunstetter, and in loving memory of her husband,
Charles Brunstetter—both have always been a beacon
of light to our family. And to our Amish friends,
the Wagler family. Thanks for your warm hospitality.

*And let us not be weary in well doing:
for in due season we shall reap, if we faint not.*
GALATIANS 6:9

Chapter 1

Topeka, Indiana

A bone-chilling wind lashed at the trees, scattering bits of debris across the yard. Elma Hochstetler drew her shawl tighter, shivering against the cold. All day long the weather had been like this. One would never know it was the first week of May. She quickened her footsteps, pausing to step around a puddle left from last night's rain. If this unpredictable, windy and gray-skied weather kept up, she'd never get the rest of her garden planted. Hurriedly, she made her way to the chicken coop, not wanting to spend any more time out here than necessary. With nightfall approaching, Elma felt the temperature dropping.

As she passed the barn, Elma heard her trusty horse, Pearl, whinny and kick the door from inside her stall. Cupping her hands around her mouth, Elma hollered, "You're okay, girl; it's just the wind." She grabbed at the scarf covering her head, hoping it wouldn't be blown away, and blinked several times when her eyes began to run because of the stinging air.

When the kicking stopped, Elma breathed a sigh of relief and hurried on. The last thing she needed was one more repair to take care of. The wind followed as she opened the door to the chicken coop, barely making it inside before it slammed shut. Loose feathers stirred up and floated slowly down as the air calmed inside. Sounds of watery clucking, claws scratching the floor, and the fluttery ruffle as a chicken preened itself greeted her. She sneezed when the odor of straw and dusty feed reached her nostrils. Elma blew a feather away from her face that until now, had been stuck in her head scarf.

Collecting eggs wasn't Elma's favorite pastime, nor did she enjoy feeding and watering the unpredictable chickens. She glanced around quickly, hoping Hector wasn't lying in wait for her this evening. The feisty multicolored rooster could be so erratic—sometimes creeping up on her in a sneak attack, other times boldly pursuing her as soon as she stepped into the coop.

Elma looked down at her leg, now sporting an itchy bandage. For no apparent reason, other than just plain orneriness, Hector had pecked her ankle and broken the skin earlier this morning when she'd entered the coop. This evening she'd brought an old broom in with her and made sure it was within reach in case she needed to defend herself. "You won't get me twice today," Elma muttered. "I'm ready for you this time, Hector."

Elma lifted her wicker basket and started down the line. "All right, ladies, what do you have for me?" She'd fed and watered the chickens this morning but hadn't taken time to collect the eggs, as she'd been in a hurry to open the store. The fabric sale going on this week was bringing more customers than they'd expected.

When Elma's twin sister lived here, taking care of the chickens had been her job. But since Thelma married Joseph and they'd moved into the house across the street, she had faced other responsibilities, not to mention the task of caring for her own chickens. And now Thelma was expecting a baby and tired easily. Even though she still helped in the store, for the last month she'd only been working part-time. This put more stress on Elma, as she couldn't manage everything on her own. Two weeks ago, she'd hired Anna Herschberger to help out during the times Thelma couldn't be there. So far, the arrangement had been working well.

"Okay, Gert, you'd better move aside." Elma gave the hen a gentle push, reached into the nesting box, and plucked out a nicely rounded tan-colored egg. "*Danki*, Gert."

Smiling, Elma moved on to the next nesting box, always wary of Hector. No sign of him yet, so she figured he hadn't come inside with the rest of the chickens when the sun began to set.

When Elma finishing gathering eggs, she hurried out the door and headed for the warmth of the house. She'd no more than stepped onto the porch when Tiger showed up. Purring in a deep, throaty rumble, the orange-and-white cat rubbed against her leg. As Elma switched the basket into her other hand, Tiger walked a figure-eight motion in and around her feet.

"Okay, okay, don't be in such a rush. At least allow me to open the door." She turned the knob, and as the door swung open, Tiger released several rapid-fire *meows* and darted in with a swish of his tail, causing Elma to trip. She regained her balance just in time to avoid dropping the eggs. "Tiger, why can't you be more patient? I could have spilled all the eggs and had a big mess to clean up."

Tiger offered a piercing *meow* and paraded off.

Elma rolled her eyes. She'd never cared much for cats, but with the mouse problem she'd had since living in her grandparents' old house, it was either allow the cat in or set traps in most of the rooms. Since Elma began letting Tiger in every evening, the mouse population had decreased, so at least something good had come from it. Elma's twin was the one who loved cats. If Thelma had her way, she'd adopt every stray cat from Topeka to Shipshewana.

Elma entered the kitchen and set the basket of eggs on the counter. She grimaced, noticing the wet tea bag she'd left on a spoon this morning before leaving to open the store. It wasn't like her to be so careless. "Guess I have too much on my mind these days," she murmured, removing her shawl and folding it neatly over the back of a chair.

Tiger, who'd joined her in the kitchen, swished his tail across the hem of Elma's long dress. *Meow. Meow.* It was a definite "I want to be fed now" meow.

"Hang on. I'll get you something to eat shortly." Elma picked up the wilted tea bag and threw it in the garbage. Then she opened a cupboard door to get the cat food. Before she could get the bowl filled, Tiger began gobbling it up.

"You greedy *katz*." Elma chuckled. "You ate breakfast this morning, so you can't be that hungry." She gave him some fresh water then took care of the eggs. Once they were put in the refrigerator, Elma took out a container of leftover vegetable-beef soup, poured it into a kettle, and placed it on her new propane-operated stove. Even unheated, the meaty scent made her stomach growl. Thank goodness the old woodstove was gone, although the kitchen wasn't as warm and toasty now. That sooty old beast had given her and Thelma so much trouble when they'd first moved here after their grandparents died. A good many desserts had flopped or ended up overly brown when they'd baked in the antiquated oven.

Elma snickered, thinking about the lopsided cake her twin sister had made and they'd taken to Shipshewana to be auctioned off. Patting her cheek, it was hard not to get flustered again. Even so, with all the time that had passed, her face grew increasingly warmer with the thought of what had transpired onstage. She could have died of embarrassment when the bidding began. Then, she stood, too stunned to speak, when someone bid one hundred dollars for their pathetic-looking cake. Turned out that Joseph Beechy had convinced his friend Delbert Gingerich to bid on the cake so he could meet Thelma. The plan worked too, because it didn't take long for Joseph and Thelma to begin courting.

As Elma stirred the soup, her thoughts drifted yet again. Slowly but surely, this old house was being transformed into a more comfortable place to live. At least Elma saw it that way. Grandma and Grandpa had been content to live here a good many years, getting by with what they had and making only a few updates. Even with the new stove, some updated kitchen cabinets, and a new water heater, Elma had a list of things she still wanted to have done. One in particular was getting someone to fix the leaky toilet in the bathroom upstairs. She also hoped to buy a new kitchen table and replace the faded kitchen linoleum, which had worn nearly through in several places—especially in front of the stove. Another project involved carpentry, so she'd need to call on Joseph's friend Delbert for that.

At one time, Delbert and Elma had been a courting couple, but things didn't work out between them. He was too set in his ways, and most likely, he thought she was too. Then Delbert's cousin Myron Bontrager came on the scene and courted Elma for a few months. Myron lived in southern Indiana, and it didn't take Elma long to realize a long-distance relationship wasn't going to work out. Besides, she and Myron didn't have much in common, so she wasn't too upset when they went their separate ways.

While waiting for the soup to heat, Elma set the table and poured a glass of water. When the soup was ready, she poured the steaming medley into a bowl, inhaling its beefy aroma. There was only enough for one helping, but it was plenty for her and certainly hearty. After adding a box of crackers and a leftover cheese ball to the setting, she took a seat and bowed her head for silent prayer. *Heavenly Father, I thank You for this food and ask You to bless it to the nourishment of my body. Be with my sister and her husband, and with our family in Sullivan, Illinois. Continue to give me the strength to keep Grandma and Grandpa's store going, and if it be Your will, bring the right man into my life. Amen.*

When Elma opened her eyes, her gaze came to rest on the vacant chair where Thelma used to sit. The chair wasn't the only thing deserted, however. The entire house seemed empty without her presence.

When Elma gave her blessing for Thelma to marry Joseph, she had no idea how lonely it would be to live in this rambling old house all alone. There was no one to converse with except the cat, and cooking for one was certainly no fun. Sometimes during a long, solitary night, Elma would cry herself to sleep. She never let on, though. No point upsetting her sister or throwing cold water on Thelma's happiness.

I need to quit feeling sorry for myself. Elma grabbed the saltshaker and sprinkled a bit on her soup. *My twin deserves to be happy with Joseph. I only wish I could find a man with whom I'd be content—someone who shares my interests and looks at life the way I do.*

Thirty-four and still unmarried, Elma had accepted her plight. Unless God brought the special man to her, she'd be an old maid for the rest of her life.

⁊

Thelma sat in the rocking chair, knitting a pair of green booties. The baby wouldn't be here for five more months, but she wanted to be prepared. She glanced at her husband, sitting across from her reading the recent edition of *The Connection* magazine, and smiled.

Returning her smile, Joseph set his magazine aside. "Is the gas lamp giving you enough light?"

"*Jah*, it's plenty."

"I was looking at you a bit ago and noticed you were squinting." He gestured to the coffee table. "You oughta be using those readers right there on the table, don't you think?"

Thelma nodded. "You're right. I'm trying to use what little sight I have without them." She wrinkled her nose. "Anyway, those glasses make me feel like I'm getting old." She began rocking in rhythm to the clicking of her knitting needles.

"You're *schee*. In fact, I think you've gotten even cuter since I married you." Joseph winked at her. "And you're even more beautiful now that you are carrying our baby. You have a glow about you."

She placed the needles in her lap and flapped her hand at him. "Go on now—you're such a tease."

Joseph left his chair and came over to give her a kiss. "I'm not teasing. I'm a lucky man to have found a woman as pretty as you. You're *schmaert* too."

Thelma bobbed her head. "Now that's one thing I'll have to agree on. I was smart enough to marry you."

He gave her another wink. "Think I'll pour myself a glass of grape juice. Can I get you anything?"

"Juice sounds good. *Danki*, Joe."

"No problem." Joseph gave Thelma another quick kiss and headed for the kitchen.

While Thelma waited for his return, she thought about some of the things she needed to get done before the week was out. Tomorrow was Thursday, and she'd be helping Elma in the store, so not much at home would get done. Friday would have to be laundry day, and Saturday she hoped to do some baking and cleaning.

Thelma felt thankful her utility room was on the main floor. She didn't miss those days of going down to the basement to wash a load of clothes. *Poor Elma. She never has liked going to the basement to do the laundry. It's too bad there isn't a place for her washing machine upstairs. Maybe Joe or Delbert could figure something out.*

Thelma glanced around the living room. She couldn't help comparing her and Joe's home to Grandpa and Grandma's old house. The fireplace mantel in this home was nicely stained, and the flooring was in tip-top shape. The prior owners had obviously kept the place up.

When Thelma and Joseph first moved in, Elma donated a few pieces of furniture, such as the rocker Thelma sat in now. Of course, Joseph brought the furniture he had in his previous home, so they didn't really need much.

She glanced at the empty cradle sitting across the room. Even though carpentry was not his specialty, Joseph had made the cradle, finishing it last week. Of course, his good friend Delbert, being a carpenter by trade, had given Joe several tips. *What a shame things didn't work out for Dell and Elma.* Thelma got the chair moving faster. *I'd always hoped when I fell in love, my twin sister would find her soul mate and fall in love too. It would be nice if Elma was also married and expecting a* boppli. *Well, at least she'll have the privilege of being an auntie soon.*

Despite Thelma's love for Joseph, it had been difficult for her to get married and move out of Grandpa and Grandma's old house, leaving Elma alone to fend for herself. Although Thelma and Joseph only lived across the street, it sometimes felt like miles between them. *I wonder what Elma is doing tonight?* Thelma paused from rocking to glance out the front window. During the day, from where she sat now, she could see across the street to the house she'd become so familiar with. Now she could only see a faint light glowing in one of the windows. *It must be lonely for her over there by herself. Well, at least she lives close and we get to see each other nearly every day.*

Thelma and Elma had always been close, and when they'd moved to Topeka two years ago, to take over Grandma and Grandpa's store and live in their house, it had drawn them even closer. She was ever so happy being married to Joseph, but oh, how Thelma wished her twin could find such a wonderful man.

"Oh, my." Thelma's eyes flew open when her neck snapped back before almost nodding off to sleep.

"You look tired, my love." Joseph set a glass of juice on the coffee table near Thelma. "Should we drink our juice and then get ready for bed?"

Thelma yawned, rubbing her neck. "I suppose it would be a good idea. The sale will continue at the store tomorrow so I need to be there early to help Elma."

Joseph's thick eyebrows rose high on his forehead. "I thought Elma hired Anna Herschberger to help out."

"She did, but one of Anna's friends is getting married tomorrow, so Anna asked for the day off." Thelma drank the juice; then, grasping the armrests, she rose from her chair.

Joseph pulled Thelma into his arms and kissed her tenderly. "I love you so much, and now that you're expecting a boppli, I want to be sure you take good care of yourself."

She tipped her head back, reaching up to stroke his soft beard. "Now don't look so worried. I'll be fine, Joe, and so will our baby."

Chapter 2

"You look tired this morning. Are you sure you feel up to working today?" Elma placed both hands on her sister's shoulders.

"I am a bit tired, but with the sale going on still, and Anna not working, you need my help." Thelma smiled, although it didn't quite reach her usual sparkling blue eyes. "Besides, I enjoy being here in the store with you and having the opportunity to visit with customers."

Elma knew all about her twin's eagerness to visit. Even when they were children, Thelma had been the outgoing one. While Elma was talkative with people she knew, her sister easily carried on conversations with complete strangers. She remembered how once, when they were ten years old, their mother had taken them shopping. As they were getting ready to leave the store, Thelma walked right up to a young English girl and asked where she'd gotten her red balloon. The next thing Elma knew, her sister and the English girl were exchanging addresses so they could write to each other. Elma had never understood why she and Thelma were different on many levels. Yet they were as close as any identical twins could possibly be.

"I have a suggestion." Elma moved to one side of the stool where her sister sat. "Why don't you sit on this stool here by the counter and wait on people? I'll take care of cutting material and restocking shelves as needed."

"Are you sure? I can help stock shelves if you need me to."

Elma shook her head determinedly. "Absolutely not! In your delicate condition, you should not be doing anything strenuous. At least here by the counter, you can stay off your feet."

"You and Joseph worry about me too much." Thelma folded her arms across her stomach. "I'm not an invalid, you know."

"Of course not, but you're thirty-four years old and expecting your first boppli. You need to be careful and not overwork." Elma glanced down at her sister's ankles then quickly looked away. She wasn't about to mention the slight swelling she'd noticed. Thelma would think she was fussing too much. But if it got any worse, she wouldn't hesitate to speak up.

Thelma sighed. "All right, I'll do as you say."

"Good to hear." Elma put the OPEN sign in the large front window and had barely gotten the door unlocked when a horse and buggy pulled up. Four Amish ladies got out, and, as soon as the horse was secured, they hurried into the store. One of them, whom Elma had not met before, held a baby in her arms. For a split second Elma felt a pang of jealousy, but she quickly got it under control.

"*Guder mariye.*" Elma greeted them with a smile.

"Good morning. How are you today, Thelma?" Clara Lehman gave Elma a hug.

Elma shook her head. "Oh, no, I'm not Thelma. I'm Elma."

Clara's cheeks reddened. "Sorry about that. You two look so much alike. Even after two years of knowing you both, it's hard to tell you apart." She looked over at Doris Miller, who stood beside her. "Don't you agree?"

"Jah, but then Thelma is the one expecting a boppli, so we should be able to tell them apart." Doris motioned to Elma's stomach and snickered. "Does she look like she's in a family way?"

"Of course not." Clara's face colored further, and Elma's cheeks heated as well. She pushed up the left sleeve of her dress, revealing a small scar on her elbow. "One way you can always tell us apart is by this scar. I got it when I was a child and fell off my bike."

"And don't forget the small mole I have behind my right ear," Thelma called from her place behind the counter. "It's one sure way to know who is who."

Clara chuckled as she moved toward the counter. "Now, now, Thelma, most people would not be likely to look behind your ear."

"Or see the scar on Elma's arm," Doris interjected.

This discussion was getting nowhere, and Elma was about to ask if either of the ladies needed help with anything, when the door opened again and two more women entered the store. From the looks of things, today would be busy. That was good; Elma liked being busy. She moved across the room to introduce herself to the young woman with the baby, while Doris, Clara, and the other women stood at the counter talking with Thelma.

❧

By noon, Thelma felt more than ready to take a break. She'd been waiting on customers all morning, and her back was beginning to hurt from sitting so long. She noticed her ankles appeared to be a bit swollen today. It was hard to believe, but twenty customers had come into the store in the last hour, all looking for material and sewing notions. Thelma wondered if every woman in their community had gone shopping today.

She stepped off the stool, and was about to seek Elma out to say she wanted to go to the back room to eat lunch, when Lizzie Yoder entered the store. Ambling over to the counter, the older woman asked breathlessly, "Does the sale you're having include everything in the store?" Her blue eyes seemed to grow larger. "I hope so, because I need a few things and don't have much money to spend."

"I'm sorry," Thelma responded, "but only the bolts of material are on sale today."

Lizzie's double chin tilted downward as she heaved a sigh. "I figured as much but had to ask. Guess I'll head on down the notions aisle."

Thelma watched Lizzie walk away. For a sixty-two-year-old who was a bit on the pudgy side, Lizzie moved pretty fast. *I hope I'm that full of energy when I'm her age.*

Once again, Thelma was on the verge of calling her sister to mind the counter when Mary Lambright entered the store. "It's good to see you. How are your boys doing these days?" Thelma asked.

Mary's eyes brightened. "Philip and Richard are doing well. They both enjoy being in school."

"I'll bet they do. Seems like just yesterday when they were sitting here in the store listening to me read them a story."

Mary bobbed her head. "My *kinner* have grown so quickly." She

209

motioned to Thelma. "Bet you're looking forward to becoming a *mudder.*"

"Oh, jah. Joseph and I are both excited about becoming parents." Thelma looked down at her growing stomach and patted it gently.

Mary smiled. "Guess I'd better get what I came in here for. If you're still at the counter when I'm ready to pay for my purchases, we can chat a bit longer."

When Mary hurried off, Thelma stepped down from the stool. She was getting ready to head to the back of the store when Lizzie showed up again. "I'm ready to check out now."

Thelma glanced around, hoping Elma was nearby and would come to her rescue, but no such luck. She must be at the back of the store.

"Umm. . .sure, I can check you out, Lizzie." Thelma stepped behind the counter again, and Lizzie placed her purchases down—a notebook, two spools of black thread, four skeins of green yarn, and a bag of jelly beans. Seeing the candy caused Thelma to think of Joseph's friend Delbert. He seemed to always have candy in his pocket. Delbert had a sweet tooth, for sure. But then from what Thelma had seen, so did Lizzie. *Good thing Elma's not waiting on her. She'd probably give Lizzie a lecture on the danger of eating too much sugar.*

"What's new with you, Lizzie?" Thelma questioned as she put the woman's purchase in a plastic bag.

Lizzie squinted over the top of her glasses. "Nothing good, that's for sure."

"What do you mean?"

"My brother, Abe, will be moving to Kentucky soon, and he's taking his whole family with him." Lizzie touched her chest. "Everyone but me."

"I didn't realize they were leaving the area. Why don't you go with them?"

"I was invited to move, but I said no, I'm staying put." Lizzie shook her head so hard her head-covering ties swished across her face. "Topeka's my home, and there's nothing in Kentucky for me."

Thelma pursed her lips. "So you'll stay here all alone?" Lizzie had never married, and it didn't seem right that she wouldn't live near her family anymore.

Lizzie shrugged her shoulders. "My friend Peggy will be moving in with me soon, and we'll share expenses. We clean houses together, so things should work out okay for both of us." She grabbed the package of jelly beans, ripped it open, and took out a few of the black ones. "These licorice jelly beans are my favorite." She offered Thelma a sheepish grin and popped a handful into her mouth.

Thelma resisted the urge to say something about eating so much candy. She'd be acting like her sister. "Will there be anything else?"

"Nope, that's all for now. I'll see you again soon though, I expect." Lizzie leaned against the counter and lowered her voice. "So how are you feeling these days? Still having morning sickness?"

"Not anymore, but I do get awful tired at times." Thelma almost snickered. *Funny how some people feel compelled to drop their voice when talking about certain topics.*

"I can't speak from experience, mind you, but I've seen plenty of women who were in a family way. Some have the morning sickness and some don't. Everyone is different." Lizzie ate several more jelly beans of various flavors. "Well, I'd better get going." She paid for her items, picked up the sack, and headed for the door. "Have a nice day, Thelma."

As Lizzie was putting the bag of candy into her satchel, a few jelly beans fell out of the opening. "Don't worry, I'll get them." Lizzie scurried to pick them up. "It's okay. I think I got them all. You take care now."

"You too." Thelma chuckled. Lizzie Yoder was quite the character. Too bad Lizzie's family would be moving to Kentucky. Thelma couldn't imagine what it would be like if Elma moved away. Of course, that wasn't likely to happen since Elma wasn't married. Even if she was, no way would Thelma's twin sister leave her—especially when she would become an aunt in five months.

⸎

When they had a small break between customers, Elma joined Thelma at the counter. "You've been up here a long while, Sister. You'd best take a break while I keep an eye on things."

"Danki. I'm more than ready for it." Thelma rose from the stool and headed for the back of the store.

Elma followed her into the back room and grabbed her lunch basket to take up front. "I'll eat this while I'm at the counter, in case any customers come in." She gave her sister's arm a gentle pat. "You relax, put your feet up, and take it easy. If I need you, I'll give a holler."

Thelma's appreciation was evident as she took a seat and smiled at Elma. "I was beginning to wonder if things would ever slow down."

Elma chuckled. "You know how it goes. We're either bored and looking for something to do, or the store is literally crawling with customers."

"Jah." Thelma pointed to the door. "You'd better get busy and eat before more people show up."

"Okay, see you soon." Elma hurried to the counter and placed her bologna and cheddar cheese sandwich, along with some carrot and celery sticks, on a napkin. As soon as she removed the thermos lid, the tangy smell of apple juice wafted up to her nose, making her mouth water.

Elma managed to eat most of her lunch before Hazel Zimmerman, one of the Mennonite women who lived close by, stopped by.

"Good day, Elma." Hazel offered a genuine smile. At least she hadn't gotten Elma mixed up with Thelma.

"How are things with you today?" Elma put her lunch basket behind the counter.

"My back has been acting up, but other than that, everything is going pretty well." Hazel reached around and rubbed her lower back.

"Sorry to hear it. I hope your back gets better soon." Elma picked up the spray cleaner and a napkin to tidy the area, while Hazel headed to the fabric section.

A short time later, Hazel returned with a bolt of pale blue, lightly printed material. "Do you happen to have more of this color in the back?"

"I'll go take a look; just give me a second." Elma stepped out from behind the counter and headed for the back room. When she entered, she spotted Thelma dozing in her chair.

Elma smiled. *I'll let her rest awhile longer. My twin needs to take care of herself and not overdo.* She found the material she'd come for and stepped quietly out of the room.

Once outside the door, Elma scurried to find the scissors to cut through the packaging tape. "This isn't going as smoothly as I had hoped," she mumbled quietly. After she had the box opened and began pulling the material out, she could see it wasn't the right material. Elma looked over at the next box sitting nearby and grabbed the scissors again. This time she had the right color, but now she'd created a mess in the back of the store.

Sighing, she heard the door out front open and close, then more voices. She hurried up front where she found Hazel leaning against the fabric table. "I believe this is what you wanted."

Hazel grinned. "Thanks, it's perfect."

Elma pushed her glasses back in place and looked toward the door, where two English women stood. "Hello, ladies."

"Hello," they said in unison.

"We saw your ad in the paper," the older of the two women said, "and we're here to check out your sale."

"Please feel free to look around." Elma gestured to the fabric section of the store.

As the women looked through the material, Elma cut Hazel's fabric and rang up the notions and thread she'd picked out.

"Are you working alone today?" Hazel picked up her bagged purchases.

"No, my sister is here, but she's taking a break." Elma glanced toward the back room, wondering if Thelma was still asleep.

"Well, tell her I said hello, and you have a good day."

"Thanks. You too."

While the two English women shopped for fabric, Elma knelt to organize the work space behind the counter. Then she heard someone step up behind her.

"Sister, how long were you going to let me sleep?" Thelma tilted her head. "Why are you looking at me so strangely?"

"Your head covering's on crooked." Elma reached out and put it back in place. "And the reason I didn't wake you is because I figured you could use some rest."

"Well, I got some. Have I missed much?" Yawning, Thelma smoothed the front of her dress.

"Hazel Zimmerman came in for material and notions, and a couple of English ladies are looking at material." Elma glanced in their direction.

"I'll pop back there and see if they have any questions."

Elma shook her head. "You should stay off your feet. I'll go see how they are doing." Elma motioned to the wooden stool.

Thelma opened her mouth as if about to argue the point, but with a slight shrug, she took a seat.

As the day wore on, so did Elma's exhaustion. She could see clearly from the distant look in her sister's eyes, and the way she sagged on the stool, that she was still quite weary.

"It's time to close up," Elma said. "Why don't you go on home now? I'll take care of everything."

Thelma didn't argue. She gathered up her things, gave Elma a hug, and with hands hanging limply, headed out the door. "See you tomorrow, Sister."

"You're not working tomorrow," Elma called to Thelma's retreating form. "Anna will be here to help me."

Thelma lifted a hand in a backward wave and shut the door behind her.

Elma slouched against the counter, supporting her head with a hand. Her muscles felt heavy, and her senses dulled. For the last hour she'd had difficulty focusing, and now all she wanted to do was go home, take a hot bath, and sit with her feet propped up. But of course, it was wishful thinking. Even though she'd collected eggs this morning and had given the chickens food and water, other animals needed tending to this evening. Somehow she would push herself to feed the barn cats and check on the horses. After those chores were done, she would grab something from the refrigerator for a quick supper, and if she had enough energy left, she'd take a bath and then put her feet up.

Pulling from deep within, Elma proceeded to turn off the gas lamps and lock up the store for the night. She missed the days when she and Thelma closed the store together then went home and shared a meal, enjoying each other's companionship and the quietness of their house. So much had changed in the last two years. Sometimes it still didn't seem possible that she now lived alone.

Heading down to the house, Elma heard Pearl whinny in the barn. "I'll be back soon to feed you, girl," Elma called.

Like clockwork, Tiger was waiting on the porch to be let in for dinner. "I know you're hungry, Tiger. So am I." Elma reached into her sweater pocket for her key chain but came up empty. She held her hands behind her back, gripping her wrists. *Oh, no. Where did I put the keys? I must have dropped them on the way down to the house.*

She looked down at the cat, who was meowing and rubbing her legs. "Sorry, Tiger, but we aren't going in yet. I have to find my keys."

Chapter 3

Tiger's plaintive *Meow!* was almost Elma's undoing. She was hungry too, and wanted to get in the house as much as he did.

"My keys have to be somewhere between the store and home." Elma's teeth clamped together when she turned and the cat darted between her legs. "Tiger, you're gonna trip me again." She clapped her hands. "Now scat!"

Elma stepped off the porch and headed back to the store, searching the ground as she went. "*Ach*, my back is throbbing." She gripped the area above her hip as she stooped over, scanning more of the area. It was like looking for a sewing needle in a field of hay. Grass, weeds, gravel, and dirt covered the path leading back to the store, and although it may have helped, she wasn't about to crawl on her hands and knees to get a closer look. Besides, the sunlight was slowly fading, making it more difficult to see anything that might be lying on the ground. Maybe the keys were inside the store. If that was the case, she was out of luck. Her key to the store was on the same chain as the one for the house, and she'd flipped the lock on the store before shutting the door. Aside from breaking a window to get inside, it could be all for nothing if the keys weren't there. Elma didn't need to add purchasing a new window to her growing project list.

"So, great!" Elma looked up at the sky in exasperation. "Now both keys are missing."

While she continued her search, Tiger meowed and pawed at the hem of her skirt.

"I'm sorry, Tiger." She bent to pet him. "But I can't feed either of us till I locate those keys. Wish you could help me find them." Elma's eyes teared up. This was a time when she missed having her twin sister at her side. Thelma would probably remain upbeat, saying something like, "Don't worry, Sister, we'll find them."

Elma choked back a sob as she searched the ground, taking small steps toward the store.

After looking for what seemed like hours, she gave up. The only sensible thing was to go over to Thelma's house and borrow her set of keys. "Don't know why I didn't think to do it sooner." She tapped the side of her head, almost knocking her head covering off.

Elma hurried down the driveway, thankful it wasn't windy this evening. She paused at the mailbox to retrieve the mail then, looking both ways, crossed the street. Joseph and Thelma's front room window faced the road, along with most of the wraparound porch. So if her sister wanted to sit outside, she could watch the customers come and go.

As Elma started up the driveway, to go around back, she heard a familiar *meow!* Looking down, she groaned. Much to her chagrin, Tiger had followed her across the street.

⁍

Thelma was about to start supper when Joseph entered the kitchen. "Don't bother fixing anything for us, 'cause I'm takin' my beautiful *fraa* out for supper this evening."

"Oh, Joseph, are you sure? I bet you had a busy day at the harness shop. Wouldn't you prefer to stay home and rest?"

"Nope." He stepped up to Thelma and gave her a hug. "I did have a busy day, but I'm guessin' you did as well. Your stooped posture and red-brimmed eyes are a good indicator of exhaustion."

Thelma nodded. "I used to be able to work five days a week and do all sorts of chores without feeling so mied."

Joseph tipped her head back so she was looking directly into his eyes. She giggled when he affectionately tweaked her nose. "But you weren't expecting a boppli back then. Which is why you need to take it easy and let me treat you to a meal out at Tiffany's."

Thelma's mouth watered thinking about the good food on the menu there, not to mention what was available on the restaurant's buffet. "All

217

right, let me wash up and get changed into a clean dress, and I'll be ready to go."

"I need to clean up and change my clothes too."

They started down the hall toward their bedroom but halted their footsteps when someone pounded on the back door. Thelma went to the door and was surprised to find her sister standing on the porch.

"Can I borrow your key so I can get into my house?" Elma spoke breathlessly, and her cheeks were bright pink.

Thelma blinked rapidly. "What happened to your key?"

"I don't know. I lost it somehow, and since the store key is on the same ring, I don't have it either. I had them when I locked up the store, so they must have slipped out of my hand somewhere between the store and home." Elma heaved a heavy sigh. "I'm tired, hungry, and so is my pestering cat, so I need to get into the house right away."

"I'll get my key for you." Thelma went to her purse and took out the key. She handed it to her sister then turned to Joseph and whispered, "Would you mind if I invited Elma to go out to supper with us?"

"Course not. She's more than welcome to join us at Tiffany's."

Elma smiled. "It's a nice offer, but I have to feed the animals yet, and..."

Joseph held up his hand. "Not a problem. I'll take care of your outside chores while you and my fraa get ready to go out. Once I'm done, I'll come back here, take a quick shower, and change into clean clothes. Then we can be off to Tiffany's."

Elma pushed an unruly strand of hair back under her head covering then picked Tiger up before he decided to venture back across the road. "If you're sure you don't mind, I'd appreciate the help, and a meal out this evening sounds *wunderbaar*."

⸎

Soon after Elma was seated at a table with her sister and brother-in-law, she spotted Delbert Gingerich coming in the door. Joseph must have seen him too, for he waved Delbert over.

After everyone greeted Delbert, Joseph pointed to the empty chair at their table. "If you're not meeting someone, we'd be glad to have you join us, Dell."

"I'm not meeting anyone, but hey, I don't mind sitting by myself. Sure don't want to interrupt your meal." Delbert rubbed the back of his neck. Shuffling his feet, he glanced at Elma then looked quickly away.

"No one should have to eat alone, especially when their friends are sitting right here." Joseph got up and pulled out the empty chair. "Now I won't take no for an answer."

"Well, umm. . ."

Delbert looked at Elma, as though needing her approval, but before she could form a response, Thelma spoke up. "We'd be pleased if you joined us, Dell. We haven't seen you in a while, and it'll be nice to catch up."

Feeling as if she had no other choice, Elma smiled and nodded. While she had nothing personal against Joseph's friend, his little quirks sometimes got on her nerves. She remembered from when Delbert courted her how stubborn and opinionated he could be. He also ate too much candy and was a poor sport whenever they played a board game with Thelma and Joseph.

Delbert's eyes brightened as he took a seat and slid his chair in close to the table. "Anyone know what the special here is tonight?"

"I'm not sure." Joseph motioned to the buffet. "But that's what I'm goin' for. It's nice to get a variety of food."

Elma glanced in that direction. Joseph was right. There were so many dishes to choose from—chicken, corn, mashed potatoes, thick noodles, a salad bar full of fresh vegetables, and some wonderfully tasty desserts.

"Guess I'll have the buffet too." Delbert grinned. "I had a busy day and worked up a hearty appetite."

"What are you going to have?" Elma asked her twin.

Thelma shrugged her shoulders. "I am kind of *hungerich*, so I may as well have the same. How about you?"

"Since everyone else is going to the buffet, I will too."

"Let's have our silent prayer before we help ourselves," Joseph suggested.

Everyone closed their eyes.

Heavenly Father, Elma prayed, *bless this food to the nourishment of our bodies, and please bless everyone at this table. Amen.*

"How are things with you these days, Elma?" Delbert asked as he followed her up to the buffet. "Are you still keeping plenty busy at the store?"

"Jah, I am, and with things at the house too." She pursed her lips. "There are many items on my list that need to be done, beginning with the upstairs toilet."

"What's wrong with it?"

"It's leaking, and I'm continually wiping up the floor."

His brows pulled together. "Not good, Elma. If you don't get it fixed soon it could damage the bathroom floor, not to mention creating a mold problem."

"I wouldn't want that to happen." She wrinkled her nose. "I've been meaning to ask Joseph, but he's been extra busy in his shop lately, so it may have to wait until things slow down for him."

"Not to worry." Delbert smiled. "I'll drop by your place and take a look at the situation. It might be something I can easily fix." He blushed; then he quickly added, "If it's okay with you, that is."

"Danki. It's kind of you to offer, and I appreciate it. I'll pay you, of course." Elma picked up a clean plate.

"We'll see how it goes. If it doesn't take too much time, I may only charge you for the part." When Delbert picked up a plate, it nearly slipped out of his hands. "Oops." He managed to grab it in time. As he started down the line, he put a glob of mashed potatoes on it then added some gravy. "Everything else okay?"

"Pretty much—except for losing the keys to my house and the store today."

"Did you find them?" He looked at her intently.

Elma shook her head. "I borrowed Thelma's key so I could get into the house, and I'll use her key to the store when I open it tomorrow." She forked a chicken thigh and put it on her plate.

"That's too bad. I hope you find it." Delbert took some of the golden-crusted meat and plopped it next to his potatoes.

"So do I." Elma added some noodles to her plate. "If I don't find them, I'll take Thelma's keys to the hardware store and have some copies made."

Delbert nudged Elma's arm with his elbow. "You can do that all right, but if someone finds the keys you lost, it could be *arig*."

She tipped her head. "Why would it be bad?"

"If the wrong person found your keys, they might break into the house or store and steal from you. If you like, I could change the locks on both doorknobs and get you another set of keys."

Elma gulped. Having Delbert around, for yet another project, could be a little unnerving. Now she was even more determined to find those lost keys.

Chapter 4

The following morning, Elma woke up with a pounding headache, as well as a stiff neck. She'd lain awake much of the night, worrying someone might have found her keys and would enter her house or rob the store. Every little noise and creak of the house put Elma on alert.

The first thing she did when she entered the kitchen was to grab a glass of water and take an aspirin. Then she stepped outdoors and took care of feeding and watering the animals in the barn. When that chore was done, she headed to the chicken coop, carrying a basket in the crook of her arm.

Hearing the shrill cry of a hawk, Elma stopped to watch it circling on the air currents. A wave of peaceful calm came over her as she paused to pray. *Lord, help me to do Your will today. Please remind me to reflect You in all I say and do.*

Things went well in the chicken coop, and Elma returned to the kitchen with six nice-sized eggs. Her head still hurt, and it almost felt as though she was in a daze. As she began to prepare breakfast, Elma wavered as pure exhaustion took over.

Holding on to the countertop, she stood quietly, until her vision cleared. Then glancing down, she noticed her furry companion, eagerly lapping the fresh water in his dish. "Sure wish I'd found those keys, Tiger."

The cat looked up at her briefly then began nibbling the food she'd given him. At least somebody was happy this morning.

Elma went to the refrigerator and took out a carton of eggs. *Think I might feel better if I had a dog to alert me to any danger. Tiger's only good for catching mice.*

As though he could read her thoughts, the cat left his dish and came over to rub against Elma's leg. She couldn't help but smile. "Okay, Tiger, you're a nice pet." Truth was, ever since Thelma moved out, Elma found herself talking to the cat as though he were a friend. At least it was better than talking to herself.

Elma got out the frying pan and cooking oil. She was about to pour some into the pan when she heard a horse's whinny. Glancing out the window, she was surprised to see Delbert's buggy pulling in. Elma watched as he secured his horse to the hitching rail and started for the house.

"Guder mariye," Elma said after opening the door. "What brings you by here this morning?"

Delbert lifted his toolbox and grinned. "Came to take a look at your leaky toilet, and maybe put a new lock on the house and at the store." He stepped into the house and followed her to the kitchen. "That is, unless you've already found your keys."

"No, I haven't, but then I haven't looked for them yet this morning." Elma gestured to the stove. "I was about to fix myself some scrambled *oier*. If you care to join me for breakfast, I'll fix enough for the both of us."

Delbert removed his straw hat and scratched his blond head. "I did have a cup of *kaffi* and a *faasnachtkuche* before I left home, but I could probably eat a plate of scrambled eggs."

Elma resisted the urge to tell Delbert that a doughnut and coffee did not make a healthy breakfast. Instead she smiled and said, "Okay, if you want to go down the hall to the bathroom and wash your hands, I'll get the eggs started."

"Okie-dokie." Delbert set his toolbox on the floor, and as he sauntered off, he sneezed.

Remembering his allergy to cats, Elma picked Tiger up and opened the door. "Sorry I have to do this, but out you go." She placed the cat on the porch and quickly shut the door.

Returning to the kitchen, Elma washed her hands at the sink and got started on the eggs. By the time they were done, Delbert was back.

"Is there a katz in the house?" He glanced around. "I started sneezing as I was going down the hall."

"Tiger was in here, but I put him out, so I hope it helps." Elma set two plates on the table, along with the platter of scrambled eggs and two glasses of orange juice.

"My allergies get so bad, sometimes all it takes is being in a house where a cat's been. It's their dander that affects me."

"I'm sorry about that. If I'd known for sure when you were coming, I would have put Tiger out before you got here."

"It's okay. I'll live." Delbert smacked his lips and pulled out a chair. "Looks good, Elma. Danki for asking me to join you."

"You're welcome." She smiled and took the seat across from him. Following Delbert's lead, Elma bowed her head for silent prayer.

When their prayers ended, they ate and talked about the weather, since Elma couldn't think of anything else to talk about. Being alone with Delbert felt strange. It made her think back to their courting days. Only then, Joseph and Thelma had been with them during all of their outings. Delbert and Elma had only been alone on a few occasions, whenever he'd come over to work on the house.

She reflected on the day he'd found carpenter ants in their porch, and how she'd appreciated his help, then and now. There were times Elma wished things could have worked out between them. *But it must not have been meant to be,* she thought. *Delbert may be a confirmed bachelor for the rest of his life, and I, quite likely, will remain an old maid.*

⸎

As Delbert began working on the toilet, his nose twitched. A musty odor in the room led him to check around. Leaning closer in at the flooring near the back wall next to the toilet base, he took the screwdriver out of his pouch to see what might be going on. Delbert knelt down and poked around the flooring near the wall. It chipped up easily as he pushed the tool into the rotted spot. *This needs to be fixed, and now I know why it smells so nasty in here.* He would bring the situation to Elma's attention when he went out to the store later on.

Delbert thought about Elma, and how tired she looked this morning. Seeing the dark circles beneath her eyes, he had a hunch she'd been working too hard and wasn't getting enough sleep. No doubt her responsibilities had increased after Thelma married Joe and moved out of their grandparents' house. In a place this old, things were bound to fall apart, which meant a lot more maintenance.

He put the screwdriver away then picked up the part he needed for the toilet and set it in place. *I wonder if Elma will ever get married. If she was a little more easygoing, like her sister, she'd have a better chance at snagging a man.* His forehead wrinkled. *She is a fine-looking woman, though. Her silky brown hair and pretty blue eyes are what attracted me to her in the beginning. If she hadn't been so persnickety, our relationship might have gone further.*

Delbert couldn't help but envy his good friend. Seeing the look of adoration that Joe and Thelma exchanged last night was enough to make any man jealous. *I don't want somebody tellin' me what to do, but it sure would be nice to have a pretty wife waiting for me at the end of the day with a sweet smile and a home-cooked meal.*

He thought about the two women he'd gone out with a couple of times since he and Elma broke up. Sarah worked at a gift shop in Shipshewana, and he'd met Millie at the hardware store in LaGrange. They were both nice enough, but the connection wasn't there, so they'd gone their separate ways rather quickly.

"Maybe I'm gettin' too old and set in my ways," Delbert muttered as he finished up with the toilet. "Might be best if I learn to be content with my life as it is now and quit hoping for something that's probably never gonna happen."

He stood and arched his back. *Guess I'd better go out to the store and let Elma know I'm done.*

⁓

Elma had just finished waiting on a customer when Delbert entered the store. "Got the toilet fixed," he announced, stepping up to the counter. "But the bad news is, you'll need some floor work done in the near future. The leak you had was dripping down and rotting out the floor behind the toilet. The bad wood will need to be taken out and replaced with new flooring. There's a disgusting odor coming from there too. I'm surprised you didn't mention it to me."

She rubbed her forehead and grimaced. "I have noticed the smell but wasn't sure of the cause."

"Well, when you're ready to do the job let me know." Delbert swiped at his brow.

Elma rested her hand on her hip. "I've wanted to replace that old flooring anyway. It's worn and faded looking."

"I'll run back to the house now and get the square footage you'll need for the new linoleum. That way you'll know how much to order." Delbert pulled his fingers through the end of his hair. "I haven't locked up yet, but I'll do that as soon as I'm finished measuring."

"Oh, good. How much do I owe you?" Elma shifted her weight, trying not to stare at his deep blue eyes.

"Nothing for my labor. I left a bill on your kitchen table for the cost of the parts. No hurry about paying me, though. After I get those floor measurements, I'll leave a note on the table with the bill."

"Danki, Delbert. I'm grateful for all you've done."

Placing both hands on the counter, he leaned close and lowered his voice. "Where do you think you lost your keys?"

Elma shook her head. "I looked all along the path between here and the house but came up empty handed." Her gaze flitted around the room. "I hope if someone else found them they'd be kind enough to say something."

"Well, you can't take any chances. I'll head over to the hardware store and get new locks for all the doors on your house, as well as the front and back door here at the store."

"Danki, Delbert." Elma placed her hand on top of his but quickly pulled it away when another customer approached the counter. "When the job's been done, let me know how much I owe you."

"Will do. See you later, Elma."

Elma smiled and lifted her hand in a brief wave. Delbert seemed a lot nicer than when they'd been courting. Maybe he'd learned a few things about how to treat a woman.

⚬⚭

As the day wore on, exhaustion set in. Yesterday had been busy, but today it seemed like even more customers had come in. Everyone was looking for a bargain, and their supply of material had diminished to less than half.

Elma sighed. *Hopefully there's another box of material in the back of the store. I should have been more prepared for our sale, but I'll make note of this for the future.* She picked up a pen and slid the notepad in front of her. She jotted down a list of supplies and noted an estimate of how much material had been sold. Her eyelids felt heavy as she released a noisy yawn. On Monday, when the store was usually closed, Elma would place an order for more fabric, as well as several other items she'd run low on.

Elma waved her hand at a pesky bee flying around her head. She noticed a few on the windows as well, buzzing and trying to get out. "With all the customers coming and going, is it any wonder there are *ieme* inside?" She opened the front door and shooed some of them out.

"Are you as mied as I am?" Elma asked when her helper joined her at the counter.

"Jah. It's been a busy, tiring day, that's for sure." Anna tugged at her apron band and cleared her throat. "Umm. . .there's something I have to tell you, Elma."

"You look so serious, Anna. What is it?"

The young woman dropped her gaze to the floor and stood silently several seconds. When she lifted her head again, Elma saw tears in Anna's blue eyes. "I find no pleasure in telling you this, but unfortunately, I can only work for you another two weeks."

Elma's posture stiffened. "How come?"

"My *daed* sold his business and my folks are relocating to Arthur, Illinois, where my grandparents live." Anna's arms hung loose at her sides, and her chin trembled slightly. "I don't really want to move, but my place is with my parents and siblings. Besides, my *grossmudder* is not well, and my *mamm*'s going to need my help to take care of Grandma."

Elma reached across the counter and clasped Anna's hand. "You'll be missed, of course, but I understand." Elma had a sinking feeling in the pit of her stomach. There was no way she could expect Thelma to work more than a few days a week, so she'd have to hire someone else.

Trouble was, she had no idea who it could be.

Chapter 5

Grabill, Indiana

Dorothy Wagler glanced at the clock above the refrigerator and frowned. If Ben didn't come in from doing his chores soon she might have to eat breakfast without him, because her driver would be here in thirty minutes.

She peered out the kitchen window but saw no sign of her son. Dorothy tapped her fingers on the edge of the sink then opened a drawer and took out two pot holders. *Sure wish he would hurry. I'm getting hungry, and smelling the buttery, browning casserole is making my mouth water.*

Dorothy went to the refrigerator, took out a pitcher of apple juice, and poured some into two glasses. She picked up her glass and brought it to her lips, savoring the cool, tangy-sweet liquid. "Ahh...this hits the spot."

Next, she removed the steaming breakfast casserole from the oven and placed it on the table, glancing at the clock one more time. *Five more minutes, Ben, and then I'm eating without you.*

After placing the silverware and napkins at each plate, Dorothy slid out her chair. She was about to take a seat at the table when her son rushed into the room. Tilting his head to one side, he pushed a piece of thick brown hair out of his eyes. "What were ya gonna do, Mom, eat *friehschtick* without me?"

Dorothy pointed to the clock. "Reba will be here soon, and if I don't eat breakfast now I won't be ready when she arrives."

"What's she's coming for? Do you have another chiropractic appointment?" He rubbed his clean-shaven chin.

"I hired Reba to drive me to Topeka to see my friend Eileen Lehman."

Dorothy's mouth slackened. "Don't you remember me telling you this during supper last night?"

Ben shrugged his broad shoulders. "Guess I must've forgot."

Dorothy lifted her gaze toward the ceiling. "Goodness gracious, son, you're only thirty-five years old. Your memory shouldn't be giving out on you already."

He grunted, moving to the sink to wash his hands. "My memory's not giving out, Mom. I just have a lot on my mind."

"I know you do, Ben, and I didn't mean to sound condemning. Sorry if I came off that way." Dorothy gestured to the table. "Please, have a seat so we can pray."

Ben pulled out the chair at the head of the table—the place his father used to occupy before he'd died of a heart attack five years ago. Since that time, Ben had taken over running the farm, while trying to keep up with his own horseshoeing business. It was a lot of responsibility for a young single man, but Ben never complained and seemed content to live at home and help his mother. Dorothy wished she had more sons to share the load, or that her daughter, Lucinda, lived closer so that her husband, James, could help out. But they'd moved to Nappanee two years ago and didn't get to visit often.

"Are you sure you wouldn't like to go with me today?" Dorothy tapped Ben's arm. "It's been a while since you've gone anywhere."

"What do you mean? Every time I get a call to shoe a horse, I have to leave the farm."

"You're right. What I should have said is, it's been a while since you went anywhere just for fun."

His brows furrowed. "A visit with your friend Eileen might be fun for you, but I wouldn't have much to say to her. Besides, your trip sounds more like a woman's day out."

"I realize that, but we'll be going out to eat lunch at one of the restaurants in Topeka." She bumped his arm again. "You always enjoy eating out."

"Maybe some other time. This isn't a good day since I have four horses to shoe." He folded his hands. "Shall we pray?"

"Of course." When Dorothy bowed her head and began her silent prayer, she asked God to bless her son and give him the desires of his heart. He was a fine man and deserved all the happiness he could get.

Perhaps someday it would include a wife, for Dorothy certainly didn't want her son to be alone after she died.

❧

Topeka

"I wish you hadn't come to work this morning." Elma pressed her lips together, watching as her sister moved toward the counter with a bolt of material. Thelma's footsteps seemed to drag with each step she took on this warm, humid first Saturday of June.

Normally, Thelma wouldn't be working at the store today, but since Anna's last day was a week ago, Elma would have been on her own today, so Thelma insisted on helping out, just as she had every day this week.

Thelma planted her feet in a wide stance. "I was not about to sit on my front porch and watch customers come and go all day, knowing you were here all alone, trying to do a million things at once."

Elma chuckled, despite her concern. "That's a bit of an exaggeration, wouldn't you say?"

Thelma giggled. "Well, I'm sure you got my meaning."

"I did, and I hope you got my meaning, as well. I'm really surprised Joseph allowed you to come over here today."

Thelma pushed her shoulders back and lifted her chin. "My husband doesn't order me about. Besides, he got up at the crack of dawn to meet Delbert for a little fishing."

Elma's eyes narrowed. "So Joseph doesn't even know you're here. Is that how it is?"

"No, he doesn't, but I'm sure he wouldn't care." Thelma placed the material on the counter. "This is for Eileen Lehman. I believe it's the right shade of green, since she described it as sort of a pine color. She'll be in sometime this morning to get it."

"Oh? When did you talk to her?" Elma brushed her hand across the counter, clearing away several strands of thread.

"Yesterday. I ran into her at the grocery store. She said she'd be coming to the store and told me what kind of material she needed."

"Oh, I see. Guess that's a good enough reason for you to come to work today."

Thelma gave no reply as she skirted around the counter and took a seat on the stool.

Elma released a long, low sigh. *If my sister is determined to be here today, then I'll make sure she doesn't work too hard. She can sit on the stool and wait on customers like she did earlier this week.*

ℰ✦

As the morning wore on, Thelma began to wish she'd stayed home and rested. Even though there were no sales, the store had been full of customers since they first opened. The balls of Thelma's feet ached, and her toes pushed against her leather shoes. She'd been on her feet too long, walking back and forth with bolts of material left on the counter after cutting fabric for some of their customers. How good it would feel to be barefoot right now. *I'll be good as a summer rain once I'm home relaxing with my feet up for a while.*

Thelma yawned, twisting her neck from side to side. *I wonder how Joe and Dell are doing. Wish I could have gone fishing with them. It would be a lot more relaxing than sitting on this hard stool, waiting on customers all morning. I don't understand why my sister won't let me help with more things.*

She glanced at the bolt of material she'd set behind the counter. It was almost noon, but there'd been no sign of Eileen Lehman. *I wonder if she forgot.*

"Are you ready to take your lunch break now?" Elma stepped up next to Thelma.

"I guess so. Sure wish we were able to eat together so we could visit. Seems like we don't get to talk much these days."

Elma placed her hand on Thelma's shoulder. "I'm sorry. With me working long hours at the store, plus having chores at home to do by myself, I don't have much free time anymore."

"Which is why you need to hire someone to help here at the store. There's way too much work for one person to do, and with me only working a few hours each day, most of the responsibility falls on you."

Elma pushed a wayward strand of hair off her face. "It's all right. I'll manage."

"I'll talk to Joseph and see if he can come over in the evenings to help with some of your outside chores."

Elma shook her head. "No, it's okay. He has enough to do at your place. Besides, the two of you need time alone to catch up on your day, make plans for the boppli, and enjoy being husband and wife."

Thelma glanced toward the ceiling at a bee trying to find a way out. Their conversation was interrupted when Eileen and another Amish woman came into the store. She couldn't help noticing the pleats in the woman's skirt and wondered if she might be from Grabill. Although she'd never been to Grabill, Elma had heard the women there wore pleated dresses.

"I'm here for my material." Eileen smiled, her dimples deepening in her slightly wrinkled cheeks. Then she motioned to the dark-haired woman beside her. "This is my friend, Dorothy Wagler. We grew up together in Shipshewana, but now she lives in Grabill and has for a good many years." Eileen gestured to the twins. "Dorothy, I'd like you to meet Thelma Beechy, and her twin sister, Elma Hochstetler."

"It's nice to meet you both." Dorothy offered a pleasant smile as she shook Thelma's and Elma's hands. "Eileen filled me in on how you both acquired this store after your grandparents died."

"Jah." Elma nodded. "It's been a challenge, but things are shaping up here at the store. My grandparents' old house, on the other hand, is still a work in progress."

Dorothy laughed. "I understand. I've lived in my home for over thirty years and still don't have everything the way I'd like it to be. My son lives with me, and his hands are full, running his own business and trying to keep the farm going. So I try not to ask him to do anything around the house unless it's absolutely necessary or something I'm not able to do myself."

"Dorothy's husband, Ray, passed away a few years ago, so trying to keep up the place has become a challenge," Eileen interjected.

"I'm sorry for your loss." Elma placed her hand on Dorothy's arm.

"Danki. It was difficult at first, but Ben and I are managing."

"We'd like to stay and visit awhile, but we're meeting two other friends for lunch, so I'd best pay for my material and get going." Eileen placed her black purse on the counter. "How much do I owe, Thelma?"

"I put your invoice next to the plastic bag." Thelma handed it to her.

While Thelma took care of ringing up Eileen's purchase, Elma waited on another customer who'd been at the back of the store.

"It's been a pleasure to meet you both," Dorothy said when Eileen was ready to go and Elma rejoined them. "Perhaps the next time I get up this way, I'll drop by your store and say hello."

"Jah, please do." Thelma waved, and Elma walked the two ladies to the door.

Elma was about to shut the door behind Eileen and her friend when Lizzie Yoder showed up.

Elma watched as Lizzie tied her horse to the hitching rail. "Are you needing more thread or material?" she asked when Lizzie stepped onto the porch.

Grinning, Lizzie shook her head. "Not today. I heard you were looking for part-time help at the store, and I'd like to apply for the job."

Elma's eyebrows lifted. "Have you had experience working in a store such as this?"

Lizzie's gray head moved quickly up and down. "I worked in a fabric store in LaGrange for a few months, and since I enjoy sewing, I think I'd be perfect for the job." Her voice lowered. "Besides, I'm living alone right now, and could certainly use some money coming in."

"You did say your brother was moving, but I thought a friend would be living with you and sharing expenses."

Lizzie's shoulders pulled inward as she released a heavy sigh. "It didn't work out. I'm on my own."

Elma slipped her arm around the older woman's ample waist, pulling her into a side hug. "Well, then, since you need a job, and I need an extra pair of hands around here, I have only two words to say: you're hired."

Lizzie's eyes brightened. "Can I begin today?"

"I don't see why not. Thelma's worked all morning, but it would be good if she could go home and rest. So you can take over for her the rest of the afternoon."

"Danki, Elma. Okay, then, if you'll show me what to do, I'll get right on it."

"Why don't you head to the room at the back of the store? I'll meet you there as soon as I tell Thelma she's free to go home."

"Okay. No problem." Lizzie's arms swung as she ambled off toward the back of the store.

"I just hired Lizzie to work here part-time." Elma grinned, joining Thelma at the counter again.

Thelma's chin jutted out. "I'm not sure that's such a good idea, Sister."

"Why not?" Elma's smile faded.

"You know as well as I do that Lizzie tends to be forgetful." Thelma spoke quietly with one hand cupped around her mouth. "She also talks too much, and at her age, I doubt she'll be able to keep up with all the work needing to be done here."

"She says she's had experience working in a fabric shop in LaGrange, so I'm sure she'll do fine." Elma placed her hands on Thelma's shoulders. "Lizzie is starting work right now, actually. So you're free to go home now and take it easy the rest of the day."

Thelma blinked. "Are you kidding me?"

"Course not. I can see the fatigue on your face, and do I need to remind you what the doctor said about making sure you get plenty of rest?"

Thelma leaned forward, elbows on the counter. "I may as well do as you say, because I'm sure I will not win this argument." She glanced toward the back of the store and whispered, "I only hope you didn't make a mistake hiring Lizzie."

Elma bit down on her bottom lip. *I hope not either, because if I did, it will be difficult to tell poor Lizzie I don't need her help anymore.*

Chapter 6

LaGrange, Indiana

"The *fisch* aren't bitin' so good today, are they?" Delbert set his pole aside and leaned back, clasping his hands behind his head.

Joseph grunted. "I wouldn't complain if I were you." He pointed at the cooler near Delbert's feet. "You've caught two more fish than I have."

"True, but you know what, Joe? Even if I didn't catch a single fish all day, I'd enjoy being here at the pond with my best friend, taking in all the sights, sounds, and smells of nature. There ain't nothing better, as the old saying goes."

"I know exactly what you mean." Joseph gestured to a line of beetles trundling along a rotten log. "Nature at its finest, jah?"

Delbert reached over and poked his friend's arm. "You enjoy watchin' a bunch of *keffer*?"

Joseph snickered. "Sure do. All kinds of bugs are interesting to watch."

"Personally, I'd rather look at a butterfly or dragonfly."

"Now you sound like my fraa and her *zwilling*. Just the other day when we had a picnic in our yard, the twins were having fun watching all the butterflies."

"I doubt they saw any big ones this early yet. The monarchs aren't usually seen till the later summer months."

"You sound like an expert on the subject." Joseph grinned. "Now I've learned something about you I didn't know before."

Delbert rolled his eyes. "Don't you remember when we were boys and I used to catch butterflies with a net so I could study them awhile before letting 'em go?"

235

"Oh, yeah, I forgot about that." Joseph removed his straw hat and fanned his face with the brim. "Seems so long ago. The biggest thing on my mind these days is making sure Thelma takes good care of herself as we anxiously await the arrival of our boppli."

"Are you *naerfich* about becoming a daed?"

"Jah, a little nervous. Never expected to get married, much less father any children." His forehead wrinkled. "Sure hope I'll be a good daed."

"Ah, you'll do fine. I know you can't compare the two, but look how good you take care of Ginger. You have a caring heart, and I know you'll be a great daed."

"Danki for giving me the vote of confidence."

Squinting against the sunlight streaming through the trees, Delbert swatted a mosquito that had landed on his arm. "Doesn't look promising for me to ever get married or have any kinner. Guess I'm too set in my ways for true romance to blossom."

Joseph gave Delbert's shoulder a squeeze. "Don't give up, my friend. The right woman's out there for you somewhere. Who knows, it could even be someone you've courted before."

Delbert's eyebrows rose as he cocked his head to one side. "Are you thinking of anyone in particular?"

With a wink, Joseph shrugged. "I'll let you figure it out."

Delbert pointed to the other side of the pond before reeling in his line. "Now there's a nice sight to see a woman and a boy fishing together."

Joseph looked in that direction. "Isn't that the widow Rachel Lambright and her son, Ryan?"

"Yep, I believe you're right." Delbert reached into his lunch-box cooler, removed two bottles of root beer, and held one out to Joseph. "Are ya thirsty?"

Joseph's eyes lit up. "Sounds good."

The two sat sipping their sodas while three young fellows walked by with their poles. The boys went a ways up from them and wasted no time getting their lines in the water.

Delbert watched in amazement as one of the boys reeled in a fish. "Did you see that, Joe? The boy got a big one right away."

Joseph cupped his hands around his mouth. "That's a keeper. Nice work!"

"Thanks," the boy called back. "This is my favorite spot for catching the good ones."

"I think he just caught your fish, Joe," Delbert teased.

Joseph bobbed his head. "Maybe we oughta try that location the next time we come here to fish."

"Jah, if someone doesn't beat us to it, that is."

$\sim$

Topeka

Thelma sat on the front porch of her home, hands clasped over her stomach as the wicker rocker moved steadily back and forth. She intended to do some mending while watching the birds eat at the feeders this morning, but her sewing basket still sat on the small table beside her. She couldn't help that her blue-skied mood had turned to gray. It was hard not to feel useless as she watched several cars, as well as horse and buggies, go up and down the driveway leading to the store up behind Elma's house.

Wish I could work there full-time again. Sure miss the connection with the customers. Now Lizzie gets to work there in my absence and visit with everyone who comes into the store. Thelma shifted slightly in her chair. *Seems at this stage in my life I need to pray for patience and learn to be content.*

Thelma rested her head comfortably for a moment, while soft breezes tickled her face. *I'm sure I won't miss it so much once the baby is born. Joseph and Elma are probably right: it's important for me to take it easy right now.*

Thelma smiled when she felt the baby kick. Oh, how she looked forward to becoming a mother.

Her gaze lowered when a wet tongue slurped her ankle. Joseph's golden retriever looked up at her with solemn brown eyes and whined.

"I know, Ginger, you're missing your master too." She combed her fingers through the dog's silky hair. Quite often when Joseph went fishing, he took Ginger along for company. But not today. This morning he'd mentioned that he planned to make a couple of stops after he and Delbert went their separate ways and didn't want Ginger waiting in the open buggy for him. In addition to the hot sun beating down on the animal, she might jump out and try to follow him into one of the stores, like she'd done once before.

Thelma closed her eyes and leaned her head against the back of the rocker as she continued to rock.

Yip! Yip!

She stopped rocking, and her eyes snapped open. "Sorry, Ginger. I didn't mean to rock on your tail." Thelma checked the dog over to be sure she was all right.

Ginger was a good companion. Talking to the dog was better than sitting here all alone. *Maybe I'm dealing with those silly hormones other pregnant women have talked about.* She patted her stomach when the baby kicked again. *There's a miracle inside me, and I need to stop feeling sorry for myself. If anyone's to be pitied, it's my sister. She works so hard and lives all alone in that big old house without a word of complaint. Sure hope Elma didn't make a mistake hiring Lizzie to help out in the store. I wonder how things are going over there this afternoon.*

Elma was relieved when things slowed down at the store after Thelma went home, because Lizzie wasn't working out quite as well as she'd hoped. In addition to moving about the store like a turtle carrying a load of bricks, the chatterbox spent too much time visiting with customers.

And I thought my sister was talkative. Lizzie could talk circles around Thelma. Elma sat on the stool behind the counter, pressing her fingers to her temples. *Maybe things will get better after she's worked here awhile. I can't expect her to do everything right on the first day. Sure hope that's how it goes, because Lizzie needs a job, and I certainly need help.*

Elma glanced at the clock on the wall across from her. One more hour and she'd be closing the store for the day. She looked forward to going to church tomorrow, and except for feeding the animals, it would be a day of rest. Most assuredly, she needed some time to let down. More than likely she'd spend Sunday afternoon with Thelma and Joseph. One more thing to look forward to.

"Yeow! *Iem schtachel!*"

Bee sting? Elma jumped off the stool and raced to the back of the store, where she found poor Lizzie wincing while holding her thumb. "When I picked up a bolt of material, I didn't notice the bee on it, until the pest stung me." She gave a slow, disbelieving shake of her head. "This has not been a good day for me. First, I dropped a box on my foot. Then

I bruised my knee when I bumped into the step stool in the back room. And now this." Lizzie's face contorted. "I hope you don't think I'm accident prone."

"No, of course not." Elma moved closer to Lizzie. "Are you okay? You're not allergic to bee stings, I hope."

Lizzie shook her head. "Never have been before, and I've been stung plenty of times over the years. It hurts like crazy, but I'm sure I'll be fine."

"Let's go in the back room, and I'll get out the first-aid kit. I have a homeopathic remedy specifically for bee stings."

"Okay." Lizzie offered Elma a weak smile. "I hope there aren't any more *ieme* in the store. One nasty sting is enough for this old lady."

Elma's lip curled, remembering the bees she'd seen here a few weeks ago. She didn't want to risk having any customers getting stung and would need to find a way to keep the bees out of the store. It probably wouldn't hurt to take a look outside around the perimeter of the store to see if there were any bee nests. She wouldn't do it without bug spray, though. There might be a can in the back of the store, or for sure, underneath the kitchen sink at the house.

Maybe Delbert could take care of the problem by putting in new screens on the windows, and possibly adding a screen door at the front of the store. Elma tapped her chin. He'd been by earlier this week and put new flooring down in the bathroom. Before Delbert left, he'd told Elma to let him know if she needed anything else. *Think I'll give him a call this evening and see when he'd be free to come by again.*

Elma stepped into the back room behind Lizzie. "If you'll take a seat, I'll have a look at your thumb."

∽

Grabill

"I hope you don't mind cold sandwiches tonight, Ben." Dorothy set a platter of lunch meat and cheese on the table. "I got back from Topeka later than expected and felt too *mied* to fix a big meal."

"It's fine, Mom. I'm tired myself, so a lighter meal is okay by me." Ben took a seat at the head of the table, and when he bowed his head, Dorothy did the same.

After they finished praying, she passed him the bread. "How'd your day go?"

"It was busy. After I got all my customers' horses shoed, I worked in the fields awhile and watered your garden."

Her cheekbones grew warm as she clasped his arm. "Danki. I meant to do it this morning, but my driver showed up, so I figured I'd have to do it when I got home."

"Now you don't have to worry about it at all." Ben helped himself to the meat and cheese then slathered his bread with mayonnaise.

"You're such a considerate son. Don't know what I'd do without you."

A flush crept across his face. "Now don't get all sentimental, Mom. I'm only doing what any good *sohn* would do for his mamm."

Dorothy handed him a bowl of strawberry gelatin. "You've made a lot of sacrifices for me since your daed's passing. A man your age ought to be married and starting his own family, instead of taking care of his old mother."

"First of all, you're not old." Ben's glass dripped with condensation as he took a drink. "And even if I had a fraa and kinner, I'd still see to your needs."

"I believe you would." Dorothy fiddled with her napkin, wondering how best to tell Ben the plans she'd made for tomorrow. He wouldn't like it if he thought she was trying to play matchmaker, but desperate times called for desperate measures.

"How come you're staring at your plate? Aren't you gonna eat, Mom?"

"Umm, jah. I was thinking, is all." She picked up a piece of bread.

"About what?" His voice muffled as he bit into his sandwich.

"About what I should fix for Sunday evening supper. Is there anything special you'd like to have?"

He lifted his broad shoulders. "Don't go to any trouble on my account. We hardly ever have a big meal on Sundays, unless we're having company."

"Well, actually. . ." Dorothy paused to make her sandwich.

"Actually, what, Mom?"

"I invited the Grabers to spend Sunday evening with us. Since they moved a few miles south, and are no longer in our church district, I thought it would be nice if we had some time to visit. I'm not sure what to fix for supper, though. What do you think about a roast with potatoes and carrots?"

Ben shrugged, popped the last of his sandwich into his mouth, and chewed. "I didn't realize you missed seeing them so much. As I recall, you and Paul's Ada were never that close."

"Maybe we're not close, but we do know each other, and. . ."

He slapped the table with his open hand, looking directly at her. "Oh, wait a minute. Think I'm beginning to understand. You invited the Grabers, hoping they'll bring their unmarried daughter along. Am I right?"

"Well. . ."

"Forget it, Mom. If it's meant for me to find a fraa, I'll do my own looking. So please don't try to match me up with Martha Graber." His forehead wrinkled. "Besides, she's ten years younger than me, not to mention we have nothing in common."

"Okay, but you need to keep an open mind."

Ben lifted his cup and sipped. "My mind is open, and I know you worry about me, Mom, but there's no need. I'm perfectly happy being single."

Dorothy wasn't sure about that, but if things didn't work out between Ben and Martha, she would keep looking. There had to be a young woman here in Grabill good enough for her son. Of course, it would have to be someone who was content to remain in Allen County, because this was Ben's home, and hers too. If he should ever decide to move, Dorothy didn't know what she would do.

Chapter 7

Topeka

"You've been quiet all evening, Thelma. Is something bothering you?" Joseph asked after opening their bedroom window.

"No, not really." Thelma pulled the bedcovers aside, breathing in the moist night air. "I've been thinking about Elma."

"Is it about her being lonely or working too hard at the store?"

Thelma took a seat on the end of the bed and removed the pins holding her bun in place. "I'm concerned about both of those things, but just now I was thinking about Elma and Delbert."

Joseph took a seat beside her and combed his fingers through her long hair as it cascaded down her back. "What about her and Delbert?"

"He's been over at her place a lot lately." She smiled, leaning back and enjoying her husband's attention. "Wouldn't it be something if he and Elma got together after all?"

"I don't think it's likely to happen. Remember how things went between them when they courted before? Like when Delbert and I met you both at the pond to fish for the first time. Do you recall how Dell chose to sit in his favorite fishing chair and left your sister alone on the blanket she'd brought along to share?"

Thelma gave a slow nod.

"I remember the tension during that moment." Joseph raised his eyebrows. "It was awkward for me, and I'm certain it was for you too."

"Jah, I admit, it was a little trying. Nonetheless, in the beginning of their relationship there was a definite attraction, and I'm sure my sister and Delbert were simply having a difficult time reading one another. Anyway, with the months that have passed since then, things could change."

Thelma sighed when Joseph picked up the brush she'd placed on the bed and began brushing her hair.

"Some things may have changed, but not necessarily them. Delbert's the same person he was two years ago, and so is your sister," Joseph reminded her.

"True, but I don't believe he'd go over there so often if he wasn't interested in her."

"Delbert's not paying social calls, Thelma. He's been doing work for Elma. A few days ago he put new screens in all the store windows, added a screen door, and took care of the bee problem."

"I realize that, but the more time they spend together, the better the chance for some little spark to be rekindled." Thelma tapped her chin while clicking her tongue. "Tomorrow's Saturday, and with the weather being so nice, I think we ought to have an evening barbecue."

"Sounds good to me. What kind of meat do you want me to cook?"

"I was thinking burgers, and we can invite Elma and Delbert to join us."

Joseph set the hairbrush down and reached over to clasp her hand. "Now don't get any ideas about playing matchmaker. If Dell and Elma are meant to be together, they don't need any help from either of us."

"I won't push, but they might need a little nudge."

He leaned over and kissed her cheek. "Let's forget about your twin sister and my best friend for now and concentrate on us."

Thelma slipped her hands around Joseph's neck and gave him a hug. "I love you, husband."

"I love you too, my dear sweet wife."

⁂

When Elma opened the store Saturday morning, she was hit with a blast of warm air. For the latter part of June the weather had gotten quite hot, with high humidity making it hard to sleep even with the windows open at night. Last night, there'd been only a little breeze. If Elma didn't get the store cooled off, any customers who came in would be miserable.

She hurried to open all the windows, thankful for the new screens Delbert had installed earlier in the week. She also made sure the front door was left open so whatever breeze might come up could blow through the new screen door too. If it got too hot, Elma would turn on a few of the battery-operated fans she had for sale in the store. Stirring up the air would help a bit more. Elma was also relieved that she no longer had bees sneaking into the store and possibly stinging someone else.

She glanced out the window. No sign of Lizzie yet. *I hope she gets here before too many customers show up. She was late yesterday too. Oh dear, those potted flowers out there on the front porch are drooping. I'd better give them a drink of water.*

She pushed the screen door open and let it slap shut. There weren't any customers yet, so Elma got under way with the job at hand. She grabbed the coiled-up hose against the side of the store and added the nozzle to the end. Then Elma hauled the hose up the stairs, yanking on it when it became caught on one of the rungs. After twisting and yanking some more, she was able to free the hose. The tired old stairs creaked and moaned under her feet. There was quite a bit of rough wood showing that needed repair.

She frowned. *I'm not happy with these treads. I wish they were new and sturdy like the front porch of my house. Guess I'll need to add that to my list of things for Delbert to do.*

Elma began watering the flowers, when suddenly the water stopped. "Now what?" She twisted and turned the nozzle. Fearing something happened to the well pump, her gaze followed the hose's length down the steps. It was then she realized there was a crimp in the hose. "Well, at least it's not the pump." Elma breathed a sigh of relief as she unkinked the section that kept the water from flowing.

After the watering was done, Elma went back inside and gave herself a quick check. Looking down at her dark brown dress, she noticed a white cobweb clinging to the skirt. After brushing it away, she spotted a small spider crawling on her hand. "Yikes!" Elma slapped the bug off and stomped on it. "I hate *schpinne!*" she grumbled under her breath.

Elma moved about the store, making sure everything was in place, until she spotted a pile of debris near the back room, next to the broom and dustpan. Before leaving for home yesterday, Lizzie said she would sweep up the mess and dispose of it properly. She'd obviously forgotten.

Elma gritted her teeth. *She either forgot or got busy talking to someone, like she's done several times since I hired her to work here. I probably should speak to Lizzie about it, but I don't want to hurt her feelings. Besides, it's good to have a friendly relationship with our customers.*

Elma grabbed the dustpan and swept up the mess. *If you want something done, you may as well do it yourself. It's the quickest way to accomplish the task.* She groaned. *But then if I do all the work, what was the point in hiring Lizzie to help out in the store?*

It was almost nine thirty when Lizzie showed up. By then, five customers stood in line at the counter. Lizzie's plump cheeks colored like a bright red rose as she limped across the room. Elma noticed the elderly woman wore one black shoe and one sandal. Lizzie's swollen big toe poked out of the open-toed sandal.

"Oh, my! What happened to your toe?" Elma asked.

Lizzie moved toward the counter, wincing as she walked. "I dropped a jar of pickles on my foot last night, and my big toe took the brunt of it."

"How awful. It must hurt a lot."

Lizzie gave a nod. "It's not broken, though—only bruised. Had my driver take me to the hospital emergency room last night to have it checked out. The doctor said to stay off my feet as much as possible and put ice on the toe."

"You should have stayed home today and rested your foot." Elma spoke in a soothing tone.

"No way was I going to leave you in the lurch." Lizzie raised her dimpled hand.

Elma stepped down from the stool. "Well, then, you'd best sit here and wait on customers today, while I take care of other things."

Lizzie didn't have to be told twice. She made her way behind the counter and took a seat on the stool. Then she got down again. "Oops, I almost forgot." Lizzie pulled a small cushion out of her satchel. "I hope you don't mind, but I brought along something soft to sit on. In fact, you can keep it here for the counter stool. It'll be comfortable for Thelma, and you can sit on it too."

"Good idea, Lizzie. Would you like to rub some Arnica on your toe?" Elma asked. "There's a tube of it in my first-aid kit. As you probably know, it's good for bruises and other injuries."

"Danki for your thoughtfulness."

"You're welcome." *Poor Lizzie,* Elma thought, as she hurried to the back of the store. *I hope coming here today won't be too much for her. Oh, I wish Thelma was free to work full-time again.*

By closing time, Elma was so tired she could barely put one foot in front of the other. While Lizzie waited on customers, she ran back and forth directing people to the items they wanted, cleaning up after anyone who dropped something on the floor, cutting material, and placing the bolts back on the shelf.

Elma was putting away the last bolt of material when she heard a deep droning noise coming from the front of the store. She set the fabric in place and hurried up front to investigate the sound. Halting her footsteps, her mouth dropped open. Lizzie was bent over, with her head on the counter. Her snores sounded like the reverberation of buggy wheels when some of the young Amish fellows got into a racing match.

Elma covered her mouth, stifling a snicker. Lizzie's fatigue wasn't what tickled her funny bone, though. It was the vibration of her snores against the wooden counter.

Sucking in a deep breath to rein in her emotions, Elma stepped around the counter and gave Lizzie's shoulders a gentle shake.

"*Was is letz do?*" Lizzie sat up with a start.

"Nothing's going on here." Elma spoke softly. "You nodded off, and I needed to wake you because it's time to close up the store and go home."

Lizzie leaned her head back and released a noisy yawn. "Oh, my, I must have been more tired than I thought." Glassy eyed, she glanced around. "Sure hope I didn't miss anyone wanting to pay for their items."

Elma shook her head. "Everyone's gone. I'm sure the last ones left before you fell asleep." *At least I hope that was the case.*

A horn tooted from outside, causing Elma to jump.

"I'll bet it's my driver. With my toe hurting so badly, I didn't want the bother of hitching my horse to the buggy this morning." Lizzie stepped off the stool and winced when her feet hit the floor. "I'm glad you let me sit up here most of the day. Don't think I'd have been able to do all the things you did today."

"Would you like me to go to the back room and get your empty lunch basket?"

Lizzie gave a quick nod. "I'd appreciate it."

As Elma headed back to get the basket, she thought about the cookout she'd been invited to at Thelma and Joseph's this evening. As tired as she was, she wouldn't be the best company, but at least it meant not having to cook a meal. If things went as they usually did whenever Thelma's husband fired up the barbecue grill, he would do all of the cooking. A little relaxation was what she needed.

When Elma entered her sister and brother-in-law's backyard, she was surprised to see Delbert standing near the barbecue grill, talking to Joseph. Ginger rolled around in the grass nearby. When Thelma invited her to join them this evening she hadn't mentioned Delbert would be here.

As Elma approached, he looked over at her and smiled. "*Guder owed*, Elma. I didn't know you'd be here this evening. But then, guess I should have figured as much, since you live right across the street, not to mention being Thelma's twin sister."

Elma smiled in return. "Good evening, Delbert. I'm surprised to see you as well." She glanced around then looked at Joseph. "Is Thelma inside?"

"Jah. She'll be bringing out the paper plates and silverware, along with the potato salad she made."

"I'll go see if she needs any help." Elma gave the men a brief nod then hurried into the house. She found Thelma in the kitchen, putting paper plates, napkins, and plastic silverware on a serving tray.

Thelma smiled. "Oh, good, I'm glad you made it. I was afraid after working in the store all day you might be too tired to come over."

Elma shook her head. "I'm never too tired to spend time with you and Joseph."

"Delbert's here too." Thelma took a bowl of potato salad from the refrigerator.

"I know. I spoke to him a few minutes before coming in here."

"I hope you don't mind that we invited him."

"Course not. It's your right to invite whomever you choose." Elma gestured to the tray. "Would you like me to carry it outside to the picnic table?"

"That'd be great. I'll bring the potato salad and condiments for the burgers on another tray."

"Maybe I should carry that one for you." Elma handed Thelma the silverware tray. "This is lighter and will be easier for you."

Thelma's brows furrowed as she pressed both hands against her hips. "I am perfectly capable of carrying the other tray. Besides, it's not that heavy."

"Okay, if you insist." Elma could see by the determined set of her sister's jaw that she was not going to give in. Thelma could be so stubborn sometimes.

"Is that a new dress you're wearing?"

"Jah. I've been eyeing the new color for a couple weeks at the store and finally decided to treat myself to a new dress." Elma gave a wide grin. "It's not my usual color choice, but I thought a change might be nice."

"That shade of lavender looks nice on you. You should wear it more often." Thelma's voice lowered. "I think Delbert's changed since we first met him, don't you?" She glanced out the kitchen window.

"Changed in what way?"

"He seems to be more even tempered."

"Maybe so. I hadn't really noticed."

Thelma turned to face her. "Maybe you should be more observant."

"What do you mean?"

"Oh, nothing." Thelma set the potato salad along with ketchup, mustard, mayonnaise, and pickles on the tray and picked it up. "Let's join the men. I think this is going to be a fun evening."

Elma wished she had her twin's enthusiasm. With Delbert here, she didn't feel like she could really be herself.

Chapter 8

Grabill

"Where are you going?" Ben's mother asked when he started for the back door Saturday evening.

"Out to the barn to groom the horses," he called over his shoulder. "Think I'll wash 'em down before I start brushing."

"Sounds good. I'm sure the animals would enjoy a good bath." Mom sipped her coffee and set the mug in front of her. "But can you wait a few minutes before you go outside? I want to talk to you about something."

"Okay." Ben snatched his straw hat from the wall hook and turned back around. "What's up, Mom?"

"As you know, with this warm weather we've been having, my garden is doing quite well."

He gave a nod, pressing his back against the counter. "Jah, those cherry tomatoes and the Early Girls you're raising are mouthwatering. Their taste is far better than the ones they pick early and ship to the markets."

"True, and I'm thinking of taking some of my produce to the farmers' market in Shipshewana next month. Maybe the second Wednesday of July."

"Wouldn't you rather set up a fruit and vegetable stand in front of our place, like you've done in years past?"

Mom shook her head. "With the abundance of produce I have, I'd never get it all sold. By going to the market, I might be able to make some extra money to put aside for something I need later. Shipshewana brings in not only the locals, but a huge number of tourists as well."

"Good point. You might check with one of our drivers who owns a truck to see if they'd be available to take you that day." Ben shifted his weight. "Anything else?"

"Umm, jah—two things, actually."

He crossed his arms, waiting for her to continue while trying to remain patient. Sometimes Mom could be a bit long winded.

Ben thought about the customers he had to see this week. He wasn't sure until he verified his schedule, but it was getting closer to the time he'd be checking in on one of his biggest clients.

"Son, are you paying attention to me?" With arms crossed, Mom's foot tapped against the shiny linoleum floor.

"Sorry, Mom. I have a lot on my mind. Now what were you saying?"

"Well, first of all. . ." She stepped forward and stroked the side of his face. "It doesn't look like you've shaved today."

"I did it first thing this morning." He wiped a hand across his stubbly chin. "I can't help it that my beard grows faster than most men's."

"If you were married, you could let your beard grow, and it wouldn't be a problem."

Ben backed away, lifting his chin. "Please don't start with that again, Mom. If the good Lord wanted me to have a wife, she would look me right in the eye and say, 'Benjamin Wagler, you're the man I love and can't live without.'"

With a shake of her head, Mom snickered. "Not many women would be so bold."

"Exactly." He turned toward the door again and put on his hat. "Now if you don't need me for anything else, I'd better get out to the barn and take care of the *geil*."

"I do have one other quick question."

Ben paused, with his hand on the doorknob. "What is it?"

"When I take my produce to the farmers' market, would you like to go along?"

"It depends on whether I have any horses to put shoes on that day."

"Can't you make sure not to schedule any? I could use some help setting up my stand, and maybe during the sale things will go well, and I'll get a lot of business."

"Okay, but if I'm not free that day, you'd better see if someone else is free to go with you."

Mom gave him a wide smile then pointed to the door. "Better not keep those horses waiting."

"You're right. I'm on my way."

⟡

When Ben went outside, Dorothy got out a notebook and pen then took a seat at the kitchen table to make a list of all the garden produce she wanted to take to the farmers' market. She had peas and beans aplenty, as well as onions, zucchini, and tomatoes. In a few more weeks, carrots, cucumbers, and maybe some beets would also be ready.

Maybe I should also pick some of my colorful flowers to sell. Surely there would be some people attending the market who might be interested in buying a lovely bouquet.

Dorothy smiled, thinking about the fuss Martha Graber had made over her flowers when she'd been here last Sunday for supper with her folks. Martha especially admired the zinnias. Dorothy couldn't blame her. Zinnias were one of her favorite flowers too. Bunched together in the flower bed, their rainbow of color was not to be missed.

Martha was as stunning as those flowers. A beautiful young woman such as her, with hair the color of straw and eyes as blue as the summer sky, would make any man stop and take notice. *How could my son not be interested in someone as lovely as her?*

Dorothy tapped the end of her pen along her jaw. *I need to have Martha over again, only this time without her parents. After supper I'll discreetly retire to my room, leaving Ben and Martha alone to visit. If they spend enough time together, surely they'll find some things they have in common.* She set the pen down and poured herself a cup of coffee. *My son's too timid for his own good. He needs to be more assertive around women.*

⟡

Ben finished washing his buggy horse, Fella, and led him back to the stall. Once inside, he grabbed the currycomb to untangle the animal's mane and tail. As Ben worked the comb slowly and carefully through Fella's hair, he couldn't help thinking about what his mom had said earlier. *"If you were married, you could let your beard grow, and it wouldn't be a problem."*

Ben sucked in a breath. *I understand why Mom wants me to find a wife, but she's trying to match me up with who she thinks is the right woman for me.* His shoulders slumped. It had been awkward the other evening when the Grabers came for supper. It was especially uncomfortable having Martha sitting across from him, and not finding much in common to talk about. *Mom means well, but I'm old enough to make my own decisions. I might decide to stay single, if that's what I choose to do with my life.*

Ben switched from the comb and used the soft-bristled brush, working it along the horse's side, while Fella munched on his hay. The sweet grassy aroma filled the air, tickling Ben's nose. The barn was quiet and peaceful—a nice area to think—just him and the horses.

Mom's buggy horse, Patsy, chewed on the hay in her stall across from them. Ben had taken care of her earlier. Patsy possessed a mild demeanor, which Dad had said he felt from the moment he'd purchased her at an auction. He brought her home for Mom so she would have an easygoing horse.

Ben preferred to take Fella out with his buggy, and sometimes he rode horseback. In addition to having more get-up-and-go, the horse always brought Ben numerous compliments. Even strangers commented on the animal's shiny, deep chestnut color. It was hard not to feel prideful.

Stepping away from Fella, Ben admired his work. All the brushing he'd done brought out a nice sheen to the horse's stunning coat. "Fella, you look good enough to take out on the town." He carried the brush and comb out of the stall and put them away. Then he went outside to where he'd given the horses their baths and returned the sponges to the shelf in the barn. Following that, Ben began coiling up the hose. When he backed up, he tripped over the bucket. Soapy water splashed out, soaking Ben's pant legs. "Oh, great!" He glanced toward the house and saw Mom looking out the window, shaking her head. *She probably thinks I'm a clumsy* dummkopp.

Heat flooded Ben's face as he retrieved the bucket and hurried back to the barn.

Topeka

"Those were some mighty good burgers, Joe. I couldn't stop at two, so I had to have three." Delbert laced his fingers together and placed his hands behind his head. "My compliments to the cook."

Joseph's face flushed a bit. "It doesn't take much to grill burgers. The real compliment should go to my fraa for her tangy potato salad. But I'm glad you enjoyed eating the meat." He paused and smiled at Thelma.

Delbert smacked his lips. "You're right. The salad was *appenditlich*. I had to have a second helping, in fact." He grinned at Thelma. "If I could find a single woman who made potato salad this good, I'd marry her tomorrow."

With little thought of what she was about to say, Thelma pointed to Elma. "My sister makes potato salad every bit as delicious as mine."

Elma's face flushed a deep crimson, while Delbert's ears turned bright pink.

Hoping to cover her slip of the tongue, Thelma changed the subject. "How did things go at the store today, Elma?"

"They were hectic, since Lizzie couldn't do any more than sit on the stool and wait on customers."

"How come? Doesn't she usually help with other things?" The question came from Joseph.

"Normally, she does, but Lizzie came to work today with a badly bruised big toe. She could barely walk, so I had no choice but to let her sit behind the counter, which meant I was on my feet most of the day. She did bring a cushion for the stool, which she said we could keep there."

"How'd she hurt her toe?" Thelma reached for her glass of iced tea, rubbing her fingers where moisture collected.

"She dropped a jar of *bickels* on it. Lizzie thought at first it might be broken, but the doctor said it was only a bad bruise." Elma sighed heavily. "I hate to say this, but Lizzie seems prone to accidents."

"That's not all." Thelma shook her head. "When I was helping at the store yesterday, I couldn't help noticing how forgetful Lizzie seemed to be. She was also quite the chatterbox with customers."

Delbert leaned forward, resting his elbows on his knees. "Sounds to me like her name oughta be 'Dizzy Lizzie.'" He chuckled and so did Joseph. Even Thelma had to hide a snicker behind her hand.

A slight muscle jumped in Elma's left cheek. "Better not say anything like that in front of poor Lizzie. She may have a few quirks, but she's really a dear soul."

"Maybe so, but from what I saw while installing new screens, that 'dear soul' is more of a hindrance than a help, Elma. If I were you, I'd look for someone more dependable to work in the store."

Elma's lips pressed together as her face tightened. "I appreciate your concern, Delbert, but as long as I'm in charge of the store, I'll decide who stays and who goes."

A sheen of sweat erupted on Delbert's forehead as he lifted his hands as if in surrender. "Okay, okay. . .no need to get all *umgerennt*."

"I am not upset." Elma folded her arms and looked the other way.

Thelma sagged in her chair, pressing a hand against her stomach. *Maybe I was wrong thinking Elma and Delbert might get together. It seems the problem between them from before is still there. If they could just learn to agree to disagree, things might go better. Well, I'm not giving up yet. Perhaps I'll try again some other time when Elma isn't so tired.*

Chapter 9

Since the store was usually closed on Mondays, Elma used this time to get caught up on things around the house and run errands. She had her lists on the kitchen table, where she'd been jotting down a few late additions.

Elma brewed some black tea and sat nibbling on blueberries that had come from her garden. "Yum. These berries are sure tasty." She added a dollop of vanilla yogurt and smacked her lips.

Tiger sat in a sunny spot on the floor not far from her. He seemed content, although he blinked his eyes against the intense light.

"I wish you could do some chores for me, Tiger. How about going out to the barn and getting the horse ready for me this morning?" Elma chuckled.

Tiger meowed; then his tongue came out as he began grooming himself. When he finished his bath, he plopped down and closed his eyes.

Elma picked up her dishes and went to the sink. She still needed to get her horse, Pearl, ready in the barn, but she needed to finish up in the kitchen first.

It would be nice if Thelma could come with me today. I'd welcome her company, and maybe she could drive Pearl while I jot down more items to my lists. Elma rinsed the blueberry juice from the bowl. *I miss the quality time we used to share.*

Today, being the last Monday in June, she'd decided to make a run to town for groceries and a few other items. One of the things she wanted to do was look for baskets she could use to display her garden produce when she went to the farmers' market next month. This would be Elma's first time renting a stand at the market, and she hoped it would be a profitable day.

In addition to selling her garden produce, Elma planned to take a few handmade items, along with flyers listing some of the things sold in the store and giving directions on how to get there. While most of the locals knew about Elma and Thelma's store, many tourists did not. So her trip to Shipshewana the second Wednesday of July would have a twofold purpose.

Joseph would take time from his harness shop that day to accompany Elma and Thelma to the market. Of course, they'd have to close the store. Elma certainly couldn't expect Lizzie to manage by herself. Thelma had agreed, saying it would be less to worry about having the store closed for the day. There were times, like the day Lizzie had come to work with a bruised toe, when the poor woman could barely function. Expecting Lizzie to run the store by herself would be asking for trouble.

Elma had already taken the buggy out of the shed in readiness for her trip to town, so she placed her purse inside on the seat and headed for the barn to get Pearl. Stepping through the tall double doors and into the building, she heard the rustle of hay and smelled nose-tickling straw, but didn't hear her horse's usual whinny-greeting or hooves scuffing the wooden floor.

The old boards creaked as she made her way over to Pearl's stall. The gate whined when she opened it and stepped inside. Pearl stood with her backside near the wall, almost as if she was leaning against it for support.

"What's the matter, girl? Are you mad at me for not putting you in the pasture this morning so you could run and kick up your heels?" Elma ran a currycomb over the curve of the mare's back. "Well, I had a good reason. I need you to take me to town."

Pearl nickered, nuzzling Elma's hand.

Elma smiled. She loved this old horse, and felt ever so thankful Dad had brought her to them a few years ago, when he and Mom came for a visit. Pearl was gentle and reliable—nothing like Rusty, the unpredictable horse they'd inherited from their grandfather when he and Grandma died, leaving them the house and store. Rusty was spirited and could be a handful at times.

Elma was glad Thelma had taken Rusty as her horse when she'd married Joseph. From the start, she'd been able to control him better than Elma could. Elma figured Rusty rightly sensed her fear. Merely thinking about the feisty gelding made her break out in a cold sweat.

Elma put Pearl's lead rope in place to take her from the stall, but the horse only snorted with huffing breaths and wouldn't budge.

"Come on, girl, now don't you be stubborn this morning." Elma gave a tug.

Pearl took a few faltering steps and halted. The horse seemed to be favoring her right back leg, appearing not to put any weight on it.

"What's the matter, Pearl?" Elma looked down, and she gasped when she saw a nasty gash on the horse's back leg. "Ach, you poor thing. No wonder you don't want to go anywhere with me."

Elma removed Pearl's leade rope and was quick to close the stall door. She'd need to call the vet immediately. Hopefully he would be free to come out right away.

Thelma hummed as she stood at the counter near the kitchen sink, preparing a pot of garden mint tea. Their bishop's wife, Lena Chupp, would be here soon, bringing some baby items one of her grandchildren had outgrown. Thelma looked forward to going through them to see what she might be able to use. It had been a while since she'd visited with Lena, so she'd invited her to stay and have lunch.

A knock sounded on the back door. Thinking it must be Lena, Thelma hurried to answer. Opening the door wide, she stepped back in surprise. Her red-faced sister stood on the porch, blowing out a series of short breaths. Elma's stooped posture and wrinkled forehead let Thelma know she was distressed about something.

"Elma, what's wrong? You look umgerennt."

"I am very upset." Elma stepped inside. "Pearl's been hurt, and she won't be able to pull my buggy for several weeks."

"Ach, my! What happened? Have you called the vet?" Thelma's body tensed.

"Pearl has a gash on her right back leg. I'm not sure when she got the cut, but I called Dr. Brown as soon as I discovered it, and he came to check

Pearl right away." She paused, her chin trembling a bit. "At first we didn't know how it had happened, but then the vet discovered a nail sticking out of one of the lower stall boards. Don't know why I didn't see it before."

"Is your *gaul* going to be all right?" Thelma's concern escalated. *If Pearl dies, Elma will be devastated. I'd miss that trusty old horse too. And then she would need to buy another buggy horse, which would be expensive.*

"Dr. Brown put medicine on the wound, wrapped it good, and gave her an antibiotic. His instructions were to keep an eye on her and watch for infection. I'll need to change her bandage once a day and apply the ointment to the gash." Tears gathered in Elma's eyes, and she blinked several times. "I hope I can do a good job for her. The doctor left medicine for Pearl, and bandages to rewrap the wound, but I'll need to pick up more sterile pads in town. I hate to say this, but if my horse doesn't recover well enough, she may not be able to pull the buggy anymore."

Thelma slipped her arms around Elma and patted her back. "Hang in there and try not to worry. I'm sure she'll be fine."

"I hope so, but in the meantime, I'll either have to ride my bike everywhere or rely on a driver to take me places. Also, I wouldn't mind some support, or at least having someone next to me while I change Pearl's bandage tomorrow. Do you think you or Joseph could come over to help?"

"Not to worry. One of us will be there. Oh, and you can borrow one of our horses until Pearl is better." Thelma gave her sister a hug.

"Danki." Elma smiled, returning the embrace. "I appreciate it. As a matter of fact, I was planning to go into town today to do some shopping, so can I borrow Joe's horse? In addition to the sterile pads for Pearl, I need groceries, plus I want to buy several baskets to display the produce I'll be taking to the farmers' market in a few weeks."

"Rusty is available, but Joseph's already left for work, so his horse isn't here this morning."

Elma's eyes widened as she pressed her hands to the sides of her head. "Oh, no, I can't take Rusty. That horse is too temperamental for me."

"Both Joseph and I have worked with him over the last two years, and he's more manageable than he was before."

Elma moved closer to Thelma. "Could you go with me today? You've always handled Rusty better than me."

"I would if I could, but Lena Chupp will be here soon, and I invited her to join me for lunch, so she'll probably stay awhile."

Elma's shoulders slumped. "Maybe I'll see if one of our drivers is available."

Thelma clasped her sister's arm. "You should take Rusty today. You need to get past your fear."

"I can't." Elma's chin trembled. "Even the thought of taking that horse makes me naerfich."

"I understand your nervousness, but as I said before, Rusty is easier to handle now."

"For you maybe, but I doubt he would be for me."

"Just keep a firm hand on the reins and let him know who's boss. I'm sure he will do fine for you."

Elma's shoulders curled forward as she clutched her arms to her chest. "Okay, I'll give Rusty a try, but if things don't go well, I will never use him again."

Thelma glanced at the clock. "Lena won't be here for another fifteen minutes, so I'll go outside with you and hitch Rusty to the buggy."

⸙

Elma's fingers ached as she clung to the reins. Other than tossing his head a few times, so far Rusty had behaved himself. Maybe the trip into town wouldn't be so bad after all.

She loosened her grip a bit and tried to relax. Rusty must have sensed it, for he stopped shaking his head. The closer Elma got to town, the more her senses heightened. The car traffic grew heavier, and some drivers got a little too close for comfort. She wondered if all this was worth putting herself through so much stress. Her thoughts raced. *What if something spooks or upsets Rusty? If he takes off and won't slow down, I'll be in a pickle.*

Elma could tell by the sweat rolling down her back that she was losing faith in her abilities. She spotted a place to pull off the road to rest and collect her thoughts for a moment. As she sat holding the reins, Elma closed her eyes to pray. *Lord, allow me the strength and safety to continue on with this day You have made. Please surround me with Your wonderful peace and help me not to be afraid. Amen.*

After a while, Elma's nerves calmed as she allowed the horse to take the lead. With all his years of experience pulling the buggy for her grandparents, Rusty certainly knew the way to town.

Elma waved to an English neighbor on a riding lawn mower, cutting his grass. She'd seen it before but still had to giggle, watching the barn swallows swoop at bugs the mower kicked up.

They'd almost made it to the first intersection in town when a car pulled out of a side street without stopping, right in front of the horse and buggy. Rusty planted his hooves, halting the buggy, before Elma could even pull back on the reins.

She blinked a couple of times. *Thank You, Lord. What an answer to prayer.* Leaning forward, she clucked to the horse. "Good boy, Rusty. You are one schmaert horse and may have just saved our lives."

Elma jumped when the driver blared his horn at her and was even more stunned when the car kept going. *How can people be so rude?*

Despite the prickling of her scalp, Elma drew a deep breath and continued in the direction of town. Rusty nickered as if to assure her that he had everything under control. If she needed to go any distance in the next few weeks, perhaps she would borrow Thelma's horse again.

Chapter 10

Shipshewana, Indiana

Entering the farmers' market, Elma's gaze came to rest on the rows of tables with bright tablecloths, filled with local seasonable produce. Many craft tables were filled with various handmade items, and food vendors were selling cookies, breads, pies, and beverages. One English man pulled his red pickup truck into one of the open spots to sell his rustic birdhouses. Cloth awnings of different colors hung behind several of the booths. While other tables sat outside her view—where numerous miscellaneous items were sold—unless Thelma and Joseph stayed at the table, it wasn't likely Elma would get to check out many of the vendors' tables.

Even though the market hadn't opened yet, an increasing number of visitors already were milling about. The aroma of fresh herbs and ripening berries mingling with fragrances from homemade soaps and creams filled Elma's senses as she drew a deep breath. She appreciated being able to take part in a rural event that nurtured the feeling of community spirit.

"Look at all the people who came to sell their wares at the market today," Joseph commented as he helped Elma set up her table. Thelma had brought a few things to sell too, but most of the proceeds from whatever they sold would go to pay for more repairs needing to be made at the house or store.

Elma inhaled sharply. It seemed the list of repairs at both places was endless. Thelma and Joseph were fortunate to have bought a place in such good shape.

Now don't start feeling sorry for yourself. Elma picked up one of the baskets she'd bought a couple of weeks ago and filled it with fresh fruits and berries. She put cucumbers, beets, peppers, and carrots in another basket and a mixture of both in a third basket. Soon, all the baskets were full, and several other items were placed on the table by themselves.

"The display looks nice." Thelma gestured to a hefty watermelon. "It's a warm day, so I'm sure lots of people will be looking for sweet-tasting summertime fruit such as this."

"I hope so. Sure don't want to haul a lot of this produce home at the end of the day and then try to figure out how we're going to eat all of it."

"Not to worry." Joseph motioned to the table. "If I were a betting man, I'd bet most of your produce will be gone by the day's end."

Thelma nodded. "I believe my husband is right."

"Well, it remains to be seen." Elma rummaged through the oversized bag she'd brought along and retrieved some chair pads she'd remembered to bring for the day. She picked out a bottle of sunscreen and set it aside for later. "It's good to be prepared and as comfortable as we can. Lizzie gave me this idea." Holding up the cushions, she placed them on the hard, wooden stools they'd also brought from home and took a seat. Thelma sat on the other stool. "My only concern," Elma admitted, "is all the other vendors with the same type of produce as mine. It may be too much competition."

❦

"I'm glad you came with me this morning." Smiling, Dorothy looked up at her son. "If things get really busy, I'll need your help at my table."

"No problem, Mom. That's why I agreed to come along." Ben glanced around. "Looks like there's a lot of other tables full of produce, though. Sure hope you're able to sell most of your things."

"I hope so too, but if not, at least I can say I tried." Dorothy placed a dark green tablecloth on the table and began setting things out.

Ben grabbed a box filled with a variety of plants Dorothy had brought to sell. "I don't see too many people selling flowers like yours, so that should help."

"Jah. Providing anyone who comes to the market today is looking for flowers." She folded her arms. "I was excited about coming here, but now a few doubts are settling in."

Ben put his hand on her shoulder. "Don't worry, Mom. Things will go okay. Just try to relax and enjoy the day."

"You're right." She smiled. "I need to keep a positive attitude."

"Good to hear." Ben set the last of her things in place. "Would ya mind if I take a look around before the market opens for business? If things get busy later on, I may not have a chance to do it."

"Go right ahead. I'll be here waiting when you get back."

"I won't be gone long," Ben called over his shoulder as he headed off.

Ben wandered around for a bit, savoring the tantalizing smells of the food vendors. He and Mom had eaten a hearty breakfast this morning, but the thought of chomping down on a juicy hot dog or bag of tasty kettle corn made his stomach growl. Well, he'd have a chance to do that later on, when it was time for lunch. For now, though, he wanted to see what some of the vendors were selling, because he might not get the opportunity again. It would be great looking around with fresh inventory sitting undisturbed at the different booths. Having first pick of things made it worth getting here early.

Ben stopped to admire some knives on display at a nearby booth. He picked one up and let it rest in his hand, feeling its weightiness. He couldn't resist running his thumb along the handle where the detailed carving of an eagle was made. *I'm glad my mamm convinced me to come and help her today. Maybe she'll sell enough produce at the market to make it worth her while.*

"What do you think about that knife there?" the bearded English vendor asked.

"It's nice. I have a few at home, but none like this one." Ben placed it on the table in front of him.

"I've collected many through the years, and passed a lot of them down to my sons."

"I'm sure they liked receiving knives like these." Ben glanced at an enclosed case next to him. "Think I'll take this one off your hands." He pointed to his choice and reached for his wallet.

"Okay." The vendor took Ben's cash and put the knife in its original box then handed it to him.

"Thanks." Ben carried his purchase along while he checked out a few more tables. The smell of food cooking filled the air, and the irresistible aroma made his mouth water. Fighting the urge to get something to eat, he headed back to their table.

His mother smiled at him. "I see you found something to buy already. What did you get?"

Ben passed the box to her. "Found a nice knife to add to my growing collection."

"That is a nice one." She touched the handle. "Your daed liked to collect coins, as you well know. He had socks with money in them inside his dresser, and little boxes containing collector coins. Of course, he ordered more the older he got. If a coin caught his eye, he'd try to get it." Her eyes misted.

Ben's mom became sentimental when it came to his dad. For that matter, so did Ben. *Bet Dad would have enjoyed being here today, and he would've gotten Mom to wander around with him to check out all the wares.* Ben winced. *They were so close. What a shame he's no longer with us.* It seemed to be getting a little easier for himself, but Ben could only imagine how difficult it had been for Mom to lose her spouse.

Ben left the knife with his mother and wandered up and down a few more aisles, checking out everything from books, household tools, straw hats, to lots of collectable things. Nothing caught his interest, until he spotted a produce stand where a young Amish woman stood placing fruits and vegetables in baskets. Thinking it might be good to check out the competition, he headed that way.

❧

"Since we're all set up, would you mind if Joseph and I walked around for a bit?" Thelma leaned close to Elma. "If things get busy at the stand later on, this may be our only chance to look at some of the other tables and booths."

"Go right ahead. If people start coming in before you get back, I'm sure I can manage." Elma gestured to the basket closest to her. "Before you leave, do you think this one looks okay, or should I add a few more pieces of fruit?"

"Looks good enough to eat." Joseph chuckled. "Not the basket—just what's inside."

Elma smiled. "You two go on now, and enjoy yourselves."

"Okay. We shouldn't be gone too long." Thelma waved and headed off with Joseph in the direction of the booths selling food.

Elma snickered. No doubt her sister had a craving for something. Thelma had confided in Elma on the drive here this morning that two nights ago she'd gotten up in the wee hours to eat a couple of brownies. Thelma needed to eat something healthier than chocolate, especially late at night. She might have ended up with heartburn, and with her being pregnant, it would be even more miserable. Elma would look through her natural desserts cookbook for a better treat to bake for her twin.

Elma took her notepad from the tote she'd brought along and jotted down a reminder. *Since Thelma craves sweets, my recipes will fill the void yet won't be bad for her. My sister has a habit of eating whatever she wants, but not always what is good for her.*

I'll probably never know what it's like to have pregnancy cravings, Elma mused. *But if I ever do, I hope it's not for sugary treats. I'll be sure to eat well, avoiding temptations, and give my unborn child the best start I possibly can.*

Elma had always been the more health conscious of the twins, although she did sometimes splurge—especially when it came to certain desserts. She'd walk a mile through the pouring rain for a piece of home-made cherry pie.

Elma smiled when a few children ran past, giggling while they gave chase to each other. She noticed some other kids sat with parents behind tables, watching with an I-want-to-play-too look in their eyes.

Oh, to be young again. Elma heaved a sigh, wishing there was a way to slow life down a bit. It seemed like yesterday she and Thelma were eager children.

Elma's thoughts drifted in another direction as she reflected on how things had been going at home, as well as inside the store. While Lizzie was not the best helper she'd ever had, having her working in the store was better than no help at all during the times Thelma couldn't be there. Lizzie kept her company, and with busy times in the store, the workdays flew by. Besides, Lizzie needed a job, and Elma didn't have the heart to let her go. It made her feel good to help the woman out, even though Elma worked like two people at times, and at lightning speed to keep up with everything.

With the exception of Tiger being a pest much of the time, things were going okay at the house. Of course, Elma still spent many hours by herself and struggled with loneliness, but it was a comfort to have her twin sister living across the street. Looking over there and seeing activity made being alone a little more tolerable. It was nice to know she could pop over from time to time if the loneliness became too unbearable.

"Looks like you have some nice produce here."

Elma jerked at the sound of a deep voice. When she looked up, a pair of brilliant blue eyes stared at her. It was difficult not to gaze back at them.

"Sorry if I startled you." The Amish man's deep-dimpled smile seemed sincere.

"It's okay. I was deep in thought when you stepped up to my table." Elma couldn't help but notice that he wasn't sporting a beard.

"I was admiring your produce and the way it's displayed." Leaning forward, he reached out to pick up an apple, but in the process, he bumped the table. The next thing Elma saw was a blur of red fruit leaving as the basket toppled over and everything spilled out. Some of the produce rolled off and under the table.

"Sorry about that." A blotch of red erupted on the man's face as he bent down and crawled under the table to retrieve the items from the upset basket. At the same time, Elma went under from her side of the table. They both reached for an apple, and their hands touched.

Elma jerked her head, bumping it on the underside of the table. "Ouch!"

"Are you okay?"

"Jah, I'm fine." Elma picked up the apple, backed out, and clambered to her feet just as her twin sister stepped up to the table.

Pursing her lips, Thelma glanced at Elma, then at the man who had been under the table but now stood facing them. Arms folded, she tilted her head, looking back at Elma. "What's going on here, Sister?"

Chapter 11

Elma's hand trembled as she gathered up the rest of the apples and placed them on the table. Between her sister's disapproving look and the Amish man's curious stare, she couldn't seem to find her voice and could hardly look her twin in the face.

Thelma nudged Elma's arm. "What's going on? How come the produce is in such disarray?"

Before Elma could respond, the man raised his hand and spoke. "It's my fault. I reached out for a piece of fruit and knocked the basket over." He picked up a few more items and placed them in the basket.

Joseph joined them at the table, squinting at the Amish man. "You look familiar to me. Have we met before?"

"I'm not sure. My name is Benjamin Wagler, and I live in Grabill." He swiped a hand across his forehead, pushing a chunk of his thick brown hair under the brim of his straw hat. "Most folks just call me Ben."

Joseph pulled his fingers through the ends of his beard; then a slow smile spread across his face. "I know where I've met you. A few years ago I was near Grabill, looking at some used harness-making equipment. The fellow who owned the farm was Abe Miller, and you were there, shoeing his horses."

Ben nodded. "That's right; I shoe horses for a living, and Abe's still one of my steady customers."

"I'm Joseph Beechy. This is my wife, Thelma, and her twin sister, Elma Hochstetler."

"It's nice to meet you," the twins said in unison while Ben shook Joseph's hand.

Ben shifted his gaze from Thelma to Elma. "You two certainly look alike. In fact, if it weren't for. . ." His face colored as he glanced at Thelma's baby bump then looked quickly away.

"People have been getting us mixed up since we were *bopplin*." Thelma chuckled. "Of course now, and for a while yet, it'll be easier to tell us apart."

Ben gave a brief nod. "Is this your produce stand, Elma? Or are you running it with a husband or some other family member?"

Elma's cheeks burned hot. Was Ben only curious, or could his question have been asked to find out if she was married?

She cleared her throat, hoping she could speak without stumbling over the words. With the exception of Delbert, it had been some time since she'd met an Amish man as attractive as Ben.

"Oh, my sister's not married," Thelma blurted before Elma could respond.

The heat Elma felt on her face radiated to her neck, chest, and arms. She tried to gather her thoughts before saying something foolish. "Umm. . .most of the produce on the table is mine, but some of the vegetables and fruit are from Thelma's garden."

"My mamm has a table too. She's selling some flowers in addition to produce from our yard." Ben gestured toward the area near the front entrance of the farmers' market.

"There seems to be lots of folks selling fresh produce today." Joseph bent down and picked up several radishes that had fallen on the ground during the mishap.

"Do you live here in Shipshewana?" Ben looked at Elma.

She shook her head. "We live in Topeka, and my sister and I run a general store."

"Well, mostly you run the store these days," Thelma put in. "I only work a few hours, a couple days a week anymore."

"It must be difficult to run the store by yourself when your sister's not working." Ben kept his focus on Elma.

"Things can get hectic," she admitted, "but I have a woman who helps out when Thelma's not there."

"When Joe and I were walking around, we stopped at one of the stands selling homemade pies and flavored coffees." Thelma placed her hand on Elma's arm. "I think I spotted cherry pie there. I know it's one of your favorites." She gave her sister a playful wink. "Why don't you go over and sample some?"

"Oh, I can't. The market will be open for business soon, and I wouldn't want to miss any prospective customers."

"Don't worry about that." Joseph put a few more pieces of fruit back on the table. "Thelma and I will watch the table. Besides, my fraa could use some shade and rest on one of these stools." He motioned for his wife to take a seat.

Shifting her weight, Elma bit her lip. "I suppose I could go check it out, but I won't be gone long."

"Would you mind if I tag along?" Ben asked. "I could use a cup of coffee, and a slice of pie sounds good too."

"Okay, that's fine with me." What else could she say? It surprised Elma when he said he wanted to go along, and it would be rude to say she preferred to go alone. Besides, she might enjoy his company.

⁓

Ben didn't normally feel a connection to a woman he'd only just met, but after visiting with Elma a short time, he felt as if he'd known her awhile. They'd been sitting on a bench, drinking coffee and eating pie for half an hour or so, and he wished it could be longer. Elma was not only intelligent and interesting to talk to, but her pleasant smile captivated him.

"Have you ever visited Grabill?" he asked.

She shook her head. "Between the store and keeping things going at my house, I don't have a lot of free time to explore other towns in the area."

"It's a small community, but it's where I grew up, so I feel comfortable there." Ben drank the last of his coffee. "How about you? Have you lived in Topeka all your life?"

"No, Thelma and I were raised in Sullivan, Illinois." She blotted her nicely shaped lips with a napkin.

"So how'd you end up here?"

Ben listened intently as Elma explained how she and her twin sister had inherited their grandparents' home, as well as their store. "I assume Thelma wasn't married to Joseph back then?"

"No. She met him not long after we moved here."

Ben was tempted to ask if Elma was being courted by anyone but thought better of it. She might think he was too forward. Since they'd both finished their pie and had places they needed to go, he rose to his feet and tossed his paper plate and cup into the nearest trash can. When Elma stood, he politely threw hers away too. "Sometime, when I'm up this way again, maybe I'll stop by your store and say hello."

She smiled. "That would be nice. The name of our store is E&T's General Store, and it's on Meadowbrook Lane."

"Good to know." He shuffled his feet a few times, kicking up dust. "It's been nice meeting you, Elma."

She gave a brief nod. "I enjoyed meeting you too."

As they parted ways, Ben paused briefly and glanced over his shoulder. *Now I need to find some excuse to visit Elma's store.* Watching Elma walk away, he gave her a smile when she briefly looked back in his direction. Even from where he stood, Ben could see Elma's cheeks had turned pink.

When Ben approached his mother's table, he was surprised to see several people clustered around. Mom's face would scrunch up; then, breathing deeply, she'd release it, as though trying to regain her calm. He recognized that look as one of frustration.

Ben wasted no time in stepping behind the table and helping to wait on customers. From the looks of things, Mom had already sold most of her flowers, and the garden produce seemed to be going fast too.

When the customers moved on, Mom turned to Ben with a frown. "Where have you been all this time? I thought you were only going to look around and wouldn't be gone long."

"Sorry, Mom. Guess the time got away from me." Ben explained the circumstances of how he'd met Elma Hochstetler and gone with her to have coffee and pie.

Mom's eyebrows squished together. "Hmm. . . That name sounds familiar. Did she say where she's from?"

He nodded. "She and her twin sister run a general store in Topeka, and. . ."

Mom snapped her fingers. "Now I remember. When I spent the day with my friend Eileen a few weeks ago, we visited a store run by a woman named Elma. I wonder if it could be the same person."

"I bet it is. I mean, how many stores could there be in Topeka run by a woman named Elma?" Ben scratched at a spot under his hat.

"Good point." Mom got out her handkerchief and wiped the perspiration from her forehead. "So how come you went off to have pie and coffee with her when you knew I was here at the table by myself?"

"Because I wanted pie and coffee, and since she was heading that way I figured I may as well tag along. It gave us a chance to get acquainted." Ben leaned against the table. "Besides, I didn't realize you had a bunch of customers. I wasn't even sure the market had officially opened." He glanced at his mother's flowers, toying with the idea of taking a potted plant over to Elma. He could say it was an apology for spilling her basket of produce.

Naw, I'd better not. He mentally shook his head. *Mom might ask me about it and give me a hard time.*

Ben's mother tipped her head from one side to the other, as though weighing the situation. "Are you sure that was all there was to it?"

"What do you mean?"

"Hearing the way you were talking about her, plus your wide-eyed expression at the mention of her name, makes me think you might be smitten with the young woman." Mom took a bag of raisins from her purse and ate a few.

"Why would you think that, Mom? I only met Elma today." *Am I really that transparent? Does Mom have any idea the strange feeling I had when I first looked in Elma's eyes?*

※

Dorothy sat for a time, but she needed to get up and take a walk. "Ben, would you mind watching our booth while I get some lemonade?"

"No problem, Mom. You go ahead and take a break."

"Do you need anything while I'm out?" She picked up her purse.

"I'm fine for now. The pie and coffee I had earlier is holding me." Ben rubbed his stomach and grinned.

"Okay, I'll be back soon." Dorothy started walking, looking further

271

down the line of vendors. The place was full of people milling around. She knew right where the food places were located, so she headed in that direction. All she really had to do was follow her nose. Besides the drink Dorothy intended to buy for herself, she smelled kettle corn being made nearby, and it called to her. About the time she finished paying for a glass of lemonade, her friend Eileen tapped her shoulder.

Dorothy smiled. "Well, hello. I was hoping to see you here."

"I'm glad I made it today. As you can see, I've been shopping." Eileen held up a large paper bag. "How's it going at your booth so far?"

"I've sold a lot of my plants, and with Ben's help, we've kept up a nice pace."

"Good to hear. I've been slowly making my way around to your booth but hadn't made it that far yet." Eileen pointed across the way. "Why don't we take a seat over there at that table?"

"All right. It'll be nice to sit and chat." Dorothy stopped first to buy a bag of kettle corn; then they both found seats.

As they sat and talked, Dorothy told Eileen about Ben leaving their booth earlier to look around. "He was gone awhile, and it got real busy for me there by myself. I felt frustrated trying to juggle everything alone."

"You poor thing. I bet it was nerve wracking."

"Jah." Dorothy held the bag of kettle corn out to her friend. "Would you like some?"

"Danki." Eileen helped herself.

"Anyway, when Ben came back to our booth, he mentioned that he'd been off having pie and coffee with an Amish woman named Elma Hochstetler from Topeka."

Eileen's eyebrows rose. "Oh, jah, you and I were in her store a couple weeks ago. She's one of the owners of E&T's General Store."

Dorothy leaned closer, lowering her voice. "I think Ben might be smitten with this young lady."

"Really? What makes you believe so?"

"When he talked about her, he seemed to brighten up." Dorothy sipped on her drink. "Of course, he only met her today, so I probably shouldn't read much into it."

"I agree. A lot of young people today seem to be moving slower than we did at that age—not wanting to hurry into marriage and start a family."

Dorothy nodded. *I'm fine with that. Ben does need to find a wife, though. But not if she lives a good distance from Grabill. My world would be so different if he were to move far from home. I don't think I could deal with it.*

Chapter 12

Topeka

It had been two weeks since Elma went to the farmers' market in Ship-shewana. She'd done fairly well with sales, but it wasn't likely she'd be able to rent another table there this month because things were busier than ever at the store. Elma couldn't help wondering if she might see Ben Wagler again if she went back to the market. He'd said he might drop by the store sometime, but he could have been making small talk or trying to be polite. More than likely, she'd probably never see him again. In the brief time they'd spent together, though, Elma found herself desiring to know Ben better. He had the kindest-looking eyes, and although his voice was deep, his tone was gentle. She could still visualize his warm smile.

Now don't start fantasizing about something that's not likely to happen, she scolded herself.

Elma glanced across the room to where Thelma sat behind the counter. Thelma looked more tired than usual today but was determined to be here for a few hours.

Lizzie was in the back, straightening some bolts of material, and then she was supposed to put out a box of thread that had just come in. Elma wasn't sure how much her helper had gotten done so far, because the last time she checked, Lizzie had been visiting with some of the customers. It wasn't a bad thing to chat with those who came into the store, but if given the chance, Lizzie could go on for hours.

With a shrug, Elma headed for the back room to check the list of supplies she needed to order. When she stepped inside, she took a seat at the desk and picked up her ordering tablet. She'd only been sitting a moment when she caught a movement out of the corner of her eye. It didn't take long for her to realize it was a little gray mouse.

Oh, great. Just what the store needs. I don't want the creepy rodent in here with me. Mice are disgusting creatures. If Tiger was in here right now, he'd go after the mouse.

Sliding her chair away from the desk, she picked up the broom in the corner of the room. "I don't need this," Elma muttered. Of course, the mouse was too quick for her and darted into a wee hole on the opposite side of the room. As much as Elma disliked the idea, she'd have to bring Tiger into the store.

❦

Delbert pulled his horse up to the hitching rail outside Joseph's harness shop and stepped down from the buggy. He'd been in the area doing carpentry work for an Amish couple, so it was a good chance to drop by and say hello to his friend.

After making sure his horse was secure, Delbert opened the door to the harness shop. When he stepped inside, he was greeted by the smells of leather, savory neat's-foot oil, and pungent dye. Piled on the cement floor were bits of leather scraps resembling spaghetti noodles. An oversized sewing machine run by an air compressor sat on a large table, and a row of tools spilled out of round wooden holders on the workbench nearby.

Delbert moved past several harnesses and bridles looped from ceiling hooks and nearly ran into an enormous sheet of loosely rolled leather. "Where are ya, Joe?" he called.

A few seconds later, his longtime friend stepped out of the back room, grinning as he ambled toward him. "Well, well, I didn't expect to see you today." Joe grinned and slapped Delbert on the back.

Delbert explained his reason for being in town then asked how things were going.

"Ya mean here or at home?"

"Either or." Delbert leaned against the sewing machine table.

"Things at home are okay, although my fraa tends to do too much." Joseph folded his arms and groaned. "Here, things have been kinda slow the last few weeks, and it's got me worried."

Delbert shook his head. "No need for that. As long as there are Amish folks living in Topeka and the surrounding area, there will be a need for your harness shop."

"You're right about there being a need for a harness shop, but what if people who used to come in here decide to take their work someplace else?"

"That's not gonna happen. You have a reputation for doing good work. Things will pick up again soon, I'm sure."

"And if they don't?" Joseph dropped his gaze to the messy floor while rubbing his neck.

"I'm sure they will, but if for some reason they don't, then you'll look for something else to do."

Joseph's bottom lip pulled in. "I don't know how to do anything but make and repair harnesses, Dell."

Tired of standing, Delbert pulled a folding chair out from the wall and took a seat. "Are you still worried about whether you can support your family?"

Joseph looked up and nodded. "It won't be just me and Thelma anymore. In a few months, I'll be a daed, and there will be another mouth to feed."

Delbert snickered. "The boppli won't be eating solid food for some time after it's born, so you don't have to worry about that for a while."

"Very funny. You know what I mean."

"The best thing you can do is pray about the situation and let God take care of the rest."

"You're right. I made that decision once already, but I keep taking it back."

"Well, quit it." Delbert stood and draped his arm across his friend's shoulders. "Just remember, I'm here for you if you need to talk. Oh, and don't worry, 'cause I'd never stand by and let my best friend and his family starve." He noticed for the first time dark circles beneath his friend's eyes.

Joseph smiled. "Danki, Dell. You really are a good *freind*."

"Hey, let me take you out to lunch. I'll even drive, since I'm ready to go." Delbert fiddled with a piece of leather lying on the counter.

"Okay. Let me close things up and hang my RETURN AFTER LUNCH sign in the window. I can sure use a break. Maybe it'll help pick up my spirits." Joseph adjusted the sign on the door.

As they headed for town, Delbert asked which restaurant Joe would like to go to for lunch. He wasn't surprised when his friend chose his favorite place—Tiffany's.

Delbert snapped the reins to get his horse to pick up the pace. "You know, if you're worried about your business and wondering if you'll be able to support a family, I could teach you how to do carpentry work."

Joseph smirked, pulling off his straw hat. "I'm not sure I could learn that type of trade easily. Besides, I like what I do."

"It was only a suggestion."

"I appreciate it, and you'll be the first person I call upon if it comes to changing careers." Joseph swatted him with the hat before placing it back on his head.

Delbert pulled his rig into the restaurant parking lot. *Sure hope my pal's worries are for nothing. I hope and pray he can keep providing for his growing family.*

ᴄᏩ

Grabill

"Sure appreciate you takin' me to LaGrange on such short notice," Ben told his driver, Dave Carlson, as they headed down the road in Dave's truck.

Dave tapped the steering wheel. "It's a good thing you caught me when you did, because I was heading out to do some fishing when the telephone rang."

Ben's jaw clenched. "Sorry about that. I would have called another driver if you'd said something."

Dave shook his bald head. "It's no big deal. I can always go fishing tomorrow." He glanced in his rearview mirror. "You sure your dog's gonna be okay back there?"

Ben turned his head to check, and he smiled at how the breeze from the moving truck made his dog's ears flap around. Nose sniffing the air, Hunter was obviously enjoying himself, watching the scenery whiz by. "Hunter's ridden in the bed of a truck before, so I'm sure he'll be fine."

Dave snickered. "I could see by the way he was carryin' on back at your place that he wanted to go along."

"Yeah, the dog thinks he should go everywhere with me, but most times, like when I'm going off to shoe a horse, he has to stay home with Mom." Ben reached into his pocket and pulled out a pack of gum. "I would have left Hunter home today, but with Mom not feeling well, I figured he'd bark and get on her nerves if I locked him in the kennel."

"You're probably right. He'd have most likely carried on the whole time you were gone."

Ben gave a nod before glancing at the cardboard box filled with flowers on the seat between them. A lady who bought some of Mom's flowers at the farmers' market two weeks ago had called and asked if she could get some more. Since Mom had come down with a bad cold and didn't feel like going out or exposing anyone, Ben had volunteered to take them. Afterward, if Dave didn't mind the detour, he planned to go to Topeka and stop by E&T's General Store to say hello. Elma had been on Ben's mind a lot since their meeting in Shipshewana. He was eager to get to know her better. At the very least, he needed to find out if she had a suitor.

❧

LaGrange

Ben was glad when he delivered the flowers to Velma Williamson, and she seemed pleased. "I was hoping your mother would have a table at the farmers' market again, but I guess she's been busy with other things." The elderly woman smiled when she gave Ben the money; then she tipped her head to one side. "Did you hear that sound?"

"What sound?"

"It came from outside, I think." She fiddled with her hearing aid. "I need a new battery for this thing. When the battery is low it buzzes sometimes."

"I didn't hear anything."

She waved a hand in the air. "Not important. Please tell your mother

I hope she feels better soon, and I might be calling again for another order."

"Yes, I will." Ben couldn't imagine why Velma would need to buy more flowers when she had some growing in her own garden. With what he'd witnessed already, she appeared to be a bit eccentric. But if she wanted to spend her money that way, who was he to question it?

Ben said goodbye to Mrs. Williamson and hopped back in Dave's truck. He was about to ask if Dave would mind going to Topeka when he glanced back and noticed Hunter was no longer in the bed of the truck. He looked over at Dave. "What happened to my dog?"

Dave lifted both hands. "He jumped out when you headed up to the house with the flowers. Then I saw him running around the yard for a bit, chasing a black-and-white cat. Figured he'd be back in the truck by now."

"Well, he's not." Ben opened his door and jumped out. Scanning the yard, he cupped his hands around his mouth. "Hunter! Hunter! Where are ya, boy?"

No sign of the dog. Not even a bark in response to his call. Surely Hunter couldn't have gone too far. But then if he was after Velma's cat, they both could have taken off down the road.

Ben called Hunter's name a few more times, but still no response. A few minutes later, a scruffy-looking black-and-white cat darted into the yard and leaped onto the front porch. Ben expected to see Hunter come bounding in on the cat's heels, but no such luck.

He called the dog's name a few more times then stepped onto the porch and knocked on Velma's door. As soon as it opened, the cat zipped inside.

Velma tipped her head back, looking up at him with a quizzical expression. "Did you forget something, Ben?"

"Yeah, my dog."

Her mouth opened slightly. "Did you say your hog?"

Taking into consideration that Velma was slightly hard of hearing, Ben repeated, a little louder, "My dog. He was in the back of my driver's truck when I brought the flowers up to you, and now he's gone." No point mentioning that Hunter had been chasing her cat.

"Well, I haven't seen your dog, but if you'll give me a description, I'll call and let you know if I see him anywhere."

Ben closed his eyes briefly and took a deep breath. Apparently, Velma thought he would go home without his dog. Well, that wasn't going to happen. If it took the rest of the morning and all afternoon, Ben would find Hunter.

Chapter 13

Grabill

"Thanks for the ride." Ben reached into his pocket and handed Dave the money he owed. "And I'm sorry for keepin' you most of the day."

Dave waved away his concerns. "Aw, that's okay. I'm just sorry we couldn't find your dog."

"Yeah, me too." Ben's neck bent forward as he sagged against the seat. "Maybe, if I'm lucky, Hunter will find his way home."

"Could be. I've heard of some dogs traveling many miles to get back to their master."

Ben nodded, although his chest felt heavy. As much as he hated to admit it, he might never see Hunter again. Ben and Dave had driven around LaGrange for several hours after leaving Velma's house, but there was no sign of his dog. In addition to the possibility of losing a good hunting dog, they'd used up so much time looking for Hunter that he hadn't made it to Topeka to see Elma. He'd have to plan a trip there some other time. One thing was certain, if Hunter should return, he wouldn't be going any distance with Ben—especially not in the bed of a pickup truck.

"Well, I'd better let you go." Ben opened the truck door and stepped out. "Thanks again, Dave, for all you did today."

"No problem. Tell your mother I said hello and that I hope she feels better soon."

"I will." As Ben watched Dave's truck pull out of the yard, his mouth twisted grimly. He dreaded telling Mom that Hunter was gone. These past few years she'd grown attached to the dog, and it went without saying that Ben had too. Unfortunately, he had a sinking feeling Hunter wasn't coming back.

Ben walked slowly toward the house; then wishful thinking made him glance toward the pastures. How many times had he and Hunter walked those fields together? Would it only be a memory now? Ben watched, almost willing Hunter to materialize and run toward him, hungry and eager to be fed his supper.

"Where are you, my furry friend?" Ben whispered, with one last look before going in. "I hope wherever you are tonight, someone will be kind to you."

LaGrange

When Delbert arrived home, he pulled his rig around back near the buggy shed and barn. The summery heat of the day made him happy to pull into some cool shade near the building. He climbed down took off his hat, and fanned himself, leaning against his rig to rest a moment. His horse, Chip, stood snorting loudly and nodding his head.

"Okay, boy. I'll see to you in a moment." Delbert noticed his shirt was sweaty under his suspenders. He couldn't wait to eat, change, and relax when all the chores were done.

After unhitching Chip, he led him to the barn for a good brushing and offered fresh water to drink.

Today had been long, and Delbert looked forward to spending a quiet evening with his feet propped up. Since he didn't feel like heating up the kitchen by using the gas stove, he'd settle for a tuna sandwich and a few pickles with chips. He'd stopped at the grocery store on the way back from Topeka and bought a gallon of root beer, so he would have a tall glass of that too. Good thing Elma wouldn't be there to watch him drink it. She'd probably have something to say about the high sugar count.

Delbert led the horse to the barn, and when he opened the stall door, the hinges squeaked. He'd need to get those oiled soon. Once the horse was inside, he grabbed the brush and currycomb. While Chip drank water and munched on some oats, Delbert wiped the animal down then began the combing and currying process.

The odor of straw tickled Delbert's nose. *Achoo! Achoo! Achoo!* He set the brush aside and pulled a hankie out of his pocket. Hay was one of the many things he was allergic to—especially as he'd gotten older. His sensitivities had worsened over the years, and he'd become intolerant to even more things than when he was young.

Sweat trickled down his face as he fought against the tangles in Chip's mane, but he persevered, despite his horse's snorting protests and hooves thumping against the wooden floor.

When the chore was done, Delbert put the comb and brush away, stepped out of the stall, and latched the door. His stomach rumbled, reminding him it was suppertime, so he would wait to put the buggy in the shed till after he'd had a bite to eat. A tuna sandwich sounded pretty good about now.

Stepping out of the barn and into the yard, Delbert paused to breathe in the fresh air. After being cooped up in the stuffy building, it felt good to be outside again.

When Delbert rounded the corner of his house, he came to a halt. "What's this?"

A German shorthair pointer, with liver-and-white spots on his head and back, lay on the porch, tongue hanging out. Delbert had never seen the hunting dog before and didn't have an inkling who the animal belonged to. Well, the critter couldn't stay here, but Delbert wouldn't let it languish in the hot sun either, even though it would be setting before long.

As soon as Delbert stepped onto the porch, the dog whimpered and looked up at him with sorrowful brown eyes.

"I know, buddy. You look hot and tired. I'll get ya some water real quick." Delbert opened the door and stepped into the house, hoping the dog wouldn't follow. The last thing he needed was dirty paw prints or dog hair floating through the rooms. He glanced back, impressed to see the dog patiently waiting.

After filling a large plastic bowl with cool water, he went back outside. Placing the dish in front of the dog, Delbert stepped aside and watched. He had to admit, the animal was beautiful and seemed well behaved. As nice looking as this one was, there must be an owner searching for it.

With no hesitation, the critter began lapping the water until it was gone. Licking his lips and wagging his short, stubby tail, the dog sat, looking at Delbert as if he needed more.

"Okay, okay." Delbert picked up the bowl, went back in the house, and filled it again. This time the dog drank half the water then flopped onto the porch with a grunt and a burp.

"My, my, that must have been good." Delbert chuckled and patted his own stomach. "I know how you feel when your belly is satisfied."

Delbert took a seat and watched the animal rest. The dog appeared friendly enough. He noticed that the shorthair wore a collar, but after inspecting it, he saw no identification. Delbert figured now that the animal had been refreshed he'd move on, but the critter put his nose between his paws and slept.

Delbert didn't want to bother the dog, and the tuna sandwich he envisioned himself eating made his mouth water. He brought his hand up to his shoulder and massaged a knot that had developed.

I can't keep this hund. Delbert rolled his neck from side to side while giving an impatient huff. He wasn't allergic to all dogs. In fact, when he was a boy, he'd had the best dog ever. *But I'll never put myself through that again. Besides, this animal is not my problem. He can stay on the porch for now. But if he's not gone by morning, I'll ask around. I'm sure someone must know who owns the mutt.*

Topeka

Elma glanced at the clock, relieved to see it was almost time to close the store for the day. No doubt there'd be something Lizzie had forgotten to do, which wasn't out of the ordinary on any given day. She could tell Lizzie's back was acting up again by the way she bent or reached in an odd position to do even the simplest of tasks.

Thelma had gone home a few hours ago, and Lizzie was in the back room gathering her things. An English woman and her son were still in the store, but Elma didn't want to rush the lady if she had more shopping to do. It wouldn't hurt to keep the store open a few minutes past closing time.

Elma went over by the garden clogs, looking at what was left from the inventory. She'd run a half-off special on the older styles so she'd have ample floor space for the newer versions. It appeared there were only two pairs left, so Elma would need to bring out the new ones with fun colors.

As mother and son approached the candy aisle, Elma overheard the young boy ask if he could have a candy bar.

"No, son," his mother responded. "You had candy earlier today, and too much sugar isn't good for you."

The boy pouted, but the mother held firm.

Elma smiled then headed to the counter to tidy up the workspace. It was nice to know she wasn't the only person who objected to sugar-laden treats. Silently, she commended the woman for not giving in to her son. She'd witnessed too many mothers who came to the store give in to a whiny child's wishes in order to keep the child quiet or from throwing a temper tantrum.

Elma pursed her lips. *If I ever become a mother, I hope I'll be able to practice tough love.* While it would be difficult not to give in to children's wants, it wouldn't be good for them to have their way all the time. Up at the front, Elma took a seat on the stool. She slid the notepad over and wrote a reminder to herself to check for healthier snacks to sell in the store. *I believe we need a good array of both types. I'd like to offer my customers something for on the go that is better for their health.*

A short time later, the English woman, wearing an ample amount of perfume, placed her purchases on the counter.

Elma held her breath. *I'll have to open up the front door and air the place out after this woman leaves.* Her nose twitched, and she glanced toward the front entrance.

As Elma rang up the items, the child darted back up the candy aisle. She was tempted to follow, but that was up to his mom. No doubt he hoped to convince his mother that he should have the candy bar he'd asked for previously.

The boy's mother, dressed in a bright green printed dress, glanced over her shoulder, then back to Elma. "When he gets something going in his mind, it's hard to reason with him. Do you have any children?"

"No." Elma reached for the next item, examining it to find the price.

"My name is Corine, and we're new to the area. Well, I'm actually not new. I lived here for a few years when I was a kid. Anyway, we're still trying to settle down from the hectic move." She cupped her hands around her mouth and turned around. "Ronnie, hurry up now!" She stuffed a hand, weighted with bold jewelry, into her large handbag and fumbled through to retrieve her billfold.

"Where are you from?" Elma questioned.

"Pennsylvania. I was married for a time, but now it's just me and my son. We came back to my old stomping grounds. Ronnie will have his grandparents and me to watch him grow." Corine smiled, showing the whitest teeth.

Once Corine's purchases were paid for and Elma had bagged everything up, the woman looked at her and said, "Thank you. I hope you have a nice evening."

Elma smiled. "And you as well."

"Come on, Ronnie, it's time to go," Corine called as she started for the front door.

A few second later, the towheaded boy ran up to his mother and followed her out the door.

Lizzie came out of the back room then and asked if Elma needed her for anything else.

"No, and I'm ready to close up for the day." Elma gave Lizzie's arm a tender squeeze. "See you tomorrow morning."

"You can count on it." Lizzie lifted her chin and sniffed the air. "Wow, that's some mighty strong toilet water someone splashed on today."

Elma rolled her eyes. "I agree. Lizzie, would you please do me a favor and prop the door open on your way out? I don't need the strong perfume odor clinging to everything in the room."

"No problem."

As soon as her helper went out the door, Elma moved from the counter and stepped up to the window, watching Lizzie disappear around the corner. She flipped over the CLOSED sign and turned off the battery-operated fans, shut off most of the gas lamps, and made sure Tiger wasn't in the store. She'd been letting him inside every morning, and it seemed to help keep the mice population down. However, she didn't want the cat to remain in the store overnight. Elma needed him in the house with her, if for nothing else but companionship.

While Elma aired out the store, she walked down the toy aisle to turn off the overhead lamp. There, she discovered a crumpled-up candy wrapper behind a wooden truck. She frowned. *I'll bet that little English boy took a candy bar and ate it, despite what his mother said. If they return to the store, I'll have to keep a closer watch on the little* schtinker.

Chapter 14

LaGrange

When Delbert got up Saturday morning, he made a decision. The dog, after three days, was still on the front porch, always looking up at him as if to say, "Please take me in."

"Guess that's what I get for feeding the mutt and letting him sleep on the porch." Delbert grimaced. Despite having asked around the area, no one knew who owned the German shorthair.

"Sorry, buddy, but I'm not a bird hunter, so I don't need a hunting dog." Delbert pulled out his hankie and blew his nose, trying not to think of the past. "In addition to that, I'm allergic to cats as well as some dogs. Maybe I'm not sensitive to you, but the last thing I need is a pet."

Delbert had vowed many years ago that he'd never own another dog. The pain he went through when he was a boy stuck with him even after all these years. How other people could go right out and get another pet after losing the one they loved was beyond him. Delbert realized it was normal for a person to outlive a pet, but he was not one of those people willing to go through such anguish again. That solemn day, as his dog of nine years lay lifeless in his arms, Delbert's heart felt as if it were torn in two. Even his dad said Sadie was the best rabbit dog he'd ever seen, but unfortunately, her zealousness was what got her killed. Delbert could still see Sadie chasing a bunny around the yard, and when it ran across the road, the dog followed. After that, it was like watching in slow motion as Sadie's life was snuffed out by an oncoming car. It was an image that to this day, Delbert would never forget.

Woof! Woof! The German shorthair wagged his tail and pawed at

Delbert's pant leg, pulling his thoughts aside.

Looking upward, he groaned. "Why me?"

Unable to resist, Delbert went down on his knees to pet the friendly animal. Its hair was short, and after scratching behind the pointer's ears for a while, Delbert was surprised he hadn't started sneezing. In fact, his nose didn't even tickle anymore.

Already this dog was worming his way into Delbert's heart as he shared a dish of leftovers from his ham and egg breakfast. "Well, it's not going to happen again." Delbert shook his head. "Since I don't know who your owner is, and I'm not gonna keep ya, it's time for me to find you a new home."

⌒

Grabill

Ben sat at the breakfast table with his head in his hands.

Dorothy tapped his shoulder. "Are you missing your hund?"

He lifted his head and gave a slow nod.

"I miss Hunter too. He was a good watchdog and kept me company when you were at work."

"Jah." Ben reached for his cup of coffee and took a drink. "I was hoping by now he'd have the good sense to find his way home, but it doesn't look like that's gonna happen."

"Maybe you should go back to LaGrange and look around some more." Dorothy handed Ben a plate of blueberry muffins.

He shook his head. "No thanks, Mom, I've had enough to eat, and I should get busy and finish the rest of my chores that I didn't get done earlier this morning."

"What about Hunter? Are you going to go looking for him?"

"I don't think so. I mean, what would be the point? He got out of Dave's truck while we were in LaGrange, but he could be anywhere by now."

"You're right." Dorothy helped herself to another muffin, grateful that her cold was better and her taste buds had returned. During the worst of her illness, not much appealed, and what she had eaten had no taste at all. To make matters worse, Dorothy's nose had been so stuffed up she'd been unable to smell any tantalizing aromas. Now, as she ate the blueberry treat, slathered with creamy butter, Dorothy enjoyed every morsel.

"Wish I'd left him home with you. It's my fault the hund is missing." Ben pushed his chair away from the table with a noisy scrape across the floor. "I'm headin' outside now, Mom. As soon as I'm done with the chores I'll be working out in the fields."

"Okay, I'll see you at lunchtime, then."

Dorothy watched her son go out the door, head down and shoulders slumped. She closed her eyes and prayed for Ben—for his dog to come home, and also that he'd find the perfect helpmate soon, because every man deserved a good wife.

Opening her eyes, Dorothy remembered she hadn't planned anything yet to include Martha Graber for a meal. *I'll call her later today and see if she'd be free to join us for supper one night next week. Maybe having Martha over will lift my son's spirits and put his mind on matters of the heart.*

Topeka

"How'd things go at the store this afternoon?" Thelma asked as she and Elma sat on her front porch, drinking ice-cold lemonade.

Elma sighed. "Busy as usual. It was hard for me and Lizzie to keep up."

"You should have let me stay and help you."

Elma shook her head. "You needed to come home and rest. Besides, we managed okay."

"You always seem to manage, but not always so easily." Thelma shifted in her chair when the baby kicked. She placed both hands against her stomach. "This little one has been quite active all day."

Elma moved her chair closer to Thelma's. "Can I feel it?"

"Of course." Thelma placed Elma's hand on the spot where the baby had been moving. "Feel that?"

Elma's eyes lit up. "I sure do. It must be wunderbaar knowing you're gonna become a mudder in a few months."

"It truly is." Thelma placed her hand over Elma's and gave it a pat. "Your turn will come. You'll see."

Elma crossed her arms, leaning back in her chair. "As much as I would like to be married, I'm not holding out hope. I am past my prime, Thelma, and the truth is, I may never find the right man."

Thelma tapped her fingernails on the arm of her chair. *Should I tell my sister about Delbert calling this morning to say he'd be coming by later in the day? Would Elma decline my offer to stay for supper if she knew I'd invited Delbert to join us?* Thelma didn't want her sister to think she was playing matchmaker, but it was only last month when she'd invited Delbert for a cookout without Elma knowing.

Thelma cleared her throat. "When Joe gets home, he's going to cook some chicken on the grill. You will stay and join us, I hope."

Elma smiled. "That'd be nice. I made some gluten-free, dark chocolate brownies that are also sugar-free before going to work this morning. I'm enjoying the recipes from the all-natural cookbook I picked up in town." Her voice grew louder. "I've even gone through the book and dog-eared several of the pages. I can bring the brownies over, and we'll have them for dessert."

Thelma licked her lips. "That sounds good, and before I forget, how is Pearl's leg? It's been a little over a month now since she cut it on the nail. Just wondered how much longer until you can start using her again."

"Well, she is still under the vet's care, but the antibiotics and salve must be working because he says she's healing pretty well. The nail seems to be staying in place too, after I hammered it back in. I sure don't want it to happen again." Elma paused. "I felt bad I didn't see that nail before."

"But everything is okay now, and that's what matters." Thelma licked her lips again. "Now, about those brownies. . . I have vanilla ice cream we can serve with them."

"Think I'll run over to my house and get them right now." Elma stood, smoothing the wrinkles in her long blue dress.

"Okay. I'll go inside and set things out to make a tossed green salad. Joseph should be here soon, and we'll eat after he grills the meat."

Elma smiled as she put the brownies in a plastic container. It would be nice to eat supper with family this evening. It had been a few weeks since they'd cooked out together, and this time Delbert wouldn't be there. Surely Thelma would have said something if she'd planned to invite him. *I need time to relax with my family. It'll be a lot better than sitting at the kitchen table by myself with Tiger staring up at me, meowing.*

Maybe I should get a dog to keep me company. Elma thought about

Joseph's dog, Ginger, and how she seemed almost human sometimes. Of course a dog couldn't carry on a conversation, or help with one's chores. But at least it wouldn't disagree with her if she said something it didn't like, and the best part was, most dogs were eager to please.

"Well, I don't have a dog, and I'm not going out of my way to look for one, so I'd better be satisfied with Tiger for now." Elma picked up the brownie container and went out the door. She'd fed and watered the chickens earlier and also checked on Pearl, so the only thing she'd need to do when she got home later this evening was let Tiger in the house and give him some food and fresh water.

Walking through the grass, Elma stopped when she stepped on something hard. Bending down to see what it was, she moved the blades about with her hands. "Ach, my keys!" After all these weeks, Elma could hardly believe her missing keys had been found. Of course, they were useless now, since Delbert had already replaced the locks. At least she had the consolation of knowing no one else had found them.

Glancing both ways before crossing the street, Elma headed up the driveway leading to Thelma and Joseph's house. As she drew closer, she saw a horse and buggy at the hitching rail near the barn. At first, she thought it belonged to Joseph, but after approaching the gelding, she recognized it as Delbert's horse, Chip. *Oh, no! Not again. I wonder what he's doing here. Is Delbert staying for supper? If so, why didn't my sister tell me?* Even though Thelma hadn't admitted it, Elma suspected her twin was hoping she and Delbert would get back together.

When Elma rounded the corner of the house, she spotted Delbert standing near the picnic table with a beautiful spotted dog at his side. As she approached cautiously, the dog's ears perked up, and he left Delbert to rub against her leg. Elma reached out to let the dog smell her hand, and right away, he licked her fingers.

"He's a friendly one." Delbert joined Elma.

"What a beautiful hund." She bent down to pet the dog's silky head. "Is he yours, Delbert?"

"No, not really. When I got home Wednesday afternoon, the critter was lying on my porch, lookin' like he was half-dead. I haven't found his owner, and I was hoping maybe Joe might take him."

Joseph stepped up to them and pointed under the picnic table, where

Ginger lay sleeping. "One hund is enough for me. Besides, if I had another, Ginger would probably be jealous."

The shorthair moved his head from side to side and slurped Elma's hand with his long, wet tongue.

Elma didn't know what she was thinking, but with one hand on the dog's head, she turned to Delbert and said, "I'll take the hund. I think he likes me."

He gave a nod. "I believe you're right."

Elma turned to Thelma when she joined them on the lawn. "Oh, guess what I found before coming over here?"

Thelma shrugged and turned both hands upward.

"Found my missing keys to the store and house."

"That's good." Thelma moved closer. "Too bad you didn't find them sooner, though."

"Hopefully you won't lose your new set of keys," Delbert put in.

Ignoring his comment, Elma lifted the container she held. "Here's the dessert I brought. Should I take it inside?"

"Jah. I'll go with you. I'm not quite done with the salad."

Elma followed her sister into the house. Nearing the open window, she tipped her head back and sniffed the air. "Smells like Joe has the meat grilling already. I can hardly wait to eat."

Thelma nodded. "I'm getting hungerich myself." She giggled, rubbing her stomach. "Or should I say *we* are getting hungry?"

Elma laughed. It was good to see her sister in a joyful mood. Being married to Joseph and now expecting her first baby—what more could she ask for to fulfill her life?

For a few seconds, Elma's jealousy took over. She and Thelma had always done everything together. It didn't seem right that Elma had no one.

Chapter 15

Grabill

When Ben came home from shoeing a horse the following Wednesday evening, he was exhausted and ready to relax. He only had a few things that needed to be done, and then he planned to put up his feet and unwind the rest of the evening.

Ben's tiredness didn't stop him from pausing to listen to the cicadas singing, however. "Sure can tell it's almost August." He reached up to rub a knot in his shoulder. Where had this year gone? Summer would soon be over.

While he listened to the insects' rhythmic chorus, he meandered toward the house. Surprised to see Martha holding a bouquet as she stood beside Mom near her flower garden, Ben halted. Assuming she must have come by to purchase the daisies, he said a quick hello and headed for the house.

"I invited Martha to join us for supper," Mom called as Ben stepped onto the porch.

Hoping to conceal his frustration, he halted and forced a smile before turning around. "I didn't realize we had company coming tonight. I was planning to muck out the barn after we eat, so I wasn't gonna take a shower till it was done."

"Can't it wait until tomorrow?" Mom's hands fluttered like she'd lost track of what she was doing. Ben recognized his mother's way of covering up her disappointment. He had a hunch she'd set this meal up so he could spend time with Martha.

"Never mind. It's no big deal." Ben waved a hand. "I'll clean out the barn after work tomorrow."

Feet shuffling as she kicked at the ground with her shoe, Martha mumbled, "Maybe I should go. I don't want to interrupt your plans."

Ben shook his head. "No, it's okay. I'll go take a shower and change clothes. Then I'll be ready for supper." He stepped into the house and closed the door. *Poor Martha. She keeps being dragged into my mother's plan to make us a couple. I doubt Martha has any more interest in me than I do her. Mom could use a new hobby to keep herself busy.* He reached up to rub his shoulder again. *Sure wish she would stop meddling. If it's meant for me to have a wife, I'd like to pick my own.*

❧

Ben couldn't wait to eat. He'd worked up a good appetite and taken his spot at the head of the table. They bowed their heads for silent prayer, and when finished, Ben's mother passed the food to him. Ben took what he wanted and passed the plates to Martha in awkward silence, unsure of what to say. Mom appeared to be compensating for his lack of conversation, as she chatted away to their guest.

Meanwhile, Ben couldn't help wondering what Elma might be doing. He nudged the potatoes on the plate with his fork, allowing his attention to keep on its detour. *I wonder what she's having for supper tonight. Can't wait to get up to Topeka to see her again.*

"Did you have many horses to shoe today?"

Ben's head jerked at Martha's question. "Uh. . .jah, I did."

"Do you enjoy shoeing horses?"

He nodded.

Mom passed him the platter of meat. "Would you like some more beef, Ben?"

"Jah, sure." He forked two pieces then handed the platter to Martha. The distraction of eating and having one's mouth full of food made it easier not to talk.

"This roast beef is so delicious and tender." Martha smiled at Mom from across the table.

"Danki. I'm glad you like it." Mom glanced at Ben, sitting at the head of the table, silently poking at his mashed potatoes. "How's your new job at Country Sales going, Martha?" Mom asked.

"It's going well. I enjoy working there." Martha blotted her lips with a napkin. Looking over at Ben, she smiled.

Mom gestured to the platter of meat. "Would you like another piece of beef?"

He stabbed one with his fork and passed the plate to Martha without making eye contact with her.

When the meal was over, he excused himself and headed for the comfort of the recliner in the living room. After Ben took a seat, he adjusted the footrest and put up his feet. "Ah, this feels good. Now I can relax and allow Mom's good meal to digest."

Ben heard his mom and Martha chatting in the other room, but he couldn't make out their words. He figured they were busy clearing away the dishes and putting the leftovers in the refrigerator.

Martha was all right, but she didn't seem mature enough for him. She was nice looking too, but in his judgment, Elma was prettier. Ben couldn't help comparing the young women.

Redirecting his thoughts, Ben remembered a customer he needed to call for a time adjustment, since he'd forgotten about his dental appointment next week. Trying to let his mind go blank, he closed his eyes. It took no time for his thoughts to return to Elma. *If she isn't being courted by anyone, I'd like to ask her to have supper with me.* Ben laced his fingers together and rested them under his head. His eyelids became heavy while he thought of the pretty young woman who lived in Topeka.

⌒⌣

Dorothy closed her eyes briefly and took a deep breath. Had Ben still been a little boy, she would have scolded him. Martha was their guest, and he should have known better than to treat her that way. She wasn't about to give up, but she couldn't force Ben to talk to Martha either. Maybe he'd be more cordial if the two of them were alone.

After Ben retired to the living room, Martha started clearing the table, beginning with the bowl of mashed potatoes.

"Oh, never mind about that." Dorothy came around the table and took the bowl from their guest. "There aren't many dishes, and I can manage fine on my own. Why don't you join Ben in the living room? It'll give you two a better chance to visit."

Martha drew her mouth into a straight line while biting down on her bottom lip. "Are—are you sure?"

"Absolutely." Dorothy gestured toward the archway leading to the other room, shooing her in that direction. "Go on now. I'll be fine."

Martha offered a quick smile and left the room. A few seconds later, she was back. "Umm. . .Ben is asleep in his chair." Before Dorothy could comment, the young woman said she would finish clearing the table.

Heaving a sigh, Dorothy ran warm water in the kitchen sink and added liquid detergent. "As soon as we finish the dishes I'll wake him up."

Martha shook her head. "Oh, no, please don't. He's obviously tired and needs his sleep. I guess he worked too hard today."

Or else he's not interested in a relationship with you. Dorothy gripped the sponge and picked up a plate. *Should I give up on this or keep trying to get Ben and Martha together?*

ↄᴼↄ

Topeka

Thelma sat beside Joseph on the couch, writing a letter to her parents. Even though she could easily make a phone call and leave a message asking to set up a time so they could talk, she liked keeping in touch through the mail. Thelma enjoyed making her own cards and stationery too. She'd made some spring-themed cards a while back, with friends and family in mind, to replenish her supply. The card she'd chosen to send her parents was detailed with flowers, like some Mom grew in her yard.

Sitting here in shared silence as their day wound down gave Thelma an opportunity to jot down her thoughts and make sure she was giving Mom and Dad all the details of what was going on in her and Joseph's life, as well as Elma's.

While Thelma wrote the letter, her husband read the latest edition of *The Budget* newspaper. He'd been quiet this evening, and Thelma wondered if something might be bothering him. A couple of times, she heard him sigh. If it was anything major, she was sure Joseph would talk about it in his own good time.

Thelma felt a flutter in her stomach, followed by a powerful kick. The baby was quite active these days. It was a good thing, though. It meant everything with her pregnancy was going as it should.

She set her card aside and clasped Joseph's arm. "I think our boppli is playing a game of shuffleboard tonight."

Squinting, he set the paper on his lap. "What do you mean?"

"He or she kicks on one side and then the other." Thelma took hold of his hand, placing it against her belly—first on the right side, then on the left. "See what I mean?"

Joseph's eyes widened, and his mouth opened slightly. "You're right. Doesn't that bother you? I mean, is it painful?"

She laughed. "No, it's not painful, and it doesn't bother me much when I'm up and about. Sometimes, though, when I'm in bed trying to sleep, all that movement can keep me awake."

He clasped her hand. "That's why it's important for you to rest during the day—to make up for lost sleep at night."

"I know. My sister reminds me to take it easy all the time."

"Speaking of Elma, how's she gettin' along with the hund Dell gave her?"

"Okay, I guess." Thelma shrugged. "I sure never expected she would want a dog—especially when she brings the katz in the house at night."

Tucking her feet under a throw pillow, Elma curled up on the couch, exhausted after another busy day at the store. Tonight, however, she didn't feel as lonely as before. Along with Tiger, she now had the companionship of a dog, and he seemed to like her as much as she did him. In fact, the German shorthair lay curled on the throw rug in front of the couch. Every once in a while, he would lift his head, look up at Elma, and whimper. In response to his bid for attention, she reached out and stroked the dog's head.

Tiger, on the other hand, wasn't fond of the new stranger and avoided the dog. The striped cat took fresh pathways lending him cover behind or under the furniture. In most cases, if the dog saw the cat, he'd do his bird dog stance before the chasing started. Much to Elma's chagrin, Tiger would leap for the countertops in the kitchen or other high places, making loud hissing noises in disapproval.

Since Elma didn't know the dog's name, she decided to call him

Freckles because of all the liver-and-white spots on his body. He was a well-behaved animal and responded eagerly to most anything she told him to do. Elma hadn't been sure how things would go the first night she'd brought Freckles into her house. It hadn't taken him long to spot Tiger and start a merry chase around the house. But when Elma clapped her hands and hollered, "Stop! Leave the poor cat alone!" Freckles dropped to the floor and put his nose between his paws. From that moment on, all Elma had to do when she wanted the dog to obey was clap her hands and say, "Stop!" Apparently his previous owner had done a good job teaching him to mind.

Elma's foot tingled when it began to fall asleep, and Freckles didn't even lift his head as she sat up to stretch her leg. After a few twirls of her ankle, the circulation returned.

She looked down at the dog and smiled when he shifted his position, never opening his eyes. "Crazy mutt." Two years ago, she'd have had a conniption if a dog or cat had come into her house, and she certainly would never have invited them in. But she'd become used to Tiger being in the house, and now here was another animal invading her domain.

I'm surprised Delbert didn't want to keep the hund, especially since Joseph has Ginger. Elma remembered how when they'd all gone fishing and Joseph brought Ginger along, Delbert seemed to like the dog. Maybe because of his work, he didn't want to be tied down with a pet. Elma had to admit she was glad he'd given the German shorthair to her.

Freckles lay contentedly as she ran her bare foot down the middle of his back, enjoying the feel of the animal's smooth, shiny coat. He thumped his tail on the floor and gave a contented grunt before going back to sleep.

I wonder where Freckles came from and who his master is. Elma yawned and lay back down, closing her eyes. *Could the person who used to own this beautiful animal be missing him tonight?*

Chapter 16

"I can hardly believe it's the first Monday of August already," Lizzie announced when she entered the store.

"I know," Elma agreed. "Seems like just the other day we turned over the calendar to the month of July. Now, here we are beginning a brand-new month." She pointed to the stand-up perpetual calendar on one end of the counter.

"Sometimes I wish I could slow the hands of time." Pursing her lips, Lizzie gave a slight shake of her head. "Then there are other times when I'm waiting for something and I wish I could speed things up." She moved closer to Elma.

"I understand." Elma left the stool where she'd been sitting. "Lizzie, why don't you sit here and take care of customers as they check out? When it's time for lunch we'll trade off."

Lizzie's eyes shone as she nodded her head. "It's fine with me."

Elma figured her helper would probably do a lot of visiting when people brought their purchases to her, but what other choice did she have? Thelma had a doctor's appointment this morning and wouldn't be available to work in the store until tomorrow, and then only for half a day. Elma had almost gotten used to Lizzie's continual chatter and sometimes eccentric ways. The customers didn't seem to mind, as they chatted with Lizzie about various things.

Elma smiled. There was no doubt about it—the elderly woman kept things interesting here in the store. There was never a dull moment with Lizzie around.

"Oh, before I forget. . ." Lizzie put her canvas tote on the counter. "My friend Miriam, from Kendallville, came to visit me on Saturday and brought a bag of peaches. There's a farm near her where you can pick your own."

"Fresh peaches. They are so good this time of year." Elma's mouth watered, thinking about their sweet, juicy taste. "I can't remember the last time I had a good peach."

"Well, think no more." Lizzie opened the bag. "I sure can't eat all of them, so I brought you some. You can share with Thelma and her husband too."

Elma watched while Lizzie laid all the peaches out on the counter. "They're beautiful." She picked one up. "I may have to wash this off right now and eat it."

Then Elma's eyes widened as Lizzie put a plastic container on the counter.

"I also made a peach pie." Lizzie beamed when she held up the pie dish. "Thought we could have some for dessert after our lunch today."

"Goodness, now I hope the morning goes fast. I'm already looking forward to lunch." Elma gave Lizzie a hug. "Danki for being so thoughtful."

"Think nothing of it. It's my pleasure." Lizzie waved her hand. "If I had kinner, I'd be baking for them all the time. Except for my brother, you and your sister are the closest thing I have to family."

"Thelma and I think a lot of you too." Elma felt fortunate to have this wonderful lady helping in the store. Not because Lizzie gave her peaches and a pie, but because Elma had begun to see Lizzie as more than an employee. She hadn't thought about it much before, but this dear woman spent extra time with customers because she was lonely and enjoyed being with people. Not that she hadn't liked Lizzie before, but from here on out, Elma would consider this caring woman a friend.

Elma couldn't imagine not having her family nearby. It was bad enough her parents lived several hours away; thank goodness Thelma was close.

"I'm going in the back to straighten a few things and unload the rest of the material that was delivered last week." Elma gathered up the peaches and pie to put with their lunches in the back. "At lunchtime, we can divvy up some of the peaches for Thelma and Joe."

Lizzie nodded. "I'll be right here if you need me."

Elma started walking, but Lizzie called out to her again. "I forgot to ask. How's that new hund of yours doing?"

Elma turned to face her. "Freckles is getting along fine. I'm keeping him in the basement when I'm here at the store, until I can hire someone to build a kennel for him. I'm not about to let the dog have free run of the house when I'm not there." Elma shook her head. "There'd be too many temptations."

"Maybe your brother-in-law could do it." Lizzie rested her dimpled hands in her lap.

"He'd probably be willing, but I may ask Delbert, since he has carpentry skills."

"You've had him do a lot of things for you, jah?" Lizzie peered over the top of her glasses with a curious expression.

Elma nodded. "Both here and in my home."

"Is there something going on between you two?" Lizzie leaned forward, rubbing her hands together.

A rush of heat covered Elma's cheeks. "Now don't get any ideas about me and Delbert. We're just friends."

Lizzie's brows jiggled up and down. "Doesn't love begin with friendship?"

"Ach, Lizzie! Now who said anything about love?"

The older woman chuckled, putting her hand over her heart. "Guess I'm an old romantic." Her brows gathered in, and she looked downward. "Although I'll never really known what it's like to fall in love."

"Now don't you fret, Lizzie. Thelma and I love you, and your family does too." It was all Elma could think to say. After all, she was in the same boat and had never known what true romantic love felt like.

Lizzie reached for a tissue and blew her nose. "Well, I mustn't keep you from what you'd planned to do. Besides, I heard a vehicle pulling in, which means we have a prospective customer."

"Right, and I'll let you take care of that while I do my thing."

"Okie-dokie."

⁂

"If you don't mind waiting for me, I shouldn't be too long," Ben told his driver when he pulled his truck up to E&T's General Store.

"No problem. Take your time." Dave picked up a paperback book. "I'll get a bit of reading done."

Ben opened the door and hopped out of the truck. After all these weeks of waiting, he looked forward to seeing Elma again. Now that he was within a short distance of her, his palms grew sweaty.

When he entered the store, he saw an older woman sitting behind the counter on a wooden stool. It certainly wasn't Elma or her twin. This had to be the right store, but maybe Elma and her sister weren't working today.

"Excuse me." Ben stepped up to the counter. "Is Elma Hochstetler here?"

The Amish woman stared at him, her eyelids blinking rapidly behind her metal-framed glasses. "Yes, she is. Would you like me to get her?"

He gave a quick nod. "If you don't mind."

"Since I have no other customers at the moment, I don't mind a'tall." She stepped off the stool and ambled toward the back of the store.

Ben rubbed a damp hand down his pant leg, taking a couple of quick breaths. He hoped he wasn't being too forward coming here. But ever since he'd met Elma at the farmers' market he had looked forward to seeing her again. Thoughts of her had come to mind each day since he'd met her. Now, as he stood leaning against the counter, he had a sudden desire to flee. What if she wasn't happy to see him? What if she thought he was being too forward coming here?

Maybe I could make some sort of excuse—say I came to buy something. Ben's muscles twitched as he took another calming breath and glanced around the store. What could be taking so long? Didn't the Amish woman know where Elma was?

Two women entered the store—one Amish, one English. They glanced at him briefly; then each headed down a different aisle.

Ben felt a trickle of sweat roll down his nose. He pulled a hankie from his pocket and wiped it away. A few seconds later, the older woman returned, but no Elma.

Ben cleared his throat. "Did you tell Elma I came to see her?"

"I did, but when she asked who you were, I said I didn't know 'cause I forgot to ask."

"I'm Ben Wagler. Elma and I met at the farmers' market a few weeks ago."

Grinning, the older woman sized him up and down then turned and ambled off once more. Ben's irrational fears began to take over again. He flexed his fingers, curling and uncurling them into the palms of his hands. Then he began cracking each knuckle. He'd come all this way and wasn't going to leave until he saw Elma.

Sure hope this green shirt I'm wearing isn't too wrinkled. Ben glanced at the bedraggled straw hat in his hands. *What was I thinking wearing this old thing today?*

While continuing to wait, he stood with his back against the counter. Looking around, he noticed how clean the place looked, although the building had an old smell to it. Everything looked quite organized too. He liked that, since he kept all his tools in place on his workbench in the barn.

He watched the English woman who'd come into the store browsing near the back with her head lowered, while her Amish friend flitted about, holding on to her list and a basket for her purchases.

Leaning back farther, Ben tried to relax. *I wish the older woman who'd been sitting up here earlier would hurry back with Elma. What could be taking so long?*

A few more minutes went by; then there was Elma—smiling sweetly and extending her hand. "It's nice to see you again, Ben. What brings you into our store today?"

Ben felt relieved, seeing her positive response to his visit. He moistened his lips while clearing his throat. "I. . .uh. . .said I might come by sometime." Ben's nerves were heightened merely looking at her.

"Yes, you did. I just wasn't sure—"

"Came to see if you'd like to go out to lunch with me." Surprised by his own boldness, Ben touched his throat. "That is, if you're not too busy."

"I'd like to, Ben, but I can't today." Elma's shoulders drooped slightly. "My helper, Lizzie, and I are the only ones working at the store right now, and I can't leave her alone in case we get busy." Elma glanced down one of the aisles toward where Lizzie was helping some customers.

"Oh, I see." Ben couldn't hide his disappointment. "Maybe another time, then."

"That would be nice." Elma grabbed a notebook and pen and jotted down her phone number. Smiling, with a sincere expression, she lowered her voice. "The next time though, please call ahead when you know you'll be in the area again, and I'll make sure my sister and Lizzie are both working here that day so I'm free to have lunch with you."

Ben smiled, speaking softer as well. "Okay, I'll do that." Well, at least she hadn't said she didn't want to be with him. He glanced around. "Since I'm here, maybe I'll do a little shopping."

She smiled. "Is there anything in particular you're looking for? Anything I can help you find?"

Ben shuffled his feet, looking anxiously about. "Well, maybe a new straw hat, if you have those here."

"We certainly do. If you'll come with me, I'll show you where they're located."

I would follow you anywhere, Elma. Ben clamped his teeth together, afraid he might blurt out the words.

Elma led the way, and Ben followed, his mouth getting drier by the minute. *Sure hope I don't say anything stupid.* He swallowed, wishing he had a bottle of water with him.

As they approached the shelf where men's hats were sold near the front of the store, Ben heard the roar of an engine outside. As the sound grew closer, he glanced out the window and watched in horror as a car approached, barreling toward the store. Before Ben could react or say anything, there was a crash, and the floor shuddered as if there'd been an earthquake. The hats vibrated off the shelf, and with a high-pitched squeal, Elma fell back into Ben's outstretched arms.

Chapter 17

"A re you all right?" Ben clasped Elma's trembling shoulders, turning her to face him.

"I—I think so." Elma wasn't sure if her limbs felt weak from the shock of the crashing sound or the nearness of Ben as he held on to her arms. "Wh–what just happened?" Her voice quivered as she stepped to one side.

"I don't know, but we'd better go see."

As Elma and Ben moved toward the front door, Lizzie joined them, her face turning ashen. "I've never heard such a commotion. What on earth happened?"

"I believe a vehicle hit the store." Ben opened the front door. "Sure hope no one was seriously injured. Let me make sure the porch and steps are still sound."

Stepping out the door, Ben bounced his weight as he checked out the structural integrity of the porch and steps. "Nothing looks damaged here, at least, but I see where the vehicle has ended up." Ben waved the ladies over, and when Elma and Lizzie looked down, they gasped. The front bumper of a car, with its motor still running, was pushed up against one side of the store's basement wall. An elderly English woman sat inside, gripping the sides of her head.

Before Elma could react, Ben leaped off the porch, jerked the car door open, and turned off the ignition. At the same time, a man sitting in a pickup truck, who Elma assumed was Ben's driver, rushed to the scene.

Elma hurried down the stairs, joining Ben by the side of the vehicle. "Is she hurt?"

"I'm okay! I'm okay!" The woman released her hands and lifted them in the air. "Just scared out of my wits, is all." She shook her head slowly. "I thought my foot was on the brake, but it must have been on the gas pedal instead."

"I'll help you get her inside and then notify the sheriff about the accident," the other man said.

"Thanks, Dave." Ben introduced him to Elma; then he and Dave helped the woman from the vehicle while Elma retrieved her purse, which was lying in a heap on the floor of her car. Elma carried the purse as the men led the distraught woman into the store.

"There's a cot in the back room. Let's take her there so she can lie down." Elma wanted to be certain the woman really hadn't been injured. How thankful she was that no one else had been in the store when the accident occurred, especially outside near the wall where it had been pushed in.

Lizzie walked ahead of them. "I'll get things ready for her."

Once they had the woman situated on the cot, Ben went back outside. Like a mother hen, Lizzie fussed over the woman, while Elma handed the purse to her, asked her name, and whether there was anyone she would like to have notified of the accident.

"My name's Opal Freemont, and my daughter lives in the little town of Emma." She gave Elma the phone number, and while Lizzie gave Opal something cold to drink, Elma hurried outside.

As she neared the phone shack, her twin arrived, breathing heavily. "I heard a crash. What happened? Was anyone hurt?" Thelma's blue eyes widened when she looked at the car up against the building.

"The driver of the car is Opal Freemont, but she only seems to be shaken up." Elma took a breath. "Opal is in our back room, lying on a cot to rest. Lizzie is there, keeping her company." She adjusted her loosened head covering.

"I'm relieved to hear she's okay. I was on my front porch reading when the noise from the crash startled me." Thelma gave her sister a hug. "Do you need my help with anything?"

"You can sit behind the counter to wait on customers while I make a phone call to Opal's daughter to let her know what happened."

"Okay, I'll see you back inside." As Thelma turned toward the store,

Ben stepped up to Elma. "The sheriff is on his way."

"Good to hear. The woman's name is Opal, and she gave me her daughter's phone number. I need to call and let her know what happened to her mother." Elma hesitated. "Oh, and after checking Opal over, I'm pleased to say she doesn't seem to be hurt."

"Good to hear." Ben crossed his arms, leaning against the small wooden building. "I'll wait outside while you make the call."

⁓

Ben didn't want to keep his driver waiting any longer, but after seeing how shook up Elma was, he didn't want to leave her either. Since he couldn't take her out to lunch today, he told Dave if he had someplace he needed to go, maybe he could come back in a few hours and pick him up.

"There's no place I need to be, but guess I could go see my friend in Shipshe for a while." Dave's arms hung loosely at his sides. "You have my cell number, so give me a call when you're ready to go home."

"Okay, thanks." Ben gave a wave and watched as his driver turned his truck around and left the yard. Then he headed back to inspect the damage the car had done to the store.

Ben felt fortunate to have Dave as his main driver. One would never know this calm-talking man held a senior executive position for a well-known company for more than twenty years. But as Dave explained when they'd first met, all the money in the world meant nothing if a person wasn't happy with what he did. Dave told Ben being vice president of the company had been exciting at first, and he was getting paid more money than he knew what to do with, but after a few years, he got burned out, and the job he'd once loved ended up being something he dreaded.

Ben couldn't imagine waking up and going to a job he detested every day. He enjoyed his job of shoeing horses, and had met many nice people in the process.

A few minutes after Ben finished looking over the damage to the store, Elma stepped out of the phone shack, halting his thoughts. "Opal's daughter is on her way." She glanced around. "Where'd your driver go?"

"He went to Shipshewana to see a friend. He'll be back later to get me."

Elma nodded her head.

After a bit of silence, Ben spoke again. "I had a chance to look over the damage to the store's basement wall."

"How bad is it?" Elma squinted her eyes with a look of dread.

"Some fixing needs to be done, but I think the sound of the crash was worse than the actual damage. Opal's car nudged the support beam in the corner of that wall pretty good, and I noticed a small crack in the beam, but it seems to be holding, at least for the time being." He rubbed his chin. "I wouldn't wait too long though, to get it fixed."

"Okay. I know someone who'll probably come over right away to fix it for me." Elma looked at Ben with those pretty blue eyes, and his heart nearly melted. "Danki, Ben, for assessing the damage." She paused and released a long sigh. "Why don't you come inside? It's much too hot out here. Besides, Lizzie made a fresh peach pie, and I think we're all deserving of a piece."

"Sounds good to me." Ben followed Elma into the store. This wasn't the way he'd planned for the day to go, but at least he could spend some time with her. For that much he was grateful. Maybe next time he came to Topeka he could take her out for a meal.

Grabill

Dorothy glanced out the kitchen window, then at the clock on the far wall. It was almost four o'clock, and still no Ben. *I wonder what could be keeping him.* When he left with Dave, he'd said he had some errands to run but hadn't said how long he would be.

She turned from the table and sat down with a huff. *I hope he's here in time for supper. Maybe I should go out to the phone shack and see if he called and left a message. I'd hate to start cooking supper and then end up eating by myself.*

She glanced at the clock one more time then rose to her feet.

Outside, Dorothy paused to look at her garden. Several mums had begun to bloom, and there were a few remaining daisies, but the lovely roses were what caught her eye. There were red, yellow, white, and pink ones too.

Dorothy bent to sniff their aroma and drew in a lingering breath. She'd miss the colorful flowers in her yard when winter set in, but for now, she would enjoy them to the fullest.

A hummingbird swooped past Dorothy's head as it hovered near one of the bright red blooms. It wouldn't be long and the tiny birds would be gone for the rest of the year.

Every season brought a new change, and at least here in Indiana, one could count on spring, summer, autumn, and winter. Each brought its own beauty. What concerned Dorothy the most were the things she couldn't count on. One of those involved Ben. What if he never found a wife? Would he be content to continue living here and seeing to his mother's needs until the day she died? If he ended up marrying Martha or some other woman in the area, would they buy a place of their own, or would his bride be willing to live here? There were many questions and so few answers.

Dorothy needed to trust God and seek His will in all things, but it was difficult to do at times. She thought about the words to Isaiah 26:3: *"Thou wilt keep him in perfect peace, whose mind is stayed on thee."* If she kept her mind on Jesus and not circumstances, she would feel more peace.

As she headed for the phone shack, Dorothy prayed for peace. She was halfway down the path when Dave's truck pulled in. Ben got out, waved goodbye to Dave, and gave Dorothy a hug.

"How'd your day go, son? Did you get all your errands run?"

"My day turned out much different than I'd planned." He gestured toward the house. "Let's go inside and I'll tell you about it."

Chapter 18

Topeka

After Elma finished breakfast, she kept an eye on the clock. The vet would be by to check on Pearl's progress soon. The horse had been on antibiotics, along with salve to heal the nasty gash on her back leg. The veterinarian wanted to give the horse a couple of more weeks to improve and had been coming by regularly to check on her. Pearl's appetite was good, and the mare appeared to be getting back to her old self. Elma was glad to see her coming along so well. It would be nice to use Pearl again, even though Rusty wasn't so bad.

Since Elma still had time before the vet showed up, she took out some furniture polish and a rag to dust the living-room furniture. Once she finished, she picked up all the throw rugs and took them outdoors to shake and air on the line.

Elma was getting ready to return to the house when the veterinarian's truck pulled up by the barn. She hurried out to meet him. They engaged in conversation before going inside the barn to check Pearl's wound.

"You've done well taking care of your horse. The wound is healing like it should." He rubbed and patted the horse's side. "You're doing well, Pearl, but you'll need to be reshod pretty soon." The vet pointed to her hooves.

"When do you think it'll be safe for me to take her out on the road again?" Elma questioned.

"Since you have another buggy horse, you should give this one a little more time to heal. We don't want her to bump that wound and undo the progress she's made. I'd say another week or two, but use your discretion. Also, remember, she's an older horse and probably would like some time off."

Elma nodded. "You're right. Pearl's been around awhile. Maybe retirement isn't too far off in her future."

⟡

It had been two weeks since Opal Freemont's car hit the store, but thanks to Delbert and his friend Sam, who did masonry work, the repairs were finished and a new support post had been set in place. Fortunately, Opal's insurance paid for the damages to her car, and she'd given Elma money to pay for the work that needed to be done to the store. One good thing came from the accident, though. Ben had been calling Elma every few days to see how she was doing and hear the progress on the repairs.

Thinking about his most recent call, inviting her to go out to supper with him this evening, caused Elma's heartbeat to quicken.

She looked down at her fingernails and couldn't believe how rough they had gotten. Elma wanted to make a nice impression on Ben—especially since this was their first real date. She went to her dresser and found an emery board and some hand lotion. Then she took a seat on the end of her bed and filed each nail until it had a nice rounded edge. After that, she worked with diligence, using the two-sided board to add a smooth, shiny surface to them. Satisfied that they looked better, she picked up her manicure kit and returned it to the dresser.

Glancing at the clock on the small table by her bed, she saw that it was five thirty, which meant Ben should be here within the next half hour. In some ways Elma wished Thelma and Joseph were going out with them. That way she'd have someone to talk to if the conversation lagged. But Ben hadn't suggested it, and it wasn't Elma's place to invite her sister and brother-in-law, so she would try to relax and think of enough things to talk about. With Ben hiring a driver to take them to and from the restaurant, it was almost like having a chaperone. If they couldn't think of anything to talk about during the drive, maybe Ben's driver would fill in the gaps. All she had to worry about was thinking of something to talk about during their meal at the restaurant.

Elma moved to stand in front of her dresser mirror, making sure her head covering was on straight and positioned correctly. She'd chosen to wear her lavender dress with matching cape and apron, since Thelma had said Elma looked good in that color. It was vain to think such thoughts, but she hoped Ben would appreciate the color of the dress and maybe even think she looked attractive.

Elma fanned her face. Was it the summer heat or being anxious to see Ben that made her cheeks flush? "Probably a little of both, don't ya think?" Elma directed her question to Freckles.

Cocking his head to one side, with ears perked, she almost felt as if the dog understood what she'd said.

When Elma heard the crunch of loose gravel from a vehicle pulling in, she peeked out her bedroom window. Instead of a truck, like the one Ben's driver had driven when he brought Ben to the store two weeks ago, she saw a minivan pulling into the yard. Either Dave had more than one vehicle, or Ben had hired someone else to bring him there this evening.

"Some watchdog you are," Elma said, nearly tripping over Freckles, who now lay in the hall outside her bedroom. He hadn't even barked. "Well, it doesn't matter. My ride is here, and you, my furry friend, must go down to the basement." With the August heat and humidity, Freckles would be in a cool, comfortable place for the evening.

Elma opened the basement door, and the dog went obediently down the stairs. She still couldn't get over how well–behaved this animal was. His previous master must have trained the dog well. She appreciated Freckles and felt thankful he'd come into her life at just the right time. Having the dog in the house during the night made her feel secure and a lot less lonely.

Elma shut the basement door, grabbed her black handbag, and hurried out the door. She met Ben as he came up the walk.

"I planned on coming up to the house to get you." Shoulders back, he held his head erect, never breaking his gaze into her eyes. "It's good to see you again, Elma."

She swallowed hard, clutching her purse against her side. "It's good to see you too."

"I talked my favorite driver into driving his van tonight." Ben started walking in the direction of the vehicle. "Figured it'd be more comfortable for you, and we can sit in the back and visit without Dave feeling like he has to be part of the conversation."

"I see. I hope he won't think we're being rude if we don't include him."

Ben shook his head. "Nope. I've gotten to know Dave real well, and he's not the least bit sensitive. Nothing ruffles him."

"Okay."

Ben opened the passenger's door in the back, and Elma slid in. Then he went around to the other side and took his seat.

"It's nice to see you, Elma." Dave turned and smiled at her.

"Nice to see you too. The seats in your minivan are comfortable."

He gave a nod. "This is really my wife's rig, but she lets me drive it whenever I need to."

"It's cool in here too," Elma commented.

"If you like, I can turn the air-conditioning off or down, but I thought it would be more comfortable with this heat," Dave offered.

"No, you don't have to. It actually feels quite good." Elma was thankful for the cooling system in Dave's van. At least it would help to keep her from perspiring, since she was a ball of nerves.

"Okay, then." Dave turned around and pulled out of the driveway.

"You look nice in that color." Ben's cheeks colored as he looked at Elma.

"Danki."

"Are you hungerich?"

"I'm getting there. Where are we going?" Elma asked when Ben's driver headed out of Topeka in the direction of Shipshewana.

Ben grinned. "Thought we'd have supper at the Blue Gate Restaurant. Have you eaten there before?"

She nodded her head. "My sister and I ate there a few years ago." She saw no need to mention that it had been with Joseph and Delbert during the time the men had been courting the twins.

"They have good food at the Blue Gate," Dave interjected, glancing back at them from his rearview mirror. "My favorite supper dish there is meatloaf shepherd's pie. It's served with a generous helping of mashed potatoes smothered in a tasty blend of cheeses." He snickered. "Course, the smoked pork chops are real good too."

"I may have to try the shepherd's pie." Elma looked at Ben. "What's your favorite meal?"

Ben smacked his lips as he gave his stomach a tap. "Anything that includes chicken. I like it fried, baked, or roasted."

"I like chicken too," Elma agreed.

"Well, then, you're both in luck. The Blue Gate has plenty of chicken dishes on the menu," Dave called over his shoulder.

Elma shifted in her seat, pulling on the seat belt buckle to make sure it was snug enough. She always felt safe when she buckled herself in. Elma sometimes wished there were seat belts in Amish buggies. Wearing one kept a person from being jostled around, not to mention being safer in the event of an accident.

"See that crossroad over there?" Ben pointed to his left.

Elma nodded.

"It leads to an Amish-run business I'd like to visit someday—Lambright Wind Chimes."

"I've never been there, but my brother-in-law, Joseph, bought one of the Lambright chimes to hang in their backyard. It has a beautiful, melodic sound." Elma leaned against the seat, feeling quite relaxed. So far things were going well between her and Ben.

"I bet it does. The hardware store in Shipshe sells them, and after listening to the quality of their tinkling sound, I became interested." Ben reached across the seat and touched her arm. "Maybe the two of us can go there sometime."

"To the hardware store?" His touch had Elma feeling so rattled she could barely think or speak.

"No, to see where Lambright's chimes are made."

"Oh." Elma's cheeks warmed. She was sure they'd turned red, and she hoped Ben wouldn't notice. "That would be nice. I'd enjoy visiting there." She glanced his way.

Ben gave her a dimpled smile. "I'll be looking forward to it. Maybe we can do it soon, when we both have some time off from our jobs."

"Okay." Elma clasped her trembling hands together in her lap. *He wants to see me again. He must enjoy my company as much as I enjoy his. I'm already looking forward to seeing Ben again.*

‿◡

"You're kind of fidgety tonight," Joseph commented as he took a seat beside Thelma on the couch. "Is the boppli kicking again and making you feel uncomfortable?"

"No, it's not the baby."

"Well, that's good." Joseph picked up a book to read. "Oh, I wanted to ask if you've been hungry for fish."

"I can always eat fish—fried or on the grill. Why? What were you thinking?"

"It's been a while since Delbert and I went fishing, and I'd like to check out the Little Elkhart River not far from here, where there's a designated trout stream. It feeds into a chain of lakes, which might be a nice area for all of us to go sometime. Maybe we could pack a picnic lunch and spend the afternoon there."

"Sounds nice, and I could surely eat some fresh trout." Thelma smiled. "Maybe we can have another cookout with Elma and Delbert—if you guys catch enough fish, that is." She poked Joseph in the ribs. Then just as quickly, she returned to her knitting and grew quiet.

"I'm sure Dell and I will bring home plenty for a supper meal." Joseph nudged Thelma's arm when she didn't respond. "Hey, all of a sudden you're like a million miles away. What's up?"

"I can't stop thinking about Elma."

"What about her?"

"She went out to supper with that Amish man from Grabill."

"You mean Ben Wagler?"

"Jah." Thelma's knitting needles clicked as she set them aside once more. "He's been calling her a lot lately, and now Ben's hired a driver to bring him all the way up here to take Elma to a restaurant." She pursed her lips. "He is moving way too fast, don't you think?"

Joseph shrugged his shoulders. "If a man knows what—or should I say who—he wants, shouldn't he go after her? After all, Ben and Elma aren't getting any younger, so what's the point in wasting time? And look at us. . .it didn't take long for you and me to realize how we felt about each other."

"That part's true." Thelma gave her husband's arm a light tap, while her shoulders tightened. "They're not that old. But I don't want my *schweschder* to get hurt."

"Why would you think your sister's going to get hurt?" Joseph's chin jutted out.

"Ben lives in Grabill, and Elma lives here. It's a long-distance relationship, Joseph, and I don't see how it can work." Thelma peered at him over the top of the glasses she wore for reading and close-up work. "If they became serious about each other, one of them would have to move."

"Oh, I see what this is about." Joseph's eyes narrowed. "You're worried your sister might move to Grabill."

She nodded. "I couldn't stand it if Elma moved away. Until I married you, she and I always lived together. I'm thankful our home is across the street from hers so we can see each other regularly."

Joseph took hold of Thelma's hand and gave her fingers a tender squeeze. "I think you're worried about nothing. First of all, Ben and Elma don't know each other well enough to be making any kind of long-term commitment. And second, have you forgotten that the relationship between Elma and Delbert's cousin didn't last? One of the reasons was because Myron lived too far from Topeka and they rarely saw each other."

"True. Danki for reminding me." Thelma grasped her knitting needles once again. *Maybe Joseph is right. This whole thing with Elma and Ben could be just a passing fancy. I certainly hope that's the case, because I couldn't stand it if my twin sister moved away. I need her living close to me.*

Chapter 19

Danki for helping me paint the boppli's room." Thelma gave her sister a hug.

"You're welcome. I'm glad I found the time to do it." Between work at the store and being courted by Ben, Elma's days were busier than ever.

Thelma opened the refrigerator and took out a pitcher of lemonade while Elma finished making tuna-salad sandwiches. "Why don't we take our lunch outside on the front porch?" Thelma suggested.

"Good idea. The fresh air will do us both some good."

Once outdoors, they took seats and bowed their heads for silent prayer. When they opened their eyes, Thelma handed Elma her sandwich and beverage.

As Elma ate and drank, she thought about how nice it was on this lovely September day, enjoying some quality time with her twin as she listened to the sounds of cows mooing in the distance. They both waved when a friend from their church district passed by in a buggy. Joseph and Thelma's porch gave a nice vantage point, enabling them to see a good ways down the road.

A slight breeze kicked up, and the wind chimes swayed with the harmony of soft, tinkling sounds.

"Those chimes sound so pretty." Elma cocked her head to listen.

"I know. I'm so glad Joseph moved them to the front porch for me. It seems lately I've been sitting out here a lot more." Thelma sighed.

"Ben wants to take me to an Amish-run business where they sell the Lambright wind chimes." Elma added. "I can't see the road from my house as well as you can, but I wouldn't mind having some wind chimes on my porch too."

Thelma nodded but didn't respond to what Elma said about Ben. "I never grow tired of sitting out here and watching the people go by. Sometimes I bring my mending or knitting, but it's easy to lose track of time." Thelma drank the rest of her lemonade.

Elma bobbed her head. "I know what you mean. Wish I had my crossword-puzzle book with me."

They sat quietly for a while as Elma watched one of the sociable barn cats Thelma had named Marble come up to the porch. Meowing, it slunk over to them and jumped into Elma's lap. She set her empty plate on the wicker table and stroked the cat's silky head.

Thelma chuckled. "I remember when you wouldn't let any of the *katze* do that."

Elma shrugged. "I still prefer dogs, but cats do have an appeal, and they're good for keeping the mice at bay."

"I'll take the dishes inside while you enjoy sitting here with Marble."

"She's a pretty little calico, and her name always makes me think of Grandpa and Grandma Hochstetler. Remember the jar of marbles spilling when I had that nasty migraine a few years ago?" Smiling, Elma stared at the home across the street that had once been their precious grandparents'.

"I'll never forget that incident. I make sure the jar I keep full of Grandpa's marbles in the center of my kitchen table has a tight-fitting lid. Sure wouldn't want it getting tipped over and spilling all over the place like they did that day." Thelma collected the plates before going inside.

Grabill

Over the past several weeks, Ben had seen Elma as often as he could. He took her out to supper several times and joined Elma at her sister's house for pizza and games. The trips to and from Topeka were costing him money, but he didn't care. It was worth every penny to be able to spend time with her. By the middle of September, Ben was convinced he'd fallen in love with Elma. It might seem too soon to some people—especially Mom—but Ben knew what he wanted. Elma Hochstetler was the woman he'd been waiting for all his life. Of course, he hadn't told her yet. It might seem too forward, and the last thing he wanted to do was scare her off.

Ben had been invited to join Elma at her sister and brother-in-law's place tonight for a barbecue. He looked forward to going and was eager to get on with his day of shoeing several horses so he could rush back home and get ready for his driver to pick him up.

"Will you be leaving for work soon?" Mom asked when Ben placed his empty coffee cup in the sink.

"Jah. I've gotta get going so I'm home on time to get ready for my evening with Elma." His face broke into a wide smile.

Mom's gaze flitted around the room as she rubbed the side of her cheek. "You've been seeing her a lot lately."

He nodded. "I enjoy Elma's company. We have a lot in common."

Her forehead wrinkled. "Such as?"

"For one thing, we both like chicken as well as some other foods."

"*Puh!* You can't base a relationship on liking the same kind of food. You need to think alike on many levels, and—"

"Sorry." Ben held up his hand. "Can we talk about this some other time? If I don't go now, it'll take all day to get the horses done."

"Okay, I understand."

Ben picked up his lunch box and moved toward the door. "See you later, Mom. I hope you have a good day." By the time the door closed, he'd begun to whistle.

⁓

Groaning, Dorothy grabbed her cup of tea and sank into a seat at the table. If she didn't do something soon, she could very well lose her son to that young woman.

She took a sip of mint tea and let it roll around on her tongue as she thought things through. *I might be worried for nothing. It's not as if Ben is making plans to get married. I'm sure he'd tell me if he was. Maybe after he's courted Elma awhile and gotten to know her better, Ben will decide she's not the right woman for him.*

Dorothy sighed. She'd been convinced Martha was the right choice for Ben, but it didn't appear that he had any interest in the young woman. For that matter, Martha didn't seem too upset when word got out in their community that Ben had begun courting a woman from Topeka.

Doesn't anyone but me care that he might move away? If he did move, would he invite me to go with him? Is there any chance at all that Elma would be willing to move here?

She stared into her cup as her mouth twisted grimly. *No way could I leave my home. And if Ben left, it would mean he'd have to start all over with his business, looking for new clients who live in or close to Topeka.*

Dorothy turned and glanced at the throw rug by the back door where Hunter used to lie. It was a shame he never made his way back home. If Ben had his dog right now, maybe he'd be too busy getting him ready for the hunting season to worry about courting.

Topeka

Elma stood at her bathroom sink, patting her hot cheeks with cold water from the faucet. For the middle of September, it was still quite warm and humid. She wondered how much longer the hot weather would last. It was a good thing Joseph and Thelma's backyard had several shade trees. It would be much cooler eating out there at the picnic table than inside the warm house.

Elma wanted to have Ben over for a meal at her house but didn't feel it would be appropriate unless Joseph and Thelma joined them. Maybe in a few weeks she would invite them all over for an evening of homemade pizza and board games.

The more Elma saw Ben and talked with him on the phone, the more she liked him. She often caught herself fantasizing about what it would be like if she were married to him. If their relationship continued and Ben eventually proposed, she couldn't imagine herself saying anything but yes. After the wedding, Ben would need to move to Topeka, of course. Elma couldn't leave her sister—especially since Thelma was expecting a baby. Elma looked forward to being an aunt and helping her twin in any way she could.

Then there was the matter of running the store their grandparents had left them. Once the baby came, Thelma could not run the business by herself.

"And she shouldn't be expected to, either," Elma murmured. Owning the store and running it was a joint effort, and Elma wouldn't think of leaving her sister with the full responsibility.

Feeling flushed, Elma patted her cheeks with a little more cool water. *I don't know why I'm even thinking about all this. Even if Ben should propose, it won't be for a while, so there's no point in me dwelling on this right now.*

After brushing her teeth and making sure her hair was neatly combed with her bun and white head covering in place, Elma left the bathroom. When she stepped into the kitchen to get the healthy dessert she would take to Thelma's, she halted. Lying on the braided throw rug in front of the sink was Freckles, with Tiger nestled right beside him.

Elma grinned. "Amazing! I believe these two animals have actually become friends." She hated to disturb them, but it was time to leave, and Freckles needed to go down to the basement.

Well, maybe it wouldn't hurt this one time if she let him stay in the house. She wouldn't be gone more than a few hours, and if the cat and dog kept sleeping peacefully, everything should be fine.

Chapter 20

When Ben's driver dropped him off at Elma's house, he was pleased and yet a bit disappointed to see her waiting for him on the front porch. He'd sort of hoped he might get to see the inside of her house, since he was curious if she kept it as neat as she did the store. Well, maybe some other time. Right now, he looked forward to spending the evening with Elma and getting to know her sister and brother-in-law better.

"Guder owed." Ben stepped onto the porch and offered her what he hoped was his best smile.

"Good evening." Elma's lips parted slightly as he took her hand, giving her fingers a gentle squeeze. What Ben really wanted to do was hug her, but he didn't want to appear too forward. Besides, Elma's sister might be watching from across the street.

"Are you ready to go?" he asked.

"Jah. I just need to get the dessert I'm taking." She gestured to the cardboard box sitting on the small table near the porch swing.

"I'll carry it for you." Ben picked up the box and stepped off the porch.

"Danki."

As Ben walked beside Elma, his thoughts ran wild. It was too soon to be thinking such things, but he couldn't help picturing her as his bride. *If we got married, would she be willing to move to Grabill? If we had children, would they resemble her or take after me?*

As they paused at the end of the driveway to look for oncoming cars, Ben looked at Elma and smiled. "How was your day?"

"It went well. Not quite so busy at the store, so it gave me a chance to do some organizing." She laughed. "Of course, that kind of work can be tiring too."

"You're right. From what I've seen of your store, it looks pretty well organized." While holding the dessert box in one hand, it felt right resting his other hand on the small of Elma's back as he escorted her across the road.

Elma waited until they'd crossed the street to reply. "I try to keep things put in their proper place, but with people coming and going and handling various items, the shelves can get a bit messy at times." She paused when they reached her sister's driveway. "Running the store is a full-time job, and with Thelma only working part-time, I couldn't do it all without Lizzie's help."

He nodded. "I don't have anyone helping me shoe horses, but there are several good neighbors I can call on when it's time to harvest our fields."

"You must keep quite busy. I'm surprised you've been able to take the time to come here for visits."

"To see you, I'm more than happy to take some time off." An empty feeling came over Ben when he dropped his hand from her back.

A blotch of red erupted on Elma's cheeks. "That's nice to hear, but I hope you're not setting your work aside on my account."

"Nope. I've planned my schedule around trips up here."

She slackened her pace and looked up at him. "Thelma and I took some time out to paint the nursery for the up-and-coming arrival."

"I'll bet it looks nice." He slowed his steps to match hers.

"Jah. The nursery will be cute with all the baby's things in it."

"I've always wanted kinner."

"Same here." Elma's cheeks reddened further.

As they continued their leisurely walk toward the house, a beautiful golden retriever pranced down the driveway to greet them, barking and wagging its tail.

"This is Joseph's dog, Ginger." Elma bent down to pat the dog's head.

"She's a good-looking hund. Do you have any pets, Elma?"

"Jah. I have a cat named Tiger, and a dog I call Freckles."

He tipped his head. "I'm surprised I haven't seen either one whenever I've dropped by the store or come to pick you up."

"Tiger often hangs out in the barn during the day, and I keep Freckles in the basement when I'm going somewhere or at work in the store. I haven't had him very long, and don't want to chance him running off."

Ben shifted the box in his hands. "I understand. My dog, Hunter, ran off when I was delivering some of my mamm's flowers to a lady who lives in—"

"Welcome, Ben." Thelma joined them on the lawn and shook Ben's hand. "I see you've met my husband's hund."

He gave a nod. "She's a real beauty."

"She can also be a *pescht*." Thelma nudged the dog with her knee. "They've had enough greeting, Ginger. Now go lie down."

The dog slunk off with its tail between its legs and found a spot to lie down on the back porch.

"I brought some dessert." Elma took the box from Ben. "Should I take it to the kitchen, Thelma?"

"Please do, and I'll go with you, since I still have a few more things to bring out to the picnic table." Thelma smiled at Ben. "Joseph's grilling steaks on the barbecue." She pointed in that direction. "Why don't you join him while Elma and I are in the kitchen? I realize you met my husband some time ago at the farmers' market, but it'll give you two a chance to get better acquainted."

"Okay, I'll do that." As the women headed into the house, Ben ambled across the yard to where Joseph stood in front of the barbecue grill.

❧

"Your cheeks are flushed," Thelma commented when Elma placed her dessert on the counter.

Elma touched her face. "I suppose they would be since it's so hot outside. Seems like summer is going to carry right into fall this year."

"Jah, I expect it will." Thelma placed her hands on her well-rounded belly. "Sure hope things are cooler when the boppli comes toward the middle of October."

Elma clasped her sister's hands. "It's hard to believe you only have one month to go."

"I know." Thelma sighed. "I hope Mom and Dad can come for a visit soon after the boppli is born."

"I'm sure they will. After all, this is their first *kinskind*, so they'll be anxious to greet the little one." Elma opened the refrigerator door and took out a jug of iced tea. "Should I take this outside, along with a bucket of ice?" Her sister almost always served iced tea when they had a cookout.

"That'd be great, but could you wait a minute? There's something I'd like to talk to you about." Thelma took a seat at the kitchen table and motioned for Elma to do the same.

"What is it?" Elma asked after she'd pulled out a chair and sat down.

"It's about you and Ben." Thelma blew out a series of short breaths.

"What about us?"

"Are you two getting serious?"

"I'm not sure. Maybe. . . I think so. Why do you ask?"

Thelma's eyebrows rose as she touched the back of her neck. "I've seen the way Ben looks at you, and I am frightened."

"Why?"

"I don't want you to move away from me, Sister. I would be lost without you, and now, with the boppli coming, I'm going to need you even more."

Elma got up and went to stand beside Thelma's chair. "You needn't worry. I'm not going anywhere." She placed her hands on Thelma's shoulders. For the first time since Ben had been courting Elma, she realized their relationship couldn't go any further. If he were to propose marriage someday, she would have to say no, because she couldn't move to Grabill and leave her twin.

⁓

As Thelma watched her sister go out the door with the jug of iced tea, a lump formed in her throat. She hoped she hadn't said too much. Elma's heavy sigh and the downward tilt of her chin gave evidence of suppressed disappointment. She was clearly infatuated with Ben and perhaps even thought she was in love with him.

But Ben isn't the right man for Elma. He lives too far away and would most likely expect her to move to Grabill if they got married. It might be selfish, but I need Elma here with me—especially with the baby coming soon.

Thelma cupped her hand under her chin. *And who would run the store if my sister moved from Topeka? I certainly can't run it by myself, and it would be a shame to sell it.*

Thelma stared at the table, unsure of what to do. All the unknowns caused many questions to run through her head. She wanted her sister's happiness, but surely Elma could find contentment with some other man. *Is it wrong for me to depend on my sister because I'm having a baby?*

She glanced at the refrigerator, remembering that Joseph had gone fishing with Delbert last Saturday, and they still hadn't eaten the trout they'd caught that morning and later froze. Maybe what she ought to do was invite Elma and Delbert for a fish fry next week. Perhaps a bit more time spent with Joseph's good friend would open her sister's eyes.

⁓

Ben's excitement over being with Elma and her family fizzled a bit as the evening progressed. For some reason, Elma, who'd been friendly and talkative earlier, had become quiet, responding only when Ben asked a question, but no longer initiating a conversation of her own. Plus, she no longer looked at him—not even when he spoke to her. Ben was perplexed by this. He hoped he hadn't said or done something to embarrass or upset her.

But if so, what did I say? I've tried to be polite and friendly to Elma and her family. He shifted on the picnic bench. *Maybe Elma's tired from working at the store all day and it's caught up to her.*

Ben pulled out his pocket watch, noting the time. His driver would be back in an hour or so, picking him up over at Elma's place, where he'd dropped him off.

"Now that we're done eating, should we play a game of horseshoes while the women get dessert ready?" Joseph nudged Ben's arm.

Startled, Ben jumped. "Jah, sure, that'd be great. I can only play thirty minutes or so, though. My driver will pick me up in an hour, and I'll need a little time to walk Elma home."

Joseph's shoulders drooped; then he straightened them again. "Okay, guess thirty minutes is better than nothing." He got up from the bench and went to get out the horseshoes.

Ben and Joseph played, with Ginger yapping every time each of them took a turn, until Thelma called them back to the picnic table to eat Elma's dessert.

"You're a good cook, Elma." Ben wiped the crumbs off his face from the blueberry crisp. "This is sure tasty."

Elma smiled, although it didn't quite reach her eyes. "I got the recipe from a harvest cookbook and altered it a bit so it doesn't have cane sugar in it. It's also gluten-free."

Joseph smacked his lips. "Well, you did real good because I'd never know it was a healthy dessert if you hadn't just said so."

"Elma has always tried to get me, as well as others, to eat a healthier diet." Thelma passed around some napkins. "But I have to say, I appreciate it—especially after trying this appenditlich dessert."

Ben looked at Elma to see her response. She merely smiled at her sister and quietly said, "Danki."

By the time they finished dessert, Ben spotted his driver pulling his truck up Elma's driveway. Dave was either early, or Ben had lost track of time.

Ben threw his legs over the bench and stood. "I hate for the evening to end, but Elma, if you're ready to go, I'll walk you home now."

She glanced at her sister, and when Thelma nodded, Elma stood too. "You can keep the dessert, Thelma." She gave her sister a hug, shook Joseph's hand, and headed down the driveway with Ben.

After crossing the street, and before approaching Dave's truck, Ben stopped walking and reached for Elma's hand. He was surprised at how cold it felt. Although the sun had begun to set, the air was still quite warm and humid. Compared to Elma's, Ben's hand seemed hot.

"I enjoyed being with you tonight," he whispered, bending close to her ear. "How would you like to come for supper at my house next Saturday? I can either have my driver pick you up, or if you prefer to have one of your drivers bring you to Grabill, I'll pay them for bringing you to my house."

Elma lowered her head a bit while clearing her throat. "Sorry, Ben, but I have plans for next Saturday."

"Oh." He couldn't hide his disappointment. "How about the Saturday after that?"

She stared down at her feet. "I'm not sure, Ben. Thelma's due to have her boppli sometime in October, and I need to be close so I'm available when it happens." She let go of his hand.

Already missing the feel of her soft skin, Ben slowly nodded. "Guess that makes sense. Well, I'll give you a call soon and see if we can work something out. Maybe I'll just come up this way again."

"All right, but please call before you come, okay?" Elma spoke so softly Ben could barely hear the words.

"I won't show up unless I've talked to you first." On impulse, Ben leaned down and gave her a quick kiss on the cheek. "*Gut nacht*, Elma."

"Good night, Ben."

As Ben got into Dave's truck a strange feeling came over him—a premonition of sorts. He couldn't be sure, but he was almost convinced something had happened tonight to make Elma pull away from him. He wished now he'd had the nerve to ask.

Chapter 21

Grabill

Shoulders slouched and head down, Ben stepped out of the phone shack. He'd left another message for Elma but didn't know why. He'd made several calls in the last three weeks, and she'd never called him back.

Jerking his hat off, he felt like throwing it on the ground. Instead, Ben ran his fingers through his hair. *I don't get it. Is there something wrong that she hasn't responded? Could Thelma have had her baby? If so, I would think Elma might have at least let me know.* Ben's jaw clenched as he leaned against the small building. *Maybe Elma doesn't want to see me anymore. She did act a bit strange when I walked her home after the cookout at her sister and brother-in-law's place. Sure hope I didn't do anything to mess things up between us. I can't picture myself with anyone else but Elma.*

Ben's boots felt like they were full of lead. Every step took great effort as he made his way back to the house.

He found his mother in the kitchen, sitting at the table, reading her Bible. As he approached, she looked up and pointed to the coffeepot on the stove. "There's still plenty of kaffi left, if you'd like a second cup."

"Okay, it does sound good. Maybe it'll help me perk up."

"Are you feeling down this morning or just tired?"

"A little of both." Ben poured himself a cup of coffee and took a seat at the table across from her.

"Want to talk about it?"

He shook his head. A few days ago he'd mentioned not hearing from Elma, and Mom had said it might be for the best, since long-distance relationships were difficult. Ben hadn't wanted to hear that, so he decided not to mention it again—at least not to his mother.

"Do you have a full work schedule today?" Mom asked while fiddling with the pleats of her dark green dress.

"No, not really."

Ben's spoon clicked against the inside of his mug as he stirred his coffee. The last thing on his mind was work. *Elma is such a nice person. Maybe ignoring my phone messages is her way of telling me it's over—sort of softening the blow.* They'd had so little time together. A solid relationship had never really gotten off the ground. But how could it with so many miles between them? Despite it all, though, this was the first time Ben had ever felt serious about a woman. Like a wildfire, it happened so fast.

Pushing his thoughts aside, Ben glanced out the window. It was a beautiful morning and still quite warm, as it had been the last couple of weeks. He noticed droplets of dew on the grass, sparkling like diamonds as the sun cast light on the blades. Looking farther out in the fields, he noticed the patchy ground fog slowly ascending into the blue sky. Ben figured by midmorning the fog clouds would disperse and temperatures would rise with the heat of the glaring sun. It was unusual having such hot weather carry into fall. *Sure would be fun sitting on a porch swing with Elma, watching the morning unfold.* He drew in a breath and let out a heavy sigh.

"So what are your plans for the day?" Mom cleared her throat a couple of times. "Son, did you hear me?"

"Uh, sorry, guess my mind was wandering."

"I asked what your plans are for today."

"I have a horse to shoe, and there are a few things I probably should do around here before it gets too hot, but I think I'm gonna let 'em wait till tomorrow."

Mom's eyes narrowed. "You know what your daed would say about that."

"Jah. He'd say, 'Benjamin, you should never put off what you'd planned to do today till tomorrow, 'cause tomorrow might never come.'" Ben blew on his coffee and took a sip. "It's good advice, but sometimes plans change and things have to wait."

Mom lifted the bottom of her apron to fan her face. "Are you thinking of anything in particular?"

Ben shrugged as his mind drifted in another direction. He had to see Elma. Needed to know what was going on.

Setting his cup on the table, he got up, said goodbye to his mother, and hurried out the back door. *Sure hope one of our drivers is available to take me to Topeka this afternoon.*

⁂

Topeka

"Joseph, it's time to go." Thelma nudged her husband's arm as he sat beside her at the breakfast table.

He looked at the clock on the kitchen wall and shook his head. "I don't have to head to the harness shop for at least another half hour."

"No, I mean it's time for us to go to the birthing center."

His eyes widened. "The b–boppli's coming?"

"Jah. I started having contractions during the night."

"Why didn't you wake me?"

"Because they weren't strong enough." Thelma grimaced as a sharp pain shot through her middle and around her back. "But they've gotten closer now."

Joseph leaped out of his chair, nearly knocking it to the floor. "I'd better call a driver. Can't take the chance of making the trip by horse and buggy." He paused and wiped his sweaty forehead. "We might not make it in time."

"Calm down and take a deep breath. I'm sure we'll be fine. But I agree, hiring a driver to take us there would be the best thing." Thelma pushed away from the table. "Oh, and after you do that, could you please run across the street and let Elma know? I want both you and her to be with me in the birthing room."

"Okay. You'd better go to the living room and lie on the couch till I get back." Joseph's face looked like all the blood had drained out. He grabbed his straw hat and rushed out the back door.

Thelma had already packed a small bag with the things she would need for herself and the baby, so all she had to do now was try to stay calm. With this being her first pregnancy, she couldn't help feeling some apprehension. Especially since the baby wasn't due for a couple of more weeks.

Elma had just finished eating breakfast when someone knocked on the back door.

"Coming!" she called.

Woof! Woof! Elma's dog raced for the door.

"Calm down, Freckles, and let me see who's there." When Elma opened the door, she was surprised to see Joseph on the porch, lips pressed together while tugging on his right ear.

His strange behavior caused her concern. "What is it, Joe? Is everything all right? You look naerfich."

"I admit. I am feeling nervous right now."

"What's wrong?"

"It—it's Thelma." Joseph's knees bent, then straightened, as his brows pulled in. "The b—boppli's coming." The poor man could hardly manage to get the words out. Elma hadn't seen him this flustered since the day he married her sister. She understood how he felt though, for she too felt naerfich right now.

"Already? B—but she's not due for two more weeks." Now Elma was the one stuttering. None of this seemed real. She felt as if she were in the middle of a dream.

"Maybe the doctor was wrong. Or perhaps the boppli decided to come early. Either way, your sister says it's time, and she wants you to go to the birthing center with us. I've already called our driver, and he's on his way right now." Joseph seemed more confident, as he puffed out his chest. "Just think, Elma, I'm about to become a daed, and you'll soon be our little one's aunt." His voice cracked. "I'm thankful my business has picked up, 'cause I have a family to care for."

Elma's mouth felt dry, and she licked her lips, hoping it might help. "It is hard to believe the day we've all been waiting for is finally here. Once the boppli makes his or her entrance into the world, none of our lives will ever be the same."

With a vigorous nod, Joseph turned to head back home. Walking backward, he hollered, "You will go with us to offer your sister support, won't ya?"

"Of course I'll go. Wild horses wouldn't keep me away. I'll be at your house lickety-split."

As she went about closing up the house, excitement welled in Elma's chest. This was the day they'd all been waiting for. She sent up a quick prayer. *Please Lord, let everything be all right—for my sister and her child.*

Grabill

Dorothy put a lid on the soup and took out the items needed to make sandwiches for when Ben arrived home for lunch. She had his routine down, and when Ben spent the morning with clients, he was always ready to eat when he got home.

Once the bread was toasted in the oven, Dorothy made a jug of iced tea. She was almost done slicing a lemon when Ben stepped in the door. He set his things down and tossed his hat on the wall peg.

"Hi, Mom. Something smells good." He took a seat by the back door and pulled off his new boots. "Ah, that feels better."

"It's never fun breaking in a pair of shoes or boots. You should do it in small phases." Dorothy removed the lid from the kettle. "I made chicken noodle soup, and I'll get us a couple fried-egg sandwiches started quickly."

Ben sat, rubbing the toes of his feet. "Okay."

"You can get washed up. It won't be long till lunch is ready." Dorothy watched her son get up from his chair and leave the room; then she turned to the stove and broke two extra-large eggs into the skillet. While they cooked, she dished up the hot soup and placed their bowls on the table.

By the time Ben returned, the sandwiches were ready, so they sat down and offered their silent prayers. Then Ben added several crackers to his soup and started in.

"Did you have a *gut mariye?*" Dorothy handed Ben his sandwich plate.

"My morning was as good as any other this week." Ben smacked his lips. "This soup is sure tasty, Mom."

"Danki. I'm glad you like it." Dorothy gestured to her bowl of soup. "I added more noodles than usual." She grabbed a napkin.

They ate in silence for a while, but Dorothy wanted some conversation. "I'll need to get some weeding done after lunch. I also have cherry tomatoes ripe enough for picking."

He nodded and continued eating.

Dorothy wondered if he had something on his mind. "Are you going back out to shoe more horses this afternoon?"

Ben glanced at the wall clock and shook his head.

Dorothy frowned. It felt as though she were having a one-way conversation.

"That was good, Mom." He stood and put his dirty dishes in the sink then sat back down to put on his boots.

"If you have no more horses to take care of, where are you going?"

"I have an errand to run, and I'd better get going. Danki for lunch. See you later."

When Ben headed out the door, grabbing his hat, Dorothy finished her meal then rose to tidy up the kitchen.

When her chore was done, she went outside and got down to business. Dorothy weeded awhile then collected an abundance of tomatoes and other vegetables. After bringing her produce inside and setting it on the table, she deposited the warm, fragrant tomatoes carefully into the sink. While rinsing them with cool water and placing each one on a towel to dry, her mind drifted.

It's strange that Ben hasn't mentioned his friend Elma the last few days. Could he be losing interest in her? Dorothy shifted her weight and kept rinsing the vegetables. *If so, it's for the best. He needs to find someone closer to home.*

Chapter 22

Topeka

When Ben stepped onto the porch of Elma and Thelma's store, he was surprised to see a CLOSED sign in the window. It was ten o'clock in the morning. The store should be open by now.

Ben sprinted back to his driver's vehicle. "The store's closed, so I need to head to Elma's house and see if she's there."

"Okay." Dave gave a nod. "I'll park my truck down by the house. Do you want to ride with me or walk over there?"

"I'll walk and meet you there." Instead of walking, however, Ben ran all the way to Elma's front door. His skin felt clammy and sweat trickled down his forehead, but he didn't care. Ben knocked several times. When no one answered, he ran around back and knocked on that door. Still no answer. The only thing he heard was the muffled sound of a dog barking. He stood listening a few seconds. It had to be his imagination, but the bark sounded familiar—almost like. . . *No, it couldn't be. That was Elma's dog, Freckles, barking.*

He stepped off the porch and ran back to Dave's truck. "Elma's not here, so I guess we oughta head back to Grabill." Groaning, he climbed into the passenger's side, wiping his face with a handkerchief.

"Maybe she's across the street at her sister's, where you had the cookout a few weeks ago." Dave turned on the air-conditioning. "If you want to check, I'll drive you over there."

"Good idea. If Elma's not there, maybe Thelma will know where she is." Ben rubbed a knot on the nape of his neck. "Sure hope everything's okay with her."

When they pulled into Joseph and Thelma's yard, Ben hopped out of the truck and ran up to the house. He knocked on the front door several times, but nobody answered. Then he ran around back to see if anyone was in the yard. No one was in sight. After knocking on the back door with no luck, Ben returned to Dave's truck. "The Beechys aren't home, either. If you don't mind taking me to Elma's again, I'll leave a note on her door. Then we may as well head home."

ornamental divider

Elma stood on one side of Thelma, wiping her sister's forehead, while Joseph stood on the other, holding her hand and giving encouragement as Thelma pushed again.

Thelma had been laboring a couple of hours since they arrived at the birthing center, but now the pains were really intense.

"Why's it taking so long?" Thelma moaned, her face red from all the pushing.

"Our little one is just being stubborn." With a calm voice, Joseph grinned. "The boppli isn't even born yet, and it's already taking after me."

That got a quick chuckle out of Thelma before her face scrunched up and she bore down again.

Elma didn't say a whole lot. She let Joseph give her sister encouragement. Elma figured it helped him too, because she knew how nervous he was. Elma wiped the cool cloth over her sister's brow again. Looking toward the other end of the bed, Elma realized she would soon be seeing her niece or nephew seconds after it came into the world.

Elma wished she could take the pain away from Thelma but was hopeful it wouldn't be much longer. She'd always heard labor pains were quick to be forgotten once the baby was put in its mother's arms. Despite the pain her sister was going through, Elma was glad to be present, watching this miracle unfold.

"All right now, the baby's coming. Bear down and give me one more good push," the midwife urged Thelma.

Elma instinctively took Thelma's other hand, while Joseph continued to hold her other.

Thelma took a deep breath, raised up, and pushed with all her might.

"It's a boy," the midwife proclaimed, "but lay back and relax a little, because you're not done."

Joseph's head jerked when his newborn son was placed into the nurse's arms, who had been standing by and assisting the midwife. "Wh—what do you mean?"

"Just relax, Joe," Elma spoke up. "She still has to deliver the afterbirth."

The midwife shook her head. "It's more than that. The monitor is indicating there's a second heartbeat."

"It has to be Thelma's heartbeat you're hearing." Joseph gave a nod. "Right?"

The midwife shook her head before examining Thelma further. "You know what? There's a second baby coming."

Joseph's eyes widened, while Elma and Thelma both gasped. "Twins?" they asked in unison.

"Yes. Now this could take some time, so just relax, Thelma. After this one is born, we will transfer you to the hospital so you and the babies can be checked out."

Thelma grunted. "It's not going to take any time at all. I need to push now."

Elma watched in amazement as, a few minutes later, a perfect baby girl made her entrance into the world. Tears welled in her eyes. What a joy to witness the miracle of her sister giving birth to not one, but two precious children. At the same time, Elma couldn't help feeling envious. She could only imagine the thrill of having a child of her own. *But it may never happen,* she reminded herself. *I need to be happy for Thelma and Joe and appreciate the joys of being an aunt.*

Elma bent close to her sister. "I'm going out to make a phone call. Mom and Dad need to know you've given birth to twins."

"Would you call my folks and leave a message for them too?" Joseph looked tenderly at the infant cradled in his arms after the nurse cleaned the baby boy.

"Jah, of course, I'll make the call." Elma watched when the nurse finished cleaning their tiny girl and laid her gently into Thelma's arms. Both Joseph and Thelma had tears in their eyes, as did Elma. Taking one last look at the happy family, she slipped quietly from the room.

❦

Thelma gazed at her twins in awe. "I had no idea there were two babies inside my womb. How come we never realized it?" she asked the nurse. "I mean, I never got that big, and no one ever said they heard two heartbeats."

The nurse pursed her lips. "We actually did hear two during your appointments, but we thought the second one was an echo of your heartbeat, because it was so faint. Also, since you didn't have an early ultrasound, the second baby was obviously hidden behind the first one."

"Guess that makes sense," Joseph put in. "Whew!" He blew out his breath in a loud puff. "Can you believe it, Thelma? We have a *bu* and a *maedel*. What are we gonna name them?"

"I don't know, but we need to make a decision soon." Thelma blinked as tears seeped out from under her lashes. "Maybe when Elma gets back from making the phone calls."

"The babies' names can be decided later," the nurse said. "The first thing we need to do is get you and the twins transferred to the hospital."

Thelma swallowed hard. From what she could tell, her son and daughter looked perfect. She hoped and prayed they would be pronounced healthy, and they could all go home soon.

❦

Elma stood in the hallway outside her sister's room after calling her parents, as well as Joseph's folks, to share the good news. She'd left messages for both couples since no one was in their phone shacks when she called.

She leaned against the wall, goose bumps erupting on her arms. *It's really happened. Thelma is officially a mamm, and I'm those precious babies' aendi. It's amazing how one's life can change in a single day. How wunderbaar to see our family growing. Someday, the children will be grown and getting married. Then I'll have the opportunity of being a greataunt.*

Elma closed her eyes. *Thank You, Lord, for giving my sister and her husband two babies to love and cherish. I pray when they get to the hospital, the doctor will pronounce them both perfectly healthy. Help me to find the time to be there for Thelma when she needs me the most. Thank You again, for all that You do. Amen.*

Chapter 23

Elma sat in her sister's rocking chair, tears welling in her eyes as she gazed at the precious baby girl in her arms. It had been a week since Thelma's twins were born, and she'd taken time off from working at the store to help out. Mom and Dad hadn't come to see the babies yet, because Mom had been down with a bad cold. But she was better now, and they'd be arriving sometime today. Once they got settled in, Mom would take care of Thelma and the babies so Elma could open the store again. Elma had thought about letting Lizzie run the place in her absence but figured that wouldn't go well, so closing it for a week had seemed like the logical thing to do.

"Looks like you've put Miriam to sleep." Thelma snuggled her son in her arms. "Charles is sleeping too."

Elma smiled. "Jah." She was pleased Joseph and Thelma chose to name their daughter after their grandma Miriam, and their son after Joseph's grandfather, Charles. It was an honor for the children to be named after a relative.

Elma stroked Miriam's soft cheek. *If I ever have a daughter I'll call her Kathryn, after my mamm. And if I had a son. . .*

A vision of Ben popped into Elma's head, as she thought about the note he'd left on her door the day the twins were born. She was sorry she had missed him, but it was probably for the best.

If I were married to Ben, what name would he choose for our son? Elma leaned her head against the back of the chair and closed her eyes. There was no point thinking about this. She and Ben were not getting married, and unless she found someone who lived closer, it wasn't likely she'd ever get married.

During the last three weeks, Ben had left messages for Elma on her voice mail, but she'd been too busy to respond—first at the store, and then helping Thelma.

I ought to call him. At least let him know Thelma had her babies and that I'm too busy to see him right now. Perhaps in time, Ben will give up on our relationship and stop calling. It would be easier than having to tell him the reason I've pulled away.

"I hear a vehicle pulling in." Thelma's eyes brightened. "I bet it's Mom and Dad with their driver."

Grabill

After Ben finished with his last client for the day, he stopped at a grocery store to grab a snack. He needed some energy to get him going again.

Ben chatted with the clerk a few minutes, paid for the items, and left the building. He went back to his buggy and sat munching on an apple, while watching customers come and go from the store. When he finished his snack, he tossed the core and the empty water bottle into the nearest trash can.

He walked over to the hitching rail and stood there, thinking about Elma, as he so often did these days. *I wonder why she hasn't returned any of my calls. Sure hope the last time we were together I didn't do something to offend her.*

Over and over he had relived the evening they were at Thelma and Joseph's. Ben remembered every word spoken between him and Elma but could not come up with anything that might have upset her. He remembered how his heart skipped a beat when he guided Elma across the road, and the way she looked at him when they talked earlier in the evening. But then something had changed in her demeanor, and she'd said very little. It was as though she'd lost interest or was preoccupied.

Forcing his thoughts aside, Ben untied his horse and paused to give him a few pats. Then he climbed into the buggy and backed up his rig before heading onto the street.

A short ways down the road, Fella threw a shoe. "Oh, great, just what

I don't need today. It's like the story of the shoemaker—always too busy taking care of everyone else to notice his children were going without good shoes." Ben clucked to his horse. "Don't worry, boy. We'll take it easy on the way home. I'll get you fixed up soon."

❧

"Look what I got while you were working today." Ben's mother grinned when he entered the kitchen, as she sat in a chair, holding a black-and-tan German shorthair puppy. "I know how much you miss Hunter, so I thought you'd like to have this cute little fella."

Ben glanced at the pup then looked away. "I appreciate the thought, but I'm not interested, Mom. No hund could ever replace the one I lost."

"Of course not, but you may end up liking this dog as much as you did Hunter." She stroked the puppy's ears. "Isn't he the cutest thing? And look how relaxed he is in my arms. Would you like to hold him?"

Ben shook his head. "He seems nice enough, but I don't want another dog." He placed his lunch box on the counter and got a drink of water. "Since you like the hund so much, he can be yours."

Her lips compressed. "But I got him for you, Ben."

He gripped his glass of water. Didn't his mother get it? Why was it so hard for her to understand?

"Any thoughts on what name the dog should have?"

He shrugged. "Whatever you want to call him is fine by me. He'll be with you most of the time anyway, so you ought to choose the name."

Rocking from side to side in her chair, almost as if she were keeping time to some unheard music, Mom smiled and said, "How about Partner? A good hunting dog should be the hunter's partner, don't you think?" With that, the puppy barked and licked Mom's nose. "Ah, you are such a cute little baby. He likes his new name." Mom cooed and continued to cuddle the puppy.

"I suppose." It was all Ben could do to keep from rolling his eyes. Mom was already stuck on this dog, and to make matters worse, she expected him to be too. Well, she could keep the mutt if she wanted, and if it made her feel better, Ben would let her think he'd accepted the animal too. It was better to go along with things than stir up a problem.

"What time's supper?" Ben asked, setting his empty glass in the sink.

"Not for another half hour or so."

"Good. It gives me time to go out and replace my horse's lost shoe. When I come back I can eat, take a shower, and change into clean clothes."

"Sorry to hear your gaul lost his shoe, but at least you can remedy the problem." Mom smiled, nuzzling the pup's head.

"It's true, but it only lengthens my workday. I didn't check the phone messages coming home today. Did I have any calls?" Ben crossed his arms.

"Only one. It was from a customer, confirming their eight o'clock appointment tomorrow morning."

"Okay, thanks." Out of respect for Mom, Ben leaned down and gave the dog a pat on the head. He had to admit, the pup was sweet. And who could resist a puppy? The animal responded by licking Ben's hand as he started to move it away.

Mom smiled up at him. "See there. . .already, Partner likes you."

"Jah, I suppose." Ben shuffled back outside and headed for the barn. Shaking his head, he couldn't help thinking, *If I don't watch out, that dog is gonna grab at my heartstrings.*

Speaking of heartstrings. . . . As he approached the barn door, a vision of Elma popped into Ben's head. *Since she still hasn't returned any of my calls, if I don't hear something from her by tomorrow, I'm gonna hire Dave to take me to Topeka so I can find out for myself if anything is wrong.*

❧

Topeka

"Such a *siess* little maedel. Oh, and I love the name you chose for your daughter," Mom said when Thelma handed Miriam to her.

Tears gathered in Mom's eyes as she stroked the top of her granddaughter's head. "I can't get over all her pretty auburn hair."

Joseph grinned. "Yep. She takes after her daed." He gestured to little Charles, being held by Thelma's father. "Can't tell for sure yet, 'cause it's kinda sparse, but it looks like he may have his mamm's brown hair."

Thelma smiled. It was good to have her folks here, making a fuss over the twins and offering their help, but she couldn't help noticing the look of longing on her sister's face. If only Elma were married and had a baby. Thelma was certain Elma had felt left out when she and Joseph got married. Now, becoming a parent was one more thing she and Elma couldn't share. It didn't seem fair that her twin had no husband. Up until Thelma fell in love with Joseph and they decided to get married, she and Elma had done everything together. Truth was, they'd made a promise to each other many years ago that neither of them would marry unless the other one did. Of course, Elma had relinquished Thelma from her promise, saying she wanted her sister's happiness and wouldn't hold her back. Thelma was so deliriously happy on her wedding day, she hadn't stopped to truly consider her twin's feelings.

"Have many visitors come to see the new bopplin so far?" Mom looked at Thelma.

"Jah, we've had some from church, and a couple of neighbors stopped in." Thelma sat back in her seat. "It's been a busy week since we brought the babies home."

"Have you had anyone from any distance come, or have they all been local?"

"Actually, our friend Delbert Gingerich came by yesterday. He used to court Elma and lives in LaGrange, although it isn't that far from here."

"Dell's been coming to Topeka to do some work for Elma. And he's been over here to our place for a few barbecues," Joseph added.

Thelma thought about Delbert, and once more, she wondered if there was a chance he and Elma might get together. Delbert had dropped by last night to see the babies and visit with Joseph, but it was after Elma had gone home. If Elma had witnessed Delbert holding little Charles, she may have seen him in a different light. Thelma was almost certain she'd seen a look of longing on his face. Even if he and Elma didn't get together, Thelma hoped Delbert would find a good wife and start a family of his own. Maybe if things worked out like she hoped, his role as a husband and father would be with Elma.

⁓

Elma watched while her parents fussed and cooed over the babies, as Thelma and Joseph stole glances at each other with pure love in their eyes. All their faces beamed, and Elma felt nothing but happiness here in her sister's living room.

Baby Charles and Miriam were her parents' first grandchildren. Elma wondered if she would ever be able to give them more. She'd never been the jealous type, but oh, how it hurt not to be in Thelma's shoes right now as a new mother. If Elma had a husband, at least children could be in her future.

Does Thelma realize the sacrifice I've made giving up my relationship with Ben? Maybe I should confide in her and explain how much Ben means to me. After all, didn't I take a chance that Thelma might move away when I told her she and Joseph belonged together?

Elma forced a smile, which really wasn't hard to do when her father stood and put the baby boy in her arms. She placed her little finger in the infant's grasp, amazed at how tiny his hand was. Her heart melted when Charles yawned and clutched her finger tighter before he fell asleep. All she could do was pray once more, that someday her own baby would be cooing and gripping her finger.

Chapter 24

Elma stepped into the phone shack and called Ben. Fully expecting his answering machine to pick up, she was surprised when he answered the phone.

"Hello, Ben, this is Elma." Her fingers grew moist with perspiration, and she wiped them across her brows. "I–I didn't expect you to pick up." Just hearing his voice caused her to stammer.

He chuckled. "You caught me a few minutes after I entered my phone shack to check for messages. It's good to hear from you, Elma. How have you been?"

"I'm fine, and I apologize for not responding to any of your messages." She shifted on her seat. "There's been a lot going on in my life these past weeks, and I've been extra busy."

"What's going on?"

"In addition to running the store, my sister gave birth to twins a week ago. She had a boy and a girl."

"Wow, that's really something! Is everyone doing well?"

"Jah, Thelma and the bopplin are fine. And Joseph. . ." Elma paused to swallow. "Well, he hasn't stopped smiling since they were born."

"No wonder you've been busy. I bet you go over to your sister's place whenever you're not working at the store to help out."

"I did at first, but now my mamm and daed are here, so Mom's taking charge of things. Dad will be heading back to Illinois tomorrow to make sure things are running smoothly at his and Mom's general store, but Mom plans to stay a few more weeks."

Ben didn't say anything for several seconds. Then he cleared his throat loudly. "I'd like to see you again, Elma. Maybe you could come to Grabill on your next day off and stay for supper. I'm sure my mamm would like to show off her new puppy too."

Elma pinched the bridge of her nose, squeezing her eyes shut. "That sounds nice, but—"

"I won't take no for an answer. I know you're busy, but since your mamm is there to help Thelma, and you've been working hard at the store, you deserve some time off. Don't you agree?"

Elma's tongue darted out to lick her lips. *Would it hurt if I went to Grabill and had supper with Ben and his mother? I should be able to see him once in a while without letting our relationship become serious.*

"Jah, visiting your place would be nice." Elma paused a second. Her throat felt so dry she could barely swallow. "My next day off is this coming Saturday. I'm having some work done inside the store, so it will be closed that day. Would that work for you?"

"Saturday's good. I'll have my driver bring me to your place around three. Maybe we can stop at your sister's before we head for Grabill. I'd like to see the twins and offer congratulations."

Hearing Ben's excited tone caused Elma to wonder if she'd done the right thing accepting his invitation. Going to his house for supper might give the impression she wanted their relationship to become serious. *Which I do,* Elma admitted to herself. *If only I could.*

⁂

When Delbert entered Elma and Thelma's store, he found Lizzie sitting on a stool behind the counter, reading a book. "Where's Elma?" he asked. "She told me she wanted some new shelves built. Since I'll be installing them this Saturday, I came by to see what size she wants."

Without looking up from her book, Lizzie popped a piece of caramel candy into her mouth and chewed on it for what seemed like forever. "Elma's not here right now," she mumbled.

Delbert frowned. Couldn't Lizzie even put the book down and look at him when she spoke? To add to his annoyance, she didn't offer him any candy, even though several pieces lay on the counter. Jelly beans were Delbert's favorite, but he would never pass up a good caramel either.

Some people could be so rude. He'd never understood why Elma hired the woman. In all the times he'd been here, he'd never seen Lizzie doing much except gabbing with the customers.

With mounting irritation, Delbert tapped the toe of his boot against the wooden floor. "Where'd Elma go, and when's she coming back?"

"She ran out to the phone shack to make a few calls and check for messages, so it could be a while."

Still no eye contact from Dizzy Lizzie. It might be wrong to think of her that way, but from all the things Delbert had heard and seen about Elma's helper, it seemed like a fitting name. Of course, he would never call Lizzie "Dizzy" to her face.

The door opened, and Delbert looked in that direction, hoping it was Elma. Instead, two Amish women he'd never met entered the store. He glanced back at Lizzie to see what she would do and was surprised when she set her book aside and greeted the women. *Sure didn't do that when I came in.*

Delbert moved toward the front of the store, where the men's straw hats were sold. He picked one up and looked it over. All his hats were in fairly good condition, so he didn't need a new one, but at least it gave him something to do while he waited for Elma.

He didn't have to wait long, for a few seconds later the door opened again, and she stepped in.

Elma looked in his direction. "Oh hello, Delbert. I wasn't expecting you until Saturday."

He couldn't help noticing her flushed cheeks. "Came by to get the measurements for the shelves you want me to put up."

She lifted both hands and touched her face. "Of course. How silly of me. You'll need to know that before you can do the work. Oh, and when you arrive on Saturday, I'll probably be here long enough to let you in, but the store will be closed the rest of the day."

Blinking rapidly, Delbert crossed his arms. "Isn't it normally open all day on Saturdays?"

She nodded. "Since you'll be working on the new shelves, I thought it would be best to close the store."

"But you'll still be here, watching me do the task, right?" Almost every time Delbert had done work for Elma, here or at her house, she'd been there, often giving suggestions as to how he should or shouldn't do certain things.

"No, I won't be here in the afternoon."

"Where are you going?"

"To Grabill."

His brows drew together. "What's in Grabill?"

Elma glanced at the counter where Lizzie sat then looked back at Delbert. "I'm going to Grabill with a friend. He wants me to see where he lives."

Delbert tipped his head. "Are you and this fellow courting? Is that what you're saying?"

Elma's gaze dropped to the floor. "Well, sort of."

"How can you sort of be courting? You either are, or you're not." Delbert was sure if Elma was being courted by someone, Joseph would have known about it. And if his friend knew, why hadn't he mentioned it?

"Well actually, Ben and I have been courting for the past couple of months." Elma spoke in a near whisper.

Delbert's toes curled inside his boots as he bit the inside of his cheek. "Oh, I see. Well, this is the first I've heard of it, but I hope it all works out." Delbert was tempted to say more on the subject but thought better of it. His one big concern was if things got serious between Elma and her suitor who lived in Grabill, would she end up moving there?

Grabill

When Ben hung up the phone, he sat for several minutes, grinning and tapping his fingers on his leg. He felt like singing or shouting. Not only would Elma get to see where he lived, but it was an opportunity for her to become acquainted with his mother.

He held his arms out wide, feeling as though he could hug the whole world. *It's too soon yet, but when the time is right, I'm going to ask Elma to marry me.*

As the realization hit that he'd invited Elma for supper and hadn't asked Mom, Ben jumped out of his chair. *I'd better get up to the house and make the announcement.*

Ben's long strides took him quickly up the path. Midway, he stopped long enough to jump and click his heels together. Then, taking the porch steps two at a time, he stepped into the house. He found Mom in the kitchen, washing the breakfast dishes.

Mom glanced over her shoulder at Ben while the puppy stood at his feet, barking up at him. "Back already? You weren't at the phone shack very long. Does that mean there were no messages?"

"I don't know. Never checked."

She dropped her sponge into the sink and turned to face him. "How come?"

"When I entered the building, the phone rang, so I answered it." Ben's hands tingled as he spoke rapidly. "Turned out to be Elma, and I. . ." He paused and took a deep breath. "I invited her to come here this Saturday, and she said yes. I'm gonna ask Dave to drive me up to Topeka to get her. Is that okay with you?"

Ben turned his attention to Partner, now tugging on his shoelace. After bending down and scooping the puppy into his arms, Ben ended up with a face full of slurpy kisses. Next, the pup licked his ear.

"Come on now, behave." Ben repositioned the dog in his arms. He hadn't grown much yet and still possessed his milky puppy breath. He couldn't help but like the critter.

Mom's eyebrows furrowed. "Since when do you need my approval to spend time with Elma?"

He scraped a hand through his hair. "Well, the thing is, I invited her for supper. Hope that's okay with you," he added sheepishly.

Mom's shoulders slumped a bit as she slowly nodded. "It's fine. What would you like me to fix?"

"I don't know. Guess you can make anything you want. I don't think Elma's fussy."

"Okay, I'm sure I can come up with something." Mom turned back to the sink and continued to wash the dishes.

Ben looked down at Partner, who had gone limp in his arms and was now asleep. Slowly, he stroked the puppy's head, hoping it would ease this awkward moment. When Mom grew quiet, he knew it best not to say anything more. Ben had a feeling his mother wasn't happy about Elma coming. But once Mom had a chance to spend time with Elma, he felt certain she'd give her blessing.

⌁

Dorothy had been hoping her son had lost interest in the young woman from Topeka. Some time had passed, and it appeared as if the romance might have died down. Now, out of the blue, Ben had invited Elma here for supper. She couldn't help feeling concerned.

Dorothy scrubbed a skillet that didn't want to come clean. She paused to let her hands go limp in the warm water and tried to relax. *I wonder what I should make for Saturday's supper. Ben likes roasted chicken with mashed potatoes. I wonder what Elma likes.*

She grabbed the sponge to wash the next dish. *Ben might be fascinated with Elma, but I still think Martha Graber would have been a better choice for him.*

"Mom, you'd better be careful where you leave things lay." Ben walked up to her, holding the pup. "I found Partner with your slipper in his mouth." He held up her fuzzy blue house shoe.

Dorothy rolled her eyes. "Guess I need to give him some of those chew sticks. He's like a baby, needing to teeth on something for his hurting gums." She chuckled.

"I'm glad you think he's cute." Ben frowned. "Where do you want this wet thing?"

"Put it in my bedroom closet." Dorothy moved from the sink and dried her hands.

"Okay." Ben set the pup on the floor and left the room.

Dorothy's thoughts returned to Elma. The least she could do was give the young woman a chance.

Chapter 25

D o you have a problem with your leg?"

Ben jerked his head to look at his driver. "Uh, no. Why do you ask, Dave?" Ever since they'd left Grabill, Ben had been in deep thought, thinking about Elma.

Dave let go of the steering wheel with one hand and pointed. "You've been bouncing that leg for the last ten miles. Are ya nervous about seeing your girl again?"

Ben placed both hands on his knee to keep it from jiggling. "Um, no, not really. Well, maybe a little. This'll be the first time Elma's been to Grabill, and I'm worried she might not like it."

"What's not to like? If you ask me, our little town's a great place to live."

Ben gave a nod. "True, but not everyone likes small towns."

"Topeka's not that big either."

"Right, but it's close to Shipshewana and several other communities. There's a lot more Amish living in Elma's area too."

"Are you sure that's all you're worried about—the size of the town and how many Amish live there?" Dave glanced at Ben with brows drawn together; then he looked back at the road again.

Ben swallowed hard while loosening the collar of his shirt. Truth was, he was worried if he and Elma got married that she'd be unwilling to leave her twin sister. But he saw no reason to share that with Dave. Instead, he glanced out his side window and commented on the herd of goats they'd just passed.

Dave gave a little grunt. His cell phone rang then, but like other times, he let it go. He'd once told Ben he didn't like being distracted while he was driving. Besides, it wasn't safe to drive while talking on the phone. Ben couldn't count all the times he'd seen other drivers with their cell phones up to their ears. It seemed to be the thing to do these days.

Ben leaned his head back, closed his eyes, and tried to relax. They'd be in Topeka soon, and he'd feel better once he saw Elma.

Topeka

Needing something to do with her hands, Elma nibbled on a handful of almonds, which probably was a mistake, because now she'd need to brush her teeth again before Ben arrived.

She glanced at her cat as he lay purring under the dining-room table.

"Wish I felt as relaxed as you look," Elma murmured before heading to the bathroom.

After brushing her teeth, she stared at her reflection in the mirror. *Kapp on straight, no cat hairs showing.* Satisfied with her appearance, she went to get her handbag. A quick glance at the clock, and she hurried out the door. The butterflies in her stomach were hard at work as she took a seat on the porch.

While Elma waited nervously for Ben's arrival, she made a mental list of everything she had done to be sure she hadn't forgotten anything. She'd put the dog in the basement a while ago and then gone out to the store to check on Delbert. He was doing fine on his own and seemed a bit perturbed when she'd come in asking questions. *But that's just Delbert. He never has liked it when he's doing a job for me and I check on him or offer suggestions.*

Elma stepped off the porch and strolled around her vegetable garden. Some potatoes, carrots, and beets remained to be dug up, but other than those areas, the garden was bare. It was just as well. She didn't have time to do much in the way of preserving right now. Dad had gone home to Illinois, and Mom would follow within the next few weeks; then Elma would need to help Thelma as often as she could, with little time for other things. So it was good she was seeing Ben this evening, because after tonight she might not have time for much socializing.

Elma's attention turned to the road when she heard a vehicle approach. Her heartbeat quickened as a van pulled in and she saw Ben inside with his driver, Dave. Elma rushed out to meet them, eager to take Ben across the street to meet her niece and nephew.

❧

Although not quite finished with his job, Delbert set his tools aside and went to the front of the store to sit on the stool behind the counter and eat the candy bar he'd brought along. After finishing the treat, he ambled over to the window and looked out. Delbert watched with interest as a van pulled into Elma's yard. A few seconds later, an Amish man got out. They stood beside each other for a bit then got into the van. The vehicle pulled across the street and up Thelma and Joe's driveway. Elma and the Amish man got out and went inside.

Delbert pressed his nose against the window. *I bet that's the man who's been courting her.* Delbert needed to get back to work, but he couldn't keep from watching. His lips grew tight as he thought about the days he'd courted Elma. Truth was, they'd never had much to say to each other unless she was scolding or questioning him about something, and he was constantly defending himself.

Delbert wondered what would have happened if he hadn't stopped courting Elma. He slapped the side of his head. *Why am I even thinking such thoughts when Elma always got under my skin and annoyed me to no end?*

Seeing Elma with another man was like watching a possibility fade away. For some reason his heart did a flip-flop and sadness quickly took over.

❧

Thelma had finished feeding and diapering the babies when a knock sounded on the door.

"I'll get it." Mom rose from the rocking chair, where she'd sat burping Miriam a few minutes ago. She hurried from the nursery.

Thelma was about to put the babies in their bassinets when Mom returned, saying Elma was here, along with an Amish man who'd introduced himself as Benjamin Wagler. "They're on their way to Grabill and said they stopped by here first to see the bopplin," she added.

Thelma frowned, brushing some baby powder off her blue dress. "I can't believe Elma agreed to go there with Ben. I told her we planned to have Delbert over this evening to finally eat those fish he and Joseph caught a few weeks ago."

Mom tipped her head. "Are you still trying to get those two together?"

"I'm not pushing things, but it would be nice if it happened." Thelma handed Charles to her mother then picked up Miriam.

Mom tapped her shoulder. "You know the old saying, 'Love has no bounds.' If your sister chooses that young man in the other room, you won't have an easy time changing her mind."

Thelma's shoulders slumped as she lowered her voice. "To tell you the truth, I'm struggling with the issue. Why can't she be content with Delbert?"

"It's not up to you to choose for her. Please think about it, and a little praying would also help. Besides, Elma didn't decide Joseph was the one for you. You did."

"You're right. Guess we'd better go out and say hello."

Upon entering the living room, Thelma's heart clenched when she saw Elma and Ben sitting on the couch, wearing big smiles as they engaged in conversation. In all the time Delbert and Elma had been courting, she'd never seen her sister look so happy and relaxed.

That's how it's always been with me and Joseph. Thelma moved toward the couch. "It's nice to see you, Ben. I understand you came by to see our twins."

His eyes brightened as he bobbed his head. "I expected to see their daed here too."

"Joseph will be home later. He had some work to get done at the harness shop today." Thelma handed Miriam to Elma then looked at Ben. "Would you like to hold our little Charlie, or do bopplin make you naerfich?"

"I'm not nervous at all." He held out his arms. "I would very much like to hold him."

Thelma put the baby in Ben's arms and was surprised to see how at ease he seemed to be as he placed Charles against his shoulder and patted the baby's back. It seemed strange that a man who had no children would appear so relaxed. Even Joseph acted nervous when he first held the twins.

"You've been blessed with two fine-looking bopplin." Ben chuckled when little Charlie let out a healthy burp. "And this one's already learning what it is to be a man."

"Miriam can burp pretty loud too," Elma interjected. "I've heard her on several occasions."

"It's amazing how small we start off when we enter the world." Ben stared at the babies.

"Jah. These little ones have a ways to go, but they will grow too quickly, I'm afraid," Mom responded.

Thelma and Mom both took seats in the chairs opposite the couch, and everyone visited awhile, with the conversation revolving mostly around the babies.

When a horn tooted outside, Ben stood and handed Charles back to Thelma. "I think my driver is getting anxious to go."

"You could invite him in," Mom suggested.

Ben shook his head. "Elma and I need to get going anyway. I want Dave to drive us around Grabill before it gets dark so Elma can see what she thinks of the area."

Elma stood too, and gave Miriam to Mom. Then she turned to face Thelma. "I don't know how late I'll be, so when Delbert finishes at the store, would you ask Joseph to go over and make sure all the doors are locked?"

"Of course. But since Delbert will be joining us for supper, we can ask if he locked up."

A rosy color erupted on Elma's cheeks. "Oh, that's right, I'd forgotten he was coming here for the evening meal."

Thelma's forehead wrinkled. *How could my sister have forgotten? It was only a few days ago when I mentioned our plans and invited her to join us for the fish fry.* Thelma determined that apparently the only thing on Elma's mind right now was spending time with Ben. Her concern over losing her sister grew as she said goodbye to Ben and Elma and watched them head outside, both all smiles. If this relationship wasn't nipped soon, she might lose her sister to Ben Wagler, as well as to the town of Grabill.

Chapter 26

Grabill

As Dave drove Ben and Elma around Grabill, Ben pointed out the various sights. They went past an Amish-run fabric store, two grocery stores—one owned by the Amish and one by the English. They also saw a feed store, buggy shop, health food store, machine shop, the local library, and two Amish schools. As they passed several buggies on the road, Ben explained that the Grabill Amish only drove open buggies.

"How interesting. I bet it can get a bit chilly in the winter," she responded.

"Jah, but we manage."

"That's Miller's Country Store over there," Dave put in. "They sell everything from housewares, shoes, sewing notions, china dishes, baby things, and vitamins." He glanced over his shoulder at Elma. "They even carry stoves and refrigerators."

Elma sucked in her breath. The exterior of the building made her and Thelma's store look small by comparison. She'd have to hire a lot more help if she and her sister owned such a big place.

"There's Nolt's Dinner House, where a lot of English folks like to go for a taste of Amish-style cooking," Ben commented as Dave turned his van onto another road. "My mom's and my place will be coming up soon."

Elma's hands grew sweaty as she clasped them tightly in her lap. *I hope this evening goes well. What if his mother doesn't like me?*

"So what do you think of Grabill?" Ben's elbow connected gently with Elma's arm. "Do you think you could ever live here?"

Unsure of how to respond, she smiled and said, "It's a lovely town—although smaller than Topeka or Shipshewana."

"But that's the beauty of it," Dave interjected. "Fewer tourists come here."

"And we can go about our lives without so many curious stares from outsiders. Not all English are like Dave," Ben was quick to say.

When he paused, Elma felt him watching her. She turned toward him, unable to look away.

"So could you ever live here?" Ben asked again.

She dropped her gaze. "I don't think so. Thelma needs me in Topeka, not to mention I have a business to run. . . . What about you?" she dared to ask. "Could you move from Grabill and start over someplace else?"

"It would be hard for me to leave." Rubbing his hand against the front of his shirt, Ben's lips pressed together in a slight grimace. "Grabill's my home, and I have a responsibility to take care of my mamm, as well as my horseshoeing business."

Elma's chest tightened. *Then why are we carrying on this long-distance relationship that can go nowhere?* She clasped her fingers tightly around her purse straps. *I should never have agreed to come here today. But oh, I do enjoy being with you, Ben. If only you lived in Topeka, or could move there to be closer to me.*

⁓

Dorothy opened the oven door to check on the roast. It poked tender, so she turned the temperature to low. After closing the oven door, she looked up at the clock above the refrigerator. Ben and his guest should be here soon, so she might as well put the potatoes on to boil. If they got done before Ben and Elma arrived, she would put the kettle on a low burner to keep them warm.

Dorothy put the fruit salad she'd made in the refrigerator and began setting the table. After placing silverware beside each plate, she heard the back door creak open and click shut. A few seconds later, Ben stepped into the room with a lovely young Amish woman at his side.

"Mom, I'd like you to meet Elma Hochstetler."

"Jah, we've met. When I went into her store once, with my friend Eileen. I'm sure I mentioned it to you, Ben." Dorothy gave Elma a hug, as she didn't want to appear unwelcoming. "It's nice to see you again."

Elma nodded. "It's nice to see you too. I didn't realize when we met that you were Ben's mamm, however. What a coincidence."

"Maybe it wasn't." Ben looked over at Elma and grinned. "It could have been fate—like the day the two of us met at the farmers' market in Shipshe."

Ben's beaming expression and glowing cheeks said it all—he was in love with Elma.

ℯ𝒸

"Is there anything I can do to help with supper?" Elma asked, setting her purse on the floor in the corner of the room.

Mom was about to respond when Partner bounded into the kitchen, yipping up a storm.

Elma raised a hand to her mouth, giggling as the puppy slid to a stop at Ben's feet.

"Hey little fellow, did ya miss me today?" Ben squatted down to greet the small dog.

Elma went on her knees beside him. "What a *lieblich* pup." Partner licked her hand when she reached out to stroke his ears.

Ben looked up at Mom in time to see her wrinkle her nose. "Oh, he's adorable all right, but not when he's stirring up mischief. He got into my knitting basket earlier and unraveled a ball of yarn. Why, the little schtinker even pulled one of Ben's *hemmer* out of the laundry basket this morning and dragged it all over the yard. I had quite the time chasing after him."

Ben chuckled. "I'll bet it was a sight to behold."

She shook her finger. "It's not funny, and you're fortunate the shirt didn't end up with more than a little dirt on it. Partner could have put a hole in the sleeve."

"Partner?" Elma tipped her head. "Is that the puppy's name?"

Ben gave a nod. "Haven't had him very long. Mom brought the pup home after my dog, Hunter, disappeared." He gave Partner a pat on the head. "It'll be a while before he's old enough to do any bird hunting, but I hope to begin early training for him later this fall. Hunter could work a field real good when he was hunting birds. I'm hoping Partner will take after him in that regard."

Elma lifted Partner's chin and gazed at him. "It's amazing how much he looks like my dog, Freckles." She shrugged her shoulders. "But then I suppose most German shorthairs look similar."

"Jah." Ben rose to his full height, and Elma stood too. "Well, now that we've both got our hands all doggied, guess we'd better wash up or Mom won't let us sit down at her supper table. You can go first, Elma."

She took a few steps forward but hesitated, looking quizzically at Ben.

"The bathroom's down the hall—second door on the right." Mom pointed in that direction.

"Okay, danki." A deep flush crept across Elma's cheeks as she hurried from the room.

⁓

A short time later, they all went to the dining room. Ben's mother directed Elma to have a seat next to Ben. The table was set with pretty pink-and-white floral china and a cream-colored tablecloth. Dorothy had obviously put some thought into this visit.

They prayed silently, and then Dorothy passed the roast and potatoes. They also circulated a mixed green salad, steamed carrots, and broccoli.

"This is a tender roast, Mom. Very good." Ben smiled in her direction. Elma nodded in agreement.

"Your daed taught me how to pick the choicest cuts of meat." Dorothy looked across the table at Elma. "This is one of Ben's favorite meals."

"I can understand why." Elma ate some potatoes. "Everything is delicious." *Ben's mamm is a good cook, and she knows how to do up a fancy table.*

"I made a blueberry and a cherry pie for dessert." Dorothy took a drink of water.

Ben scooted his chair in closer. "Wait till you taste my mamm's pies. She's the best baker."

"It sounds tempting. I hope I'll have room for it after all this supper."

Dorothy gave a quick wave of her hand. "Well, if you don't, I'll send some home with you."

Elma smiled. "Danki."

"Mom's also quite the yodeler."

"Is that so?" Elma's ears perked up. "I've always admired people who could yodel."

"It's part of Swiss Amish heritage here in Grabill. Maybe she'll sing and yodel for us after supper." Ben looked at his mother with expectancy.

"We'll see about that." Her cheeks colored. "I understand Ben showed you around our small town. What did you think of Grabill, Elma?"

"It's a nice place. There seems to be plenty of shops, plus a few restaurants." Elma took a bite of mashed potatoes.

"At times I go with my friends to one of the larger towns. The variety we get here can't match those of the larger stores."

Ben picked up a pretty etched-glass dish and spooned some of its contents onto his plate. "My mamm makes some good apple butter. If you have room, give it a try on a piece of bread." He placed the small jar near Elma.

Elma scooped a spoonful and put it near her salad. She ate some mixed with the lettuce. "This is good."

Dorothy beamed then changed the conversation back to shopping.

Elma remained quiet during most of the drive home. She'd enjoyed spending time with Ben this evening and getting to know his mother. The meal had been good, and after Dorothy sang and yodeled a few songs, they'd had fun eating popcorn while working on a puzzle for a short time. Partner had taken a liking to her and had even fallen asleep in her lap. She meshed okay with Dorothy too, although Ben's mother seemed a bit reserved when they talked. Deep down, Elma's feelings were growing for Ben, but she couldn't stop thinking about what he'd told her earlier—that his home was in Grabill and he bore responsibility for his mom. Ben obviously had no plans to move.

Well, neither do I. She folded her arms, staring out the van window into the darkened sky. *So where does that leave us? Certainly not with a future together.*

Elma felt the warmth of his skin as he took hold of her hand. She felt certain he cared for her. But was it enough to leave Grabill and move to Topeka? Ben hadn't said anything about marriage, so it would be improper to bring the topic up. But what was the point in continuing to see him when neither of them were willing or able to relocate?

She squeezed her eyes shut. *Should I tell him when he walks me to my door that I don't think we should see each other anymore? I should never have agreed to spend the afternoon and evening with Ben. I let my feelings for him get in the way of good sense, and now saying goodbye will be that much harder.*

Elma's skin tingled as Ben stroked her hand tenderly with his thumb. *I can't tell him tonight. I'll wait a few days, or even a week, and then write Ben a letter, explaining why I can't see him anymore. Surely he'll understand and won't call or come around. It's best for both of us if we don't carry this relationship any further.*

Chapter 27

T he next Friday evening, after Ben finished working for the day, it was all he could do to put his horse away. Bending over to shoe for a good many hours had caused his back to spasm. "I should go see the local chiropractor," he mumbled. "My back's in bad shape." As much as he enjoyed his line of work, Ben figured he might have to give it up someday. But for now, it helped pay the bills, along with what they got from farming, as well as the sale of Mom's garden produce and flowers.

Gritting his teeth, Ben limped toward the house. All he wanted to do was eat a little something, take a long hot bath, and stretch out on his bed. He didn't have much appetite for food and hoped Mom hadn't cooked a big meal.

Tomorrow, if his back felt better and his driver was available, Ben planned to head up to Topeka to see Elma. Last night he'd called and left a message, saying he hoped to come by on Saturday, and if she was free, he wanted to take her out for supper.

Sure wish Topeka was closer. Ben reached around to rub the sorest spot on his back. *At least I could go with my horse and buggy instead of spending the money to hire Dave or one of our other drivers.*

When Ben reached the back porch, he paused to reflect on the conversation he'd had with Elma last Saturday when they'd been driving around Grabill. She'd made it clear that she had no intention of relocating, and since he didn't plan to move either, there was no point in continuing to pursue her—unless he could convince Elma to change her mind about moving. And that could only happen if he kept seeing her.

Ben grasped the door handle and stepped inside. He sat on the bench inside the utility room and removed his boots, being careful not to strain his back further.

Still wearing his stockings, Ben made his way to the kitchen.

"Hey, Ben. Supper will be ready soon. Oh, and there's a letter for you from Elma." Mom turned from where she stood at the stove and pointed to the kitchen table. "It came in today's mail."

Eager to see what Elma had written, Ben took a seat and tore the envelope open.

Bending his neck forward, he pressed his hands to his temples as he silently read her message:

Dear Ben:
There's no easy way to say this, but I've come to the conclusion that we should stop seeing each other. Your place is in Grabill with your mother, and mine is here in Topeka, with my twin sister and her family.
You are a kindhearted man, who deserves to be happy, and I wish you all the best in the days to come.

Fondly,
Elma

"Is everything okay?" Mom asked. "You look umgerennt."

At a loss for words, Ben turned away, covering his mouth.

Mom placed a lid on the kettle she'd been stirring and moved over to the table. "Did Elma say something upsetting?" She put both hands on Ben's shoulders.

He swallowed hard. "She doesn't want to see me anymore."

"Really? How come?"

"Elma wants to stay in Topeka, and my place is here, so she's right—there's no point in continuing to see each other, since we have no future together."

Mom massaged his tense shoulders. "Maybe it's for the best, son. A long-distance relationship is difficult, and since neither of you is free to move. . ."

Ben pushed his chair away from the table. "My back hurts, Mom. I'm gonna take a bath and go to bed."

"What about supper?"

"Sorry, but I'm not hungerich. Maybe I can have some of what you made for lunch or supper tomorrow, since I won't be going to Topeka like I'd planned." Holding his back, he bent slightly forward and shuffled out of the room. He needed to be alone to rest and sort things out.

❧

Topeka

"Are you hungry, boy?" Elma placed a bowl of dog food on the floor next to Freckles' water dish. She'd finished eating supper herself and still needed to do the dishes, but she wanted to get Freckles and Tiger fed first.

Elma still thought it was surprising how Freckles had acted last week after Ben and Dave dropped her off. When she'd taken the dog outside and sat on the porch steps to wait, instead of Freckles going into the yard, he didn't leave her side. He sniffed her from head to toe. At first, she thought it was normal, with the scent from Dorothy's puppy lingering on her clothes. But it wasn't only that—it was how Freckles kept whining that seemed so odd and caused Elma to wonder why it took the dog a while to settle down.

She shook her head. *If only animals could talk.*

While Freckles ate, Elma poured Tiger his food, placing it in the opposite corner of the room. If she didn't keep her pets' dishes separated, they would often try to horn in on each other's food.

Once that chore was done, Elma went to the sink and filled it with warm, soapy water. As she sloshed the sponge over each dirty dish, her thoughts went to Ben. *I wonder if he received my letter yet? If so, what was his reaction?* Her nose and throat burned with unshed tears. *I hope he understands and doesn't try to contact me. If I see him again, it'll only make things harder.*

A few minutes later, Tiger left his dish and came over to sit beside Elma, swishing his fluffy tail against her leg. *Meow! Meow!*

Elma looked down. "Did you come here to offer me comfort, or are you needing some attention?"

The cat looked up at her and purred.

Elma smiled, despite her melancholy mood. "I'll take that as a yes to both."

⌾

"Did you notice how sullen your sister seemed when she was here for supper last night?" Mom commented as she sat beside Thelma on the living-room couch, each of them holding a baby.

Thelma shook her head. "To tell you the truth, I was so busy with the bopplin, I hadn't noticed. Did she say anything was bothering her?"

Mom shook her head. "No. She just wasn't her usual perky self."

"Maybe she was mied. Since I'm not able to help at the store anymore, Elma's been working longer hours, which would make anyone tired." Thelma placed Miriam tummy-down across her lap and patted the infant's back. Sometimes that position worked best to get her to burp. "What my sister needs to do is hire another helper. Lizzie's a nice person, but she can't do many things and tends to talk too much when she should be working." Once Miriam burped, Thelma cradled the baby in her arms. "I'm not saying Elma should let Lizzie go—just hire an additional person."

Mom slowly nodded. "I'd hoped to help out in the store while I was here, but my first priority is to help you with the twins." She patted little Charlie on the back and smiled when he let out a healthy burp.

Tears welled in Thelma's eyes. "Having you here has meant a lot to me. I can't thank you enough."

"It's been my pleasure. I only wish I could stay longer."

Thelma swallowed hard, determined not to give in to her tears. "Dad needs you back home, and when you leave next week, we'll manage on our own, just as you did after Elma and I were born."

Mom's forehead wrinkled. "That was a little different. I had four sisters plus my mamm to help me back then. All you have is Elma, and because of the store, she can't be over here all the time."

"Which is why I am going to ask some of the women in our church district to help out. Several have volunteered already, so it shouldn't be a problem."

Mom reached over and touched Thelma's arm. "Your daed and I will be back for Christmas. Maybe we can stay till New Year's too."

"That'd be nice. It'll give Elma and me something to look forward to. Hopefully Joseph's parents can be here too, although they will probably spend part of the holidays with other family members." Thelma sighed. "It's important for family to be together as often as they can."

Chapter 28

Grabill

Throughout the holidays Ben moped around, spending much of his free time in his bedroom. He'd gone in for a few chiropractic treatments because of his back. They seemed to help, and he experienced less discomfort while he worked.

As Ben stood in front of his bedroom closet, he thought about his job and wondered what other kind of work he could do. He enjoyed meeting people and keeping informed on things. He also needed a job that would pay a decent wage. Here it was, the first of January already, and a whole new year lay ahead—a year in which he had nothing to look forward to.

It was hard to think about going through the rest of his life without Elma. Even though he'd known her a short time, his heart told him he'd never feel for any other woman what he did for her. But if she wouldn't leave Topeka, being together was out of the question, for Ben couldn't leave his mother in the lurch. In addition to needing to support herself, she'd be lonely living in this big old house alone.

Maybe Mom had been right when she'd said it was better this way. Elma had an obligation to her family, same as him. Truth was, Ben wished he'd never met her at the farmers' market. If he hadn't been looking at the produce on her table and had a little mishap, he wouldn't feel like there was a hole in his heart right now.

Ben stopped pacing to look out his window. He stared at the swirling snow which was quickly covering the ground. It was the first snowfall they'd had this winter, but the beautiful trees in their yard, wearing blankets of white, did nothing to lift his spirits. Back when Ben was a boy, he loved playing in the snow. Even as a young man, it was fun to romp in the white stuff with his dog.

Ben didn't know how he'd made it through the holidays. All he could think about was the fun he and Elma were missing out on, enjoying the snow together. First Hunter, and now Elma—both of them gone from his life.

"Hunter," Ben murmured, pressing his forehead against the cold window glass. "I hope you found a new master who's been taking good care of you."

While Partner had filled a void in Ben's life, he'd never felt as close to the pup as he had to Hunter. As far as Ben was concerned, the puppy was more Mom's dog than his. But that was okay. She needed the pup's companionship whenever Ben was away.

Compelled to seek God's will for his life, Ben took a seat on the end of his bed, reflecting on Proverbs 16:9, a verse he'd committed to memory some time ago: *"A man's heart deviseth his way: but the LORD directeth his steps."*

He bowed his head. *Heavenly Father, please guide and direct my life in the year ahead, and if Your will is for me to get married, send the right woman into my life who'll be happy living in Grabill, or help me to be content as a bachelor. Amen.*

Topeka

As Elma sat watching her parents hold Miriam and Charles, a deep sadness welled in her soul. In addition to feeling bad because Mom was going home tomorrow, she struggled with envy yet again because she had no children. Mom's nonstop talk about how much the babies had grown and how she was going to miss them when she went home only added to Elma's resentment.

Her parents had experienced the joy of raising twins, and now Thelma and Joseph had been given the same opportunity. Elma didn't even have a husband, much less the prospect of becoming a parent.

She glanced across the room to where Delbert and Joseph sat playing checkers. Elma wondered if Delbert had been invited to join them for a meal and to spend the evening playing games because he was lonely, or if

Thelma had planned it to try and get her and Delbert back together. Elma was pretty sure it was the latter, since this wasn't the first time Delbert had been invited to her sister's house when she was there for a meal. Somehow it always worked out so that Elma was seated next to or directly across the table from him.

Delbert's blond hair seemed a bit thinner these days, and Elma noticed he had a patch of eczema on the back of his neck. *Probably from eating too many sugar-laden sweets and unhealthy snacks. He needs a wife to cook him some decent meals.*

"King me! That's it—I won!" Delbert clapped his hands, causing everyone in the room to jump except Elma. Delbert was a sharp cookie when it came to most games, and it didn't surprise her in the least that he'd beaten Joseph at checkers. Delbert always got excited when he won too.

She glanced at the babies and was surprised they'd both slept through the noise.

"Hey, Elma, why don't ya come over here and see if you can beat me at checkers? As I recall, you're pretty good at this game."

Unable to say no to the challenge, Elma rose from her comfortable chair and took Joseph's seat at the dining-room table. Joseph winked at Elma before settling himself in the love seat beside Thelma.

And who might you be cheering for? she almost asked out loud.

Delbert insisted Elma begin the game, and as things got started, a desire to win crept in. She'd always liked a good challenge, and playing against Delbert was definitely that. Elma had to think fast while calculating each move in order to stay up with him.

When his next turn came, Delbert took some time then slid his game piece.

Elma studied the board, wondering why he'd moved it there. She made her next move and took another one of his checkers. "Your turn, Delbert."

He squinted, looking at her suspiciously. "Again? How are you doing that?"

She smiled, feeling a bit smug. "I know how to play this game, and you seem to be losing your edge."

"I'm doing fine. I only slipped up a little," Delbert mumbled.

Halfway through the game, Thelma and Joseph left the room to make popcorn.

Despite the challenge of trying to outsmart Delbert, for the first time all day, Elma was enjoying herself. The icing on the cake, so to speak, was that for the first time in many weeks, Ben Wagler was not at the center of her thoughts.

ℹℹ

Thelma smiled at Joseph as he got out the popcorn maker and placed it on the stove. She felt grateful to have a husband who enjoyed being with her and was willing to help. She chuckled to herself. *Of course, his enjoyment of popcorn might have something to do with his eagerness to make it.*

She handed him the container of coconut oil—a Christmas gift from Elma. Her sister might have thought she was being subtle, but Thelma knew the reason for this particular gift was to make sure she was cooking with a healthy oil. As always, Thelma's twin was looking out for her welfare.

While Joseph took care of the popcorn, Thelma brewed a pot of coffee and sliced some pumpkin bread Mom had made yesterday. What a joy it had been to have her mother with them from Christmas to New Year's. Thelma looked forward to spring, when she and Joseph hoped to take their little ones on their first trip to see their grandparents in Sullivan, Illinois. It would also be nice to introduce Miriam and Charles to all the aunts, uncles, and cousins she and Elma had grown up with.

After all the doting and holding our twins will get, they'll be spoiled by the time we come home, she mused.

When the corn was done popping and Thelma had a tray filled with pumpkin bread ready, she took cups and small plates down from the cupboard.

"If you want to carry the popcorn and bread to the dining-room table, I'll bring the coffeepot, plates, and silverware," Joseph offered. "Oh, and some napkins too."

She nodded. "I'll do that in a minute, but first I'd like to ask you something."

He turned to face her. "What is it, my dear fraa?"

Thelma smiled at his endearing words. "It's about Delbert."

"You think he's taken all of Elma's checker pieces by now?"

"Probably, but that's not what I was going to ask." She moved closer to him and spoke in a low tone. "Do you think Delbert might still be interested in my sister?"

His eyes widened. "Now what would make you ask such a question?"

She lifted her shoulders. "Oh, I don't know. Maybe it's wishful thinking on my part, but it does seem like he and Elma are getting along better these days. Remember how she laughed at all his jokes when he stopped by on Christmas Eve?"

"Jah, but then we all were laughing." Joseph placed both hands on Thelma's shoulders. "I wouldn't make too much of it if I were you."

"Oh, I'm not. I just think. . ."

Joseph bent his head and kissed the end of her nose. "If Dell and Elma are meant to be together, it'll happen without any help from either of us. Now let's get back there and watch those two play the rest of the game. I'm sure if one of 'em had won, we'd have heard a bit of commotion by now."

Thelma snickered. "You're right about that." She picked up the bowl of popcorn and tray full of pumpkin bread and entered the dining room in time to hear Elma shout, "King me, Delbert! End of game!"

Chapter 29

By the middle of March, Thelma had settled into a routine with the twins. It was hard to believe they were five and a half months old already. Time seemed to be slipping by so quickly.

Thelma sat in the rocker, mending a pair of Joseph's trousers, but glanced up every once in a while to check on the babies. They were both wide awake, rolling and scooching around in their playpen, while making all sorts of unintelligible baby noises.

She chuckled when little Charlie reached for a rattle and Miriam grabbed ahold of it first. It looked like a bit of sibling rivalry had already begun. No doubt, it would get worse as they grew. Of course, she and Joseph, as any good parents, would teach the twins to share and try to work out their problems.

Thelma reflected on her and Elma's childhood. For the most part, they'd gotten along well, and being identical twins, they usually were treated the same. However, Thelma recalled how one time, when she'd gone shopping with Dad, he'd bought her an ice-cream cone. After returning home, she'd mentioned getting the treat, and Elma became upset. There'd also been a little rivalry whenever Thelma and Elma played games. Most times, though, Thelma let her sister win in order to keep the peace.

She glanced at her babies again and smiled. They'd both fallen asleep, only now Charlie held the favorite rattle. As the children grew, it would be interesting to see who would become the more dominant twin.

A clap of thunder in the distance drove Thelma's thoughts aside. The howling wind and patter of rain hitting the window indicated a storm was brewing. As the skies darkened, so did the inside of the house. Thelma got up and lit the gas lamp hanging overhead. She went to the kitchen and lit that one too. Dinner cooked in the oven, and the smell of roasting chicken made her mouth water. The warm glow emanating from the lamp felt soothing.

Thelma got out some carrots and cucumbers to go with the meal. Once she'd finished cutting the veggies, she returned to the other room to check on her little ones. They were both still sleeping, so she quietly took a seat in her rocker.

After mending Joseph's pants, she reached for one of her knitting projects. She'd started a peach-colored pot holder the other day and couldn't wait to finish it.

Thelma looked up at the clock on the fireplace mantel. Joseph would be getting off work soon. She hoped the rain would let up before he headed home. Well, at least he'd be driving his closed-in buggy this evening. It was never fun to ride in an open buggy and get caught in the rain. She wondered how the Amish who lived in Grabill managed in their open buggies during rainy and snowy weather.

Thoughts of Grabill made Thelma think about Elma and how she'd told her that she had broken things off with Ben Wagler. In the long run, it was for the best, since they lived so far from each other. Still, it distressed Thelma to see her sister unhappy. But these last few months, Elma seemed more relaxed. Maybe the pain of breaking up with Ben had eased.

⁂

"How's it going today, Lizzie?" Delbert asked as he entered the store and crossed over to the counter where the older woman sat working on a crossword puzzle. At least this time she wasn't reading a book or munching on candy—although he couldn't figure out why she was sitting here at all, since there were no customers to wait on at the moment. Shouldn't she be stocking shelves or something?

Lizzie looked at him and blinked several times. "Well, Delbert. I didn't realize you'd come into the store."

"Just got here, and I asked you a question." He folded his arms. "Apparently you didn't hear me, though."

Her cheeks reddened, and she set the crossword puzzle aside. "Sorry about that. Guess I was a little preoccupied."

His eyebrows pinched together. *What else is new?*

"What was your question?"

"I asked how it's going."

She smiled. "Everything's fine and dandy here. Oh, and if you're look-ing for Elma, she's in the back room." Lizzie motioned in that direction with her head.

"I'll head back there now." Delbert paused and tapped the countertop lightly with the palm of his hand. "Don't work too hard, Lizzie."

Before she could comment, he scurried down the nearest aisle. He was at the door of the back room when Elma stepped out, nearly colliding with him.

"Ach, I didn't know you were there." A flush of pink crept across her cheeks as he clasped her arms to keep them from bumping into each other.

"Sorry about that. Are you okay?"

"Jah. You just surprised me, is all."

He wiggled his brows. "That's me—always full of surprises."

She smiled. "I assume you're on your way home from somewhere. Did you stop by the store for a reason or to get out of the rain till it passes?"

"The rain doesn't bother me, but I have another reason for stopping. I'm hungerich and don't want to wait till I get back to LaGrange to eat supper." He released his hold on her arms and took a step back. "I was wondering if you'd like to go out to supper with me. We can either go to Tiffany's or one of the Mexican restaurants in town."

She looked down, then back up at him again while shuffling her feet. "I don't have anything definite planned for supper, so jah, I'd be happy to accept your invitation. But what about the nasty weather we're having?"

Delbert grinned. "Don't worry about that. See. . ." He pointed toward the window. "It's a steady rain now and not blowing like it was before. I'll hang around here till you're ready to close the store. Then we can head to the restaurant of your choice. Oh, and you might want to bring an umbrella with you."

"I'll need to let Freckles outside for a while before we go. He's been in the basement most of the day, except when I went home for a short time around noon. I'm sure the thunder has him worked up by now too."

"No problem. I can wait. You know what though, Elma?"

"What?"

"You oughta let me build a doghouse and a chain-link fence around it so the dog can be outside during the day when you're not home. It's not good for a hund—especially one his size—to be cooped up in the basement for hours on end."

Elma nodded. "You're right. I'd thought about asking but wasn't sure if you'd have the time."

"Even if I didn't, I would make the time." He brushed his hand lightly over her arm. "That's what friends are for." Truth was, Delbert had come to see Elma as a good friend.

⚮

"Sure am glad the rain's stopped. It was comin' down pretty hard for a while there," Delbert commented as he and Elma entered El Zorrito's Mexican Restaurant.

Elma nodded, holding her wet umbrella away from her dress. "The sky still looks a bit ominous."

He tipped his head. "Ominous?"

"Jah—threatening."

"Oh, you mean the dark, low-hanging clouds that seem to be moving toward LaGrange?"

"Right. Sure hope we don't get a really bad storm—or worse yet a tornado."

"It's been some time since one touched down around these parts." Delbert led Elma to a table near the window. "Think the last tornado I heard about here in Indiana happened in Kokomo. There was a bad one in Nappanee several years ago too. Many of us Amish in the area went there afterward to help repair the damage. That was before you and Thelma moved here, though."

Leaning toward the window, Elma shivered as she took another look at the sky. She bit her lips when she noticed, off in the distance, how its color had changed to a sickly green. The air had felt strange when they'd gotten out of the buggy and walked through the parking lot—like a quiet calm settling over the area. The eerie silence had been unnerving, as though a prelude of something about to happen.

Elma glanced toward one of the trees near the hitching rail where Delbert's buggy was parked. Not a single branch moved. Nothing in the air was stirring, not even a bird. Although a few tornadoes had touched down in her home state of Illinois, including Sullivan, none had ever hit her parents' home, for which she felt grateful.

Another shiver went up Elma's spine as she forced herself to look away.

Delbert reached across the table and patted her outstretched hand. "Don't look so worried. I'm sure we'll be fine. Just remember, as long as we don't hear about any tornado warnings or sirens, there's nothing to worry about." He picked up his menu. "Now let's try to relax and enjoy the evening. Think I'll have the arroz con pollo. What sounds good to you?"

"I might have the chicken fajitas." Thinking about how good this restaurant's food was made Elma's mouth water. Even the chips they served were good, although the salsa was a bit too hot for her liking.

Her mind went back to an evening a few years ago when she, Thelma, Joseph, and Delbert had shared pizza together. Delbert had added hot sauce to his, and Elma foolishly tried some. She'd never forget the burning sensation. It felt like her whole mouth was on fire.

When a waiter came to take their orders, Elma asked for a side order of mild salsa to go with the chips he'd placed on the table. The lights flickered overhead, and a murmur went through the restaurant.

"Sure hope we don't lose power." Their dark-haired waiter frowned. "We don't have a generator, so when the power goes out we can't cook. Hopefully it won't happen tonight." He turned to put in their orders and returned a few minutes later with their beverages.

There weren't any more disturbances with the lights, and everything seemed to be fine. Elma and Delbert bowed their heads for silent prayer, and then, while they munched on the chips, Delbert brought up the topic of Elma's dog again.

"Sure am glad you were willing to take Freckles. When he showed up at my house, I didn't know what to do with him."

She leaned both elbows on the table, gazing across at him. "I'm curious about something, Delbert."

"What's that?"

"You seem to like the dog. How come you didn't want to keep him?"

He shifted in his chair, looking down at the table. "Other than Joe, I've never told anyone this before, but I used to have a good hunting dog when I was a teenager." His voice faltered. "After she got hit by a car and died in my arms, I swore I'd never own another hund. *Es hot arig wehgeduh*, and I never want to get attached to another pet and put myself through something like that."

Her heart went out to him. "I understand that it was very painful. Loss is always hard, but life goes on. As Christians, we need to enjoy each new day and thank the Lord for all He's given us."

"I do thank Him. Just don't want to put myself in the position to lose another hund."

Elma was about to respond when their waiter, wearing a grim expression, returned to the table with two glasses of iced tea. "Just heard on the radio that a tornado struck some area in LaGrange. Doesn't sound like it's heading this way, though. But I'd keep an eye on the weather out there."

Delbert's eyes widened. "LaGrange? Ach, I hope my house is still standing."

Elma's heart pounded, and she squeezed her eyes shut. *Heavenly Father, please let everyone there be okay.*

Chapter 30

Grabill

Did ya hear the news about the tornado that hit LaGrange last night?" Dave asked when he picked Ben up to take him to a chiropractic appointment the following morning.

Eyes widening, Ben shook his head. "How bad was it? Did anyone get hurt?" He thought about the woman he'd delivered Mom's flowers to a few months back.

"There were several injuries, but I don't think any lives were lost." Dave's forehead creased. "Lots of destruction to some homes and barns in that area, though. I can only imagine what those poor families are going through today. They're gonna need help rebuilding."

Ben drew in a deep breath and blew it out quickly. "A group of Amish men from our area will likely go, and I plan to be with them."

Dave turned his head, looking at Ben through half-closed eyelids. "You sure your back's up to it? The pain you've been dealing with is the reason you're going to the chiropractor's, isn't it?"

Ben nodded. "I'm certain after Dr. Stevens works me over, I'll be good as new. Sure can't sit around here when there's work to be done and people are in need of our help. I'm gonna get there as quickly as possible."

LaGrange

Delbert rubbed a fist against his aching chest as he stared at the area where his house used to be. What had once been a cozy abode for him to live in was now nothing but a pile of rubble. Winds that had blown up to 180 miles per hour had wreaked havoc throughout several parts of his town.

"Thank the Lord you weren't at home when the tornado struck." Joseph draped his arm across Delbert's shoulder. "Most likely you would have been killed."

"It's strange to look at that heap of rubble and know it was once my house. I'd like to sift through it to see if there's anything worth salvaging." Delbert reached in his pocket for a hankie and wiped his nose. "The Lord giveth and He taketh away. It's all according to His plans, and maybe I'll have something better when it's all said and done. Jah, it could have been worse." He spread his arms open wide. "This can all be replaced. Guess my time here on earth isn't meant to be over just yet."

His good friend nodded. "The community will help you rebuild, as well as assist others in the area who lost their property. I have it on good authority that a crew from Topeka will be coming here later today to get started. And I'm sure other communities in the state, and perhaps beyond, will send workers too."

Delbert's vision blurred as he held his arms close to his body. "I'll appreciate all the help I can get." He turned to face Joseph. "Danki for letting me stay at your house last night after I learned that my home was gone. Don't know what I'd do without a good friend like you."

Joseph's eyes welled with tears. "You'd do the same for me if the boot was on the other foot."

Delbert stared at the ground. Joe was right—there wasn't anything he wouldn't do to help his best friend.

ஃ

Topeka

"With everything there is to do at the store, are you sure you want to go to LaGrange to help out?"

Thelma's question drove Elma's thoughts aside, and she set her paper and pen on the coffee table. "I am absolutely certain. Joseph and many other men from our area have gone there to help out, and they'll need to be fed. I'm sure there are other chores I can do there too." She clasped her hands together. "Remember, Galatians 6:9 says: 'And let us not be weary in well doing: for in due season we shall reap, if we faint not.'"

"You're right. But what about the store? Who's going to take care of things there?" Thelma gestured to her little ones, sleeping peacefully in their playpen across the room. "I'd work in the store while you're gone, but I wouldn't get anything done if I took the bopplin along."

Elma smiled. "No, but they'd sure get a lot of attention from customers."

"True. So what are you going to do?"

Elma lifted her hands. "It's all taken care of. I asked Doris Miller if she'd help Lizzie while I'm gone, and she agreed. In fact, she's probably on her way now, since I'll be leaving soon."

"Will you be coming home each day?" Thelma asked.

"Most likely I'll stay. I can get more things done that way. Many people will open their homes for the workers, so I'm sure I'll find a place to stay at night."

"How many days will be you be there?"

Elma shrugged. "I don't know. As long as they need cooks, I'll stay— at least till someone comes along to replace me." Elma paused. "There is something you can do to help me, though. Will you watch my dog while I'm gone?"

"Of course. You can bring him over here when you're done packing."

"Danki. Between Doris and Lizzie, the cat will be taken care of, and they'll also feed and water my horse and the chickens. I made sure to warn the ladies about Hector, the feisty rooster. He can be a little schtinker. Hector almost got me the other day with his long spurs." Elma grimaced. "As usual, it gave me a scare, so I let Doris and Lizzie know to keep the broom handy."

Thelma smiled. "Good thinking. You wouldn't feel right if that naughty chicken hurt either of those nice women." She rolled her eyes. "Why don't you get rid of that despicable old chicken?"

"I'll admit, he's a handful, but the other chickens—especially the hens, get along fine with him."

"Well, it's nice of Lizzie and Doris to take care of the critters. And please don't worry about Freckles. He can hang out here with Ginger for a few days."

"I bet he will enjoy having another dog to play with."

"It's a shame about Delbert's house." Thelma slumped in her chair. "I can't imagine how he must feel right now."

∼

About an hour after Elma left, Freckles started to whine.

"It's okay, boy, she'll be back." Thelma felt sorry for the dog. He'd grown quite attached to Elma.

Freckles pawed at her leg, and she reached down to pat his head.

Ginger, who lay under the kitchen table, got up and drank some water from her dish. Thelma figured Freckles might follow suit, but he continued to sit at her feet and whine.

After a while, it got on her nerves. She went to the cupboard and got him a dog bone. Of course, Ginger's ears perked up and she had to have one too. Their bodies poised, both dogs sat waiting for their tasty treat.

Thelma smiled while watching the dogs crunch on their bones. She enjoyed Joseph's dog, but since the twins were born, poor Ginger had taken a backseat. Maybe Ginger would gain more attention as Charles and Miriam grew.

After the dogs were through with their treats, Thelma heard the babies crying from the other room. It probably wouldn't be long before her sister's dog started whining again.

"How would you two like to go out in the yard and play?" Thelma moved toward the door.

Both dogs' ears perked up, and Ginger raced to the door. Freckles followed.

Thelma opened the door a crack and checked to see that the fence gate was closed before letting the dogs out. It was, so she opened it wider and was nearly knocked off her feet when Freckles and Ginger dashed outside.

Those silly critters. Shaking her head, she closed the door behind them and went to take care of the twins.

Sometime later, after the babies were fed and changed, Thelma heard scratching at the back door. When she opened it, she was surprised to see only Ginger on the porch.

She glanced around but saw no sign of Freckles.

"Here, Freckles! Come here, boy!" She clapped her hands.

No response.

"That's strange. I wonder if he found his way into the barn." Thelma stepped off the porch and was about to head in that direction when she noticed the fence gate hung open. "Oh, great! It must not have been securely latched."

She ran up to the fence and cupped her hands around her mouth. "Freckles! Where are you, boy?"

Not a sound and no sign of the dog.

Her heart pounded. *Oh, dear. That hund had better be back before Elma gets home.*

Elma had become attached to the dog and would be upset if she lost him. Even Delbert seemed to like Freckles. The last time they'd had him over for supper, he'd asked about the dog.

Thelma called for Freckles several more times but finally gave up and went inside. Hopefully by the time Elma returned, Freckles would be here waiting. If not, Thelma would have some explaining to do, and she didn't look forward to that.

Chapter 31

LaGrange

Elma took a break from the food table where she'd been helping ever since arriving a few hours ago. She pulled her shawl tightly around her shoulders, her heart heavy from all the devastation she saw. Despite the shawl's heaviness, Elma's body felt cold. But it wasn't the chilly March air causing her to tremble. It was the sight of so many somber-faced people who had lost their homes. Her heart ached for them.

It was surprising how the storm hit only certain houses but skipped others. For some, it was a miracle, but for the unfortunate ones like Delbert, not only had their homes been flattened, but bits and pieces of furniture and personal belongings were scattered everywhere.

One scene made Elma's eyes spill over with tears when she stopped to watch a little girl who'd found one of her dolls. Like a loving mother, the child rocked back and forth, comforting and whispering to her doll, holding it as gently as if it were a real baby.

Elma tore her gaze away as she took in more of the destruction. She noticed missing shingles and blown-out windows in several houses and barns. Tree branches lay scattered about, while some trees had been sheared off into stumps. Yet despite the rubble and mess, no lives had been lost, and only a few people were slightly injured. Temporary shelters had been set up in some of the buildings in town, and as Elma suspected, many people had opened their homes. Upon hearing of the disaster, Amish and English folks started working together to help those whose lives had been upended. Some brought in food, the way Elma did, while others offered supplies and began clearing debris and helping people put their homes back together.

"Thank You, God," she murmured, watching two Amish men working side by side with an English man who'd lost his barn.

She spotted Delbert talking to Joseph and hurried over to them. Elma could hardly believe the sight before her. Delbert's house was gone, as well as part of his woodworking shop. As horrible as it seemed, at least Delbert was alive and unhurt.

As Elma stepped up to Delbert, she was overcome with the need to give him a hug. Unsure of how he might take it, she placed her hand on his arm and gave it a tender squeeze. "I'm sorry for your loss." Her words seemed so insignificant, for she could not imagine the emotions going through him right now.

He dropped his gaze to the ground. "My home and material things can be replaced; I'm *dankbaar* to be alive."

"I am thankful too." When Elma glanced to the right, her breath caught in her throat. Ben Wagler had come, and he was heading her way.

"Excuse me, Delbert, I see someone I know and should go say hello."

"Of course. Go right ahead."

She moved slowly toward Ben. "Wh–what are you doing here?" Elma could barely find her voice, and her gaze fixed on him. The sight of Ben coming toward her caused Elma to shiver even more. She noticed that he walked a bit slower than normal.

"Came to help out, like all the others." He motioned to a crew of men picking up debris. "I didn't expect to see you here, Elma."

She lifted her chin. "I came for the same reason you did. To help wherever I can." Elma pointed to the rubble that used to be Delbert's house. "My friend Delbert's home was one of the many places that were totally destroyed."

"Is he the man you were talking to?"

"Jah. Delbert and my brother-in-law have been friends a good many years."

"I see." He took a few steps toward her and winced.

"Are you okay?"

"My back's been acting up lately, but it's some better after seeing my chiropractor."

"Maybe you shouldn't have come." Elma bit the inside of her lip.

"What if you injure your back even more?"

"There's a lot of work that needs to be done here, and I can help in many ways. Just have to watch myself." He stared at her, his eyes never moving. "It's good to see you, Elma. I've been wondering how you were doing." He reached out and touched her arm.

Goose bumps erupted all the way up to her neck. The mere sight of him filled Elma's heart with regrets. "I'm fine. How are you?"

"Other than my back, I'm doin' okay, I guess." He leaned on the table where the paper plates and cups had been set. "But I'd be even better if I was with you."

His bold statement caused her to jerk.

"Sorry if I offended you. It's just that—"

She shook her head briskly. "No, no, I wasn't offended. You took me by surprise."

His voice lowered as he leaned a bit closer. "Do you feel the same about me?"

Elma felt like a mouse caught between a cat's paws. Ben knew why they couldn't be together. Why was he bringing this up now?

She parted her lips, about to respond, when an exuberant German shorthair pointer showed up, out of nowhere, barking frantically and wagging his tail.

"Freckles!"

"Hunter!"

Ben and Elma spoke at the same time.

Elma looked at Ben and blinked.

"Freckles?" Ben tipped his head to the side. "Is this your dog, Elma? The one you told me about?"

Reaching down to pet the dog's head, Elma nodded. "But you just called him Hunter."

"Jah. This is my hund, I'm sure of it." Ben slapped his knee and called the dog. "Come here, Hunter. Come on, boy."

The dog darted over to Ben and pawed at his pant leg.

Elma clapped her hands. "Come here, Freckles! Come to me."

Obediently, the animal ambled over to her.

Elma's mouth opened wide. So did Ben's.

Ben pointed to the dog. "Where and when did you get him?"

"Delbert offered him to me several months ago." Elma looked toward Joseph and Delbert, down on their knees, sorting through the rubble. "The dog showed up at his house, and when he couldn't locate its owner, I volunteered to take him."

"So you named him Freckles?"

She bobbed her head. "With all his liver spots, it seemed like a fitting name."

Ben reached under his straw hat and scratched the side of his head. "I lost my hund when I was delivering flowers to a woman in LaGrange. The crazy critter jumped out of the truck, and after looking for him several hours with no luck, I finally gave up and went home."

"So the dog is yours, and his name is Hunter?"

"Jah." Ben motioned to the dog's collar. "I bought that for him last year."

Elma couldn't deny it was Ben's lost dog, but the idea of giving him up put an ache in her heart. "He's obviously your dog, but I can't figure out how he got here. I left him in Topeka with my sister this morning. Guess he must have gotten away somehow and run off—although I can't imagine what directed him here."

"I'm thinkin' he wanted to be with the two people he loves, so he sought us out." Ben offered a thumbs-up.

She giggled. "You really believe he could do that?"

"Sure do. I've heard of other dogs traveling farther than this to find their way back to their owner. And ya know what else, Elma?"

She shook her head.

"We can't make him choose between us, so as far as I can tell, there's only one answer to the problem."

"What would it be?"

"We're gonna have to get married so Hunter/Freckles can live with both of us."

Elma swallowed hard. "Ben, you know that's not possible. Your home is in Grabill, and mine's—"

He put his finger against her lips. "I can move to Topeka and start over."

She shook her head vigorously. "Oh no, Ben, I couldn't ask you to do that."

"You didn't ask. It was my suggestion."

"But your business is there, and so is your mamm. It wouldn't be fair to her if you moved."

"Mom can move with me. And if you need more assistance in the store, maybe she can help out. Who knows? After I retire from horseshoeing, you might put me to work in your store too. With my back issues, I may not be shoeing horses much longer." Ben clasped Elma's arm. "Please say you'll at least think about it."

As far as Elma was concerned, there was nothing to think about. She would love it if Ben moved to Topeka and they got married. His mother, however, might not want to move—in which case, he should remain in Grabill to look after her needs.

She fiddled with her head-covering ties, weighing her choices. As much as Elma loved Ben, she had an obligation to Thelma, so moving to Grabill would be difficult, if not impossible.

Ben moved his hand from Elma's arm to take hold of her hand. "I believe God brought us together today for a reason, and our meeting and little mishap at the farmers' market in Shipshe last spring was no accident." He brought her hand to his lips and kissed it softly. Looking tenderly into Elma's eyes, Ben grew serious. "Maybe Hunter, or Freckles, did bring us together again today. I could use that as a reason, but truthfully speaking, I've been miserable ever since I received your letter. You have been on my mind since I first saw you, and there hasn't been a day since meeting you in Shipshe that I haven't thought of you. I've prayed that somehow we'd find each other again."

Elma's heart beat wildly when Ben took both of her hands. "Elma, I love you."

As if to reaffirm what he'd said, Hunter gave a loud *Woof! Woof!* before slurping both of their hands.

Elma was about to respond when Ben added, "As soon as I return home, I'm going to talk to my mamm. I feel confident she'll be willing to move. She knows how much I love you." Ben wet his lips and looked tenderly at Elma. "Will you marry me?"

Her mind racing as she thought of the possibility, all Elma could do was nod. *If Dorothy Wagler agrees to Ben's plan, I'll be forever grateful.*

Epilogue

One year later

Sitting beside her groom at their corner table, all Elma could think about was how fortunate she was to have met a man as wonderful as Ben. She smiled at him, as he looked so handsome in his wedding suit. He smiled in return and squeezed her fingers under the table. Elma's heart was filled with gratitude over his mother's willingness to move to Topeka. Everything had fallen into place, as though it was meant to be. An Amish couple with five children bought the Waglers' farm in Grabill, and Ben retired from horseshoeing. He would now be helping Elma run the store, and Dorothy would work part-time there too, as well as Lizzie. This would allow Ben and Elma time off in order to go on trips or do other fun things together.

Elma glanced across the room to where her sister and brother-in-law sat eating their meal. Charlie sat on Joseph's lap, and Miriam was seated on Thelma's lap. Mom and Dad sat across from them, all smiles. Ben's mother was seated at another table, along with Ben's sister and her family. Everyone seemed to be having a good time, which only added to Elma's pleasure.

Her gaze went to Delbert, sitting at the same table with the widow Rachel Lambright and her seven-year-old son, Ryan. He'd begun courting her six months ago, and if things continued on the same path, Elma suspected before the year was out, they might be celebrating another wedding. She could tell Ryan was warming up to Delbert by the boy's big grin as the two interacted. Elma also noticed warm smiles being exchanged between Dell and Rachel. She was glad things were working out for her friend. After the tornado, with the help of those in the community and even outside the area, Delbert's house had been rebuilt in only a few weeks.

Despite the chilly March winds blowing outside Joseph's barn where the afternoon wedding meal was taking place, blue skies and puffy white clouds made the day perfect.

While Elma enjoyed the delicious meal with her new husband, Thelma got up from her seat and handed Miriam to her grandmother. Then she picked up a large wicker basket sitting on the floor and made her way to the wedding couple's table. Thelma placed it in front of them, and then, one by one, guests started filing up and putting pieces of fresh fruit inside.

Elma looked at Ben with her mouth gaping open as apples, oranges, bananas, and a few pears quickly had the basket full of colorful produce. After the last person came up to put fruit in the basket, Thelma topped it off with some deep purple grapes then gave Elma a big grin.

Elma smiled as her husband stood, cleared his throat, and started to thank everyone. His little speech no sooner got started when he gestured to the overflowing basket and accidentally bumped it with his hand. The basket toppled over, and all the vibrant fruit spilled out, bouncing and rolling off in different directions.

A hush went among the guests, but Ben was quick to say, "It's okay." He chuckled, bending down to pick up an apple then handing it to Elma. "This little mishap is a pleasant reminder of how we met at the farmers' market in Shipshewana two years ago." He smiled at Elma. "You were so kind to me that day when I made my little blunder. I could not be more fortunate to have found a woman who cares about others and goes around doing good. I feel truly blessed."

"And I've never grown weary of following the Lord's example, for in due season, I truly have reaped a blessed reward." Tears welled in her eyes as she looked at her groom. "And I too, feel doubly blessed."

Elma's Healthy Blueberry Crisp

Ingredients:

5 cups fresh or frozen
   blueberries
1¼ cups coconut sugar, divided
2 tablespoons instant tapioca
½ cup water

1 teaspoon lemon juice
½ cup melted butter
1 cup gluten-free flour
1 cup gluten-free quick oats

Combine berries, ¾ cup coconut sugar, tapioca, water, and lemon juice. Pour into greased 9x13 baking dish. In bowl, mix butter, ½ cup coconut sugar, flour, and oats. Sprinkle over blueberry mixture. Bake at 350 degrees for 40 minutes. Serve plain or with vanilla ice cream or whipped topping.

Thelma's Tasty Potato Salad

Ingredients:

12 cups potatoes, boiled
12 eggs, boiled
2 cups celery, chopped
1½ cups onion, chopped
3 cups mayonnaise

3 tablespoons vinegar
3 tablespoons mustard
4 teaspoons salt
1½ cups sugar
½ cup milk

Shred cooked potatoes and eggs into bowl. Add celery and onion. In separate bowl, mix mayonnaise, vinegar, mustard, salt, sugar, and milk. Pour over potato mixture and combine gently. Best when made up the day before or several hours before serving.

New York Times bestselling and award-winning author **Wanda E. Brunstetter** is one of the founders of the Amish fiction genre. Wanda's ancestors were part of the Anabaptist faith, and her novels are based on personal research intended to accurately portray the Amish way of life. Her books are well read and trusted by many Amish, who credit her for giving readers a deeper understanding of the people and their customs. When Wanda visits her Amish friends, she finds herself drawn to their peaceful lifestyle, sincerity, and close family ties. Wanda enjoys photography, ventriloquism, gardening, bird-watching, beachcombing, and spending time with her family. She and her husband, Richard, have been blessed with two grown children, six grandchildren, and two great-grandchildren. To learn more about Wanda, visit her website at www.wandabrunstetter.com.